Richard Wells is an illustrator and graphic designer. Primarily working in the television industry, he has provided graphic props for the likes of *Poldark*, *Sherlock*, *Doctor Who* and BBC adaptations of Bram Stoker's *Dracula* and M. R. James's 'The Mezzotint'. Outside of his television work, he makes and sells his own darkly folkloric artwork, often lino-cut and hand-printed.

DAMNABLE TALES

A

FOLK HORROR

ANTHOLOGY

Selected & Illustrated by

RICHARD WELLS

unbound

First published in 2021
This paperback edition first published in 2022

Unbound
Level 1, Devonshire House,
One Mayfair Place, London W 1J 8AJ

www.unbound.com

Selection and illustration © Richard Wells, 2021

Foreword © Benjamin Myers, 2021

Contributions © the individual authors and estates

While every effort has been made to trace the owners of copyright
material reproduced herein, the publisher would like to apologise for any
omissions and will be pleased to incorporate missing acknowledgements in
any further editions. All copyright notices can be found on pages 465–6.

Typeset by Patty Rennie

A CIP record for this book is available from the British Library

ISBN 978-1-80018-182-3 (paperback)
ISBN 978-1-80018-060-4 (hardback)
ISBN 978-1-80018-061-1 (ebook)

Printed and bound by Clays Ltd, Elcograf S.p.A.

5 7 9 8 6 4

CONTENTS

FOREWORD

Benjamin Myers

FEAR NOURISHES. FEAR can comfort. It can provide succour, take us to the hinterlands of the imagination or jolt us back into being.

There are only really two types of fear that we might experience: rational fears and irrational fears, and it is somewhere in the space between the two that the best horror stories grow like mould in the dank cellars of our psyches. For centuries they have been shared, from fireside to ebook.

But wait, something is changing. All the old fears that we once held as sacred and which, even at their murkiest, still followed a code of sorts – those strange and familiar fears that are the bedrock upon which the best tales of the uncanny are built – are being superseded by new fears, for which such rules or signifiers are not so easily recognisable.

As the world moves deeper into dystopian realities that few of us imagined would ever exist away from the pages of fiction, and technological advancements allow us to live in ways that reach far beyond the pace that evolution has prepared us for, new fears emerge. Fears most modern. The digital realm of today presents a dark new landscape that simply did not exist just three or four decades ago. It is a shadowland whose architecture is ever-expanding in all directions and is stalked by hordes of face-swapping ghouls, cynical manipulators and algorithmic revenants preying upon the vulnerable, all watched over by a chorus of continuously chattering voices offering a feverish running commentary on our thoughts and actions.

Infinite and nightmarish, the digital sphere is far from the utopia it might have been. Suddenly trolls are real. They have crawled out from beneath their bridges and now they're in our bedrooms, they are in our beds. We carry them in our pockets. True horror.

New fears begat new mythical creatures then. Meanwhile, just outside our front doors: unstoppable viruses, senseless terror attacks, raging conflicts, growing divisions. Even the things we once held as sacred and irrefutable – scientific and historic fact, *truth* – are now routinely called into question, and have resulted in an anxiety epidemic on an unprecedented scale. That this has all happened in the same amount of time it takes, for example, a pine sapling to grow to the height of a house, should be cause for alarm. Simply put, we have not been sufficiently prepared for the epoch we now find ourselves inhabiting. Things have accelerated too quickly, and, in our confusion, we are clinging on for our dear lives.

It is little wonder then that so many of us retreat into those fears we at least partially recognise, and willingly submit to. Old fears. The fear of the weird and the inexplicable. The fear of the land that rises up around us once the sun has set and the orchestra of night plays its dreary lament.

In *Damnable Tales*, Richard Wells has curated and illustrated a selection of stories that steers us into the dark recesses of landscapes both literal and imaginative. These stories unfold in the aforementioned no man's land between the rational and the irrational, a dusty interzone where doubt reigns supreme, and collectively form an ur-text for the folk-horror genre. They take place in worlds we recognise as once-removed from our realities. These are the settings of our ancestors, and therefore are still carried somewhere deep within us now: remote villages and darkened lanes, lonely woodlands, obscure country houses and crumbling cemeteries. Places where the crepuscular light is eternally fading and in which the inanimate or the dormant is slowly stirring.

It is no coincidence that the twenty-first century has birthed a major resurgence in the reading and writing of what we might call tales of the uncanny, a catch-all description that takes in ghost stories, the occult, hauntings, the supernatural and the peculiar, and the tropes of what has more recently been dubbed 'eerie England' or, more broadly, folk horror. Circumstances have made it so. We have become so far removed from the land we once farmed that we now fear it. This is the essence of folk horror, though as these stories demonstrate, this sense of unease is as old as the hills themselves.

The genre is thriving in cinema and music too, part of a broader nod towards nostalgia for those bold and beguiling television programmes that unnerved a generation in the 1960s and 1970s, and which have since found new life on the internet. But it is here in these stories that the seeds of folk horror were first sown. From these seeds surely sprouted *The Wicker Man*, *The Owl Service* and all manner of other key works that most readers will already be familiar with. Here in classic literature are the old fears to distract us from the new fears. And they remain as profane and potent as ever.

Arranged chronologically, from a masterful Sheridan Le Fanu work of 1872 through to a Robert Aickman story first published in 1964, *Damnable Tales* draws on the greats of the proto-folk-horror genre – though the term itself had sporadically appeared in print over the decades, it was only popularised in the twenty-first century – but also offers plenty of delights and surprises along the way. It's worthy of note that half the collection is clustered around the dying years of the nineteenth century, a time in which the ghost story was enjoying a golden period, though often these pieces reach back to an earlier era. Robert Louis Stevenson's 'Thrawn Janet', for example, was published in 1881 but set in 1712, a time both pre-industrialisation and pre-Enlightenment, and therefore free of the advancements that Darwinism and social reform might have brought about in the interim.

It is perhaps for this exact same reason that we now find ourselves reaching back to immerse ourselves in stories that occur before such things as the motor car, telephones, television, the internet and flight were commonplace. Unhindered by modern rationale and practical plot spoilers, the evil forces in each story are instead allowed to fester.

Such explorations of earlier, darker days are perhaps best represented by the work of M. R. James, whose stories followed an unerring formula that can generally be distilled into three words – an outsider meddles – and manage to handle plots that could be comically absurd in the hands of lesser writers, but which today remain timeless, powerful and as utterly sinister as when they were first read aloud by candlelight in his King's College, Cambridge study. Such is the residual power of his stories, 'Jamesian' is now an adjective to describe works where atmosphere and setting are everything. Monty, as his fans call him, is represented here with his chilling 1904 tale 'The Ash-Tree'.

Elsewhere are stories that tell of strange practices, thwarted desires and vengeful forms; here are scenarios where witches push pins through hearts, then throw them on to fires, or silent stone statues (as in Edith Nesbit's 'Man-size in Marble') rise on one night of the year. Reason has no place in this collection. One must simply submit.

Running through the marrow of each story is the understated power of language to disturb and confound, often in one key sentence. An example is right there on the very first page of Sheridan Le Fanu's opening story, 'Laura Silver Bell':

The sun is sinking blood-red in the west. His disk has touched the broad black level of the moor, and his parting beams glare athwart the gaunt figure of the old beldame, as she strides homeward stick in hand, and bring into relief the folds of her mantle, which gleam like the draperies of a bronze image in the light of a fire. For a few moments this light floods the air – tree, gorse, rock, and bracken glare; and then it is out, and gray twilight over everything.

This is writing at its most powerful – controlled, poetic and ornate, yes, but gripped by a growing sense of foreboding that will deliver us, the readers, to a conclusion that we are certain will be both disturbing and satisfying.

And where else might the mysterious Arthur Machen, a man whose work directly influenced not only the magic realist writing of Jorge Luis Borges but also the occultist declarations of Mark E. Smith of the post-punk group The Fall and today's wandering psychogeographers (from Iain Sinclair and Alan Moore onwards), sit comfortably alongside the queen of American weirdness, Shirley Jackson, or Thomas Hardy, whose inclusion, 'The Withered Arm', may well be his best short-form work?

The answer is nowhere but here in *Damnable Tales*.

We should acknowledge that a good many of these stories were written at time when the war-to-end-all-wars had not yet happened. Those writers and artists who survived the trenches, poisonous gases and grotesque disfigurements of 1914–1918 would go on to reshape the culture of the twentieth century accordingly. Yet so many tales of the uncanny that followed still favoured old fears over new fears, just as we today might pluck our trusted copy of M. R. James's *Ghost Stories of an Antiquary* or Henry James's *The Turn of the Screw* from the shelf at the first turning of the leaves, or when the scent of woodsmoke is brought in on the October easterlies.

Because fear nourishes. Fear comforts. As we approach the uncanny we do so with certain expectations in mind. We lick a fingertip and turn the page, ready to have our notions of normality and reality challenged. We want to be baffled and beguiled, gently victimised, even. We seek to be spooked – but just enough so that we can still sleep at night.

Damnable Tales fulfils these ancient needs. Here are the old fears.

BENJAMIN MYERS

DAMNABLE
TALES

LAURA SILVER BELL

by

Sheridan Le Fanu

First published in the *Belgravia Annual*
1872

IN THE FIVE Northumbrian counties you will scarcely find so
bleak, ugly, and yet, in a savage way, so picturesque a moor as
Dardale Moss. The moor itself spreads north, south, east, and west,
a great undulating sea of black peat and heath.

What we may term its shores are wooded wildly with birch,
hazel, and dwarf-oak. No towering mountains surround it, but
here and there you have a rocky knoll rising among the trees, and
many a wooded promontory of the same pretty, because utterly
wild, forest, running out into its dark level.

Habitations are thinly scattered in this barren territory, and a
full mile away from the meanest was the stone cottage of Mother
Carke.

Let not my southern reader who associates ideas of comfort
with the term 'cottage' mistake. This thing is built of shingle, with
low walls. Its thatch is hollow; the peat-smoke curls stingily from
its stunted chimney. It is worthy of its savage surroundings.

The primitive neighbours remark that no rowan-tree grows
near, nor holly, nor bracken, and no horseshoe is nailed on the door.

Not far from the birches and hazels that straggle about the
rude wall of the little enclosure, on the contrary, they say, you may

discover the broom and the rag-wort, in which witches mysteriously delight. But this is perhaps a scandal.

Mall Carke was for many a year the *sage femme* of this wild domain. She has renounced practice, however, for some years; and now, under the rose, she dabbles, it is thought, in the black art, in which she has always been secretly skilled, tells fortunes, practises charms, and in popular esteem is little better than a witch.

Mother Carke has been away to the town of Willarden, to sell knit stockings, and is returning to her rude dwelling by Dardale Moss. To her right, as far away as the eye can reach, the moor stretches. The narrow track she has followed here tops a gentle upland, and at her left a sort of jungle of dwarf-oak and brushwood approaches its edge. The sun is sinking blood-red in the west. His disk has touched the broad black level of the moor, and his parting beams glare athwart the gaunt figure of the old beldame, as she strides homeward stick in hand, and bring into relief the folds of her mantle, which gleam like the draperies of a bronze image in the light of a fire. For a few moments this light floods the air – tree, gorse, rock, and bracken glare; and then it is out, and gray twilight over everything.

All is still and sombre. At this hour the simple traffic of the thinly peopled country is over, and nothing can be more solitary.

From this jungle, nevertheless, through which the mists of evening are already creeping, she sees a gigantic man approaching her.

In that poor and primitive country robbery is a crime unknown. She, therefore, has no fears for her pound of tea, and pint of gin, and sixteen shillings in silver which she is bringing home in her pocket. But there is something that would have frighted another woman about this man.

He is gaunt, sombre, bony, dirty, and dressed in a black suit which a beggar would hardly care to pick out of the dust.

This ill-looking man nodded to her as he stepped on the road.

'I don't know you,' she said.

He nodded again.

'I never sid ye neyawheere,' she exclaimed sternly.

'Fine evening, Mother Carke,' he says, and holds his snuff-box toward her.

She widened the distance between them by a step or so, and said again sternly and pale,

'I hev nowt to say to thee, whoe'er thou beest.'

'You know Laura Silver Bell?'

'That's a byneyam; the lass's neyam is Laura Lew,' she answered, looking straight before her.

'One name's as good as another for one that was never christened, mother.'

'How know ye that?' she asked grimly; for it is a received opinion in that part of the world that the fairies have power over those who have never been baptised.

The stranger turned on her a malignant smile.

'There is a young lord in love with her,' the stranger says, 'and I'm that lord. Have her at your house to-morrow night at eight o'clock, and you must stick cross pins through the candle, as you have done for many a one before, to bring her lover thither by ten, and her fortune's made. And take this for your trouble.'

He extended his long finger and thumb toward her, with a guinea temptingly displayed.

'I have nowt to do wi' thee. I nivver sid thee afoore. Git thee awa'! I earned nea goold o' thee, and I'll tak' nane. Awa' wi' thee, or I'll find ane that will mak' thee!'

The old woman had stopped, and was quivering in every limb as she thus spoke.

He looked very angry. Sulkily he turned away at her words, and strode slowly toward the wood from which he had come; and as he approached it, he seemed to her to grow taller and taller, and stalked into it as high as a tree.

'I conceited there would come something o't,' she said to

herself. 'Farmer Lew must git it done nesht Sunda'. The a'ad awpy!'

Old Farmer Lew was one of that sect who insist that baptism shall be but once administered, and not until the Christian candidate had attained to adult years. The girl had indeed for some time been of an age not only, according to this theory, to be baptised, but if need be to be married.

Her story was a sad little romance. A lady some seventeen years before had come down and paid Farmer Lew for two rooms in his house. She told him that her husband would follow her in a fortnight, and that he was in the mean time delayed by business in Liverpool.

In ten days after her arrival her baby was born, Mall Carke acting as *sage femme* on the occasion; and on the evening of that day the poor young mother died. No husband came; no weddingring, they said, was on her finger. About fifty pounds was found in her desk, which Farmer Lew, who was a kind old fellow and had lost his two children, put in bank for the little girl, and resolved to keep her until a rightful owner should step forward to claim her.

They found half-a-dozen love-letters signed 'Francis', and calling the dead woman 'Laura'.

So Farmer Lew called the little girl Laura; and her *sobriquet* of 'Silver Bell' was derived from a tiny silver bell, once gilt, which was found among her poor mother's little treasures after her death, and which the child wore on a ribbon round her neck.

Thus, being very pretty and merry, she grew up as a Northcountry farmer's daughter; and the old man, as she needed more looking after, grew older and less able to take care of her; so she was, in fact, very nearly her own mistress, and did pretty much in all things as she liked.

Old Mall Carke, by some caprice for which no one could account, cherished an affection for the girl, who saw her often, and paid her many a small fee in exchange for the secret indications of the future.

It was too late when Mother Carke reached her home to look for a visit from Laura Silver Bell that day.

About three o'clock next afternoon, Mother Carke was sitting knitting, with her glasses on, outside her door on the stone bench, when she saw the pretty girl mount lightly to the top of the stile at her left under the birch, against the silver stem of which she leaned her slender hand, and called,

'Mall, Mall! Mother Carke, are ye alane all by yersel'?'

'Ay, Laura lass, we can be clooas enoo, if ye want a word wi' me,' says the old woman, rising, with a mysterious nod, and beckoning her stiffly with her long fingers.

The girl was, assuredly, pretty enough for a 'lord' to fall in love with. Only look at her. A profusion of brown rippling hair, parted low in the middle of her forehead, almost touched her eyebrows, and made the pretty oval of her face, by the breadth of that rich line, more marked. What a pretty little nose! what scarlet lips, and large, dark, long-fringed eyes!

Her face is transparently tinged with those clear Murillo tints which appear in deeper dyes on her wrists and the backs of her hands. These are the beautiful gipsy-tints with which the sun dyes young skins so richly.

The old woman eyes all this, and her pretty figure, so round and slender, and her shapely little feet, cased in the thick shoes that can't hide their comely proportions, as she stands on the top of the stile. But it is with a dark and saturnine aspect.

'Come, lass, what stand ye for atoppa t' wall, whar folk may chance to see thee? I hev a thing to tell thee, lass.'

She beckoned her again.

'An' I hev a thing to tell *thee*, Mall.'

'Come hidder,' said the old woman peremptorily.

'But ye munna gie me the creepin's' (make me tremble). 'I winna look again into the glass o' water, mind ye.'

The old woman smiled grimly, and changed her tone.

'Now, hunny, git tha down, and let ma see thy canny feyace,' and she beckoned her again.

Laura Silver Bell did get down, and stepped lightly toward the door of the old woman's dwelling.

'Tak this,' said the girl, unfolding a piece of bacon from her apron, 'and I hev a silver sixpence to gie thee, when I'm gaen away heyam.'

They entered the dark kitchen of the cottage, and the old woman stood by the door, lest their conference should be lighted on by surprise.

'Afoore ye begin,' said Mother Carke (I soften her patois), 'I mun tell ye there's ill folk watchin' ye. What's auld Farmer Lew about, he doesna get t' sir' (the clergyman) 'to baptise thee? If he lets Sunda' next pass, I'm afeared ye'll never be sprinkled nor signed wi' cross, while there's a sky aboon us.'

'Agoy!' exclaims the girl, 'who's lookin' after me?'

'A big black fella, as high as the kipples, came out o' the wood near Deadman's Grike, just after the sun gaed down yester e'en; I knew weel what he was, for his feet ne'er touched the road while he made as if he walked beside me. And he wanted to gie me snuff first, and I wouldna hev that; and then he offered me a gowden guinea, but I was no sic awpy, and to bring you here to-night, and cross the candle wi' pins, to call your lover in. And he said he's a great lord, and in luve wi' thee.'

'And you refused him?'

'Well for thee I did, lass,' says Mother Carke.

'Why, it's every word true!' cries the girl vehemently, starting to her feet, for she had seated herself on the great oak chest.

'True, lass? Come, say what ye mean,' demanded Mall Carke, with a dark and searching gaze.

'Last night I was coming heyam from the wake, wi' auld Farmer Dykes and his wife and his daughter Nell, and when we came to the stile, I bid them good-night, and we parted.'

'And ye came by the path alone in the night-time, did ye?' exclaimed old Mall Carke sternly.

'I wasna afeared, I don't know why; the path heyam leads down by the wa'as o' auld Hawarth Castle.'

'I knaa it weel, and a dowly path it is; ye'll keep indoors o' nights for a while, or ye'll rue it. What saw ye?'

'No freetin, mother; nowt I was feared on.'

'Ye heard a voice callin' yer neyame?'

'I heard nowt that was dow, but the hullyhoo in the auld castle wa's,' answered the pretty girl. 'I heard nor sid nowt that's dow, but mickle that's conny and gladsome. I heard singin' and laughin' a long way off, I consaited; and I stopped a bit to listen. Then I walked on a step or two, and there, sure enough in the Pie-Mag field, under the castle wa's, not twenty steps away, I sid a grand company; silks and satins, and men wi' velvet coats, wi' gowd-lace striped over them, and ladies wi' necklaces that would dazzle ye, and fans as big as griddles; and powdered footmen, like what the shirra hed behind his coach, only these was ten times as grand.'

'It was full moon last night,' said the old woman.

'Sa bright 'twould blind ye to look at it,' said the girl.

'Never an ill sight but the deaul finds a light,' quoth the old woman. 'There's a rinnin brook thar – you were at this side, and they at that; did they try to mak ye cross over?'

'Agoy! didn't they? Nowt but civility and kindness, though. But ye mun let me tell it my own way. They was talkin' and laughin', and eatin', and drinkin' out o' long glasses and goud cups, seated on the grass, and music was playin'; and I keekin' behind a bush at all the grand doin's; and up they gits to dance; and says a tall fella I didna see afoore, "Ye mun step across, and dance wi' a young lord that's faan in luv wi' thee, and that's mysel," and sure enow I keeked at him under my lashes and a conny lad he is, to my teyaste, though he be dressed in black, wi' sword and sash, velvet twice as fine as they sells in the shop at Gouden Friars; and keekin' at me again

7

fra the corners o' his een. And the same fella telt me he was mad in luv wi' me, and his fadder was there, and his sister, and they came all the way from Catstean Castle to see me that night; and that's t' other side o' Gouden Friars.'

'Come, lass, yer no mafflin; tell me true. What was he like? Was his feyace grimed wi' sut? a tall fella wi' wide shouthers, and lukt like an ill-thing, wi' black clothes amaist in rags?'

'His feyace was long, but weel-faured, and darker nor a gipsy; and his clothes were black and grand, and made o' velvet, and he said he was the young lord himsel'; and he lukt like it.'

'That will be the same fella I sid at Deadman's Grike,' said Mall Carke, with an anxious frown.

'Hoot, mudder! how cud that be?' cried the lass, with a toss of her pretty head and a smile of scorn. But the fortune-teller made no answer, and the girl went on with her story.

'When they began to dance,' continued Laura Silver Bell, 'he urged me again, but I wudna step o'er; 'twas partly pride, coz I wasna dressed fine enough, and partly contrairiness, or something, but gaa I wudna, not a fut. No but I more nor half wished it a' the time.'

'Weel for thee thou dudstna cross the brook.'

'Hoity-toity, why not?'

'Keep at heyame after nightfall, and don't ye be walking by yersel' by daylight or any light lang lonesome ways, till after ye're baptised,' said Mall Carke.

'I'm like to be married first.'

'Tak care *that* marriage won't hang i' the bell-ropes,' said Mother Carke.

'Leave me alane for that. The young lord said he was maist daft wi' luv o' me. He wanted to gie me a conny ring wi' a beautiful stone in it. But, drat it, I was sic an awpy I wudna tak it, and he a young lord!'

'Lord, indeed! are ye daft or dreamin'? Those fine folk, what

8

were they? I'll tell ye. Dobies and fairies; and if ye don't du as yer bid, they'll tak ye, and ye'll never git out o' their hands again while grass grows,' said the old woman grimly.

'Od wite it!' replies the girl impatiently, 'who's daft or dreamin' noo? I'd a bin dead wi' fear, if 'twas any such thing. It cudna be; all was sa luvesome, and bonny, and shaply.'

'Weel, and what do ye want o' me, lass?' asked the old woman sharply.

'I want to know – here's t' sixpence – what I sud du,' said the young lass. ''Twud be a pity to lose such a marrow, hey?'

'Say yer prayers, lass; *I* can't help ye,' says the old woman darkly. 'If ye gaa wi' *the* people, ye'll never come back. Ye munna talk wi' them, nor eat wi' them, nor drink wi' them, nor tak a pin's-worth by way o' gift fra them – mark weel what I say – or ye're *lost*!'

The girl looked down, plainly much vexed.

The old woman stared at her with a mysterious frown steadily, for a few seconds.

'Tell me, lass, and tell me true, are ye in luve wi' that lad?'

'What for sud I?' said the girl with a careless toss of her head, and blushing up to her very temples.

'I see how it is,' said the old woman, with a groan, and repeated the words, sadly thinking; and walked out of the door a step or two, and looked jealously round. 'The lass is witched, the lass is witched!'

'Did ye see him since?' asked Mother Carke, returning.

The girl was still embarrassed; and now she spoke in a lower tone, and seemed subdued.

'I thought I sid him as I came here, walkin' beside me among the trees; but I consait it was only the trees themsels that lukt like rinnin' one behind another, as I walked on.'

'I can tell thee nowt, lass, but what I telt ye afoore,' answered the old woman peremptorily. 'Get ye heyame, and don't delay on the way; and say yer prayers as ye gaa; and let none but good thoughts come nigh ye; and put nayer foot autside the door-steyan again till ye gaa to be christened; and get that done a Sunda' next.'

And with this charge, given with grizzly earnestness, she saw her over the stile, and stood upon it watching her retreat, until the trees quite hid her and her path from view.

The sky grew cloudy and thunderous, and the air darkened rapidly, as the girl, a little frightened by Mall Carke's view of the case, walked homeward by the lonely path among the trees.

A black cat, which had walked close by her – for these creatures sometimes take a ramble in search of their prey among the woods and thickets – crept from under the hollow of an oak, and was again with her. It seemed to her to grow bigger and bigger as the darkness deepened, and its green eyes glared as large as halfpennies in her affrighted vision as the thunder came booming along the heights from the Willarden-road.

She tried to drive it away; but it growled and hissed awfully, and set up its back as if it would spring at her, and finally it skipped up into a tree, where they grew thickest at each side of her path, and accompanied her, high over head, hopping from bough to bough as if meditating a pounce upon her shoulders. Her fancy being full of strange thoughts, she was frightened, and she fancied that it was haunting her steps, and destined to undergo some hideous transformation, the moment she ceased to guard her path with prayers.

She was frightened for a while after she got home. The dark looks of Mother Carke were always before her eyes, and a secret dread prevented her passing the threshold of her home again that night.

Next day it was different. She had got rid of the awe with which Mother Carke had inspired her. She could not get the tall dark-featured lord, in the black velvet dress, out of her head. He had 'taken her fancy'; she was growing to love him. She could think of nothing else.

Bessie Hennock, a neighbour's daughter, came to see her that day, and proposed a walk toward the ruins of Hawarth Castle, to gather 'blaebirries'. So off the two girls went together.

In the thicket, along the slopes near the ivied walls of Hawarth Castle, the companions began to fill their baskets. Hours passed. The sun was sinking near the west, and Laura Silver Bell had not come home.

Over the hatch of the farm-house door the maids leant ever and anon with outstretched necks, watching for a sign of the girl's return, and wondering, as the shadows lengthened, what had become of her.

At last, just as the rosy sunset gilding began to overspread the landscape, Bessie Hennock, weeping into her apron, made her appearance without her companion.

Her account of their adventures was curious.

I will relate the substance of it more connectedly than her agitation would allow her to give it, and without the disguise of the rude Northumbrian dialect.

The girl said, that, as they got along together among the brambles that grow beside the brook that bounds the Pie-Mag field, she on a sudden saw a very tall big-boned man, with an ill-favoured smirched face, and dressed in worn and rusty black, standing at the other side of a little stream. She was frightened; and while looking at this dirty, wicked, starved figure, Laura Silver Bell touched her, gazing at the same tall scarecrow, but with a countenance full of confusion and even rapture. She was peeping through the bush behind which she stood, and with a sigh she said:

'Is na that a conny lad? Agoy! See his bonny velvet clothes, his sword and sash; that's a lord, I can tell ye; and weel I know who he follows, who he luves, and who he'll wed.'

Bessie Hennock thought her companion daft.

'See how luvesome he luks!' whispered Laura.

Bessie looked again, and saw him gazing at her companion

with a malignant smile, and at the same time he beckoned her to approach.

'Darrat ta! gaa not near him! He'll wring thy neck!' gasped Bessie in great fear, as she saw Laura step forward with a look of beautiful bashfulness and joy.

She took the hand he stretched across the stream, more for love of the hand than any need of help, and in a moment was across and by his side, and his long arm about her waist.

'Fares te weel, Bessie, I'm gain my ways,' she called, leaning her head to his shoulder; 'and tell gud Fadder Lew I'm gain my ways to be happy, and may be, at lang last, I'll see him again.'

And with a farewell wave of her hand, she went away with her dismal partner; and Laura Silver Bell was never more seen at home, or among the 'coppies' and 'wickwoods', the bonny fields and bosky hollows, by Dardale Moss.

Bessie Hennock followed them for a time.

She crossed the brook, and though they seemed to move slowly enough, she was obliged to run to keep them in view; and she all the time cried to her continually, 'Come back, come back, bonnie Laurie!' until, getting over a bank, she was met by a white-faced old man, and so frightened was she, that she thought she fainted outright. At all events, she did not come to herself until the birds were singing their vespers in the amber light of sunset, and the day was over.

No trace of the direction of the girl's flight was ever discovered. Weeks and months passed, and more than a year.

At the end of that time, one of Mall Carke's goats died, as she suspected, by the envious practices of a rival witch who lived at the far end of Dardale Moss.

All alone in her stone cabin the old woman had prepared her charm to ascertain the author of her misfortune.

The heart of the dead animal, stuck all over with pins, was burnt in the fire; the windows, doors, and every other aperture of the house being first carefully stopped. After the heart, thus prepared with suitable incantations, is consumed in the fire, the first person who comes to the door or passes by it is the offending magician.

Mother Carke completed these lonely rites at dead of night. It was a dark night, with the glimmer of the stars only, and a melancholy night-wind was soughing through the scattered woods that spread around.

After a long and dead silence, there came a heavy thump at the door, and a deep voice called her by name.

She was startled, for she expected no man's voice; and peeping from the window, she saw, in the dim light, a coach and four horses, with gold-laced footmen, and coachman in wig and cocked hat, turned out as if for a state occasion.

She unbarred the door; and a tall gentleman, dressed in black, waiting at the threshold, entreated her, as the only *sage femme* within reach, to come in the coach and attend Lady Lairdale, who was about to give birth to a baby, promising her handsome payment.

Lady Lairdale! She had never heard of her.

'How far away is it?'

'Twelve miles on the old road to Golden Friars.'

Her avarice is roused, and she steps into the coach. The footman claps-to the door; the glass jingles with the sound of a laugh. The tall dark-faced gentleman in black is seated opposite; they are driving at a furious pace; they have turned out of the road into a narrower one, dark with thicker and loftier forest than she was accustomed to. She grows anxious; for she knows every road and by-path in the country round, and she has never seen this one.

He encourages her. The moon has risen above the edge of the horizon, and she sees a noble old castle. Its summit of tower, watchtower and battlement glimmers faintly in the moonlight. This is their destination.

She feels on a sudden all but overpowered by sleep; but although she nods, she is quite conscious of the continued motion, which has become even rougher.

She makes an effort, and rouses herself. What has become of the coach, the castle, the servants? Nothing but the strange forest remains the same.

She is jolting along on a rude hurdle, seated on rushes, and a tall, big-boned man, in rags, sits in front, kicking with his heel the ill-favoured beast that pulls them along, every bone of which sticks out, and holding the halter which serves for reins. They stop at the door of a miserable building of loose stone, with a thatch so sunk and rotten that the roof-tree and couples protrude in crooked corners, like the bones of the wretched horse, with enormous head and ears, that dragged them to the door.

The long gaunt man gets down, his sinister face grimed like his hands.

It was the same grimy giant who had accosted her on the lonely road near Deadman's Grike. But she feels that she 'must go through with it' now, and she follows him into the house.

Two rushlights were burning in the large and miserable room, and on a coarse ragged bed lay a woman groaning piteously.

'That's Lady Lairdale,' says the gaunt dark man, who then began to stride up and down the room rolling his head, stamping furiously, and thumping one hand on the palm of the other, and talking and laughing in the corners, where there was no one visible to hear or to answer.

Old Mall Carke recognised in the faded half-starved creature who lay on the bed, as dark now and grimy as the man, and looking as if she had never in her life washed hands or face, the once blithe and pretty Laura Lew.

The hideous being who was her mate continued in the same odd fluctuations of fury, grief, and merriment; and whenever she uttered a groan, he parodied it with another, as Mother Carke thought, in saturnine derision.

At length he strode into another room, and banged the door after him.

In due time the poor woman's pains were over, and a daughter was born.

Such an imp! with long pointed ears, flat nose, and enormous restless eyes and mouth. It instantly began to yell and talk in some unknown language, at the noise of which the father looked into the room, and told the *sage femme* that she should not go unrewarded.

The sick woman seized the moment of his absence to say in the ear of Mall Carke:

'If ye had not been at ill work tonight, he could not hev fetched ye. Tak no more now than your rightful fee, or he'll keep ye here.'

At this moment he returned with a bag of gold and silver coins, which he emptied on the table, and told her to help herself.

She took four shillings, which was her primitive fee, neither more nor less; and all his urgency could not prevail with her to take a farthing more. He looked so terrible at her refusal that she rushed out of the house.

He ran after her.

'You'll take your money with you,' he roared, snatching up the bag, still half full, and flung it after her.

It lighted on her shoulder; and partly from the blow, partly from terror, she fell to the ground; and when she came to herself, it was morning, and she was lying across her own door-stone.

It is said that she never more told fortune or practised spell. And though all that happened sixty years ago and more, Laura Silver Bell, wise folk think, is still living, and will so continue till the day of doom among the fairies.

MAN-SIZE IN MARBLE

by

Edith Nesbit

First published in the December edition
of *Home Chimes* magazine

1887

ALTHOUGH EVERY WORD of this story is as true as despair, I do not expect people to believe it. Nowadays a 'rational explanation' is required before belief is possible. Let me then, at once, offer the 'rational explanation' which finds most favour among those who have heard the tale of my life's tragedy. It is held that we were 'under a delusion', Laura and I, on that 31st of October; and that this supposition places the whole matter on a satisfactory and believable basis. The reader can judge, when he, too, has heard my story, how far this is an 'explanation', and in what sense it is 'rational'. There were three who took part in this: Laura and I and another man. The other man still lives, and can speak to the truth of the least credible part of my story.

I never in my life knew what it was to have as much money as I required to supply the most ordinary needs – good colours, books, and cab-fares – and when we were married we knew quite well that we should only be able to live at all by 'strict punctuality and attention to business'. I used to paint in those days, and Laura used to write, and we felt sure we could keep the pot at least simmering.

Living in town was out of the question, so we went to look for a cottage in the country, which should be at once sanitary and picturesque. So rarely do these two qualities meet in one cottage that our search was for some time quite fruitless. We tried advertisements, but most of the desirable rural residences which we did look at proved to be lacking in both essentials, and when a cottage chanced to have drains it always had stucco as well and was shaped like a tea-caddy. And if we found a vine or rose-covered porch, corruption invariably lurked within. Our minds got so befogged by the eloquence of house-agents and the rival disadvantages of the fever-traps and outrages to beauty which we had seen and scorned, that I very much doubt whether either of us, on our wedding morning, knew the difference between a house and a haystack. But when we got away from friends and house-agents, on our honeymoon, our wits grew clear again, and we knew a pretty cottage when at last we saw one. It was at Brenzett – a little village set on a hill over against the southern marshes. We had gone there, from the seaside village where we were staying, to see the church, and two fields from the church we found this cottage. It stood quite by itself, about two miles from the village. It was a long, low building, with rooms sticking out in unexpected places. There was a bit of stone-work – ivy-covered and moss-grown, just two old rooms, all that was left of a big house that had once stood there – and round this stone-work the house had grown up. Stripped of its roses and jasmine it would have been hideous. As it stood it was charming, and after a brief examination we took it. It was absurdly cheap. The rest of our honeymoon we spent in grubbing about in second-hand shops in the county town, picking up bits of old oak and Chippendale chairs for our furnishing.

We wound up with a run up to town and a visit to Liberty's, and soon the low oak-beamed lattice-windowed rooms began to be home. There was a jolly old-fashioned garden, with grass paths, and no end of hollyhocks and sunflowers, and big lilies. From the window you could see the marsh-pastures, and beyond them the blue, thin line of the sea. We were as happy as the summer was glorious, and settled down into work sooner than we ourselves expected. I was never tired of sketching the view and the wonderful cloud effects from the open lattice, and Laura would sit at the table and write verses about them, in which I mostly played the part of foreground.

We got a tall old peasant woman to do for us. Her face and figure were good, though her cooking was of the homeliest; but she understood all about gardening, and told us all the old names of the coppices and cornfields, and the stories of the smugglers and highwaymen, and, better still, of the 'things that walked', and of the 'sights' which met one in lonely glens of a starlight night. She was a great comfort to us, because Laura hated housekeeping as much as I loved folklore, and we soon came to leave all the domestic business to Mrs Dorman, and to use her legends in little magazine stories which brought in the jingling guinea.

We had three months of married happiness, and did not have a single quarrel. One October evening I had been down to smoke a pipe with the doctor – our only neighbour – a pleasant young Irishman. Laura had stayed at home to finish a comic sketch of a village episode for the *Monthly Marplot*. I left her laughing over her own jokes, and came in to find her a crumpled heap of pale muslin, weeping on the window seat.

'Good heavens, my darling, what's the matter?' I cried, taking her in my arms. She leaned her little dark head against my shoulder and went on crying. I had never seen her cry before – we had always been so happy, you see – and I felt sure some frightful misfortune had happened.

'What *is* the matter? Do speak.'

'It's Mrs Dorman,' she sobbed.

'What has she done?' I enquired, immensely relieved.

'She says she must go before the end of the month, and she says her niece is ill; she's gone down to see her now, but I don't believe that's the reason, because her niece is always ill. I believe someone has been setting her against us. Her manner was so queer—'

'Never mind, Pussy,' I said; 'whatever you do, don't cry, or I shall have to cry too, to keep you in countenance, and then you'll never respect your man again!'

She dried her eyes obediently on my handkerchief, and even smiled faintly.

'But you see,' she went on, 'it is really serious, because these village people are so sheepy, and if one won't do a thing, you may be quite sure none of the others will. And I shall have to cook the dinners, and wash up the hateful greasy plates; and you'll have to carry cans of water about, and clean the boots and knives – and we shall never have any time for work, or earn any money, or anything. We shall have to work all day, and only be able to rest when we are waiting for the kettle to boil!'

I represented to her that even if we had to perform these duties, the day would still present some margin for other toils and recreations. But she refused to see the matter in any but the greyest light. She was very unreasonable, my Laura, but I could not have loved her any more if she had been as reasonable as Whately.

'I'll speak to Mrs Dorman when she comes back, and see if I can't come to terms with her,' I said. 'Perhaps she wants a rise in her screw. It will be all right. Let's walk up to the church.'

The church was a large and lonely one, and we loved to go there, especially upon bright nights. The path skirted a wood, cut through it once, and ran along the crest of the hill through two meadows, and round the churchyard wall, over which the old yews loomed in black masses of shadow. This path, which was partly paved, was called 'the bier-balk', for it had long been the way by which the corpses had been carried to burial. The churchyard was richly treed, and was shaded by great elms which stood just outside and stretched their majestic arms in benediction over the happy dead. A large, low porch let one into the building by a Norman doorway and a heavy oak door studded with iron. Inside, the arches rose into darkness, and between them the reticulated windows, which stood out white in the moonlight. In the chancel, the windows were of rich glass, which showed in faint light their noble colouring, and made the black oak of the choir pews hardly more solid than the shadows. But on each side of the altar lay a grey marble figure of a knight in full plate armour lying upon a low slab, with hands held up in everlasting prayer, and these figures, oddly enough, were always to be seen if there was any glimmer of light in the church. Their names were lost, but the peasants told of them that they had been fierce and wicked men, marauders by land and sea, who had been the scourge of their time, and had been guilty of deeds so foul that the house they had lived in – the big house, by the way, that had stood on the site of our cottage – had been stricken by lightning and the vengeance of Heaven. But for all that, the gold of their heirs had bought them a place in the church. Looking at the bad hard faces reproduced in the marble, this story was easily believed.

The church looked at its best and weirdest on that night, for the shadows of the yew trees fell through the windows upon the floor of the nave and touched the pillars with tattered shade. We sat down together without speaking, and watched the solemn beauty of the old church, with some of that awe which inspired its early builders. We walked to the chancel and looked at the sleeping warriors. Then we rested some time on the stone seat in the porch, looking out over the stretch of quiet moonlit meadows, feeling in every fibre of our being the peace of the night and of our happy love; and came away at last with a sense that even scrubbing and blackleading were but small troubles at their worst.

Mrs Dorman had come back from the village, and I at once invited her to a *tête-à-tête*.

'Now, Mrs Dorman,' I said, when I had got her into my painting room, 'what's all this about your not staying with us?'

'I should be glad to get away, sir, before the end of the month,' she answered, with her usual placid dignity.

'Have you any fault to find, Mrs Dorman?'

'None at all, sir; you and your lady have always been most kind, I'm sure—'

'Well, what is it? Are your wages not high enough?'

'No, sir, I gets quite enough.'

'Then why not stay?'

'I'd rather not' – with some hesitation – 'my niece is ill.'

'But your niece has been ill ever since we came.'

No answer. There was a long and awkward silence. I broke it.

'Can't you stay for another month?' I asked.

'No, sir. I'm bound to go by Thursday.'

And this was Monday!

'Well, I must say, I think you might have let us know before. There's no time now to get any one else, and your mistress is not fit to do heavy housework. Can't you stay till next week?'

'I might be able to come back next week.'

I was now convinced that all she wanted was a brief holiday, which we should have been willing enough to let her have, as soon as we could get a substitute.

'But why must you go this week?' I persisted. 'Come, out with it.'

Mrs Dorman drew the little shawl, which she always wore, tightly across her bosom, as though she were cold. Then she said, with a sort of effort—

'They say, sir, as this was a big house in Catholic times, and there was a many deeds done here.'

The nature of the 'deeds' might be vaguely inferred from the inflection of Mrs Dorman's voice – which was enough to make one's blood run cold. I was glad that Laura was not in the room. She was always nervous, as highly strung natures are, and I felt that

22

these tales about our house, told by this old peasant woman, with her impressive manner and contagious credulity, might have made our home less dear to my wife.

'Tell me all about it, Mrs Dorman,' I said; 'you needn't mind about telling me. I'm not like the young people who make fun of such things.'

Which was partly true.

'Well, sir' – she sank her voice – 'you may have seen in the church, beside the altar, two shapes.'

'You mean the effigies of the knights in armour,' I said cheerfully.

'I mean them two bodies, drawed out man-size in marble,' she returned, and I had to admit that her description was a thousand times more graphic than mine, to say nothing of a certain weird force and uncanniness about the phrase 'drawed out man-size in marble'.

'They do say, as on All Saints' Eve them two bodies sits up on their slabs, and gets off of them, and then walks down the aisle, *in their marble*' – (another good phrase, Mrs Dorman) – 'and as the church clock strikes eleven they walks out of the church door, and over the graves, and along the bier-balk, and if it's a wet night there's the marks of their feet in the morning.'

'And where do they go?' I asked, rather fascinated.

'They comes back here to their home, sir, and if any one meets them—'

'Well, what then?' I asked.

But no – not another word could I get from her, save that her niece was ill and she must go. After what I had heard I scorned to discuss the niece, and tried to get from Mrs Dorman more details of the legend. I could get nothing but warnings.

'Whatever you do, sir, lock the door early on All Saints' Eve, and make the cross-sign over the doorstep and on the windows.'

'But has any one ever seen these things?' I persisted.

'That's not for me to say. I know what I know, sir.'

'Well, who was here last year?'

'No one, sir; the lady as owned the house only stayed here in summer, and she always went to London a full month afore *the* night. And I'm sorry to inconvenience you and your lady, but my niece is ill and I must go on Thursday.'

I could have shaken her for her absurd reiteration of that obvious fiction, after she had told me her real reasons.

She was determined to go, nor could our united entreaties move her in the least.

I did not tell Laura the legend of the shapes that 'walked in their marble', partly because a legend concerning our house might perhaps trouble my wife, and partly, I think, from some more occult reason. This was not quite the same to me as any other story, and I did not want to talk about it till the day was over. I had very soon ceased to think of the legend, however. I was painting a portrait of Laura, against the lattice window, and I could not think of much else. I had got a splendid background of yellow and grey sunset, and was working away with enthusiasm at her lace. On Thursday Mrs Dorman went. She relented, at parting, so far as to say—

'Don't you put yourself about too much, ma'am, and if there's any little thing I can do next week, I'm sure I shan't mind.'

From which I inferred that she wished to come back to us after Hallowe'en. Up to the last she adhered to the fiction of the niece with touching fidelity.

Thursday passed off pretty well. Laura showed marked ability in the matter of steak and potatoes, and I confess that my knives, and the plates, which I insisted upon washing, were better done than I had dared to expect.

Friday came. It is about what happened on that Friday that this is written. I wonder if I should have believed it, if any one had told it to me. I will write the story of it as quickly and plainly as I can. Everything that happened on that day is burnt into my brain. I shall not forget anything, nor leave anything out.

I got up early, I remember, and lighted the kitchen fire, and had just achieved a smoky success, when my little wife came running down, as sunny and sweet as the clear October morning itself. We prepared breakfast together, and found it very good fun. The housework was soon done, and when brushes and brooms and pails were quiet again, the house was still indeed. It is wonderful what a difference one makes in a house. We really missed Mrs Dorman, quite apart from considerations concerning pots and pans. We spent the day in dusting our books and putting them straight, and dined gaily on cold steak and coffee. Laura was, if possible, brighter and gayer and sweeter than usual, and I began to think that a little domestic toil was really good for her. We had never been so merry since we were married, and the walk we had that afternoon was, I think, the happiest time of all my life. When we had watched the deep scarlet clouds slowly pale into leaden grey against a pale-green sky, and saw the white mists curl up along the hedgerows in the distant marsh, we came back to the house, silently, hand in hand.

'You are sad, my darling,' I said, half-jestingly, as we sat down together in our little parlour. I expected a disclaimer, for my own silence had been the silence of complete happiness. To my surprise she said—

'Yes. I think I am sad, or rather I am uneasy. I don't think I'm very well. I have shivered three or four times since we came in, and it is not cold, is it?'

'No,' I said, and hoped it was not a chill caught from the treacherous mists that roll up from the marshes in the dying light. No – she said, she did not think so. Then, after a silence, she spoke suddenly—

'Do you ever have presentiments of evil?'

'No,' I said, smiling, 'and I shouldn't believe in them if I had.'

'I do,' she went on; 'the night my father died I knew it, though he was right away in the north of Scotland.' I did not answer in words.

She sat looking at the fire for some time in silence, gently stroking my hand. At last she sprang up, came behind me, and, drawing my head back, kissed me.

'There, it's over now,' she said. 'What a baby I am! Come, light the candles, and we'll have some of these new Rubinstein duets.'

And we spent a happy hour or two at the piano.

At about half-past ten I began to long for the good-night pipe, but Laura looked so white that I felt it would be brutal of me to fill our sitting-room with the fumes of strong cavendish.

'I'll take my pipe outside,' I said.

'Let me come, too.'

'No, sweetheart, not to-night; you're much too tired. I shan't be long. Get to bed, or I shall have an invalid to nurse to-morrow as well as the boots to clean.'

I kissed her and was turning to go, when she flung her arms round my neck, and held me as if she would never let me go again. I stroked her hair.

'Come, Pussy, you're over-tired. The housework has been too much for you.'

She loosened her clasp a little and drew a deep breath.

'No. We've been very happy to-day, Jack, haven't we? Don't stay out too long.'

'I won't, my dearie.'

I strolled out of the front door, leaving it unlatched. What a night it was! The jagged masses of heavy dark cloud were rolling at intervals from horizon to horizon, and thin white wreaths covered the stars. Through all the rush of the cloud river, the moon swam, breasting the waves and disappearing again in the darkness. When now and again her light reached the woodlands they seemed to be slowly and noiselessly waving in time to the swing of the clouds above them. There was a strange grey light over all the earth; the fields had that shadowy bloom over them which only comes from the marriage of dew and moonshine, or frost and starlight.

I walked up and down, drinking in the beauty of the quiet earth and the changing sky. The night was absolutely silent. Nothing seemed to be abroad. There was no skurrying of rabbits, or twitter of the half-asleep birds. And though the clouds went sailing across the sky, the wind that drove them never came low enough to rustle the dead leaves in the woodland paths. Across the meadows I could see the church tower standing out black and grey against the sky. I walked there thinking over our three months of happiness – and of my wife, her dear eyes, her loving ways. Oh, my little girl! my own little girl; what a vision came then of a long, glad life for you and me together!

I heard a bell-beat from the church. Eleven already! I turned to go in, but the night held me. I could not go back into our little warm rooms yet. I would go up to the church. I felt vaguely that it would be good to carry my love and thankfulness to the sanctuary whither so many loads of sorrow and gladness had been borne by the men and women of the dead years.

I looked in at the low window as I went by. Laura was half lying on her chair in front of the fire. I could not see her face, only her little head showed dark against the pale blue wall. She was quite still. Asleep, no doubt. My heart reached out to her, as I went on. There must be a God, I thought, and a God who was good. How otherwise could anything so sweet and dear as she have ever been imagined?

I walked slowly along the edge of the wood. A sound broke the stillness of the night, it was a rustling in the wood. I stopped and listened. The sound stopped too. I went on, and now distinctly heard another step than mine answer mine like an echo. It was a poacher or a wood-stealer, most likely, for these were not unknown in our Arcadian neighbourhood. But whoever it was, he was a fool not to step more lightly. I turned into the wood, and now the foot-step seemed to come from the path I had just left. It must be an echo, I thought. The wood looked perfect in the moonlight. The large dying ferns and the brushwood showed where through thinning foliage the pale light came down. The tree trunks stood up like Gothic columns all around me. They reminded me of the church, and I turned into the bier-balk, and passed through the corpsegate between the graves to the low porch. I paused for a moment on the stone seat where Laura and I had watched the fading landscape. Then I noticed that the door of the church was open, and I blamed myself for having left it unlatched the other night. We were the only people who ever cared to come to the church except on Sundays, and I was vexed to think that through our carelessness the damp autumn airs had had a chance of getting in and injuring the old fabric. I went in. It will seem strange, perhaps, that I should have gone half-way up the aisle before I remembered – with a sudden chill, followed by as sudden a rush of self-contempt – that this was the very day and hour when, according to tradition, the 'shapes drawed out man-size in marble' began to walk.

Having thus remembered the legend, and remembered it with a shiver, of which I was ashamed, I could not do otherwise than walk up towards the altar, just to look at the figures – as I said to myself; really what I wanted was to assure myself, first, that I did not believe the legend, and, secondly, that it was not true. I was rather glad that I had come. I thought now I could tell Mrs Dorman how vain her fancies were, and how peacefully the marble figures slept on through the ghastly hour. With my hands in my pockets I passed up the aisle. In the grey dim light the eastern end of the church looked larger than usual, and the arches above the two tombs looked larger too. The moon came out and showed me the reason. I stopped short, my heart gave a leap that nearly choked me, and then sank sickeningly.

The 'bodies drawed out man-size' *were gone*, and their marble slabs lay wide and bare in the vague moonlight that slanted through the east window.

Were they really gone? or was I mad? Clenching my nerves, I

stooped and passed my hand over the smooth slabs, and felt their flat unbroken surface. Had someone taken the things away? Was it some vile practical joke? I would make sure, anyway. In an instant I had made a torch of a newspaper, which happened to be in my pocket, and lighting it, held it high above my head. Its yellow glare illumined the dark arches and those slabs. The figures were gone. And I was alone in the church; or was I alone?

And then a horror seized me, a horror indefinable and indes-cribable – an overwhelming certainty of supreme and accom-plished calamity. I flung down the torch and tore along the aisle and out through the porch, biting my lips as I ran to keep myself from shrieking aloud. Oh, was I mad – or what was this that possessed me? I leaped the churchyard wall and took the straight cut across the fields, led by the light from our windows. Just as I got over the first stile, a dark figure seemed to spring out of the ground. Mad still with that certainty of misfortune, I made for the thing that stood in my path, shouting, 'Get out of the way, can't you!'

But my push met with a more vigorous resistance than I had expected. My arms were caught just above the elbow and held as in a vice, and the raw-boned Irish doctor actually shook me.

'Would ye?' he cried, in his own unmistakable accents – 'would ye, then?'

'Let me go, you fool,' I gasped. 'The marble figures have gone from the church; I tell you they've gone.'

He broke into a ringing laugh. 'I'll have to give ye a draught to-morrow, I see. Ye've bin smoking too much and listening to old wives' tales.'

'I tell you, I've seen the bare slabs.'

'Well, come back with me. I'm going up to old Palmer's – his daughter's ill; we'll look in at the church and let me see the bare slabs.'

'You go, if you like,' I said, a little less frantic for his laughter; 'I'm going home to my wife.'

'Rubbish, man,' said he; 'd'ye think I'll permit of that? Are ye to go saying all yer life that ye've seen solid marble endowed with vitality, and me to go all me life saying ye were a coward? No, sir – ye shan't do ut.'

The night air – a human voice – and I think also the physical contact with this six feet of solid common sense, brought me back a little to my ordinary self, and the word 'coward' was a mental shower-bath.

'Come on, then,' I said sullenly; 'perhaps you're right.'

He still held my arm tightly. We got over the stile and back to the church. All was still as death. The place smelt very damp and earthy. We walked up the aisle. I am not ashamed to confess that I shut my eyes: I knew the figures would not be there. I heard Kelly strike a match.

'Here they are, ye see, right enough; ye've been dreaming or drinking, asking yer pardon for the imputation.'

I opened my eyes. By Kelly's expiring vesta I saw two shapes lying 'in their marble' on their slabs. I drew a deep breath, and caught his hand.

'I'm awfully indebted to you,' I said. 'It must have been some trick of light, or I have been working rather hard, perhaps that's it. Do you know, I was quite convinced they were gone.'

'I'm aware of that,' he answered rather grimly; 'ye'll have to be careful of that brain of yours, my friend, I assure ye.'

He was leaning over and looking at the right-hand figure, whose stony face was the most villainous and deadly in expression.

'By Jove,' he said, 'something has been afoot here – this hand is broken.'

And so it was. I was certain that it had been perfect the last time Laura and I had been there.

'Perhaps some one has *tried* to remove them,' said the young doctor.

'That won't account for my impression,' I objected.

'Too much painting and tobacco will account for that, well enough.'

'Come along,' I said, 'or my wife will be getting anxious. You'll come in and have a drop of whisky and drink confusion to ghosts and better sense to me.'

'I ought to go up to Palmer's, but it's so late now I'd best leave it till the morning,' he replied. 'I was kept late at the Union, and I've had to see a lot of people since. All right, I'll come back with ye.'

I think he fancied I needed him more than did Palmer's girl, so, discussing how such an illusion could have been possible, and deducing from this experience large generalities concerning ghostly apparitions, we walked up to our cottage. We saw, as we walked up the garden-path, that bright light streamed out of the front door, and presently saw that the parlour door was open too. Had she gone out?

'Come in,' I said, and Dr Kelly followed me into the parlour. It was all ablaze with candles, not only the wax ones, but at least a dozen guttering, glaring tallow dips, stuck in vases and ornaments in unlikely places. Light, I knew, was Laura's remedy for nervousness. Poor child! Why had I left her? Brute that I was.

We glanced round the room, and at first we did not see her. The window was open, and the draught set all the candles flaring one way. Her chair was empty and her handkerchief and book lay on the floor. I turned to the window. There, in the recess of the window, I saw her. Oh, my child, my love, had she gone to that window to watch for me? And what had come into the room behind her? To what had she turned with that look of frantic fear and horror? Oh, my little one, had she thought that it was I whose step she heard, and turned to meet – what?

She had fallen back across a table in the window, and her body lay half on it and half on the window-seat, and her head hung down over the table, the brown hair loosened and fallen to the carpet.

Her lips were drawn back, and her eyes wide, wide open. They saw nothing now. What had they seen last?

The doctor moved towards her, but I pushed him aside and sprang to her, caught her in my arms and cried—

'It's all right, Laura! I've got you safe, wifie.'

She fell into my arms in a heap. I clasped her and kissed her, and called her by all her pet names, but I think I knew all the time that she was dead. Her hands were tightly clenched. In one of them she held something fast. When I was quite sure that she was dead, and that nothing mattered at all any more, I let him open her hand to see what she held.

It was a grey marble finger.

THRAWN JANET

by

Robert Louis Stevenson

First published in the October edition
of *Cornhill Magazine*

1881

T HE REVEREND MURDOCH Soulis was long minister of the
moorland parish of Balweary, in the vale of Dule. A severe,
bleak-faced old man, dreadful to his hearers, he dwelt in the last
years of his life, without relative or servant or any human company, in the small and lonely manse under the Hanging Shaw.
In spite of the iron composure of his features, his eye was wild,
scared, and uncertain; and when he dwelt, in private admonitions,
on the future of the impenitent, it seemed as if his eye pierced
through the storms of time to the terrors of eternity. Many young
persons, coming to prepare themselves against the season of the
Holy Communion, were dreadfully affected by his talk. He had
a sermon on 1st Peter, v. and 8th, 'The devil as a roaring lion', on
the Sunday after every seventeenth of August, and he was accustomed to surpass himself upon that text both by the appalling
nature of the matter and the terror of his bearing in the pulpit.
The children were frightened into fits, and the old looked more
than usually oracular, and were, all that day, full of those hints that
Hamlet deprecated. The manse itself, where it stood by the water
of Dule among some thick trees, with the Shaw overhanging it on

the one side, and on the other many cold, moorish hilltops rising towards the sky, had begun, at a very early period of Mr Soulis's ministry, to be avoided in the dusk hours by all who valued themselves upon their prudence; and guidmen sitting at the clachan alehouse shook their heads together at the thought of passing late by that uncanny neighbourhood. There was one spot, to be more particular, which was regarded with especial awe. The manse stood between the high road and the water of Dule, with a gable to each; its back was towards the kirk-town of Balweary, nearly half a mile away; in front of it, a bare garden, hedged with thorn, occupied the land between the river and the road. The house was two storeys high, with two large rooms on each. It opened not directly on the garden, but on a causewayed path, or passage, giving on the road on the one hand, and closed on the other by the tall willows and elders that bordered on the stream. And it was this strip of causeway that enjoyed among the young parishioners of Balweary so infamous a reputation. The minister walked there often after dark, sometimes groaning aloud in the instancy of his unspoken prayers; and when he was from home, and the manse door was locked, the more daring schoolboys ventured, with beating hearts, to 'follow my leader' across that legendary spot.

This atmosphere of terror, surrounding, as it did, a man of God of spotless character and orthodoxy, was a common cause of wonder and subject of enquiry among the few strangers who were led by chance or business into that unknown, outlying country. But many even of the people of the parish were ignorant of the strange events which had marked the first year of Mr Soulis's ministrations; and among those who were better informed, some were naturally reticent, and others shy of that particular topic. Now and again, only, one of the older folk would warm into courage over his third tumbler, and recount the cause of the minister's strange looks and solitary life.

✦ ✦ ✦

Fifty years syne, when Mr Soulis cam first into Ba'weary, he was still a young man – a callant, the folk said – fu' o' book learnin' and grand at the exposition, but, as was natural in sae young a man, wi' nae leevin' experience in religion. The younger sort were greatly taken wi' his gifts and his gab; but auld, concerned, serious men and women were moved even to prayer for the young man, whom they took to be a self-deceiver, and the parish that was like to be sae ill-supplied. It was before the days o' the moderates – weary fa' them; but ill things are like guid – they baith come bit by bit, a pickle at a time; and there were folk even then that said the Lord had left the college professors to their ain devices, an' the lads that went to study wi' them wad hae done mair and better sittin' in a peat-bog, like their forbears of the persecution, wi' a Bible under their oxter and a speerit o' prayer in their heart. There was nae doubt, onyway, but that Mr Soulis had been ower lang at the college. He was careful and troubled for mony things besides the ae thing needful. He had a feck o' books wi' him – mair than had ever been seen before in a' that presbytery; and a sair wark the carrier had wi' them, for they were a' like to have smoored in the Deil's Hag between this and Kilmackerlie. They were books o' divinity, to be sure, or so they ca'd them; but the serious were o' opinion there was little service for sae mony, when the hail o' God's Word would gang in the neuk of a plaid. Then he wad sit half the day and half the nicht forbye, which was scant decent – writin', nae less; and first, they were feared he wad read his sermons; and syne it proved he was writin' a book himsel', which was surely no fittin' for ane of his years an' sma' experience.

Onyway, it behoved him to get an auld, decent wife to keep the manse for him an' see to his bit denners; and he was recommended to an auld limmer – Janet M'Clour, they ca'd her – and sae far left to himsel' as to be ower persuaded. There was mony advised him to the contrar, for Janet was mair than suspeckit by the best folk in Ba'weary. Lang or that, she had had a wean to a dragoon; she hadnae come forrit for maybe thretty year; and bairns had seen her mumblin' to hersel' up on Key's Loan in the gloamin', whilk was an unco time an' place for a God-fearin' woman. Howsoever, it was the laird himsel' that had first tauld the minister o' Janet; and in thae days he wad have gane a far gate to pleesure the laird. When folk tauld him that Janet was sib to the deil, it was a' superstition by his way of it; an' when they cast up the Bible to him an' the witch of Endor, he wad threep it doun their thrapples that thir days were a' gane by, and the deil was mercifully restrained.

Weel, when it got about the clachan that Janet M'Clour was to be servant at the manse, the folk were fair mad wi' her an' him thegether; and some o' the guidwives had nae better to dae than get round her door cheeks and chairge her wi' a' that was ken't again her, frae the sodger's bairn to John Tamson's twa kye. She was nae great speaker; folk usually let her gang her ain gate, an' she let them gang theirs, wi' neither Fair-guid-een nor Fair-guid-day; but when she buckled to, she had a tongue to deave the miller. Up she got, an' there wasnae an auld story in Ba'weary but she gart somebody lowp for it that day; they couldnae say ae thing but she could say twa to it; till, at the hinder end, the guidwives up and claught haud of her, and clawed the coats aff her back, and pu'd her doun the clachan to the water o' Dule, to see if she were a witch or no, soum or droun. The carline skirled till ye could hear her at the Hangin' Shaw, and she focht like ten; there was mony a guidwife bure the mark of her neist day an' mony a lang day after; and just in the hettest o' the collieshangie, wha suld come up (for his sins) but the new minister.

'Women,' said he (and he had a grand voice), 'I charge you in the Lord's name to let her go.'

Janet ran to him – she was fair wud wi' terror – an' clang to him, an' prayed him, for Christ's sake, save her frae the cummers; an' they, for their pairt, tauld him a' that was ken't, and maybe mair.

'Woman,' says he to Janet, 'is this true?'

'As the Lord sees me,' says she, 'as the Lord made me, no a word o't. Forbye the bairn,' says she, 'I've been a decent woman a' my days.'

'Will you,' says Mr Soulis, 'in the name of God, and before me, His unworthy minister, renounce the devil and his works?'

Weel, it wad appear that when he askit that, she gave a girn that fairly frichtit them that saw her, an' they could hear her teeth play dirl thegither in her chafts; but there was naething for it but the ae way or the ither; an' Janet lifted up her hand and renounced the deil before them a'.

'And now,' says Mr Soulis to the guidwives, 'home with ye, one and all, and pray to God for His forgiveness.'

And he gied Janet his arm, though she had little on her but a sark, and took her up the clachan to her ain door like a leddy of the land; an' her scrieghin' and laughin' as was a scandal to be heard.

There were mony grave folk lang ower their prayers that nicht; but when the morn cam' there was sic a fear fell upon a' Ba'weary that the bairns hid theirsels, and even the men folk stood and keekit frae their doors. For there was Janet comin' doun the clachan – her or her likeness, nane could tell – wi' her neck thrawn, and her heid on ae side, like a body that has been hangit, and a girn on her face like an unstreakit corp. By an' by they got used wi' it, and even speered at her to ken what was wrang; but frae that day forth she couldnae speak like a Christian woman, but slavered and played click wi' her teeth like a pair o' shears; and frae that day forth the name o' God cam never on her lips. Whiles she wad try to say it, but it michtnae be. Them that kenned best said least; but they never gied that Thing the name o' Janet M'Clour; for the auld Janet, by their way o't, was in muckle hell that day. But the minister was neither to haud nor to bind; he preached about naething but the folk's cruelty that had gi'en her a stroke of the palsy; he skelpt the bairns that meddled her; and he had her up to the manse that same nicht, and dwalled there a' his lane wi' her under the Hangin' Shaw.

Weel, time gaed by: and the idler sort commenced to think mair lichtly o' that black business. The minister was weel thocht o'; he was aye late at the writing, folk wad see his can'le doon by the Dule water after twal' at e'en; and he seemed pleased wi' himsel' and upsitten as at first, though a' body could see that he was dwining. As for Janet, she cam an' she gaed; if she didnae speak muckle afore, it was reason she should speak less then; she meddled naebody; but she was an eldritch thing to see, an' nane wad hae mistrysted wi' her for Ba'weary glebe.

About the end o' July there cam' a spell o' weather, the like o't never was in that country side; it was lown an' het an' heartless; the herds couldnae win up the Black Hill, the bairns were ower weariet to play; an' yet it was gousty too, wi' claps o' het wund that rumm'led in the glens, and bits o' shouers that slockened naething. We aye thocht it but to thun'er on the morn; but the morn cam, an' the morn's morning, and it was aye the same uncanny weather, sair on folks and bestial. Of a' that were the waur, nane suffered like Mr Soulis; he could neither sleep nor eat, he tauld his elders; an' when he wasnae writin' at his weary book, he wad be stravaguin' ower a' the countryside like a man possessed, when a' body else was blythe to keep caller ben the house.

Abune Hangin' Shaw, in the bield o' the Black Hill, there's a bit enclosed grund wi' an iron yett; and it seems, in the auld days, that was the kirkyaird o' Ba'weary, and consecrated by the Papists before the blessed licht shone upon the kingdom. It was a great howff o' Mr Soulis's, onyway; there he would sit an' consider his sermons; and indeed it's a bieldy bit. Weel, as he cam ower the wast end o' the Black Hill, ae day, he saw first twa, an syne fower, an' syne seeven corbie craws fleein' round an' round abune the auld kirkyaird. They flew laigh and heavy, an' squawked to ither as they gaed; and it was clear to Mr Soulis that something had put them frae their ordinar. He wasnae easy fleyed, an' gaed straucht up to the wa's; an' what suld he find there but a man, or the appearance of a man, sittin' in the inside upon a grave. He was of a great stature, an' black as hell, and his e'en were singular to see. Mr Soulis had heard tell o' black men, mony's the time; but there was something unco about this black man that daunted him. Het as he was, he took a kind o' cauld grue in the marrow o' his banes; but up he spak for a' that; an' says he: 'My friend, are you a stranger in this place?' The black man answered never a word; he got upon his feet, an' begude to hirsle to the wa' on the far side; but he aye lookit at the minister; an' the minister stood an' lookit back; till a' in a meenute the black man was ower the wa' an' rinnin' for the bield o' the trees. Mr Soulis, he hardly kenned why, ran after him; but he was sair forjaskit wi' his walk an' the het, unhalesome weather; and rin as he likit, he got nae mair than a glisk o' the black man amang the birks, till he won doun to the foot o' the hill-side, an' there he saw him ance mair, gaun, hap, step, an' lowp, ower Dule water to the manse.

Mr Soulis wasnae weel pleased that this fearsome gangrel suld mak' sae free wi' Ba'weary manse; an' he ran the harder, an', wet shoon, ower the burn, an' up the walk; but the deil a black man was there to see. He stepped out upon the road, but there was naebody there; he gaed a' ower the gairden, but na, nae black man. At the hinder end, and a bit feared as was but natural, he lifted the hasp and into the manse; and there was Janet M'Clour before his een, wi' her thrawn craig, and nane sae pleased to see him. And he aye minded sinsyne, when first he set his een upon her, he had the same cauld and deidly grue.

'Janet,' says he, 'have you seen a black man?'

'A black man?' quo' she. 'Save us a'! Ye're no wise, minister. There's nae black man in a Ba'weary.'

But she didnae speak plain, ye maun understand; but yam-yammered, like a powney wi' the bit in its moo.

'Weel,' says he, 'Janet, if there was nae black man, I have spoken with the Accuser of the Brethren.'

And he sat down like ane wi' a fever, an' his teeth chittered in his heid.

'Hoots,' says she, 'think shame to yoursel', minister;' an' gied him a drap brandy that she keepit aye by her.

Syne Mr Soulis gaed into his study amang a' his books. It's a lang, laigh, mirk chalmer, perishin' cauld in winter, an' no very dry even in the tap o' the simmer, for the manse stands near the burn. Sae doun he sat, and thocht of a' that had come an' gane since he was in Ba'weary, an' his hame, an' the days when he was a bairn an' ran daffin' on the braes; and that black man aye ran in his heid like the ower-come of a sang. Aye the mair he thocht, the mair he thocht o' the black man. He tried the prayer, an' the words wouldnae come to him; an' he tried, they say, to write at his book, but he could nae mak' nae mair o' that. There was whiles he thocht the black man was at his oxter, an' the swat stood upon him cauld as well-water; and there was other whiles, when he cam to himsel' like a christened bairn and minded naething.

The upshot was that he gaed to the window an' stood glowrin' at Dule water. The trees are unco thick, an' the water lies deep an' black under the manse; an' there was Janet washin' the cla'es wi' her coats kilted. She had her back to the minister, an' he, for his pairt, hardly kenned what he was lookin' at. Syne she turned round, an' shawed her face; Mr Soulis had the same cauld grue as twice that day afore, an' it was borne in upon him what folk said, that Janet was deid lang syne, an' this was a bogle in her clay-cauld flesh. He drew back a pickle and he scanned her narrowly. She was tramp-trampin' in the cla'es, croonin' to hersel'; and eh! Gude guide us, but it was a fearsome face. Whiles she sang louder, but there was nae man born o' woman that could tell the words o' her sang; an' whiles she lookit side-lang doun, but there was naething there for her to look at. There gaed a scunner through the flesh upon his banes; and that was Heeven's advertisement. But Mr Soulis just blamed himsel', he said, to think sae ill of a puir, auld afflicted wife that hadnae a freend forbye himsel'; an' he put up a bit prayer for him and her, an' drank a little caller water – for his heart rose again the meat – an' gaed up to his naked bed in the gloaming.

That was a nicht that has never been forgotten in Ba'weary, the nicht o' the seeventeenth of August, seventeen hun'er' an' twal'. It had been het afore, as I hae said, but that nicht it was hetter than ever. The sun gaed doun amang unco-lookin' clouds; it fell as mirk as the pit; no a star, no a breath o' wund; ye couldnae see your han' afore your face, and even the auld folk cuist the covers frae their beds and lay pechin' for their breath. Wi' a' that he had upon his mind, it was gey and unlikely Mr Soulis wad get muckle sleep. He lay an' he tummled; the gude, caller bed that he got into brunt his very banes; whiles he slept, and whiles he waukened; whiles he heard the time o' nicht, and whiles a tyke yowlin' up the muir, as if somebody was deid; whiles he thocht he heard bogles claverin' in his lug, an' whiles he saw spunkies in the room. He behoved, he judged, to be sick; an' sick he was – little he jaloosed the sickness.

At the hinder end, he got a clearness in his mind, sat up in his sark on the bed-side, and fell thinkin' ance mair o' the black man an' Janet. He couldnae weel tell how – maybe it was the cauld to his feet – but it cam' in upon him wi' a spate that there was some connection between thir twa, an' that either or baith o' them were bogles. And just at that moment, in Janet's room, which was neist to his, there cam' a stramp o' feet as if men were wars'lin', an' then a loud bang; an' then a wund gaed reishling round the fower quarters of the house; an' then a' was aince mair as seelent as the grave.

Mr Soulis was feared for neither man nor deevil. He got his tinder-box, an' lit a can'le, an' made three steps o't ower to Janet's door. It was on the hasp, an' he pushed it open, an' keeked bauldly in. It was a big room, as big as the minister's ain, an' plenished wi' grand, auld, solid gear, for he had naething else. There was a fower-posted bed wi' auld tapestry; and a braw cabinet of aik, that was fu' o' the minister's divinity books, an' put there to be out o' the gate; an' a wheen duds o' Janet's lying here and there about the floor. But nae Janet could Mr Soulis see; nor ony sign of a contention. In he gaed (an' there's few that wad ha'e followed him) an' lookit a' round, an' listened. But there was naethin' to be heard, neither inside the manse nor in a' Ba'weary parish, an' naethin' to be seen but the muckle shadows turnin' round the can'le. An' then a' at aince, the minister's heart played dunt an' stood stock-still; an' a cauld wund blew amang the hairs o' his heid. Whaten a weary sicht was that for the puir man's een! For there was Janet hangin' frae a nail beside the auld aik cabinet: her heid aye lay on her shoother, her een were steeked, the tongue projekit frae her mouth, and her heels were twa feet clear abune the floor.

'God forgive us all!' thocht Mr Soulis; 'poor Janet's dead.'

He cam' a step nearer to the corp; an' then his heart fair whammled in his inside. For by what cantrip it wad ill-beseem a man to judge, she was hingin' frae a single nail an' by a single wursted thread for darnin' hose.

It's an awfu' thing to be your lane at nicht wi' siccan prodigies o' darkness; but Mr Soulis was strong in the Lord. He turned an' gaed his ways oot o' that room, and lockit the door ahint him; and step by step, doon the stairs, as heavy as leed; and set doon the can'le on the table at the stairfoot. He couldnae pray, he couldnae think, he was dreepin' wi' caul' swat, an' naething could he hear but the dunt-dunt-duntin' o' his ain heart. He micht maybe have stood there an hour, or maybe twa, he minded sae little; when a' o' a sudden, he heard a laigh, uncanny steer upstairs; a foot gaed to an' fro in the cha'mer whaur the corp was hingin'; syne the door was opened, though he minded weel that he had lockit it; an' syne there was a step upon the landin', an' it seemed to him as if the corp was lookin' ower the rail and doun upon him whaur he stood.

He took up the can'le again (for he couldnae want the licht), and as saftly as ever he could, gaed straucht out o' the manse an' to the far end o' the causeway. It was aye pit-mirk; the flame o' the can'le, when he set it on the grund, brunt steedy and clear as in a room; naething moved, but the Dule water seepin' and sabbin' doon the glen, an' yon unhaly footstep that cam' ploddin doun the stairs inside the manse. He kenned the foot over weel, for it was Janet's; and at ilka step that cam' a wee thing nearer, the cauld got deeper in his vitals. He commanded his soul to Him that made an' keepit him; 'and O Lord,' said he, 'give me strength this night to war against the powers of evil.'

By this time the foot was comin' through the passage for the door; he could hear a hand skirt alang the wa', as if the fearsome thing was feelin' for its way. The saughs tossed an' maned thegether, a lang sigh cam' ower the hills, the flame o' the can'le was blawn aboot; an' there stood the corp of Thrawn Janet, wi' her grogram goun an' her black mutch, wi' the heid aye upon the shouther, an' the girn still upon the face o't – leevin', ye wad hae said – deid, as Mr Soulis weel kenned – upon the threshold o' the manse.

It's a strange thing that the saul of man should be that thirled into his perishable body; but the minister saw that, an' his heart didnae break.

She didnae stand there lang; she began to move again an' cam' slowly towards Mr Soulis whaur he stood under the saughs. A' the life o' his body, a' the strength o' his speerit, were glowerin' frae his een. It seemed she was gaun to speak, but wanted words, an' made a sign wi' the left hand. There cam' a clap o' wund, like a cat's fuff; oot gaed the can'le, the saughs skrieghed like folk; an' Mr Soulis kenned that, live or die, this was the end o't.

'Witch, beldame, devil!' he cried, 'I charge you, by the power of God, begone – if you be dead, to the grave – if you be damned, to hell.'

An' at that moment the Lord's ain hand out o' the Heevens struck the Horror whaur it stood; the auld, deid, desecrated corp o' the witch-wife, sae lang keepit frae the grave and hirsled round by deils, lowed up like a brunstane spunk and fell in ashes to the grund; the thunder followed, peal on dirling peal, the rairing rain upon the back o' that; and Mr Soulis lowped through the garden hedge, and ran, wi' skelloch upon skelloch, for the clachan.

That same mornin', John Christie saw the black man pass the Muckle Cairn as it was chappin' six; before eicht, he gaed by the change-house at Knockdow; an' no lang after, Sandy M'Lellan saw him gaun linkin' doun the braes frae Kilmackerlie. There's little doubt but it was him that dwalled sae lang in Janet's body; but he was awa' at last; and sinsyne the deil has never fashed us in Ba'weary.

But it was a sair dispensation for the minister; lang, lang he lay ravin' in his bed; and frae that hour to this, he was the man ye ken the day.

THE WITHERED ARM

by

Thomas Hardy

First published in the January edition
of *Blackwood's* magazine

1888

I

A Lorn Milkmaid

IT WAS AN eighty-cow dairy, and the troop of milkers, regular
and supernumerary, were all at work; for, though the time
of year was as yet but early April, the feed lay entirely in water-
meadows, and the cows were 'in full pail'. The hour was about six
in the evening, and three-fourths of the large, red, rectangular animals having been finished off, there was opportunity for a little
conversation.

'He do bring home his bride tomorrow, I hear. They've come as
far as Anglebury today.'

The voice seemed to proceed from the belly of the cow called
Cherry, but the speaker was a milking-woman, whose face was
buried in the flank of that motionless beast.

'Hav' anybody seen her?' said another.

There was a negative response from the first. 'Though they say she's a rosy-cheeked, tisty-tosty little body enough,' she added; and as the milkmaid spoke she turned her face so that she could glance past her cow's tail to the other side of the barton, where a thin, fading woman of thirty milked somewhat apart from the rest.

'Years younger than he, they say,' continued the second, with also a glance of reflectiveness in the same direction.

'How old do you call him, then?'

'Thirty or so.'

'More like forty,' broke in an old milkman near, in a long white pinafore or 'wropper', and with the brim of his hat tied down, so that he looked like a woman. 'A was born before our Great Weir was builded, and I hadn't man's wages when I laved water there.'

The discussion waxed so warm that the purr of the milkstreams became jerky, till a voice from another cow's belly cried with authority, 'Now then, what the Turk do it matter to us about Farmer Lodge's age, or Farmer Lodge's new mis'ess? I shall have to pay him nine pound a year for the rent of every one of these milchers, whatever his age or hers. Get on with your work, or 'twill be dark afore we have done. The evening is pinking in a'ready.' This speaker was the dairyman himself; by whom the milkmaids and men were employed.

Nothing more was said publicly about Farmer Lodge's wedding, but the first woman murmured under her cow to her next neighbour. ''Tis hard for *she*,' signifying the thin worn milkmaid aforesaid.

'O no,' said the second. 'He ha'n't spoke to Rhoda Brook for years.'

When the milking was done they washed their pails and hung them on a many-forked stand made of the peeled limb of an oak-tree, set upright in the earth, and resembling a colossal antlered horn. The majority then dispersed in various directions homeward. The thin woman who had not spoken was joined by a boy of twelve or thereabout, and the twain went away up the field also.

Their course lay apart from that of the others, to a lonely spot high above the water-meads, and not far from the border of Egdon Heath, whose dark countenance was visible in the distance as they drew nigh to their home.

'They've just been saying down in barton that your father brings his young wife home from Anglebury tomorrow,' the woman observed. 'I shall want to send you for a few things to market, and you'll be pretty sure to meet 'em.'

'Yes, Mother,' said the boy. 'Is father married then?'

'Yes . . . You can give her a look, and tell me what she's like, if you do see her.'

'Yes, Mother.'

'If she's dark or fair, and if she's tall – as tall as I. And if she seems like a woman who has ever worked for a living, or one that has been always well off, and has never done anything, and shows marks of the lady on her, as I expect she do.'

'Yes.'

They crept up the hill in the twilight and entered the cottage. It was built of mud-walls, the surface of which had been washed by many rains into channels and depressions that left none of the original flat face visible, while here and there in the thatch above, a rafter showed like a bone protruding through the skin.

She was kneeling down in the chimney-corner, before two pieces of turf laid together with the heather inwards, blowing at the red-hot ashes with her breath till the turves flamed. The radiance lit her pale cheek, and made her dark eyes, that had once been handsome, seem handsome anew. 'Yes,' she resumed, 'see if she is dark or fair, and if you can, notice if her hands be white; if not, see if they look as though she had ever done housework, or are milker's hands like mine.'

The boy again promised, inattentively this time, his mother not observing that he was cutting a notch with his pocket-knife in the beech-backed chair.

II

The Young Wife

The road from Anglebury to Holmstoke is in general level; but there is one place where a sharp ascent breaks its monotony. Farmers homeward-bound from the former market-town, who trot all the rest of the way, walk their horses up this short incline.

The next evening, while the sun was yet bright, a handsome new gig, with a lemon-coloured body and red wheels, was spinning westward along the level highway at the heels of a powerful mare. The driver was a yeoman in the prime of life, cleanly shaven like an actor, his face being toned to that bluish-vermilion hue which so often graces a thriving farmer's features when returning home after successful dealings in the town. Beside him sat a woman, many years his junior – almost, indeed, a girl. Her face too was fresh in colour, but it was of a totally different quality – soft and evanescent, like the light under a heap of rose-petals.

Few people travelled this way, for it was not a main road; and the long white riband of gravel that stretched before them was empty, save of one small scarce-moving speck, which presently resolved itself into the figure of a boy, who was creeping on at a snail's pace, and continually looking behind him – the heavy bundle he carried being some excuse for, if not the reason of, his dilatoriness. When the bouncing gig-party slowed at the bottom of the incline above mentioned, the pedestrian was only a few yards in front. Supporting the large bundle by putting one hand on his hip, he turned and looked straight at the farmer's wife as though he would read her through and through, pacing along abreast of the horse.

The low sun was full in her face, rendering every feature, shade, and colour distinct, from the curve of her little nostril to the colour of her eyes. The farmer, though he seemed annoyed at the boy's persistent presence, did not order him to get out of the way; and thus the lad preceded them, his hard gaze never leaving her, till they reached the top of the ascent, when the farmer trotted on with relief in his lineaments – having taken no outward notice of the boy whatever.

'How that poor lad stared at me!' said the young wife.

'Yes, dear; I saw that he did.'

'He is one of the village, I suppose?'

'One of the neighbourhood. I think he lives with his mother a mile or two off.'

'He knows who we are, no doubt?'

'O yes. You must expect to be stared at just at first, my pretty Gertrude.'

'I do – though I think the poor boy may have looked at us in the hope we might relieve him of his heavy load, rather than from curiosity.'

'O no,' said her husband off-handedly. 'These country lads will carry a hundredweight once they get it on their backs; besides his pack had more size than weight in it. Now, then, another mile and I shall be able to show you our house in the distance – if it is not too dark before we get there.' The wheels spun round, and particles flew from their periphery as before, till a white house of ample dimensions revealed itself, with farm-buildings and ricks at the back.

Meanwhile the boy had quickened his pace, and turning up a by-lane some mile and a half short of the white farmstead, ascended towards the leaner pastures, and so on to the cottage of his mother.

She had reached home after her day's milking at the outlying dairy, and was washing cabbage at the doorway in the declining light. 'Hold up the net a moment,' she said, without preface, as the boy came up.

He flung down his bundle, held the edge of the cabbage-net, and as she filled its meshes with the dripping leaves she went on, 'Well, did you see her?'

'Yes; quite plain.'

'Is she ladylike?'

'Yes; and more. A lady complete.'

'Is she young?'

'Well, she's growed up, and her ways be quite a woman's.'

'Of course. What colour is her hair and face?'

'Her hair is lightish, and her face as comely as a live doll's.'

'Her eyes, then, are not dark like mine?'

'No – of a bluish turn, and her mouth is very nice and red; and when she smiles, her teeth show white.'

'Is she tall?' said the woman sharply.

'I couldn't see. She was sitting down.'

'Then do you go to Holmstoke church tomorrow morning: she's sure to be there. Go early and notice her walking in, and come home and tell me if she's taller than I.'

'Very well, Mother. But why don't you go and see for yourself?'

'*I* go to see her! I wouldn't look up at her if she were to pass my window this instant. She was with Mr Lodge, of course. What did he say or do?'

'Just the same as usual.'

'Took no notice of you?'

'None.'

Next day the mother put a clean shirt on the boy, and started him off for Holmstoke church. He reached the ancient little pile when the door was just being opened, and he was the first to enter. Taking his seat by the font, he watched all the parishioners file in. The well-to-do Farmer Lodge came nearly last; and his young wife, who accompanied him, walked up the aisle with the shyness natural to a modest woman who had appeared thus for the first time. As all other eyes were fixed upon her, the youth's stare was not noticed now.

When he reached home his mother said, 'Well?' before he had entered the room.

'She is not tall. She is rather short,' he replied.

'Ah!' said his mother, with satisfaction.

'But she's very pretty – very. In fact, she's lovely.' The youthful freshness of the yeoman's wife had evidently made an impression even on the somewhat hard nature of the boy.

'That's all I want to hear,' said his mother quickly. 'Now, spread the table-cloth. The hare you wired is very tender; but mind nobody catches you. You've never told me what sort of hands she had.'

'I have never seen 'em. She never took off her gloves.'

'What did she wear this morning?'

'A white bonnet and a silver-coloured gownd. It whewed and whistled so loud when it rubbed against the pews that the lady coloured up more than ever for very shame at the noise, and pulled it in to keep it from touching; but when she pushed into her seat, it whewed more than ever. Mr Lodge, he seemed pleased, and his waistcoat stuck out, and his great golden seals hung like a lord's; but she seemed to wish her noisy gownd anywhere but on her.'

'Not she! However, that will do now.'

These descriptions of the newly-married couple were continued from time to time by the boy at his mother's request, after any chance encounter he had had with them. But Rhoda Brook, though she might easily have seen young Mrs Lodge for herself by walking a couple of miles, would never attempt an excursion towards the quarter where the farmhouse lay. Neither did she, at the daily milking in the dairyman's yard on Lodge's outlying second farm, ever speak on the subject of the recent marriage. The dairyman, who rented the cows of Lodge, and knew perfectly the tall milkmaid's history, with manly kindliness always kept the gossip in the cow-barton from annoying Rhoda. But the atmosphere thereabout was full of the subject the first days of Mrs Lodge's arrival; and from her boy's description and the casual words of the other milkers, Rhoda Brook could raise a mental image of the unconscious Mrs Lodge that was realistic as a photograph.

III

A Vision

One night, two or three weeks after the bridal return, when the boy had gone to bed, Rhoda sat a long time over the turf ashes that she had raked out in front of her to extinguish them. She contemplated so intently the new wife, as presented to her in her mind's eye over the embers, that she forgot the lapse of time. At last, wearied by her day's work, she too retired.

But the figure which had occupied her so much during this and the previous days was not to be banished at night. For the first time Gertrude Lodge visited the supplanted woman in her dreams. Rhoda Brook dreamed – since her assertion that she really saw, before falling asleep, was not to be believed – that the young wife, in the pale silk dress and white bonnet, but with features shockingly distorted, and wrinkled as by age, was sitting upon her chest as she lay. The pressure of Mrs Lodge's person grew heavier; the blue eyes peered cruelly into her face; and then the figure thrust forward its left hand mockingly, so as to make the wedding-ring it wore glitter in Rhoda's eyes. Maddened mentally, and nearly suffocated by pressure, the sleeper struggled; the incubus, still regarding her, withdrew to the foot of the bed, only, however, to come forward by degrees, resume her seat, and flash her left hand as before.

Gasping for breath, Rhoda, in a last desperate effort, swung out her right hand, seized the confronting spectre by its obtrusive left arm, and whirled it backward to the floor, starting up herself as she did so with a low cry.

'O, merciful heaven!' she cried, sitting on the edge of the bed in a cold sweat; 'that was not a dream – she was here!'

She could feel her antagonist's arm within her grasp even now – the very flesh and bone of it, as it seemed. She looked on the floor whither she had whirled the spectre, but there was nothing to be seen.

Rhoda Brook slept no more that night, and when she went milking at the next dawn they noticed how pale and haggard she looked. The milk that she drew quivered into the pail; her hand had not calmed even yet, and still retained the feel of the arm. She came home to breakfast as wearily as if it had been suppertime.

'What was that noise in your chimmer, mother, last night?' said her son. 'You fell off the bed. surely?'

'Did you hear anything fall? At what time?'

'Just when the clock struck two.'

She could not explain, and when the meal was done went silently about her household work, the boy assisting her, for he hated going afield on the farms, and she indulged his reluctance. Between eleven and twelve the garden-gate clicked, and she lifted her eyes to the window. At the bottom of the garden, within the gate, stood the woman of her vision. Rhoda seemed transfixed.

'Ah, she said she would come!' exclaimed the boy, also observing her.

'Said so – when? How does she know us?'

'I have seen and spoken to her. I talked to her yesterday.'

'I told you,' said the mother, flushing indignantly, 'never to speak to anybody in that house, or go near the place.'

'I did not speak to her till she spoke to me. And I did not go near the place. I met her in the road.'

'What did you tell her?'

'Nothing. She said, "Are you the poor boy who had to bring

the heavy load from market?" And she looked at my boots, and said they would not keep my feet dry if it came on wet, because they were so cracked. I told her I lived with my mother, and we had enough to do to keep ourselves, and that's how it was; and she said then, "I'll come and bring you some better boots, and see your mother." She gives away things to other folks in the meads besides us.'

Mrs Lodge was by this time close to the door – not in her silk, as Rhoda had seen her in the bed-chamber, but in a morning hat, and gown of common light material, which became her better than silk. On her arm she carried a basket.

The impression remaining from the night's experience was still strong. Brook had almost expected to see the wrinkles, the scorn and the cruelty on her visitor's face.

She would have escaped an interview, had escape been possible. There was, however, no backdoor to the cottage, and in an instant the boy had lifted the latch to Mrs Lodge's gentle knock.

'I see I have come to the right house,' said she, glancing at the lad, and smiling. 'But I was not sure till you opened the door.'

The figure and action were those of the phantom; but her voice was so indescribably sweet, her glance so winning, her smile so tender, so unlike that of Rhoda's midnight visitant, that the latter could hardly believe the evidence of her senses. She was truly glad that she had not hidden away in sheer aversion, as she had been inclined to do. In her basket Mrs Lodge brought the pair of boots that she had promised to the boy, and other useful articles.

At these proofs of a kindly feeling towards her and hers, Rhoda's heart reproached her bitterly. This innocent young thing should have her blessing and not her curse. When she left them a light seemed gone from the dwelling. Two days later she came again to know if the boots fitted; and less than a fortnight after paid Rhoda another call. On this occasion the boy was absent.

'I walk a good deal,' said Mrs Lodge, 'and your house is the nearest outside our own parish. I hope you are well. You don't look quite well.'

Rhoda said she was well enough; and, indeed, though the paler of the two, there was more of the strength that endures in her well-defined features and large frame than in the soft-cheeked young woman before her. The conversation became quite confidential as regarded their powers and weaknesses; and when Mrs Lodge was leaving, Rhoda said, 'I hope you will find this air agree with you, ma'am, and not suffer from the damp of the water-meads.'

The younger one replied that there was not much doubt of her general health being usually good. 'Though, now you remind me,' she added, 'I have one little ailment which puzzles me. It is nothing serious, but I cannot make it out.'

She uncovered her left hand and arm; and their outline confronted Rhoda's gaze as the exact original of the limb she had beheld and seized in her dream. Upon the pink round surface of the arm were faint marks of an unhealthy colour, as if produced by a rough grasp. Rhoda's eyes became riveted on the discolorations; she fancied that she discerned in them the shape of her own four fingers.

'How did it happen?' she said mechanically.

'I cannot tell,' replied Mrs Lodge, shaking her head. 'One night when I was sound asleep, dreaming I was away in some strange place, a pain suddenly shot into my arm there, and was so keen as to awaken me. I must have struck it in the daytime, I suppose, though I don't remember doing so.' She added, laughing, 'I tell my dear husband that it looks just as if he had flown into a rage and struck me there. O, I daresay it will soon disappear.'

'Ha, ha! Yes . . . On what night did it come?'

Mrs Lodge considered, and said it would be a fortnight ago on the morrow. 'When I awoke I could not remember where I was,' she added, 'till the clock striking two reminded me.'

She had named the night and hour of Rhoda's spectral encounter, and Brook felt like a guilty thing. The artless disclosure startled her; she did not reason on the freaks of coincidence; and all the scenery of that ghastly night returned with double vividness to her mind.

'O, can it be,' she said to herself, when her visitor had departed, 'that I exercise a malignant power over people against my own will?' She knew that she had been slyly called a witch since her fall; but never having understood why that particular stigma had been attached to her, it had passed disregarded. Could this be the explanation, and had such things as this ever happened before?

IV

A Suggestion

The summer drew on, and Rhoda Brook almost dreaded to meet Mrs Lodge again, notwithstanding that her feeling for the young wife amounted well-nigh to affection. Something in her own individuality seemed to convict Rhoda of crime. Yet a fatality sometimes would direct the steps of the latter to the outskirts of Holmstoke whenever she left her house for any other purpose than her daily work; and hence it happened that their next encounter was out of doors. Rhoda could not avoid the subject which had so mystified her, and after the first few words she stammered, 'I hope your – arm is well again, ma'm?' She had perceived with consternation that Gertrude Lodge carried her left arm stiffly.

'No; it is not quite well. Indeed it is no better at all; it is rather worse. It pains me dreadfully sometimes.'

'Perhaps you had better go to a doctor, ma'am.'

She replied that she had already seen a doctor. Her husband had insisted upon her going to one. But the surgeon had not seemed to understand the afflicted limb at all; he had told her to bathe it in hot water, and she had bathed it, but the treatment had done no good.

'Will you let me see it?' said the milkwoman.

Mrs Lodge pushed up her sleeve and disclosed the place, which was a few inches above the wrist. As soon as Rhoda Brook saw it, she could hardly preserve her composure. There was nothing of the nature of a wound, but the arm at that point had a shrivelled look, and the outline of the four fingers appeared more distinct than at the former time. Moreover, she fancied that they were imprinted in precisely the relative position of her clutch upon the arm in the trance; the first finger towards Gertrude's wrist, and the fourth towards her elbow.

What the impress resembled seemed to have struck Gertrude herself since their last meeting. 'It looks almost like finger-marks,' she said; adding with a faint laugh, 'my husband says it is as if some witch, or the devil himself, had taken hold of me there, and blasted the flesh.'

Rhoda shivered. 'That's fancy,' she said hurriedly. 'I wouldn't mind it, if I were you.'

'I shouldn't so much mind it,' said the younger, with hesitation, 'if – if I hadn't a notion that it makes my husband dislike me – no, love me less. Men think so much of personal appearance.'

'Some do – he for one.'

'Yes; and he was very proud of mine, at first.'

'Keep your arm covered from his sight.'

'Ah – he knows the disfigurement is there!' She tried to hide the tears that filled her eyes.

'Well, ma'am, I earnestly hope it will go away soon.'

And so the milkwoman's mind was chained anew to the subject by a horrid sort of spell as she returned home. The sense of having been guilty of an act of malignity increased, affect as she might to ridicule her superstition. In her secret heart Rhoda did not altogether object to a slight diminution of her successor's beauty, by whatever means it had come about; but she did not wish to inflict upon her physical pain. For though this pretty young woman had rendered impossible any reparation which Lodge might have made Rhoda for his past conduct, everything like resentment at the unconscious usurpation had quite passed away from the elder's mind.

If the sweet and kindly Gertrude Lodge only knew of the scene in the bed-chamber, what would she think? Not to inform her of it seemed treachery in the presence of her friendliness; but tell she could not of her own accord – neither could she devise a remedy.

She mused upon the matter the greater part of the night; and the next day, after the morning milking, set out to obtain another glimpse of Gertrude Lodge if she could, being held to her by a gruesome fascination. By watching the house from a distance, the milkmaid was presently able to discern the farmer's wife in a ride she was taking alone – probably to join her husband in some distant field. Mrs Lodge perceived her, and cantered in her direction.

'Good morning, Rhoda!' Gertrude said, when she had come up. 'I was going to call.'

Rhoda noticed that Mrs Lodge held the reins with some difficulty.

'I hope – the bad arm,' said Rhoda.

'They tell me there is possibly one way by which I might be able to find out the cause, and so perhaps the cure of it,' replied the other anxiously. 'It is by going to some clever man over in Egdon Heath. They did not know if he was still alive – and I cannot remember his name at this moment; but they said that you knew more of his movements than anybody else hereabout, and could tell me if he were still to be consulted. Dear me – what was his name? But you know.'

'Not Conjuror Trendle?' said her thin companion, turning pale.

'Trendle – yes. Is he alive?'

'I believe so,' said Rhoda, with reluctance.

'Why do you call him conjuror?'

'Well – they say – they used to say he was a – he had powers other folks have not.'

'O, how could my people be so superstitious as to recommend a man of that sort! I thought they meant some medical man. I shall think no more of him.'

Rhoda looked relieved, and Mrs Lodge rode on. The milk-woman had inwardly seen, from the moment she heard of her having been mentioned as a reference for this man, that there must exist a sarcastic feeling among the work-folk that a sorceress would know the whereabouts of the exorcist. They suspected her, then. A short time ago this would have given no concern to a woman of her common sense. But she had a haunting reason to be superstitious now; and she had been seized with sudden dread that this Conjuror Trendle might name her as the malignant influence which was blasting the fair person of Gertrude, and so lead her friend to hate her for ever, and to treat her as some fiend in human shape.

But all was not over. Two days after, a shadow intruded into the window-pattern thrown on Rhoda Brook's floor by the afternoon sun. The woman opened the door at once, almost breathlessly.

'Are you alone?' said Gertrude. She seemed to be no less harassed and anxious than Brook herself.

'Yes,' said Rhoda.

'The place on my arm seems worse, and troubles me!' the young farmer's wife went on. 'It is so mysterious! I do hope it will not be an incurable wound. I have again been thinking of what they said about Conjuror Trendle. I don't really believe in such men, but I should not mind just visiting him, from curiosity – though on no account must my husband know. Is it far to where he lives?'

'Yes – five miles,' said Rhoda backwardly. 'In the heart of Egdon.'

'Well, I should have to walk. Could not you go with me to show me the way – say tomorrow afternoon?'

'O, not I – that is,' the milkwoman murmured, with a start of dismay. Again the dread seized her that something to do with her fierce act in the dream might be revealed, and her character in the eyes of the most useful friend she had ever had be ruined irretrievably.

Mrs Lodge urged, and Rhoda finally assented, though with much misgiving. Sad as the journey would be to her, she could not conscientiously stand in the way of a possible remedy for her patron's strange affliction. It was agreed that, to escape suspicion of their mystic intent, they should meet at the edge of the heath at the corner of a plantation which was visible from the spot where they now stood.

V

Conjuror Trendle

By the next afternoon Rhoda would have done anything to escape this inquiry. But she had promised to go. Moreover, there was a horrid fascination at times in becoming instrumental in throwing such possible light on her own character as would reveal her to be something greater in the occult world than she had ever herself suspected.

She started just before the time of day mentioned between them, and half an hour's brisk walking brought her to the south-eastern extension of the Egdon tract of country, where the fir plantation was. A slight figure, cloaked and veiled, was already there. Rhoda recognised, almost with a shudder, that Mrs Lodge bore her left arm in a sling.

They hardly spoke to each other, and immediately set out on

their climb into the interior of this solemn country, which stood high above the rich alluvial soil they had left half an hour before. It was a long walk; thick clouds made the atmosphere dark, though it was as yet only early afternoon; and the wind howled dismally over the slopes of the heath – not improbably the same heath which had witnessed the agony of the Wessex King Ina, presented to after-ages as Lear. Gertrude Lodge talked most, Rhoda replying with monosyllabic preoccupation. She had a strange dislike to walking on the side of her companion where hung the afflicted arm, moving round to the other when inadvertently near it. Much heather had been brushed by their feet when they descended upon a cart-track, beside which stood the house of the man they sought.

He did not profess his remedial practices openly, or care anything about their continuance, his direct interests being those of a dealer in furze, turf, 'sharp sand', and other local products. Indeed, he affected not to believe largely in his own powers, and when warts that had been shown him for cure miraculously disappeared – which it must be owned they infallibly did – he would say lightly, 'O, I only drink a glass of grog upon 'em – perhaps it's all chance,' and immediately turn the subject.

He was at home when they arrived, having in fact seen them descending into his valley. He was a grey-bearded man, with a reddish face, and he looked singularly at Rhoda the first moment he beheld her. Mrs Lodge told him her errand; and then with words of self-disparagement he examined her arm.

'Medicine can't cure it,' he said promptly. ''Tis the work of an enemy.'

Rhoda shrank into herself, and drew back.

'An enemy? What enemy?' asked Mrs Lodge.

He shook his head. 'That's best known to yourself,' he said. 'If you like, I can show the person to you, though I shall not myself know who it is. I can do no more; and don't wish to do that.'

She pressed him; on which he told Rhoda to wait outside

where she stood, and took Mrs Lodge into the room. It opened immediately from the door; and, as the latter remained ajar, Rhoda Brook could see the proceedings without taking part in them. He brought a tumbler from the dresser, nearly filled it with water, and fetching an egg, prepared it in some private way; after which he broke it on the edge of the glass, so that the white went in and the yolk remained. As it was getting gloomy, he took the glass and its contents to the window, and told Gertrude to watch the mixture closely. They leant over the table together, and the milkwoman could see the opaline hue of the egg-fluid changing form as it sank in the water, but she was not near enough to define the shape that it assumed.

'Do you catch the likeness of any face or figure as you look?' demanded the conjuror of the young woman.

She murmured a reply, in tones so low as to be inaudible to Rhoda, and continued to gaze intently into the glass. Rhoda turned, and walked a few steps away.

When Mrs Lodge came out, and her face was met by the light, it appeared exceedingly pale – as pale as Rhoda's – against the sad dun shades of the upland's garniture. Trendle shut the door behind her, and they at once started homeward together. But Rhoda perceived that her companion had quite changed.

'Did he charge much?' she asked tentatively.

'O no – nothing. He would not take a farthing,' said Gertrude.

'And what did you see?' inquired Rhoda.

'Nothing I – care to speak of.' The constraint in her manner was remarkable; her face was so rigid as to wear an oldened aspect, faintly suggestive of the face in Rhoda's bed-chamber.

'Was it you who first proposed coming here?' Mrs Lodge suddenly inquired, after a long pause. 'How very odd, if you did!'

'No. But I am not very sorry we have come, all things considered,' she replied. For the first time a sense of triumph possessed her, and she did not altogether deplore that the young thing at her side should learn that their lives had been antagonised by other influences than their own.

The subject was no more alluded to during the long and dreary walk home. But in some way or other a story was whispered about the many-dairied lowland that winter that Mrs Lodge's gradual loss of the use of her left arm was owing to her being 'overlooked' by Rhoda Brook. The latter kept her own counsel about the incubus, but her face grew sadder and thinner; and in the spring she and her boy disappeared from the neighbourhood of Holmstoke.

VI

A Second Attempt

Half-a-dozen years passed away, and Mr and Mrs Lodge's married experience sank into prosiness, and worse. The farmer was usually gloomy and silent: the woman whom he had wooed for her grace and beauty was contorted and disfigured in the left limb; moreover, she had brought him no child, which rendered it likely that he would be the last of a family who had occupied that valley for some two hundred years. He thought of Rhoda Brook and her son; and feared this might be a judgement from heaven upon him.

The once blithe-hearted and enlightened Gertrude was changing into an irritable, superstitious woman, whose whole time was given to experimenting upon her ailment with every quack remedy she came across. She was honestly attached to her husband, and was ever secretly hoping against hope to win back his heart again by regaining some at least of her personal beauty. Hence it arose that her closet was lined with bottles, packets, and ointment-pots of every description – nay, bunches of mystic herbs, charms, and books of necromancy, which in her schoolgirl time she would have ridiculed as folly.

'Damned if you won't poison yourself with these apothecary messes and witch mixtures some time or other,' said her husband, when his eye chanced to fall upon the multitudinous array.

She did not reply, but turned her sad, soft glance upon him in such heart-swollen reproach that he looked sorry for his words, and added, 'I only meant it for your good, you know, Gertrude.'

'I'll clear out the whole lot, and destroy them,' said she huskily, 'and try such remedies no more!'

'You want somebody to cheer you,' he observed. 'I once thought of adopting a boy; but he is too old now. And he is gone away I don't know where.'

She guessed to whom he alluded; for, Rhoda Brook's story had in the course of years become known to her; though not a word had ever passed between her husband and herself on the subject. Neither had she ever spoken to him of her visit to Conjuror Trendle, and of what was revealed to her, or she thought was revealed to her, by that solitary heath-man.

She was now five-and-twenty; but she seemed older.

'Six years of marriage, and only a few months of love,' she sometimes whispered to herself. And then she thought of the apparent cause, and said, with a tragic glance at her withering limb, 'If I could only be again as I was when he first saw me!'

She obediently destroyed her nostrums and charms; but there remained a hankering wish to try something else – some other sort of cure altogether. She had never revisited Trendle since she had been conducted to the house of the solitary by Rhoda against her will; but it now suddenly occurred to Gertrude that she would, in a last desperate effort at deliverance from this seeming curse, again seek out the man, if he yet lived. He was entitled to a certain credence, for the indistinct form he had raised in the glass had undoubtedly resembled the only woman in the world who – as she now knew, though not then – could have a reason for bearing her ill-will. The visit should be paid.

This time she went alone, though she nearly got lost on the heath, and roamed a considerable distance out of her way. Trendle's house was reached at last, however: he was not indoors, and instead of waiting at the cottage, she went to where his bent figure was pointed out to her at work a long way off. Trendle remembered her, and laying down the handful of furze-roots which he was gathering and throwing into a heap, he offered to accompany her in the homeward direction, as the distance was considerable and the days were short. So they walked together, his head bowed nearly to the earth, and his form of a colour with it.

'You can send away warts and other excrescences, I know,' she said; 'why can't you send away this?' And the arm was uncovered.

'You think too much of my powers!' said Trendle; 'and I am old and weak now, too. No, no; it is too much for me to attempt in my own person. What have ye tried?'

She named to him some of the hundred medicaments and counterspells which she had adopted from time to time. He shook his head.

'Some were good enough,' he said approvingly; 'but not many of them for such as this. This is of the nature of a blight, not of the nature of a wound; and if you ever do throw it off, it will be all at once.'

'If I only could!'

'There is only one chance of doing it known to me. It has never failed in kindred afflictions, – that I can declare. But it is hard to carry out, and especially for a woman.'

'Tell me!' said she.

'You must touch with the limb the neck of a man who's been hanged.'

She started a little at the image he had raised.

'Before he's cold – just after he's cut down,' continued the conjuror impassively.

'How can that do good?'

'It will turn the blood and change the constitution. But, as I say, to do it is hard. You must go to the jail when there's a hanging, and wait for him when he's brought off the gallows. Lots have done it, though perhaps not such pretty women as you. I used to send dozens for skin complaints. But that was in former times. The last I sent was in '13 – near twenty years ago.'

He had no more to tell her; and, when he had put her into a straight track homeward, turned and left her, refusing all money as at first.

VII

A Ride

The communication sank deep into Gertrude's mind. Her nature was rather a timid one; and probably of all remedies that the white wizard could have suggested there was not one which would have filled her with so much aversion as this, not to speak of the immense obstacles in the way of its adoption.

Casterbridge, the county-town, was a dozen or fifteen miles off; and though in those days, when men were executed for horse-stealing, arson, and burglary, an assize seldom passed without a hanging, it was not likely that she could get access to the body of the criminal unaided. And the fear of her husband's anger made her reluctant to breathe a word of Trendle's suggestion to him or to anybody about him.

She did nothing for months, and patiently bore her disfigurement as before. But her woman's nature, craving for renewed love, through the medium of renewed beauty (she was but twenty-five), was ever stimulating her to try what, at any rate, could hardly do her any harm. 'What came by a spell will go by a spell surely,' she would say. Whenever her imagination pictured the act she shrank in terror from the possibility of it: then the words of the conjuror, 'It will turn your blood,' were seen to be capable of a scientific no less than ghastly interpretation; the mastering desire returned, and urged her on again.

There was at this time but one county paper, and that her husband only occasionally borrowed. But old-fashioned days had old-fashioned means, and news was extensively conveyed by word of mouth from market to market, or from fair to fair, so that, whenever such an event as an execution was about to take place, few within a radius of twenty miles were ignorant of the coming sight; and, so far as Holmstoke was concerned, some enthusiasts had been known to walk all the way to Casterbridge and back in one day, solely to witness the spectacle. The next assizes were in March; and when Gertrude Lodge heard that they had been held, she inquired stealthily at the inn as to the result, as soon as she could find opportunity.

She was, however, too late. The time at which the sentences were to be carried out had arrived, and to make the journey and obtain permission at such short notice required at least her husband's assistance. She dared not tell him, for she had found by delicate experiment that these smouldering village beliefs made him furious if mentioned, partly because he half entertained them himself. It was therefore necessary to wait for another opportunity.

Her determination received a fillip from learning that two epileptic children had attended from this very village of Holmstoke many years before with beneficial results, though the experiment had been strongly condemned by the neighbouring clergy. April, May, June, passed; and it is no overstatement to say that by the end of the last-named month Gertrude well-nigh longed for the death of a fellow-creature. Instead of her formal prayers each night, her unconscious prayer was, 'O Lord, hang some guilty or innocent person soon!'

This time she made earlier inquiries, and was altogether more systematic in her proceedings. Moreover, the season was summer, between the haymaking and the harvest, and in the leisure thus afforded him, her husband had been holiday-taking away from home.

The assizes were in July, and she went to the inn as before. There was to be one execution – only one – for arson.

Her greatest problem was not how to get to Casterbridge, but what means she should adopt for obtaining admission to the jail. Though access for such purposes had formerly never been denied, the custom had fallen into desuetude; and in contemplating her possible difficulties, she was again almost driven to fall back upon her husband. But, on sounding him about the assizes, he was so uncommunicative, so more than usually cold, that she did not proceed, and decided that whatever she did she would do alone.

Fortune, obdurate hitherto, showed her unexpected favour. On the Thursday before the Saturday fixed for the execution, Lodge remarked to her that he was going away from home for another day or two on business at a fair, and that he was sorry he could not take her with him.

She exhibited on this occasion so much readiness to stay at home that he looked at her in surprise. Time had been when she would have shown deep disappointment at the loss of such a jaunt. However, he lapsed into his usual taciturnity, and on the day named left Holmstoke.

It was now her turn. She at first had thought of driving, but on reflection held that driving would not do, since it would necessitate her keeping to the turnpike-road, and so increase by tenfold the risk of her ghastly errand being found out. She decided to ride, and avoid the beaten track, notwithstanding that in her husband's stables there was no animal just at present which by any stretch of imagination could be considered a lady's mount, in spite of his promise before marriage to always keep a mare for her. He had, however, many cart-horses, fine ones of their kind; and among the rest was a serviceable creature, an equine Amazon, with a back as broad as a sofa, on which Gertrude had occasionally taken an airing when unwell. This horse she chose.

On Friday afternoon one of the men brought it round. She was dressed, and before going down looked at her shrivelled arm. 'Ah!' she said to it, 'if it had not been for you this terrible ordeal would have been saved me!'

When strapping up the bundle in which she carried a few articles of clothing, she took occasion to say to the servant, 'I take these in case I should not get back to-night from the person I am going to visit. Don't be alarmed if I am not in by ten, and close up the house as usual. I shall be home tomorrow for certain.' She meant then to privately tell her husband: the deed accomplished was not like the deed projected. He would almost certainly forgive her.

And then the pretty, palpitating Gertrude Lodge went from her husband's homestead; but though her goal was Casterbridge, she did not take the direct route thither through Stickleford. Her cunning course at first was in precisely the opposite direction. As soon as she was out of sight, however, she turned to the left, by a road which led into Egdon, and on entering the heath wheeled round, and set out in the true course, due westerly. A more private way down the county could not be imagined; and as to direction, she had merely to keep her horse's head to a point a little to the right of the sun. She knew that she would light upon a furze-cutter or cottager of some sort from time to time, from whom she might correct her bearing.

Though the date was comparatively recent, Egdon was much less fragmentary in character than now. The attempts – successful and otherwise – at cultivation on the lower slopes, which intrude and break up the original heath into small detached heaths, had not been carried far; Enclosure Acts had not taken effect, and the banks and fences which now exclude the cattle of those villagers who formerly enjoyed rights of commonage thereon, and the carts of those who had turbary privileges which kept them in firing all the year round, were not erected. Gertrude, therefore, rode along with no other obstacles than the prickly furze bushes, the mats of heather, the white water-courses, and the natural steeps and declivities of the ground.

Her horse was sure, if heavy-footed and slow, and though a draught animal, was easy-paced; had it been otherwise, she was not a woman who could have ventured to ride over such a bit of country with a half-dead arm. It was therefore nearly eight o'clock when she drew rein to breathe her bearer on the last outlying high point of heath-land towards Casterbridge, previous to leaving Egdon for the cultivated valleys.

She halted before a pool called Rushy-pond, flanked by the ends of two hedges; a railing ran through the centre of the pond, dividing it in half. Over the railing she saw the low green country; over the green trees the roofs of the town; over the roofs a white flat facade, denoting the entrance to the county jail. On the roof of this front, specks were moving about; they seemed to be workmen erecting something. Her flesh crept. She descended slowly, and was soon amid corn-fields and pastures. In another half-hour, when it was almost dusk, Gertrude reached the White Hart, the first inn of the town on that side.

Little surprise was excited by her arrival; farmers' wives rode on horseback then more than they do now; though, for that matter, Mrs Lodge was not imagined to be a wife at all; the innkeeper supposed her some harum-scarum young woman who had come to attend 'hang-fair' next day. Neither her husband nor herself ever dealt in Casterbridge market, so that she was unknown. While dismounting she beheld a crowd of boys standing at the door of a harness-maker's shop just above the inn, looking inside it with deep interest.

'What is going on there?' she asked of the ostler.

'Making the rope for tomorrow.'

She throbbed responsively, and contracted her arm.

'Tis sold by the inch afterwards,' the man continued. 'I could get you a bit, miss, for nothing, if you'd like?'

She hastily repudiated any such wish, all the more from a curious creeping feeling that the condemned wretch's destiny was becoming interwoven with her own; and having engaged a room for the night, sat down to think.

Up to this time she had formed but the vaguest notions about her means of obtaining access to the prison. The words of the cunning-man returned to her mind. He had implied that she should use her beauty, impaired though it was, as a pass-key. In her inexperience she knew little about jail functionaries; she had heard of a high-sheriff and an under-sheriff, but dimly only. She knew, however, that there must be a hangman, and to the hangman she determined to apply.

VIII

A Water-side Hermit

At this date, and for several years after, there was a hangman to almost every jail. Gertrude found, on inquiry, that the Casterbridge official dwelt in a lonely cottage by a deep slow river flowing under the cliff on which the prison buildings were situated – the stream being the self-same one, though she did not know it, which watered the Stickleford and Holmstoke meads lower down in its course.

Having changed her dress, and before she had eaten or drunk – for she could not take her ease till she had ascertained some particulars – Gertrude pursued her way by a path along the water-side to the cottage indicated. Passing thus the outskirts of the jail, she discerned on the level roof over the gateway three rectangular lines against the sky, where the specks had been moving in her distant view; she recognised what the erection was, and passed quickly on. Another hundred yards brought her to the executioner's house, which a boy pointed out. It stood close to the same stream, and was hard by a weir, the waters of which emitted a steady roar.

While she stood hesitating, the door opened, and an old man came forth shading a candle with one hand. Locking the door on the outside, he turned to a flight of wooden steps fixed against the end of the cottage, and began to ascend them, this being evidently the staircase to his bedroom. Gertrude hastened forward, but by the time she reached the foot of the ladder he was at the top. She called to him loudly enough to be heard above the roar of the weir; he looked down and said, 'What d'ye want here?'

'To speak to you a minute.'

The candle-light, such as it was, fell upon her imploring, pale, upturned face, and Davies (as the hangman was called) backed down the ladder. 'I was just going to bed,' he said; '"Early to bed and early to rise," but I don't mind stopping a minute for such a one as you. Come into the house.' He reopened the door, and preceded her to the room within.

The implements of his daily work, which was that of a jobbing gardener, stood in a corner, and seeing probably that she looked rural, he said, 'If you want me to undertake country work, I can't come, for I never leave Casterbridge for gentle nor simple – not I. My real calling is officer of justice,' he added formally.

'Yes, yes! That's it. To-morrow!'

'Ah! I thought so. Well, what's the matter about that? 'Tis no use to come here about the knot – folks do come continually, but I tell 'em one knot is as merciful as another if ye keep it under the ear. Is the unfortunate man a relation; or, I should say, perhaps' (looking at her dress) 'a person who's been in your employ?'

'No. What time is the execution?'

'The same as usual – twelve o'clock, or as soon after as the

London mail-coach gets in. We always wait for that, in case of a reprieve.'

'O – a reprieve – I hope not!' she said involuntarily.

'Well, – hee, hee! – as a matter of business, so do I! But still, if ever a young fellow deserved to be let off, this one does; only just turned eighteen, and only present by chance when the rick was fired. Howsomever, there's not much risk of that, as they are obliged to make an example of him, there having been so much destruction of property that way lately.'

'I mean,' she explained, 'that I want to touch him for a charm, a cure of an affliction, by the advice of a man who has proved the virtue of the remedy.'

'O yes, miss! Now I understand. I've had such people come in past years. But it didn't strike me that you looked of a sort to require blood-turning. What's the complaint? The wrong kind for this, I'll be bound.'

'My arm.' She reluctantly showed the withered skin.

'Ah! – 'tis all a-scram!' said the hangman, examining it.

'Yes,' said she.

'Well,' he continued, with interest, 'that *is* the class o' subject, I'm bound to admit! I like the look of the place; it is as suitable for the cure as any I ever saw. 'Twas a knowing-man that sent 'ee, whoever he was.'

'You can contrive for me all that's necessary?' she said breathlessly.

'You should really have gone to the governor of the jail, and your doctor with 'ee, and given your name and address – that's how it used to be done, if I recollect. Still, perhaps, I can manage it for a trifling fee.'

'O, thank you! I would rather do it this way, as I should like it kept private.'

'Lover not to know, eh?'

'No – husband.'

'Aha! Very well. I'll get 'ee a touch of the corpse.'

'Where is it now?' she said, shuddering.

'It? – *he*, you mean; he's living yet. Just inside that little small winder up there in the glum.' He signified the jail on the cliff above.

She thought of her husband and her friends. 'Yes, of course,' she said; 'and how am I to proceed?'

He took her to the door. 'Now, do you be waiting at the little wicket in the wall, that you'll find up there in the lane, not later than one o'clock. I will open it from the inside, as I shan't come home to dinner till he's cut down. Good-night. Be punctual; and if you don't want anybody to know 'ee, wear a veil. Ah – once I had such a daughter as you!'

She went away, and climbed the path above, to assure herself that she would be able to find the wicket next day. Its outline was soon visible to her – a narrow opening in the outer wall of the prison precincts. The steep was so great that, having reached the wicket, she stopped a moment to breathe: and, looking back upon the water-side cot, saw the hangman again ascending his outdoor staircase. He entered the loft or chamber to which it led, and in a few minutes extinguished his light.

The town clock struck ten, and she returned to the White Hart as she had come.

IX

A Rencounter

It was one o'clock on Saturday. Gertrude Lodge, having been admitted to the jail as above described, was sitting in a waiting-room within the second gate, which stood under a classic archway of ashlar, then comparatively modern, and bearing the inscription, 'COVNTY JAIL: 1793'. This had been the façade she saw from the heath the day before. Near at hand was a passage to the roof on which the gallows stood.

The town was thronged, and the market suspended; but Gertrude had seen scarcely a soul. Having kept her room till the hour of the appointment, she had proceeded to the spot by a way which avoided the open space below the cliff where the spectators had gathered; but she could, even now, hear the multitudinous babble of their voices, out of which rose at intervals the hoarse croak of a single voice uttering the words, 'Last dying speech and confession!' There had been no reprieve, and the execution was over; but the crowd still waited to see the body taken down.

Soon the persistent girl heard a trampling overhead, then a hand beckoned to her, and, following directions, she went out and crossed the inner paved court beyond the gatehouse, her knees trembling so that she could scarcely walk. One of her arms was out of its sleeve, and only covered by her shawl.

On the spot at which she had now arrived were two trestles, and before she could think of their purpose she heard heavy feet descending stairs somewhere at her back. Turn her head she would not, or could not, and, rigid in this position, she was conscious of a rough coffin passing her shoulder, borne by four men. It was open, and in it lay the body of a young man, wearing the smockfrock of a rustic, and fustian breeches. The corpse had been thrown into the coffin so hastily that the skirt of the smockfrock was hanging over. The burden was temporarily deposited on the trestles.

By this time the young woman's state was such that a grey mist seemed to float before her eyes, on account of which, and the veil she wore, she could scarcely discern anything: it was as though she had nearly died, but was held up by a sort of galvanism.

'Now!' said a voice close at hand, and she was just conscious that the word had been addressed to her.

By a last strenuous effort she advanced, at the same time hearing persons approaching behind her. She bared her poor curst arm; and

Davies, uncovering the face of the corpse, took Gertrude's hand, and held it so that her arm lay across the dead man's neck, upon a line the colour of an unripe blackberry, which surrounded it.

Gertrude shrieked: 'the turn o' the blood', predicted by the conjuror, had taken place. But at that moment a second shriek rent the air of the enclosure: it was not Gertrude's, and its effect upon her was to make her start round.

Immediately behind her stood Rhoda Brook, her face drawn, and her eyes red with weeping. Behind Rhoda stood Gertrude's own husband; his countenance lined, his eyes dim, but without a tear.

'D—n you! what are you doing here?' he said hoarsely.

'Hussy – to come between us and our child now!' cried Rhoda. 'This is the meaning of what Satan showed me in the vision! You are like her at last!' And clutching the bare arm of the younger woman, she pulled her unresistingly back against the wall. Immediately Brook had loosened her hold, the fragile young Gertrude slid down against the feet of her husband. When he lifted her up she was unconscious.

The mere sight of the twain had been enough to suggest to her that the dead young man was Rhoda's son. At that time the relatives of an executed convict had the privilege of claiming the body for burial, if they chose to do so; and it was for this purpose that Lodge was awaiting the inquest with Rhoda. He had been summoned by her as soon as the young man was taken in the crime, and at different times since; and he had attended in court during the trial. This was the 'holiday' he had been indulging in of late. The two wretched parents had wished to avoid exposure; and hence had come themselves for the body, a wagon and sheet for its conveyance and covering being in waiting outside.

Gertrude's case was so serious that it was deemed advisable to call to her the surgeon who was at hand. She was taken out of the jail into the town; but she never reached home alive. Her delicate vitality, sapped perhaps by the paralysed arm, collapsed under the double shock that followed the severe strain, physical and mental, to which she had subjected herself during the previous twenty-four hours. Her blood had been 'turned' indeed – too far. Her death took place in the town three days after.

Her husband was never seen in Casterbridge again; once only in the old market-place at Anglebury, which he had so much frequented, and very seldom in public anywhere. Burdened at first with moodiness and remorse, he eventually changed for the better, and appeared as a chastened and thoughtful man. Soon after attending the funeral of his poor wife he took steps towards giving up the farms in Holmstoke and the adjoining parish, and, having sold every head of his stock, he went away to Port-Bredy, at the other end of the county, living there in solitary lodgings till his death two years later of a painless decline. It was then found that he had bequeathed the whole of his not inconsiderable property to a reformatory for boys, subject to the payment of a small annuity to Rhoda Brook, if she could be found to claim it.

For some time she could not be found; but eventually she reappeared in her old parish – absolutely refusing, however, to have anything to do with the provision made for her. Her monotonous milking at the dairy was resumed, and followed for many long years, till her form became bent, and her once abundant dark hair white and worn away at the forehead – perhaps by long pressure against the cows. Here, sometimes, those who knew her experiences would stand and observe her, and wonder what sombre thoughts were beating inside that impassive, wrinkled brow, to the rhythm of the alternating milk-streams.

PALLINGHURST BARROW

by

Grant Allen

First published in *The Illustrated London News*

1892

I

RUDOLPH REEVE SAT by himself on the Old Long Barrow on Pallinghurst Common. It was a September evening, and the sun was setting. The west was all aglow with a mysterious red light, very strange and lurid – a light that reflected itself in glowing purple on the dark brown heather and the dying bracken. Rudolph Reeve was a journalist and a man of science; but he had a poet's soul for all that, in spite of his avocations, neither of which is usually thought to tend towards the spontaneous development of a poetic temperament. He sat there long, watching the livid hues that incarnadined the sky – redder and fiercer than anything he ever remembered to have seen since the famous year of the Krakatoa sunsets – though he knew it was getting late, and he ought to have gone back long since to the manor-house to dress for dinner. Mrs Bouverie-Barton, his hostess, the famous Woman's Rights woman, was always such a stickler for punctuality and dispatch and all the other unfeminine virtues! But in spite of Mrs Bouverie-Barton,

Rudolph Reeve sat on. There was something about that sunset and the lights on the bracken – something weird and unearthly – that positively fascinated him.

The view over the Common, which stands high and exposed, a veritable waste of heath and gorse, is strikingly wide and expansive. Pallinghurst Ring, or the 'Old Long Barrow', a well-known landmark familiar by that name from time immemorial to all the country-side, crowns its actual summit, and commands from its top the surrounding hills far into the shadowy heart of Hampshire. On its terraced slope Rudolph sat and gazed out, with all the artistic pleasure of a poet or a painter (for he was a little of both) in the exquisite flush of the dying reflections from the dying sun upon the dying heather. He sat and wondered to himself why death is always so much more beautiful, so much more poetical, so much calmer than life – and why you invariably enjoy things so very much better when you know you ought to be dressing for dinner.

He was just going to rise, however, dreading the lasting wrath of Mrs Bouverie-Barton, when of a sudden a very weird yet definite feeling caused him for one moment to pause and hesitate. Why he felt it he knew not; but even as he sat there on the grassy tumulus, covered close with short sward of subterranean clover, that curious, cunning plant that buries its own seeds by automatic action, he was aware, through an external sense, but by pure internal consciousness, of something or other living and moving within the barrow. He shut his eyes and listened. No; fancy, pure fancy! Not a sound broke the stillness of early evening, save the drone of insects – those dying insects, now beginning to fail fast before the first chill breath of approaching autumn. Rudolph opened his eyes again and looked down on the ground. In the little boggy hollow by his feet innumerable plants of sundew spread their murderous rosettes of sticky red leaves, all bedewed with viscid gum, to catch and roll round the straggling flies that wrenched their tiny limbs in vain efforts to free themselves. But that was all. Nothing else was astir. In spite of sight and sound, however, he was still deeply thrilled by this strange consciousness as of something living and moving in the barrow underneath; something living and moving – or was it moving and dead? Something crawling and creeping, as the long arms of the sundews crawled and crept around the helpless flies, whose juices they sucked out. A weird and awful feeling, yet strangely fascinating! He hated the vulgar necessity for going back to dinner. Why do people dine at all? So material! So commonplace! And the universe all teeming with strange secrets to unfold! He knew not why, but a fierce desire possessed his soul to stop and give way to this overpowering sense of the mysterious and the marvellous in the dark depths of the barrow.

With an effort he roused himself and put on his hat, which he had been holding in his hand, for his forehead was burning. The sun had now long set, and Mrs Bouverie-Barton dined at 7.30 punctually. He must rise and go home. Something unknown pulled him down to detain him. Once more he paused and hesitated. He was not a superstitious man, yet it seemed to him as if many strange shapes stood by unseen and watched with great eagerness to see whether he would rise and go away, or yield to the temptation of stopping and indulging his curious fancy. Strange! – he saw and heard absolutely nobody and nothing; yet he dimly realised that unseen figures were watching him close with bated breath and anxiously observing his every movement, as if intent to know whether he would rise and move on, or remain to investigate this causeless sensation.

For a minute or two he stood irresolute; and all the time he so stood the unseen bystanders held their breath and looked on in an agony of expectation. He could feel their outstretched necks; he could picture their strained attention. At last he broke away. 'This is nonsense,' he said aloud to himself, and turned slowly homeward. As he did so, a deep sigh, as of suspense relieved, but relieved in the wrong direction, seemed to rise – unheard, impalpable, spiritual –

from the invisible crowd that gathered around him immaterial. Clutched hands seemed to stretch after him and try to pull him back. An unreal throng of angry and disappointed creatures seemed to follow him over the moor, uttering speechless imprecations on his head, in some unknown tongue – ineffable, inaudible. This horrid sense of being followed by unearthly foes took absolute possession of Rudolph's mind. It might have been merely the lurid redness of the afterglow, or the loneliness of the moor, or the necessity for being back not one minute late for Mrs Bouverie-Barton's dinner-hour; but, at any rate, he lost all self-control for the moment, and ran – ran wildly, at the very top of his speed, all the way from the barrow to the door of the manor-house garden. There he stopped and looked round with a painful sense of his own stupid cowardice. This was positively childish: he had seen nothing, heard nothing, had nothing definite to frighten him; yet he had run from his own mental shadow, like the veriest schoolgirl, and was trembling still from the profundity of his sense that somebody unseen was pursuing and following him. 'What a precious fool I am,' he said to himself, half angrily, 'to be so terrified at nothing! I'll go round there by-and-by just to recover my self-respect, and to show, at least, I'm not really frightened.'

And even as he said it he was internally aware that his baffled foes, standing grinning their disappointment with gnashed teeth at the garden-gate, gave a chuckle of surprise, delight, and satisfaction at his altered intention.

II

There's nothing like light for dispelling superstitious terrors. Pallinghurst Manor-house was fortunately supplied with electric light, for Mrs Bouverie-Barton was nothing if not intensely modern. Long before Rudolph had finished dressing for dinner, he was smiling once more to himself at his foolish conduct. Never in his life before – at least, since he was twenty – had he done such a thing; and he knew why he'd done it now. It was nervous breakdown. He had been overworking his brain in town with those elaborate calculations for his *Fortnightly* article on 'The Present State of Chinese Finances'; and Sir Arthur Boyd, the famous specialist on diseases of the nervous system, had earned three honest guineas cheap by recommending him 'a week or two's rest and change in the country'. That was why he had accepted Mrs Bouverie-Barton's invitation to form part of her brilliant autumn party at Pallinghurst Manor, and that was also doubtless why he had been so absurdly frightened at nothing at all just now on the Common. Memorandum: Never to overwork his brain in future; it doesn't pay. And yet, in these days, how earn bread and cheese at literature without overworking it?

He went down to dinner, however, in very good spirits. His hostess was kind; she permitted him to take in that pretty American. Conversation with the soup turned at once on the sunset. Conversation with the soup is always on the lowest and most casual plane; it improves with the fish, and reaches its culmination with the sweets and the cheese, after which it declines again to the fruity level. 'You were on the barrow about seven, Mr Reeve,' Mrs Bouverie-Barton observed severely, when he spoke of the after-glow. 'You watched that sunset close. How fast you must have walked home! I was almost half afraid you were going to be late for dinner.'

Rudolph coloured up slightly; 'twas a girlish trick, unworthy of a journalist; but still he had it. 'Oh, dear, no, Mrs Bouverie-Barton,' he answered gravely. 'I may be foolish, but not, I hope, criminal. I know better than to do anything so weak and wicked as that at Pallinghurst Manor. I *do* walk rather fast, and the sunset – well, the sunset was just too lovely.'

'Elegant,' the pretty American interposed, in her own language. 'It always is, this night every year,' little Joyce said quietly, with the air of one who retails a well-known scientific fact. 'It's the night, you know, when the light burns bright on the Old Long Barrow.'

Joyce was Mrs Bouverie-Barton's only child – a frail and pretty little creature, just twelve years old, very light and fairylike, but with a strange cowed look which, nevertheless, somehow curiously became her.

'What nonsense you talk, my child!' her mother exclaimed, darting a look at Joyce which made her relapse forthwith into instant silence. 'I'm ashamed of her, Mr Reeve; they pick up such nonsense as this from their nurses.' For Mrs Bouverie-Barton was modern, and disbelieved in everything. 'Tis a simple creed; one clause concludes it.

But the child's words, though lightly whispered, had caught the quick ear of Archie Cameron, the distinguished electrician. He made a spring upon them at once; for the merest suspicion of the supernatural was to Cameron irresistible. 'What's that, Joyce?' he cried, leaning forward across the table. 'No, Mrs Bouverie-Barton, I really must hear it. What day is this to-day, and what's that you just said about the sunset and the light on the Old Long Barrow?'

Joyce glanced pleadingly at her mother, and then again at Cameron. A very faint nod gave her grudging leave to proceed with her tale, under maternal disapprobation, for Mrs Bouverie-Barton didn't carry her belief in Woman's Rights quite so far as to apply them to the case of her own daughter. We must draw a line somewhere.

Joyce hesitated and began. 'Well, this is the night, you know,' she said, 'when the sun turns, or stands still, or crosses the tropic, or goes back again, or something.'

Mrs Bouverie-Barton gave a dry little cough. 'The autumnal equinox,' she interposed severely, 'at which, of course, the sun does nothing of the sort you suppose. We shall have to have your astronomy looked after, Joyce; such ignorance is exhaustive. But go on with your myth, please, and get it over quickly.'

'The autumnal equinox; that's just it,' Joyce went on, unabashed.
'I remember that's the word, for old Rachel, the gipsy, told me so.
Well, on this day every year, a sort of glow comes up on the moor;
oh! I know it does, Mother, for I've seen it myself; and the rhyme
about it goes—

> Every year on Michael's night,
> Pallinghurst Barrow burneth bright.

'Only the gipsy told me it was Baal's night before it was St
Michael's, and it was somebody else's night, whose name I forget,
before it was Baal's. And the somebody was a god to whom you
must never sacrifice anything with iron, but always with flint or
with a stone hatchet.'

Cameron leaned back in his chair and surveyed the child critic-
ally. 'Now, this is interesting,' he said; 'profoundly interesting. For
here we get, what is always so much wanted, first-hand evidence.
And you're quite sure, Joyce, you've really seen it?'

'Oh! Mr Cameron, how can you?' Mrs Bouverie-Barton cried,
quite pettishly; for even advanced ladies are still feminine enough
at times to be distinctly pettish. 'I take the greatest trouble to keep
all such rubbish out of Joyce's way; and then you men of science
come down here and talk like this to her, and undo all the good I've
taken months in doing.'

'Well, whether Joyce has ever seen it or not,' Rudolph Reeve
said gravely, 'I can answer for it myself that I saw a very curious
light on the Long Barrow tonight; and, furthermore, I felt a most
peculiar sensation.'

'What was that?' Cameron asked, bending over towards him
eagerly. For all the world knows that Cameron, though a disbe-
liever in most things (except the Brush light), still retains a quaint
tinge of Highland Scotch belief in a good ghost story.

'Why, as I was sitting on the barrow,' Rudolph began, 'just after sunset, I was dimly conscious of something stirring inside, not visible or audible, but—'

'Oh, I know, I know!' Joyce put in, leaning forward, with her eyes staring curiously; 'a sort of a feeling that there was somebody somewhere, very faint and dim, though you couldn't see or hear them; they tried to pull you down, clutching at you like this: and when you ran away, frightened, they seemed to follow you and jeer at you. Great gibbering creatures! Oh, I know what all that is! I've been there, and felt it.'

'Joyce!' Mrs Bouverie-Barton put in with a warning frown, 'what nonsense you talk! You're really too ridiculous. How can you suppose Mr Reeve ran away – a man of science like him – from an imaginary terror?'

'Well, I won't quite say I ran away,' Rudolph answered, sheepishly. 'We never do admit these things, I suppose, after twenty. But I certainly did hurry home at the very top of my speed – not to be late for dinner, you know, Mrs Bouverie-Barton; and I will admit, Joyce, between you and me only, I was conscious by the way of something very much like your grinning followers behind me.'

Mrs Bouverie-Barton darted him another look of intense displeasure. 'I think,' she said, in that chilly voice that has iced whole committees, 'at a table like this, and with such thinkers around, we might surely find something rather better to discuss than such worn-out superstitions. Professor Spence, did you light upon any fresh palæoliths in the gravel-pit this morning?'

III

In the drawing-room, a little later, a small group collected by the corner bay, remotest from Mrs Bouverie-Barton's own presidential chair, to hear Rudolph and Joyce compare experiences on the light above the barrow. When the two dreamers of dreams and seers of visions had finished, Mrs Bruce, the esoteric Buddhist and hostess of Mahatmas (they often dropped in on her, it was said, quite informally, for afternoon tea), opened the flood-gates of her torrent speech with triumphant vehemence. 'This is just what I should have expected,' she said, looking round for a sceptic, that she might turn and rend him. 'Novalis was right. Children are early men. They are freshest from the truth. They are freshest to us from the truth. Little souls just let loose from the free expanse of God's sky see more than we adults do – at least, except a few of us. We ourselves, what are we but accumulated layers of phantasmata? Spirit-light rarely breaks in upon our grimed charnel of flesh. The dust of years overlies us. But the child, bursting new upon the dim world of Karma, trails clouds of glory from the beatific vision. So Wordsworth held; so the Masters of Tibet taught us, long ages before Wordsworth.'

'It's curious,' Professor Spence put in, with a scientific smile, re-strained at the corners, 'that all this should have happened to Joyce and to our friend Reeve at a long barrow. For you've seen Mac-Ritchie's last work, I suppose? No? Well, he's shown conclusively that long barrows, which are the graves of the small, squat people who preceded the inroad of Aryan invaders, are the real originals of all the fairy hills and subterranean palaces of popular legend. You know the old story of how Childe Roland to the dark tower came, of course, Cameron? Well, that dark tower was nothing more or less than a long barrow; perhaps Pallinghurst Barrow itself, per-haps some other, and Childe Roland went into it to rescue his sister Burd Ellen, who had been stolen by the fairy king, after the fashion of his kind, for a human sacrifice. The Picts, you recollect, were a deeply religious people, who believed in human sacrifice. They felt they derived from it high spiritual benefit. And the queerest part of it all is that in order to see the fairies you must go round the barrow *widdershins* – that is to say, Miss Quackenboss, as Cameron will explain to you, the opposite way from the way of the sun – on this very night of all the year, Michaelmas Eve, which was the accepted old date of the autumnal equinox.'

'All long barrows have a chamber of great stones in the centre, I believe,' Cameron suggested, tentatively.

'Yes, all or nearly all; megalithic, you know; unwrought; and that chamber's the subterranean palace, lit up with the fairy light that's so constantly found in old stories of the dead, and which Joyce and you, alone among moderns, have been permitted to see, Reeve.'

'It's a very odd fact,' Dr Porter, the materialist, interposed musingly, 'that the only ghosts people ever see are the ghosts of a generation very, very close to them. One hears of lots of ghosts in eighteenth-century costumes, because everybody has a clear idea of wigs and small-clothes from pictures and fancy dresses. One hears of far fewer in Elizabethan dress, because the class most given to beholding ghosts are seldom acquainted with ruffs and farthingales; and one meets with none at all in Anglo-Saxon or Ancient British or Roman costumes, because those are only known to a comparatively small class of learned people, and ghosts, as a rule, avoid the learned – except you, Mrs Bruce – as they would avoid prussic acid. Millions of ghosts of remote antiquity must swarm about the world, though, after a hundred years or thereabouts, they retire into obscurity and cease to annoy people with their nasty cold shivers. But the queer thing about these long-barrow ghosts is that they must be the spirits of men and women who died thousands and thousands of years ago, which is exceptional longevity for a spiritual being; don't you think so, Cameron?'

'Europe must be chock-full of them!' the pretty American assented, smiling, 'though America hasn't had time, so far, to collect any considerable population of spirits.'

But Mrs Bruce was up in arms at once against such covert levity, and took the field in full force for her beloved spectres. 'No, no,' she said, 'Dr Porter, there you mistake your subject. You should read what I have written in "The Mirror of Trismegistus". Man is the focus of the glass of his own senses. There are other landscapes in the fifth and sixth dimensions of space than the one presented to him. As Carlyle said truly, each eye sees in all things just what each eye brings with it the power of seeing. And this is true spiritually as well as physically. To Newton and Newton's dog Diamond what a different universe! One saw the great vision of universal gravitation, the other saw – a little mouse under a chair, as the wise old nursery rhyme so philosophically puts it. Nursery rhymes summarise for us the gain of centuries. Nothing was ever destroyed, nothing was ever changed, and nothing new is ever created. All the spirits of all that is, or was, or ever will be, people the universe everywhere, unseen, around us, and each of us sees of them those only he himself is adapted to seeing. The rustic or the clown meets no ghosts of any sort save the ghosts of the persons he knows about otherwise; if a man like yourself saw a ghost at all – which isn't likely – for you starve your spiritual side by blindly shutting your eyes to one whole aspect of nature – you'd be just as likely to see the ghost of a Stone Age chief as the ghost of a Georgian or Elizabethan exquisite.'

'Did I catch the word ghost?' Mrs Bouverie-Barton put in, coming up unexpectedly with her angry glower. 'Joyce, my child, go to bed. This is no talk for you. And don't go chilling yourself by standing at the window in your nightdress, looking out on the Common to search for the light on the Old Long Barrow, which is all pure moonshine. You nearly caught your death of cold last year with that nonsense. It's always so. These superstitions never do any good to anyone.'

And, indeed, Rudolph felt a faint glow of shame himself at having discussed such themes in the hearing of that nervous and high-strung little creature.

IV

In the course of the evening, Rudolph's head began to ache, as, to say the truth, it often did; for was he not an author? and sufferance is the badge of all our tribe. His head generally ached: the intervals he employed upon magazine articles. He knew that headache well; it was the worst neuralgic kind – the wet-towel variety – the sort that keeps you tossing the whole night long without hope of respite. About eleven o'clock, when the men went into the smoking-room, the pain became unendurable. He called Dr Porter aside. 'Can't you give me anything to relieve it?' he asked piteously, after describing his symptoms.

'Oh, certainly,' the doctor answered with that brisk medical confidence we all know so well. 'I'll bring you up a draught that will put that all right in less than half an hour. What Mrs Bruce calls Soma – the fine old crusted remedy of our Aryan ancestor; there's nothing like it for cases of nervous inanition.'

Rudolph went up to his room, and the doctor followed him a few minutes later with a very small phial of a very thick green viscid liquid. He poured ten drops carefully into a measured medicine-glass, and filled it up with water. It amalgamated badly. 'Drink that off,' he said, with the magisterial air of the cunning leech. And Rudolph drank it.

'I'll leave you the bottle,' the doctor went on, laying it down on the dressing-table, 'only use it with caution. Ten drops in two hours if the pain continues. Not more than ten, recollect. It's a powerful narcotic – I daresay you know its name: it's Cannabis Indica.'

Rudolph thanked him inarticulately, and flung himself on the bed without undressing. He had brought up a book with him – that delicious volume, Joseph Jacobs's 'English Fairy Tales' – and he tried in some vague way to read the story of Childe Roland, to which Professor Spence had directed his attention. But his head ached so much he could hardly read it; he only gathered with difficulty that Childe Roland had been instructed by witch or war-lock to come to a green hill surrounded with terrace-rings – like Pallinghurst Barrow – to walk round it thrice, widdershins, saying each time—

> Open door, open door,
> And let me come in,

– and when the door opened to enter unabashed the fairy king's palace. And the third time the door did open; and Childe Roland entered a court, all lighted with a fairy light or gloaming; and then he went through a long passage, till he came at last to two wide stone doors; and beyond them lay a hall – stately, glorious, magnificent – where Burd Ellen sat combing her golden hair with a comb of amber. And the moment she saw her brother, up she stood, and she said—

> Woe worth the day, ye luckless fool,
> Or ever that ye were born;
> For come the King of Elfland in,
> Your fortune is forlorn.

When Rudolph had read so far his head ached so much he could read no further; so he laid down the book, and reflected once more in some half-conscious mood on Mrs Bruce's theory that each man could see only the ghosts he expected. That seemed reasonable enough, for according to our faith is it unto us always. If so, then these ancient and savage ghosts of the dim old Stone Age, before bronze or iron, must still haunt grassy barrows under the waving pines where legend declared they were long since buried; and the mystic light over Pallinghurst moor must be the local evidence and symbol of their presence.

How long he lay there he hardly quite knew; but the clock

struck twice, and his head was aching so fiercely now that he helped himself plentifully to a second dose of the thick green mixture. His hand shook too much to be Puritanical to a drop or two. For a while it relieved him, then the pain grew worse again. Dreamily he moved over to the big north oriel to cool his brow with the fresh night air. The window stood open. As he gazed out, a curious sight met his eye. At another oriel in the wing, which ran in an L-shaped bend from the part of the house where he had been put, he saw a child's white face gaze appealingly across to him. It was Joyce, in her white nightdress, peering with all her might, in spite of her mother's prohibition, on the mystic common. For a second she started. Her eyes met his. Slowly she raised one pale forefinger and pointed. Her lips opened to frame an inaudible word; but he read it by sight. 'Look!' she said simply. Rudolph looked where she pointed.

A faint blue light hung lambent over the Old Long Barrow. It was ghostly and vague, like matches rubbed on the palm. It seemed to rouse and call him.

He glanced towards Joyce. She waved her hand to the barrow. Her lips said 'Go.' Rudolph was now in that strange semi-mesmeric state of self-induced hypnotism when a command, of whatever sort or by whomever given, seems to compel obedience. Trembling he rose, and taking his bed-room candle in his hand, descended the stair noiselessly. Then, walking on tip-toe across the tile-paved hall, he reached his hat from the rack, and opening the front door stole out into the garden.

The Soma had steadied his nerves and supplied him with false courage, but even in spite of it he felt a weird and creepy sense of mystery and the supernatural. Indeed, he would have turned back even now, had he not chanced to look up and see Joyce's pale face still pressed close against the window and Joyce's white hand still motioning him mutely onward. He looked once more in the direction where she pointed. The spectral light now burnt clearer and bluer, and more unearthly than ever, and the illimitable moor seemed haunted from end to end by innumerable invisible and uncanny creatures.

Rudolph groped his way on. His goal was the barrow. As he went, speechless voices seemed to whisper unknown tongues encouragingly in his ear; horrible shapes of elder creeds appeared to crowd round him and tempt him with beckoning fingers to follow them. Alone, erect, across the darkling waste, stumbling now and again over roots of gorse and heather, but steadied, as it seemed, by invisible hands, he staggered slowly forward, till at last, with aching head and trembling feet, he stood beside the immemorial grave of the savage chieftain. Away over in the east the white moon was just rising.

After a moment's pause, he began to walk round the tumulus. But something clogged and impeded him. His feet wouldn't obey his will; they seemed to move of themselves in the opposite direction. Then all at once he remembered he had been trying to go the way of the sun, instead of widdershins. Steadying himself, and opening his eyes, he walked in the converse sense. All at once his feet moved easily, and the invisible attendants chuckled to themselves so loud that he could almost hear them. After the third round his lips parted, and he murmured the mystic words: 'Open door! Open door! Let me come in.' Then his head throbbed worse than ever with exertion and giddiness, and for two or three minutes more he was unconscious of anything.

When he opened his eyes again a very different sight displayed itself before him. Instantly he was aware that the age had gone back upon its steps ten thousand years, as the sun went back upon the dial of Ahaz; he stood face to face with a remote antiquity. Planes of existence faded; new sights floated over him; new worlds were penetrated; new ideas, yet very old, undulated centrically towards him from the universal flat of time and space and matter and motion. He was projected into another sphere and saw by fresh senses. Everything was changed, and he himself changed with it.

The blue light over the barrow now shone clear as day, though infinitely more mysterious. A passage lay open through the grassy slope into a rude stone corridor. Though his curiosity by this time was thoroughly aroused, Rudolph shrank with a terrible shrinking from his own impulse to enter this grim black hole, which led at once, by an oblique descent, into the bowels of the earth. But he couldn't help himself. For, O God! looking round him, he saw, to his infinite terror, alarm, and awe, a ghostly throng of naked and hideous savages. They were spirits, yet savages. Eagerly they jostled and hustled him, and crowded round him in wild groups, exactly as they had done to the spiritual sense a little earlier in the evening, when he couldn't see them. But now he saw them clearly with the outer eye; saw them as grinning and hateful barbarian shadows, neither black nor white, but tawny-skinned and low-browed; their tangled hair falling unkempt in matted locks about their receding foreheads; their jaws large and fierce; their eyebrows shaggy and protruding like a gorilla's; their loins just girt with a few scraps of torn skin; their whole mien inexpressibly repulsive and blood-thirsty.

They were savages, yet they were ghosts. The two most terrible and dreaded foes of civilised experience seemed combined at once in them. Rudolph Reeve crouched powerless in their intangible hands; for they seized him roughly with incorporeal fingers, and pushed him bodily into the presence of their sleeping chieftain. As they did so they raised loud peals of discordant laughter. It was hollow, but it was piercing. In that hateful sound the triumphant whoop of the Red Indian and the weird mockery of the ghost were strangely mingled into some appalling harmony.

Rudolph allowed them to push him in; they were too many to resist; and the Soma had sucked all strength out of his muscles. The women were the worst: ghastly hags of old, witches with pendent breasts and bloodshot eyes, they whirled round him in triumph, and shouted aloud in a tongue he had never before heard, though he understood it instinctively, 'A victim! A victim! We hold him! We have him!'

Even in the agonised horror of that awful moment Rudolph knew why he understood those words, unheard till then. They were the first language of our race – the natural and instinctive mother-tongue of humanity.

They haled him forward by main force to the central chamber, with hands and arms and ghostly shreds of buffalo-hide. Their wrists compelled him as the magnet compels the iron bar. He entered the palace. A dim phosphorescent light, like the light of a churchyard or of decaying paganism, seemed to illumine it faintly. Things loomed dark before him; but his eyes almost instantly adapted themselves to the gloom, as the eyes of the dead on the first night in the grave adapt themselves by inner force to the strange-ness of their surroundings. The royal hall was built up of cyclopean stones, each as big as the head of some colossal Sesostris. They were of ice-worn granite and a dusky-grey sandstone, rudely piled on one another, and carved in relief with representations of serpents, concentric lines, interlacing zigzags, and the mystic swastika. But all these things Rudolph only saw vaguely, if he saw them at all; his attention was too much concentrated on devouring fear and the horror of his situation.

In the very centre, a skeleton sat crouching on the floor in some loose, huddled fashion. Its legs were doubled up, its hands clasped round its knees, its grinning teeth had long been blackened by time or by the indurated blood of human victims. The ghosts approached it with strange reverence, in impish postures.

'See! We bring you a slave, great king!' they cried in the same barbaric tongue – all clicks and gutturals. 'For this is the holy night of your father, the Sun, when he turns him about on his yearly course through the stars and goes south to leave us. We bring you a slave to renew your youth. Rise! Drink his hot blood! Rise! Kill and eat him!'

The grinning skeleton turned its head and regarded Rudolph from its eyeless orbs with a vacant glance of hungry satisfaction. The sight of human meat seemed to create a soul beneath the ribs of death in some incredible fashion. Even as Rudolph, held fast by the immaterial hands of his ghastly captors, looked and trembled for his fate, too terrified to cry out or even to move and struggle, he beheld the hideous thing rise and assume a shadowy shape, all pallid blue light, like the shapes of his jailers. Bit by bit, as he gazed, the skeleton seemed to disappear, or rather to fade into some unsubstantial form, which was nevertheless more human, more corporeal, more horrible than the dry bones it had come from. Naked and yellow like the rest, it wore round its dim waist just an apron of dry grass, or, what seemed to be such, while over its shoulders hung the ghost of a bearskin mantle. As it rose, the other spectres knocked their foreheads low on the ground before it, and grovelled with their long locks in the ageless dust, and uttered elfin cries of inarticulate homage.

The great chief turned, grinning, to one of his spectral henchmen. 'Give a knife!' he said curtly, for all that these strange shades uttered was snapped out in short, sharp sentences, and in a monosyllabic tongue, like the bark of jackals or the laugh of the striped hyena among the graves at midnight.

The attendant, bowing low once more, handed his liege a flint flake, very keen-edged, but jagged, a rude and horrible instrument of barbaric manufacture. But what terrified Rudolph most was the fact that this flake was no ghostly weapon, no immaterial shred, but a fragment of real stone, capable of inflicting a deadly gash or long, torn wound. Hundreds of such fragments, indeed, lay loose on the concreted floor of the chamber, some of them roughly chipped, others ground and polished. Rudolph had seen such things in museums many times before; with a sudden rush of horror he recognised now for the first time in his life with what object the savages of that far-off day had buried them with their dead in the chambered barrows.

With a violent effort he wetted his parched lips with his tongue, and cried out thrice in his agony the one word 'Mercy!'

At that sound the savage king burst into a loud and fiendish laugh. It was a hideous laugh, halfway between a wild beast's and a murderous maniac's: it echoed through the long hall like the laughter of devils when they succeed in leading a fair woman's soul to eternal perdition. 'What does he say?' the king cried, in the same transparently natural words, whose import Rudolph could understand at once. 'How like birds they talk, these white-faced men, whom we get for our only victims since the years grew foolish! "Mu-mu-mu-moo!" they say, "Mu-mu-mu-moo!" more like frogs than men and women!'

Then it came over Rudolph instinctively, through the maze of his terror, that he could understand the lower tongue of these elfish visions because he and his ancestors had once passed through it, but they could not understand his, because it was too high and too deep for them.

He had little time for thought, however. Fear bounded his horizon. The ghosts crowded round him, gibbering louder than before. With wild cries and heathen screams they began to dance about their victim. Two advanced with measured skips and tied his hands and feet with a ghostly cord. It cut into the flesh like the stab of a great sorrow. They bound him to a stake which Rudolph felt conscious was no earthly and material wood but a piece of intangible shadow; yet he could no more escape from it than from the iron chain of an earthly prison. On each side the stake two savage hags, long-haired, ill-favoured, inexpressibly cruel-looking, set two small plants of Enchanter's Nightshade. Then a fierce orgiastic shout went up to the low roof from all the assembled people. Rushing forward together, they covered his body with what seemed to be oil and butter; they hung grave-flowers round his neck; they quarrelled among themselves with clamorous cries for hairs and rags torn from his head and clothing. The women, in particular, whirled round him with frantic Bacchanalian gestures, crying aloud as they circled: 'O great chief! O my king! we offer you this victim; we offer you new blood to prolong your life. Give us in return sound sleep, dry graves, sweet dreams, fair seasons!'

They cut themselves with flint knives. Ghostly ichor streamed copious.

The king meanwhile kept close guard over his victim, whom he watched with hungry eyes of hideous cannibal longing. Then, at a given signal, the crowd of ghosts stood suddenly still. There was an awesome pause. The men gathered outside, the women crouched low in a ring close up to him. Dimly at that moment Rudolph noticed almost without noticing it that each of them had a wound on the side of his own skull; and he understood why: they had themselves been sacrificed in the dim long ago to bear their king company to the world of spirits. Even as he thought that thought, the men and women with a loud whoop raised hands aloft in unison. Each grasped a sharp flake, which he brandished savagely. The king gave the signal by rushing at him with a jagged and sawlike knife. It descended on Rudolph's head. At the same moment the others rushed forward, crying aloud in their own tongue, 'Carve the flesh from his bones! Slay him! hack him to pieces!'

Rudolph bent his head to avoid the blows. He cowered in abject terror. Oh! what fear would any Christian ghost have inspired by the side of these incorporeal pagan savages! Ah! mercy! mercy! They would tear him limb from limb! They would rend him in pieces!

At that instant he raised his eyes, and, as by a miracle of fate, saw another shadowy form floating vague before him. It was the form of a man in sixteenth-century costume, very dim and uncertain. It might have been a ghost – it might have been a vision – but it raised its shadowy hand and pointed towards the door. Rudolph saw it was unguarded. The savages were now upon him, their ghostly breath blew chill on his cheek. 'Show them iron!' cried the shadow in an English voice. Rudolph struck out with both elbows and made a fierce effort for freedom. It was with difficulty he roused himself, but at last he succeeded. He drew his pocket-knife and opened it. At sight of the cold steel, which no ghost or troll or imp can endure to behold, the savages fell back, muttering. But 'twas only for a moment. Next instant, with a howl of vengeance even louder than before, they crowded round him and tried to intercept him. He shook them off with wild energy, though they jostled and hustled him, and struck him again and again with their sharp flint edges. Blood was flowing freely now from his hands and arms – red blood of this world; but still he fought his way out by main force with his sharp steel blade towards the door and the moonlight. The nearer he got to the exit, the thicker and closer the ghosts pressed around, as if conscious that their power was bounded by their own threshold. They avoided the knife, meanwhile; with superstitious terror. Rudolph elbowed them fiercely aside, and lunging at them now and again, made his way to the door. With one supreme effort he tore himself madly out, and stood once more on the open heath, shivering like a greyhound. The ghosts gathered grinning by the open vestibule, their fierce teeth, like a wild beast's, confessing their impotent anger. But Rudolph started to run, all wearied as he was, and ran a few hundred yards before he fell and fainted. He dropped on a clump of white heather by a sandy ridge, and lay there unconscious till well on into the morning.

V

When the people from the manor-house picked him up next day, he was hot and cold, terribly pale from fear, and mumbling incoherently. Dr Porter had him put to bed without a moment's delay. 'Poor fellow!' he said, leaning over him, 'he's had a very narrow escape indeed of a bad brain fever. I oughtn't to have exhibited Cannabis in his excited condition; or, at any rate, if I did, I ought, at least, to have watched its effect more closely. He must be kept very quiet now, and on no account whatever, Nurse, must either Mrs Bruce or Mrs Bouverie-Barton be allowed to come near him.'

But late in the afternoon Rudolph sent for Joyce.

The child came creeping in with an ashen face. 'Well?' she murmured, soft and low, taking her seat by the bedside; 'so the King of the Barrow very nearly had you!'

'Yes,' Rudolph answered, relieved to find there was somebody to whom he could talk freely of his terrible adventure. 'He nearly had me. But how did you come to know it?'

'About two by the clock,' the child replied, with white lips of terror, 'I saw the fires on the moor burn brighter and bluer: and then I remembered the words of a terrible old rhyme the gipsy woman taught me—

> Pallinghurst Barrow – Pallinghurst Barrow!
> Every year one heart thou'lt harrow!
> Pallinghurst Ring – Pallinghurst Ring!
> A bloody man is thy ghostly king.
> Men's bones he breaks, and sucks their marrow
> In Pallinghurst Ring on Pallinghurst Barrow.

'—and just as I thought it, I saw the lights burn terribly bright and clear for a second, and I shuddered for horror. Then they died down low at once, and there was moaning on the moor, cries of despair, as from a great crowd cheated, and at that I knew that you were not to be the Ghost-King's victim.'

DEVIL OF THE MARSH

by

H. B. Marriott-Watson

First published in the collection *Diogenes of London, and other Fantasies and Sketches*

1893

IT WAS NIGH upon dusk when I drew close to the Great Marsh, and already the white vapours were about, riding across the sunken levels like ghosts in a churchyard. Though I had set forth in a mood of wild delight, I had sobered in the lonely ride across the moor and was now uneasily alert. As my horse jerked down the grassy slopes that fell away to the jaws of the swamp, I could see thin streams of mist rise slowly, hover like wraiths above the long rushes, and then, turning gradually more material, go blowing heavily away across the flat. The appearance of the place at this desolate hour, so remote from human society and so darkly significant of evil presences, struck me with a certain wonder that she should have chosen this spot for our meeting. She was a familiar of the moors, where I had invariably encountered her; but it was like her arrogant caprice to test my devotion by some such dreary assignation. The wide and horrid prospect depressed me beyond reason, but the fact of her neighbourhood drew me on, and my spirits mounted at the thought that at last she was to put me in possession of herself. Tethering my horse upon the verge of the swamp, I soon discovered the path that crossed it, and entering, struck out boldly for the heart. The track could have been little used, for the reeds, which stood high above the level of my eyes upon either side, straggled everywhere across in low arches, through which I dodged, and broke my way with some inconvenience and much impatience. A full half hour I was solitary in that wilderness, and when at last a sound other than my own footsteps broke the silence, the dusk had fallen.

I was moving very slowly at the time, with a mind half disposed to turn from the melancholy expedition, which it seemed to me now must surely be a cruel jest she had played upon me. While some such reluctance held me, I was suddenly arrested by a hoarse croaking which broke out upon my left, sounding somewhere from the reeds in the black mire. A little further it came again from close at hand, and when I had passed on a few more steps in wonder and perplexity, I heard it for the third time. I stopped and listened, but the marsh was as a grave, and so taking the noise for the signal of some raucous frog, I resumed my way. But in a little the croaking was repeated, and coming quickly to a stand I pushed the reeds aside and peered into the darkness. I could see nothing, but at the immediate moment of my pause I thought I detected the sound of some body trailing through the rushes. My distaste for the adventure grew with this suspicion, and had it not been for my delirious infatuation, I had assuredly turned back and ridden home. The ghastly sound pursued me at intervals along the track, until at last, irritated beyond endurance by the sense of this persistent and invisible company, I broke into a sort of run. This, it seemed, the creature (whatever it was) could not achieve, for I heard no more of it, and continued my way in peace. My path at length ran out from among the reeds upon the smooth flat of which she had spoken, and here my heart quickened, and the gloom of the dreadful place lifted. The flat lay in the very centre of the marsh, and here and there in it a gaunt bush or withered tree rose like a spectre against the white mists. At the further end I fancied some kind of building loomed up; but the fog which had been gathering ever since my entrance upon the passage sailed down upon me at that moment and the prospect went out with suddenness. As I stood waiting for the clouds to pass, a voice cried to me out of its centre, and I saw her next second with bands of mist swirling about her body, come rushing to me from the darkness. She put her long arms about me, and, drawing her close, I looked into her deep eyes. Far down in them, it seemed to me, I could discern a mystic laughter dancing in the wells of light, and I had that ecstatic sense of nearness to some spirit of fire which was wont to possess me at her contact.

'At last,' she said, 'at last, my beloved!' I caressed her.

'Why,' said I, tingling at the nerves, 'why have you put this dolorous journey between us? And what mad freak is your presence in this swamp?' She uttered her silver laugh, and nestled to me again.

'I am the creature of this place,' she answered. 'This is my home. I have sworn you should behold me in my native sin ere you ravished me away.'

'Come, then,' said I; 'I have seen; let there be an end of this. I know you, what you are. This marsh chokes up my heart. God forbid you should spend more of your days here. Come.'

'You are in haste,' she cried. 'There is yet much to learn. Look, my friend,' she said, 'you who know me, what I am. This is my prison, and I have inherited its properties. Have you no fear?'

For answer I pulled her to me, and her warm lips drove out the horrid humours of the night; but the swift passage of a flickering mockery over her eyes struck me as a flash of lightning, and I grew chill again.

'I have the marsh in my blood,' she whispered: 'the marsh and the fog of it. Think ere you vow to me, for I am the cloud in a starry night.'

A lithe and lovely creature, palpable of warm flesh, she lifted her magic face to mine and besought me plaintively with these words. The dews of the nightfall hung on her lashes, and seemed to plead with me for her forlorn and solitary plight.

'Behold!' I cried, 'witch or devil of the marsh, you shall come with me! I have known you on the moors, a roving apparition of beauty; nothing more I know, nothing more I ask. I care not what this dismal haunt means; not what these strange and mystic eyes. You have powers and senses above me; your sphere and habits are as mysterious and incomprehensible as your beauty. But that,' I said, 'is mine, and the world that is mine shall be yours also.'

She moved her head nearer to me with an antic gesture, and her gleaming eyes glanced up at me with a sudden flash, the similitude (great heavens!) of a hooded snake. Starting, I fell away, but at that moment she turned her face and set it fast towards the fog that came rolling in thick volumes over the flat. Noiselessly the great cloud crept down upon us, and all dazed and troubled I watched her watching it in silence. It was as if she awaited some omen of horror, and I too trembled in the fear of its coming.

Then suddenly out of the night issued the hoarse and hideous croaking I had heard upon my passage. I reached out my arm to take her hand, but in an instant the mists broke over us, and I was groping in the vacancy. Something like panic took hold of me, and, beating through the blind obscurity, I rushed over the flat, calling upon her. In a little the swirl went by, and I perceived her upon the margin of the swamp, her arm raised as in imperious command. I ran to her, but stopped, amazed and shaken by a fearful sight. Low by the dripping reeds crouched a small squat thing, in the likeness of a monstrous frog, coughing and choking in its throat. As I stared, the creature rose upon its legs and disclosed a horrid human resemblance. Its face was white and thin, with long black hair; its body gnarled and twisted as with the ague of a thousand years. Shaking, it whined in a breathless voice, pointing a skeleton finger at the woman by my side.

'Your eyes were my guide,' it quavered. 'Do you think that after all these years I have no knowledge of your eyes? Lo, is there aught of evil in you I am not instructed in? This is the Hell you designed for me, and now you would leave me to a greater.'

The wretch paused, and panting leaned upon a bush, while she stood silent, mocking him with her eyes, and soothing my terror with her soft touch.

'Hear!' he cried, turning to me, 'hear the tale of this woman that you may know her as she is. She is the Presence of the marshes. Woman or Devil I know not, but only that the accursed marsh has crept into her soul and she herself is become its Evil Spirit; she herself, that lives and grows young and beautiful by it, has its full power to blight and chill and slay. I, who was once as you are, have this knowledge. What bones lie deep in this black swamp who can say but she? She has drained of health, she has drained of mind and of soul; what is between her and her desire that she should not drain also of life? She has made me a devil in her Hell, and now she would leave me to my solitary pain, and go search for another victim. But she shall not!' he screamed through his chattering teeth; 'she shall not! My Hell is also hers! She shall not!'

Her smiling untroubled eyes left his face and turned to me: she put out her arms, swaying towards me, and so fervid and so great a light glowed in her face that, as one distraught of superhuman means, I took her into my embrace. And then the madness seized me.

'Woman or devil,' I said, 'I will go with you! Of what account this pitiful past? Blight me even as that wretch, so be only you are with me.'

She laughed, and, disengaging herself, leaned, half-clinging to me, towards the coughing creature by the mire.

'Come,' I cried, catching her by the waist. 'Come!' She laughed again a silver-ringing laugh. She moved with me slowly across the flat to where the track started for the portals of the marsh. She laughed and clung to me.

But at the edge of the track I was startled by a shrill, hoarse screaming; and behold, from my very feet, that loathsome creature rose up and wound his long black arms about her, shrieking and crying in his pain. Stooping, I pushed him from her skirts, and with one sweep of my arm drew her across the pathway; as her face passed mine her eyes were wide and smiling. Then of a sudden the still mist enveloped us once more; but ere it descended I had a glimpse of that contorted figure trembling on the margin, the white face drawn and full of desolate pain. At the sight an icy shiver ran through me. And then through the yellow gloom the shadow of her darted past me to the further side. I heard the hoarse cough, the dim noise of a struggle, a swishing sound, a thin cry, and then the sucking of the slime over something in the rushes. I leapt forward: and once again the fog thinned, and I beheld her, woman or devil, standing upon the verge, and peering with smiling eyes into the foul and sickly bog. With a sharp cry wrung from my nerveless soul, I turned and fled down the narrow way from that accursed spot; and as I ran the thickening fog closed round me, and I heard far off and lessening still the silver sound of her mocking laughter.

THE SIN-EATER

by

Fiona Macleod

First published in the collection
The Sin-Eater, and Other Tales

1895

SIN.
Taste this bread, this substance: tell me
Is it bread or flesh?

[The Senses approach.]

THE SMELL.
Its smell
Is the smell of bread.

SIN.
Touch, come. Why tremble?
Say what's this thou touchest?

THE TOUCH.
Bread.

SIN.
Sight, declare what thou discernest
In this object.

THE SIGHT.
Bread alone.

—CALDERON
Los Encantos de la Culpa

A WET WIND OUT of the south mazed and mooned through the sea-mist that hung over the Ross. In all the bays and creeks was a continuous weary lapping of water. There was no other sound anywhere.

Thus was it at daybreak; it was thus at noon; thus was it now in the darkening of the day. A confused thrusting and falling of sounds through the silence betokened the hour of the setting. Curlews wailed in the mist; on the seething limpet-covered rocks the skuas and terns screamed, or uttered hoarse, rasping cries. Ever and again the prolonged note of the oyster-catcher shrilled against the air, as an echo flying blindly along a blank wall of cliff. Out of weedy places, wherein the tide sobbed with long, gurgling moans, came at intervals the barking of a seal.

Inland, by the hamlet of Contullich, there is a reedy tarn called the Loch-a-chaoruinn.* By the shores of this mournful water a man moved. It was a slow, weary walk, that of the man Neil Ross. He had come from Duninch, thirty miles to the eastward, and had not rested foot, nor eaten, nor had word of man or woman, since his going west an hour after dawn.

At the bend of the loch nearest the clachan he came upon an old woman carrying peat. To his reiterated question as to where he was, and if the tarn were Feur-Lochan above Fionnaphort that is on the strait of Iona on the west side of the Ross of Mull, she did not at first make any answer. The rain trickled down her withered brown face, over which the thin grey locks hung limply. It was only in the deep-set eyes that the flame of life still glimmered, though that dimly.

The man had used the English when first he spoke, but as though mechanically. Supposing that he had not been understood, he repeated his question in the Gaelic.

---

* Contullich: i.e. Ceann-nan-tulaich, 'the end of the hillocks'. Loch-a-chaoruinn means 'the loch of the rowan-trees'.

After a minute's silence the old woman answered him in the native tongue, but only to put a question in return.

'I am thinking it is a long time since you have been in Iona?'

The man stirred uneasily.

'And why is that, mother?' he asked, in a weak voice hoarse with damp and fatigue; 'how is it you will be knowing that I have been in Iona at all?'

'Because I knew your kith and kin there, Neil Ross.'

'I have not been hearing that name, mother, for many a long year. And as for the old face o' you, it is unbeknown to me.'

'I was at the naming of you, for all that. Well do I remember the day that Silis Macallum gave you birth; and I was at the house on the croft of Ballyrona when Murtagh Ross – that was your father – laughed. It was an ill laughing that.'

'I am knowing it. The curse of God on him!'

''Tis not the first, nor the last, though the grass is on his head three years agone now.'

'You that know who I am will be knowing that I have no kith or kin now on Iona?'

'Ay; they are all under grey stone or running wave. Donald your brother, and Murtagh your next brother, and little Silis, and your mother Silis herself, and your two brothers of your father, Angus and Ian Macallum, and your father Murtagh Ross, and his lawful childless wife, Dionaid, and his sister Anna – one and all, they lie beneath the green wave or in the brown mould. It is said there is a curse upon all who live at Ballyrona. The owl builds now in the rafters, and it is the big sea-rat that runs across the fireless hearth.'

'It is there I am going.'

'The foolishness is on you, Neil Ross.'

'Now it is that I am knowing who you are. It is old Sheen Macarthur I am speaking to.'

'*Tha mise* . . . it is I.'

'And you will be alone now, too, I am thinking, Sheen?'

'I am alone. God took my three boys at the one fishing ten years ago; and before there was moonrise in the blackness of my heart my man went. It was after the drowning of Anndra that my croft was taken from me. Then I crossed the Sound, and shared with my widow sister Elsie McVurie till *she* went; and then the two cows had to go; and I had no rent, and was old.'

In the silence that followed, the rain dribbled from the sodden bracken and dripping loneroid. Big tears rolled slowly down the deep lines on the face of Sheen. Once there was a sob in her throat, but she put her shaking hand to it, and it was still.

Neil Ross shifted from foot to foot. The ooze in that marshy place squelched with each restless movement he made. Beyond them a plover wheeled, a blurred splatch in the mist, crying its mournful cry over and over and over.

It was a pitiful thing to hear – ah, bitter loneliness, bitter patience of poor old women. That he knew well. But he was too weary, and his heart was nigh full of its own burthen. The words could not come to his lips. But at last he spoke.

'*Tha mo chridhe goirt,*' he said, with tears in his voice, as he put his hand on her bent shoulder; 'my heart is sore.'

She put up her old face against his.

''*S tha e ruidhinn mo chridhe,*' she whispered; 'it is touching my heart you are.'

After that they walked on slowly through the dripping mist, each dumb and brooding deep.

'Where will you be staying this night?' asked Sheen suddenly, when they had traversed a wide boggy stretch of land; adding, as by an afterthought – 'Ah, it is asking you were if the tarn there were Feur-Lochan. No; it is Loch-a-chaoruinn, and the clachan that is near is Contullich.'

'Which way?'

'Yonder, to the right.'

'And you are not going there?'

'No. I am going to the steading of Andrew Blair. Maybe you are for knowing it? It is called the Baile-na-Chlais-nambuidheag.'*

'I do not remember. But it is remembering a Blair I am. He was Adam, the son of Adam, the son of Robert. He and my father did many an ill deed together.'

'Ay, to the stones be it said. Sure, now, there was, even till this weary day, no man or woman who had a good word for Adam Blair.'

'And why that . . . why till this day?'

'It is not yet the third hour since he went into the silence.'

Neil Ross uttered a sound like a stifled curse. For a time he trudged wearily on.

'Then I am too late,' he said at last, but as though speaking to himself. 'I had hoped to see him face to face again, and curse him between the eyes. It was he who made Murtagh Ross break his troth to my mother, and marry that other woman, barren at that, God be praised! And they say ill of him, do they?'

'Ay, it is evil that is upon him. This crime and that, God knows; and the shadow of murder on his brow and in his eyes. Well, well, 'tis ill to be speaking of a man in corpse, and that near by. 'Tis Himself only that knows, Neil Ross.'

'Maybe ay and maybe no. But where is it that I can be sleeping this night, Sheen Macarthur?'

'They will not be taking a stranger at the farm this night of the nights, I am thinking. There is no place else for seven miles yet, when there is the clachan, before you will be coming to Fionnaphort. There is the warm byre, Neil, my man; or, if you can bide by my peats, you may rest, and welcome, though there is no bed for you, and no food either save some of the porridge that is over.'

'And that will do well enough for me, Sheen; and Himself bless you for it.'

And so it was. ✦ ✦ ✦

---

* 'The farm in the hollow of the yellow flowers'.

After old Sheen Macarthur had given the wayfarer food – poor food at that, but welcome to one nigh starved, and for the heart-some way it was given, and because of the thanks to God that was upon it before even spoon was lifted – she told him a lie. It was the good lie of tender love.

'Sure now, after all, Neil, my man,' she said, 'it is sleeping at the farm I ought to be, for Maisie Macdonald, the wise woman, will be sitting by the corpse, and there will be none to keep her company. It is there I must be going; and if I am weary, there is a good bed for me just beyond the dead-board, which I am not minding at all. So, if it is tired you are sitting by the peats, lie down on my bed there, and have the sleep; and God be with you.'

With that she went, and soundlessly, for Neil Ross was already asleep, where he sat on an upturned *claar*, with his elbows on his knees, and his flame-lit face in his hands.

The rain had ceased; but the mist still hung over the land, though in thin veils now, and these slowly drifting seaward. Sheen stepped wearily along the stony path that led from her bothy to the farm-house. She stood still once, the fear upon her, for she saw three or four blurred yellow gleams moving beyond her, eastward, along the dyke. She knew what they were – the corpse-lights that on the night of death go between the bier and the place of burial. More than once she had seen them before the last hour, and by that token had known the end to be near.

Good Catholic that she was, she crossed herself, and took heart. Then muttering

> Crois nan naoi aingeal leam
> 'O mhullach mo chinn
> Gu craican mo bhonn.

> (The cross of the nine angels be about me,
> From the top of my head
> To the soles of my feet),

she went on her way fearlessly.

When she came to the White House, she entered by the milk-shed that was between the byre and the kitchen. At the end of it was a paved place, with washing-tubs. At one of these stood a girl that served in the house – an ignorant lass called Jessie McFall, out of Oban. She was ignorant, indeed, not to know that to wash clothes with a newly dead body near by was an ill thing to do. Was it not a matter for the knowing that the corpse could hear, and might rise up in the night and clothe itself in a clean white shroud?

She was still speaking to the lassie when Maisie Macdonald, the deid-watcher, opened the door of the room behind the kitchen to see who it was that was come. The two old women nodded silently. It was not till Sheen was in the closed room, midway in which something covered with a sheet lay on a board, that any word was spoken.

'*Duit sìth mòr, Beann Macdonald.*'

'And deep peace to you, too, Sheen; and to him that is there.'

'*Och, ochone, mise 'n diugh*; 'tis a dark hour this.'

'Ay; it is bad. Will you have been hearing or seeing anything?'

'Well, as for that, I am thinking I saw lights moving betwixt here and the green place over there.'

'The corpse-lights?'

'Well, it is calling them that they are.'

'I *thought* they would be out. And I have been hearing the noise of the planks – the cracking of the boards, you know, that will be used for the coffin to-morrow.'

A long silence followed. The old women had seated themselves by the corpse, their cloaks over their heads. The room was fireless, and was lit only by a tall wax death-candle, kept against the hour of the going.

At last Sheen began swaying slowly to and fro, crooning low the while. 'I would not be for doing that, Sheen Macarthur,' said the deid-watcher in a low voice, but meaningly; adding, after a moment's pause, '*The mice have all left the house.*'

Sheen sat upright, a look half of terror, half of awe in her eyes.

'God save the sinful soul that is hiding,' she whispered.

Well she knew what Maisie meant. If the soul of the dead be a lost soul, it knows its doom. The house of death is the house of sanctuary; but before the dawn that follows the death-night the soul must go forth, whosoever or whatsoever wait for it in the homeless, shelterless plains of air around and beyond. If it be well with the soul, it need have no fear; if it be not ill with the soul, it may fare forth with surety; but if it be ill with the soul, ill will the going be. Thus is it that the spirit of an evil man cannot stay, and yet dare not go; and so it strives to hide itself in secret places any-where, in dark channels and blind walls; and the wise creatures that live near man smell the terror, and flee. Maisie repeated the saying of Sheen, then, after a silence, added—

'Adam Blair will not lie in his grave for a year and a day because of the sins that are upon him; and it is knowing that, they are here. He will be the Watcher of the Dead for a year and a day.'

'Ay, sure, there will be dark prints in the dawn-dew over yonder.'

Once more the old women relapsed into silence. Through the night there was a sighing sound. It was not the sea, which was too far off to be heard save in a day of storm. The wind it was, that was dragging itself across the sodden moors like a wounded thing, moaning and sighing.

Out of sheer weariness, Sheen twice rocked forward from her stool, heavy with sleep. At last Maisie led her over to the niche-bed opposite, and laid her down there, and waited till the deep furrows in the face relaxed somewhat, and the thin breath laboured slow across the fallen jaw.

'Poor old woman,' she muttered, heedless of her own grey hairs and greyer years; 'a bitter, bad thing it is to be old, old and weary. 'Tis the sorrow, that. God keep the pain of it!'

As for herself, she did not sleep at all that night, but sat between the living and the dead, with her plaid shrouding her. Once, when Sheen gave a low, terrified scream in her sleep, she rose, and in a loud voice cried, '*Sheeach-ad! Away with you!*' And with that she lifted the shroud from the dead man, and took the pennies off the eyelids, and lifted each lid; then, staring into these filmed wells, muttered an ancient incantation that would compel the soul of Adam Blair to leave the spirit of Sheen alone, and return to the cold corpse that was its coffin till the wood was ready.

The dawn came at last. Sheen slept, and Adam Blair slept a deeper sleep, and Maisie stared out of her wan, weary eyes against the red and stormy flares of light that came into the sky.

When, an hour after sunrise, Sheen Macarthur reached her bothy, she found Neil Ross, heavy with slumber, upon her bed. The fire was not out, though no flame or spark was visible; but she stooped and blew at the heart of the peats till the redness came, and once it came it grew. Having done this, she kneeled and said a rune of the morning, and after that a prayer, and then a prayer for the poor man Neil. She could pray no more because of the tears. She rose and put the meal and water into the pot for the porridge to be ready against his awaking. One of the hens that was there came and pecked at her ragged skirt. 'Poor beastie,' she said. 'Sure, that will just be the way I am pulling at the white robe of the Mother o' God. 'Tis a bit meal for you, cluckie, and for me a healing hand upon my tears. O, och, ochone, the tears, the tears!'

It was not till the third hour after sunrise of that bleak day in that winter of the winters, that Neil Ross stirred and arose. He ate in silence. Once he said that he smelt the snow coming out of the north. Sheen said no word at all.

After the porridge, he took his pipe, but there was no tobacco. All that Sheen had was the pipeful she kept against the gloom of the Sabbath. It was her one solace in the long weary week. She gave him this, and held a burning peat to his mouth, and hungered over the thin, rank smoke that curled upward.

It was within half-an-hour of noon that, after an absence, she returned.

'Not between you and me, Neil Ross,' she began abruptly, 'but just for the asking, and what is beyond. Is it any money you are having upon you?'

'No.'

'Nothing?'

'Nothing.'

'Then how will you be getting across to Iona? It is seven long miles to Fionnaphort, and bitter cold at that, and you will be needing food, and then the ferry, the ferry across the Sound, you know.'

'Ay, I know.'

'What would you do for a silver piece, Neil, my man?'

'You have none to give me, Sheen Macarthur; and, if you had, it would not be taking it I would.'

'Would you kiss a dead man for a crown-piece – a crown-piece of five good shillings?'

Neil Ross stared. Then he sprang to his feet.

'It is Adam Blair you are meaning, woman! God curse him in death now that he is no longer in life!'

Then, shaking and trembling, he sat down again, and brooded against the dull red glow of the peats.

But, when he rose, in the last quarter before noon, his face was white.

'The dead are dead, Sheen Macarthur. They can know or do nothing. I will do it. It is willed. Yes, I am going up to the house there. And now I am going from here. God Himself has my thanks to you, and my blessing too. They will come back to you. It is not forgetting you I will be. Good-bye.'

'Good-bye, Neil, son of the woman that was my friend. A south wind to you! Go up by the farm. In the front of the house you will see what you will be seeing. Maisie Macdonald will be there. She will tell you what's for the telling. There is no harm in it, sure; sure, the dead are dead. It is praying for you I will be, Neil Ross. Peace to you!'

'And to you, Sheen.'

And with that the man went.

When Neil Ross reached the byres of the farm in the wide hollow, he saw two figures standing as though awaiting him, but separate, and unseen of the other. In front of the house was a man he knew to be Andrew Blair; behind the milk-shed was a woman he guessed to be Maisie Macdonald.

It was the woman he came upon first.

'Are you the friend of Sheen Macarthur?' she asked in a whisper, as she beckoned him to the doorway.

'I am.'

'I am knowing no names or anything. And no one here will know you, I am thinking. So do the thing and begone.'

'There is no harm to it?'

'None.'

'It will be a thing often done, is it not?'

'Ay, sure.'

'And the evil does not abide?'

'No. The . . . the . . . person . . . the person takes them away, and . . .'

'*Them?*'

'For sure, man! Them . . . the sins of the corpse. He takes them away; and are you for thinking God would let the innocent suffer for the guilty? No . . . the person . . . the Sin-Eater, you know . . . takes them away on himself, and one by one the air of heaven washes them away till he, the Sin-Eater, is clean and whole as before.'

'But if it is a man you hate . . . if it is a corpse that is the corpse of one who has been a curse and a foe . . . if . . .'

'*Sst!* Be still now with your foolishness. It is only an idle saying, I am thinking. Do it, and take the money and go. It will be hell enough for Adam Blair, miser as he was, if he is for knowing that five good shillings of his money are to go to a passing tramp because of an old, ancient silly tale.'

Neil Ross laughed low at that. It was for pleasure to him.

'Hush wi' ye! Andrew Blair is waiting round there. Say that I have sent you round, as I have neither bite nor bit to give.'

Turning on his heel, Neil walked slowly round to the front of the house. A tall man was there, gaunt and brown, with hairless face and lank brown hair, but with eyes cold and grey as the sea.

'Good day to you, an' good faring. Will you be passing this way to anywhere?'

'Health to you. I am a stranger here. It is on my way to Iona I am. But I have the hunger upon me. There is not a brown bit in my pocket. I asked at the door there, near the byres. The woman told me she could give me nothing – not a penny even, worse luck – nor, for that, a drink of warm milk. 'Tis a sore land this.'

'You have the Gaelic of the Isles. Is it from Iona you are?'

'It is from the Isles of the West I come.'

'From Tiree . . . from Coll?'

'No.'

'From the Long Island . . . or from Uist . . . or maybe from Benbecula?'

'No.'

'Oh well, sure it is no matter to me. But may I be asking your name?'

'Macallum.'

'Do you know there is a death here, Macallum?'

'If I didn't I would know it now, because of what lies yonder.'

Mechanically Andrew Blair looked round. As he knew, a rough

bier was there, that was made of a dead-board laid upon three milking-stools. Beside it was a *claar*, a small tub to hold potatoes. On the bier was a corpse, covered with a canvas sheeting that looked like a sail.

'He was a worthy man, my father,' began the son of the dead man, slowly; 'but he had his faults, like all of us. I might even be saying that he had his sins, to the Stones be it said. You will be knowing, Macallum, what is thought among the folk ... that a stranger, passing by, may take away the sins of the dead, and that, too, without any hurt whatever ... any hurt whatever.'

'Ay, sure.'

'And you will be knowing what is done?'

'Ay.'

'With the bread ... and the water ... ?'

'Ay.'

'It is a small thing to do. It is a Christian thing. I would be doing it myself, and that gladly, but the ... the ... passer-by who ...'

'It is talking of the Sin-Eater you are?'

'Yes, yes, for sure. The Sin-Eater as he is called – and a good Christian act it is, for all that the ministers and the priests make a frowning at it – the Sin-Eater must be a stranger. He must be a stranger, and should know nothing of the dead man – above all, bear him no grudge.'

At that Neil Ross's eyes lightened for a moment.

'And why that?'

'Who knows? I have heard this, and I have heard that. If the Sin-Eater was hating the dead man he could take the sins and fling them into the sea, and they would be changed into demons of the air that would harry the flying soul till Judgment-Day.'

'And how would that thing be done?'

The man spoke with flashing eyes and parted lips, the breath coming swift. Andrew Blair looked at him suspiciously; and hesitated, before, in a cold voice, he spoke again.

'That is all folly, I am thinking, Macallum. Maybe it is all folly, the whole of it. But, see here, I have no time to be talking with you. If you will take the bread and the water you shall have a good meal if you want it, and . . . and . . . yes, look you, my man, I will be giving you a shilling too, for luck.'

'I will have no meal in this house, Anndramhic-Adam; nor will I do this thing unless you will be giving me two silver half-crowns. That is the sum I must have, or no other.'

'Two half-crowns! Why, man, for one half-crown . . .'

'Then be eating the sins o' your father yourself, Andrew Blair! It is going I am.'

'Stop, man! Stop, Macallum. See here – I will be giving you what you ask.'

'So be it. Is the . . . Are you ready?'

'Ay, come this way.'

With that the two men turned and moved slowly towards the bier.

In the doorway of the house stood a man and two women; farther in, a woman; and at the window to the left, the serving-wench, Jessie McFall, and two men of the farm. Of those in the doorway, the man was Peter, the half-witted youngest brother of Andrew Blair; the taller and older woman was Catreen, the widow of Adam, the second brother; and the thin, slight woman, with staring eyes and drooping mouth, was Muireall, the wife of Andrew. The old woman behind these was Maisie Macdonald.

Andrew Blair stooped and took a saucer out of the *claar*. This he put upon the covered breast of the corpse. He stooped again, and brought forth a thick square piece of new-made bread. That also he placed upon the breast of the corpse. Then he stooped again, and with that he emptied a spoonful of salt alongside the bread.

'I must see the corpse,' said Neil Ross simply.

'It is not needful, Macallum.'

'I must be seeing the corpse, I tell you – and for that, too, the bread and the water should be on the naked breast.'

'No, no, man; it . . .'

But here a voice, that of Maisie the wise woman, came upon them, saying that the man was right, and that the eating of the sins should be done in that way and no other.

With an ill grace the son of the dead man drew back the sheeting. Beneath it, the corpse was in a clean white shirt, a death-gown long ago prepared, that covered him from his neck to his feet, and left only the dusky yellowish face exposed.

While Andrew Blair unfastened the shirt and placed the saucer and the bread and the salt on the breast, the man beside him stood staring fixedly on the frozen features of the corpse. The new laird had to speak to him twice before he heard.

'I am ready. And you, now? What is it you are muttering over against the lips of the dead?'

'It is giving him a message I am. There is no harm in that, sure?'

'Keep to your own folk, Macallum. You are from the West you say, and we are from the North. There can be no messages between you and a Blair of Strathmore, no messages for you to be giving.'

'He that lies here knows well the man to whom I am sending a message' – and at this response Andrew Blair scowled darkly. He would fain have sent the man about his business, but he feared he might get no other.

'It is thinking I am that you are not a Macallum at all. I know all of that name in Mull, Iona, Skye, and the near isles. What will the name of your naming be, and of your father, and of his place?'

Whether he really wanted an answer, or whether he sought only to divert the man from his procrastination, his question had a satisfactory result.

'Well, now, it's ready I am, Anndra-mhic-Adam.'

With that, Andrew Blair stooped once more and from the *claar* brought a small jug of water. From this he filled the saucer.

'You know what to say and what to do, Macallum.'

There was not one there who did not have a shortened breath because of the mystery that was now before them, and the fearfulness of it. Neil Ross drew himself up, erect, stiff, with white, drawn face. All who waited, save Andrew Blair, thought that the moving of his lips was because of the prayer that was slipping upon them, like the last lapsing of the ebb-tide. But Blair was watching him closely, and knew that it was no prayer which stole out against the blank air that was around the dead.

Slowly Neil Ross extended his right arm. He took a pinch of the salt and put it in the saucer, then took another pinch and sprinkled it upon the bread. His hand shook for a moment as he touched the saucer. But there was no shaking as he raised it towards his lips, or when he held it before him when he spoke.

'With this water that has salt in it, and has lain on thy corpse, *O Adam mhic Anndra mhic Adam Mòr*, I drink away all the evil that is upon thee . . .'

There was throbbing silence while he paused.

'. . . And may it be upon me and not upon thee, if with this water it cannot flow away.'

Thereupon, he raised the saucer and passed it thrice round the head of the corpse sunways; and, having done this, lifted it to his lips and drank as much as his mouth would hold. Thereafter he poured the remnant over his left hand, and let it trickle to the ground. Then he took the piece of bread. Thrice, too, he passed it round the head of the corpse sunways.

He turned and looked at the man by his side, then at the others, who watched him with beating hearts.

With a loud clear voice he took the sins.

'*Thoir dhomh do ciontachd, O Adam mhic Anndra mhic Adam Mòr!* Give me thy sins to take away from thee! Lo, now, as I stand here, I break this bread that has lain on thee in corpse, and I am eating it, I am, and in that eating I take upon me the sins of thee, O man that was alive and is now white with the stillness!'

Thereupon Neil Ross broke the bread and ate of it, and took upon himself the sins of Adam Blair that was dead. It was a bitter swallowing, that. The remainder of the bread he crumbled in his hand, and threw it on the ground, and trod upon it. Andrew Blair gave a sigh of relief. His cold eyes lightened with malice.

'Be off with you, now, Macallum. We are wanting no tramps at the farm here, and perhaps you had better not be trying to get work this side Iona; for it is known as the Sin-Eater you will be, and that won't be for the helping, I am thinking! There – there are the two half-crowns for you . . . and may they bring you no harm, you that are *Scapegoat* now!'

The Sin-Eater turned at that, and stared like a hill-bull. *Scapegoat!* Ay, that's what he was. Sin-Eater, Scapegoat! Was he not, too, another Judas, to have sold for silver that which was not for the selling? No, no, for sure Maisie Macdonald could tell him the rune that would serve for the easing of this burden. He would soon be quit of it.

Slowly he took the money, turned it over, and put it in his pocket.

'I am going, Andrew Blair,' he said quietly, 'I am going now. I will not say to him that is there in the silence, *A chuid do Pharas da!* – nor will I say to you, *Gu'n gleidheadh Dia thu* – nor will I say to this dwelling that is the home of thee and thine, *Gu'n beannaic-headh Dia an tigh!*'*

Here there was a pause. All listened. Andrew Blair shifted uneasily, the furtive eyes of him going this way and that, like a ferret in the grass.

'But, Andrew Blair, I will say this: when you fare abroad, *Droch*

---

*   *A chuid do Pharas da!* 'His share of heaven be his.' *Gu'n gleidheadh Dia thu,* 'May God preserve you.' *Gu'n beannaic-headh Dia an tigh!* 'God's blessing on this house.'

caoidh ort! and when you go upon the water, *Gaoth gun direadh ort!*
Ay, ay, *Anndra-mhic-Adam, Dia ad aghaidh 's ad aodann . . . agus bas
dunach ort! Dhonas 's dholas ort, agus leat-sa!* *

The bitterness of these words was like snow in June upon all
there. They stood amazed. None spoke. No one moved.

Neil Ross turned upon his heel, and, with a bright light in his
eyes, walked away from the dead and the living. He went by the
byres, whence he had come. Andrew Blair remained where he was,
now glooming at the corpse, now biting his nails and staring at the
damp sods at his feet.

When Neil reached the end of the milk-shed he saw Maisie
Macdonald there, waiting.

'These were ill sayings of yours, Neil Ross,' she said in a low
voice, so that she might not be overheard from the house.

'So, it is knowing me you are.'

'Sheen Macarthur told me.'

'I have good cause.'

'That is a true word. I know it.'

'Tell me this thing. What is the rune that is said for the throwing
into the sea of the sins of the dead? See here, Maisie Macdonald.
There is no money of that man that I would carry a mile with me.
Here it is. It is yours, if you will tell me that rune.'

Maisie took the money hesitatingly. Then, stooping, she said
slowly the few lines of the old, old rune.

'Will you be remembering that?'

'It is not forgetting it I will be, Maisie.'

'Wait a moment. There is some warm milk here.'

With that she went, and then, from within, beckoned to him
to enter.

---

* *Droch caoidh ort!* 'May a fatal accident happen to you' (lit. 'bad moan on you'). *Gaoth gun
direadh ort!* 'May you drift to your drowning' (lit. 'wind without direction on you'). *Dia ad
aghaidh*, etc., 'God against thee and in thy face . . . and may a death of woe be yours . . . Evil
and sorrow to thee and thine!'

'There is no one here, Neil Ross. Drink the milk.'

He drank; and while he did so she drew a leather pouch from some hidden place in her dress.

'And now I have this to give you.'

She counted out ten pennies and two farthings.

'It is all the coppers I have. You are welcome to them. Take them, friend of my friend. They will give you the food you need, and the ferry across the Sound.'

'I will do that, Maisie Macdonald, and thanks to you. It is not forgetting it I will be, nor you, good woman. And now, tell me, is it safe that I am? He called me a "scapegoat", he, Andrew Blair! Can evil touch me between this and the sea?'

'You must go to the place where the evil was done to you and yours – and that, I know, is on the west side of Iona. Go, and God preserve you. But here, too, is a *sian* that will be for the safety.'

Thereupon, with swift mutterings she said this charm: an old, familiar *sian* against Sudden Harm:

Sian a chuir Moire air Mac ort,
Sian ro' marbhadh, sian ro' lot ort,
Sian eadar a' chlioch 's a' ghlun,
Sian nan Tri ann an aon ort,
O mhullach do chinn gu bonn do chois ort:
Sian seachd eadar a h-aon ort,
Sian seachd eadar a dha ort,
Sian seachd eadar a tri ort,
Sian seachd eadar a ceithir ort,
Sian seachd eadar a coig ort,
Sian seachd eadar a sia ort,
Sian seachd paidir nan seach paidir dol deiseil ri diugh narach ort,
    ga do ghleidheadh bho bheud 's bho mhi-thapadh!

Scarcely had she finished before she heard heavy steps approaching.

'Away with you,' she whispered, repeating in a loud, angry tone, 'Away with you! *Seachad! Seachad!'*

And with that Neil Ross slipped from the milk-shed and crossed the yard, and was behind the byres before Andrew Blair, with sullen mien and swift, wild eyes, strode from the house.

It was with a grim smile on his face that Neil tramped down the wet heather till he reached the high road, and fared thence as through a marsh because of the rains there had been.

For the first mile he thought of the angry mind of the dead man, bitter at paying of the silver. For the second mile he thought of the evil that had been wrought for him and his. For the third mile he pondered over all that he had heard and done and taken upon him that day.

Then he sat down upon a broken granite heap by the way, and brooded deep till one hour went, and then another, and the third was upon him.

A man driving two calves came towards him out of the west. He did not hear or see. The man stopped; spoke again. Neil gave no answer. The drover shrugged his shoulders, hesitated, and walked slowly on, often looking back.

An hour later a shepherd came by the way he himself had tramped. He was a tall, gaunt man with a squint. The small, pale-blue eyes glittered out of a mass of red hair that almost covered his face. He stood still, opposite Neil, and leaned on his *cromak.*

'*Latha math leat,*' he said at last; 'I wish you good day.'

Neil glanced at him, but did not speak.

'What is your name, for I seem to know you?'

But Neil had already forgotten him. The shepherd took out his snuff-mull, helped himself, and handed the mull to the lonely way-farer. Neil mechanically helped himself.

'*Am bheil thu 'dol do Fhionphort?*' tried the shepherd again: 'Are you going to Fionnaphort?'

'*Tha mise 'dol a dh' I-challum-chille,*' Neil answered, in a low, weary voice, and as a man adream: 'I am on my way to Iona.'

'I am thinking I know now who you are. You are the man Macallum.'

Neil looked, but did not speak. His eyes dreamed against what the other could not see or know. The shepherd called angrily to his dogs to keep the sheep from straying; then, with a resentful air, turned to his victim.

'You are a silent man for sure, you are. I'm hoping it is not the curse upon you already.'

'What curse?'

'Ah, *that* has brought the wind against the mist! I was thinking so!'

'What curse?'

'You are the man that was the Sin-Eater over there?'

'Ay.'

'The man Macallum?'

'Ay.'

'Strange it is, but three days ago I saw you in Tobermory, and heard you give your name as Neil Ross to an Iona man that was there.'

'Well?'

'Oh, sure, it is nothing to me. But they say the Sin-Eater should not be a man with a hidden lump in his pack.'*

'Why?'

'For the dead know, and are content. There is no shaking off any sins, then – for that man.'

'It is a lie.'

'Maybe ay and maybe no.'

'Well, have you more to be saying to me? I am obliged to you for your company, but it is not needing it I am, though no offence.'

---

* i.e. with a criminal secret, or an undiscovered crime.

'Och, man, there's no offence between you and me. Sure, there's Iona in me, too; for the father of my father married a woman that was the granddaughter of Tomais Macdonald, who was a fisherman there. No, no; it is rather warning you I would be.'

'And for what?'

'Well, well, just because of that laugh I heard about.'

'What laugh?'

'The laugh of Adam Blair that is dead.'

Neil Ross stared, his eyes large and wild. He leaned a little forward. No word came from him. The look that was on his face was the question.

'Yes, it was this way. Sure, the telling of it is just as I heard it. After you ate the sins of Adam Blair, the people there brought out the coffin. When they were putting him into it, he was as stiff as a sheep dead in the snow – and just like that, too, with his eyes wide open. Well, someone saw you trampling the heather down the slope that is in front of the house, and said, "It is the Sin-Eater!" With that, Andrew Blair sneered, and said – "Ay, 'tis the scapegoat he is!" Then, after a while, he went on, "The Sin-Eater they call him; ay, just so; and a bitter good bargain it is, too, if all's true that's thought true!" And with that he laughed, and then his wife that was behind him laughed, and then . . .'

'Well, what then?'

'Well, 'tis Himself that hears and knows if it is true! But this is the thing I was told: – After that laughing there was a stillness and a dread. For all there saw that the corpse had turned its head and was looking after you as you went down the heather. Then, Neil Ross, if that be your true name, Adam Blair that was dead put up his white face against the sky, and laughed.'

At this, Ross sprang to his feet with a gasping sob.

'It is a lie, that thing!' he cried, shaking his fist at the shepherd. 'It is a lie.'

'It is no lie. And by the same token, Andrew Blair shrank back white and shaking, and his woman had the swoon upon her, and who knows but the corpse might have come to life again had it not been for Maisie Macdonald, the deid-watcher, who clapped a handful of salt on his eyes, and tilted the coffin so that the bottom of it slid forward, and so let the whole fall flat on the ground, with Adam Blair in it sideways, and as likely as not cursing and groaning, as his wont was, for the hurt both to his old bones and his old ancient dignity.'

Ross glared at the man as though the madness was upon him. Fear and horror and fierce rage swung him now this way and now that.

'What will the name of you be, shepherd?' he stuttered huskily.

'It is Eachainn Gilleasbuig I am to ourselves; and the English of that for those who have no Gaelic is Hector Gillespie; and I am Eachainn mac Ian mac Alasdair of Strathsheean, that is where Sutherland lies against Ross.'

'Then take this thing – and that is, the curse of the Sin-Eater! And a bitter bad thing may it be upon you and yours.'

And with that Neil the Sin-Eater flung his hand up into the air, and then leaped past the shepherd, and a minute later was running through the frightened sheep, with his head low, and a white foam on his lips, and his eyes red with blood as a seal's that has the death-wound on it.

On the third day of the seventh month from that day, Aulay Macneill, coming into Balliemore of Iona from the west side of the island, said to old Ronald MacCormick, that was the father of his wife, that he had seen Neil Ross again, and that he was 'absent' – for though he had spoken to him, Neil would not answer, but only gloomed at him from the wet weedy rock where he sat.

The going back of the man had loosed every tongue that was in Iona. When, too, it was known that he was wrought in some terrible way, if not actually mad, the islanders whispered that it was because of the sins of Adam Blair. Seldom or never now did they speak of him by his name, but simply as 'The Sin-Eater'. The thing was not so rare as to cause this strangeness, nor did many (and perhaps none did) think that the sins of the dead ever might or could abide with the living who had merely done a good Christian charitable thing. But there was a reason.

Not long after Neil Ross had come again to Iona, and had settled down in the ruined roofless house on the croft of Ballyrona, just like a fox or a wild-cat, as the saying was, he was given fishing-work to do by Aulay Macneill, who lived at Ard-an-teine, at the rocky north end of the *machar* or plain that is on the west Atlantic coast of the island.

One moonlit night, either the seventh or the ninth after the earthing of Adam Blair at his own place in the Ross, Aulay Macneill saw Neil Ross steal out of the shadow of Ballyrona and make for the sea. Macneill was there by the rocks, mending a lobster-creel. He had gone there because of the sadness. Well, when he saw the Sin-Eater, he watched.

Neil crept from rock to rock till he reached the last fang that churns the sea into yeast when the tide sucks the land just opposite.

Then he called out something that Aulay Macneill could not catch. With that he springs up, and throws his arms above him.

'Then,' says Aulay when he tells the tale, 'it was like a ghost he was. The moonshine was on his face like the curl o' a wave. White! there is no whiteness like that of the human face. It was whiter than the foam about the skerry it was; whiter than the moon shining; whiter than . . . well, as white as the painted letters on the black boards of the fishing-cobles. There he stood, for all that the sea was about him, the slip-slop waves leapin' wild, and the tide making, too, at that. He was shaking like a sail two points off the wind. It was then that, all of a sudden, he called in a womany, screamin' voice—

"I am throwing the sins of Adam Blair into the midst of ye, white dogs o' the sea! Drown them, tear them, drag them away out into the black deeps! Ay, ay, ay, ye dancin' wild waves, this is the third time I am doing it, and now there is none left; no, not a sin, not a sin!

"O-hi O-ri, dark tide o' the sea,
I am giving the sins of a dead man to thee!
By the Stones, by the Wind, by the Fire, by the Tree,
From the dead man's sins set me free, set me free!
Adam mhic Anndra mhic Adam and me,
Set us free! Set us free!"

'Ay, sure, the Sin-Eater sang that over and over; and after the third singing he swung his arms and screamed—

"And listen to me, black waters an' running tide,
That rune is the good rune told me by Maisie the wise,
And I am Neil the son of Silis Macallum
By the black-hearted evil man Murtagh Ross,
That was the friend of Adam mac Anndra, God against him!"

'And with that he scrambled and fell into the sea. But, as I am Aulay mac Luais and no other, he was up in a moment, an' swimmin' like a seal, and then over the rocks again, an' away back to that lonely roofless place once more, laughing wild at times, an' muttering an' whispering.'

It was this tale of Aulay Macneill's that stood between Neil Ross and the isle-folk. There was something behind all that, they whispered one to another.

So it was always the Sin-Eater he was called at last. None sought him. The few children who came upon him now and again fled at his approach, or at the very sight of him. Only Aulay Macneill saw him at times, and had word of him.

After a month had gone by, all knew that the Sin-Eater was

wrought to madness because of this awful thing: the burden of Adam Blair's sins would not go from him! Night and day he could hear them laughing low, it was said.

But it was the quiet madness. He went to and fro like a shadow in the grass, and almost as soundless as that, and as voiceless. More and more the name of him grew as a terror. There were few folk on that wild west coast of Iona, and these few avoided him when the word ran that he had knowledge of strange things, and converse, too, with the secrets of the sea.

One day Aulay Macneill, in his boat, but dumb with amaze and terror for him, saw him at high tide swimming on a long rolling wave right into the hollow of the Spouting Cave. In the memory of man, no one had done this and escaped one of three things: a snatching away into oblivion, a strangled death, or madness. The islanders know that there swims into the cave, at full tide, a Mar-Tarbh, a dreadful creature of the sea that some call a kelpie; only it is not a kelpie, which is like a woman, but rather is a sea-bull, offspring of the cattle that are never seen. Ill indeed for any sheep or goat, ay, or even dog or child, if any happens to be leaning over the edge of the Spouting Cave when the Mar-tarbh roars; for, of a surety, it will fall in and straightway be devoured.

With awe and trembling Aulay listened for the screaming of the doomed man. It was full tide, and the sea-beast would be there.

The minutes passed, and no sign. Only the hollow booming of the sea, as it moved like a baffled blind giant round the cavern-bases; only the rush and spray of the water flung up the narrow shaft high into the windy air above the cliff it penetrates.

At last he saw what looked like a mass of seaweed swirled out on the surge. It was the Sin-Eater. With a leap, Aulay was at his oars. The boat swung through the sea. Just before Neil Ross was about to sink for the second time, he caught him and dragged him into the boat.

But then, as ever after, nothing was to be got out of the Sin-

Eater save a single saying: *Tha e lamhan fuar! Tha e lamhan fuar!* – 'It has a cold, cold hand!'

The telling of this and other tales left none free upon the island to look upon the 'scapegoat' save as one accursed.

It was in the third month that a new phase of his madness came upon Neil Ross.

The horror of the sea and the passion for the sea came over him at the same happening. Oftentimes he would race along the shore, screaming wild names to it, now hot with hate and loathing, now as the pleading of a man with the woman of his love. And strange chants to it, too, were upon his lips. Old, old lines of forgotten runes were overheard by Aulay Macneill, and not Aulay only; lines wherein the ancient sea-name of the island, *Ioua*, that was given to it long before it was called Iona, or any other of the nine names that are said to belong to it, occurred again and again.

The flowing tide it was that wrought him thus. At the ebb he would wander across the weedy slabs or among the rocks, silent, and more like a lost *duinshee* than a man.

Then again after three months a change in his madness came. None knew what it was, though Aulay said that the man moaned and moaned because of the awful burden he bore. No drowning seas for the sins that could not be washed away, no grave for the live sins that would be quick till the day of the Judgment!

For weeks thereafter he disappeared. As to where he was, it is not for the knowing.

Then at last came that third day of the seventh month when, as I have said, Aulay Macneill told old Ronald MacCormick that he had seen the Sin-Eater again.

It was only a half-truth that he told, though. For, after he had seen Neil Ross upon the rock, he had followed him when he rose, and wandered back to the roofless place which he haunted now as of yore. Less wretched a shelter now it was, because of the summer that was come, though a cold, wet summer at that.

'Is that you, Neil Ross?' he had asked, as he peered into the shadows among the ruins of the house.

'That's not my name,' said the Sin-Eater; and he seemed as strange then and there, as though he were a castaway from a foreign ship.

'And what will it be, then, you that are my friend, and sure knowing me as Aulay mac Luais – Aulay Macneill that never grudges you bit or sup?'

'*I am Judas.*'

'And at that word,' says Aulay Macneill, when he tells the tale, 'at that word the pulse in my heart was like a bat in a shut room. But after a bit I took up the talk.

'"Indeed," I said; "and I was not for knowing that. May I be so bold as to ask whose son, and of what place?"

'But all he said to me was, "*I am Judas.*"

'Well, I said, to comfort him, "Sure, it's not such a bad name in itself, though I am knowing some which have a more home-like sound." But no, it was no good.

'"I am Judas. And because I sold the Son of God for five pieces of silver . . ."

'But here I interrupted him and said, "Sure, now, Neil – I mean, Judas – it was eight times five." Yet the simpleness of his sorrow prevailed, and I listened with the wet in my eyes.

'"I am Judas. And because I sold the Son of God for five silver shillings, He laid upon me all the nameless black sins of the world. And that is why I am bearing them till the Day of Days."'

And this was the end of the Sin-Eater; for I will not tell the long story of Aulay Macneill, that gets longer and longer every winter; but only the unchanging close of it.

I will tell it in the words of Aulay.

✦ ✦ ✦

'A bitter, wild day it was, that day I saw him to see him no more. It was late. The sea was red with the flamin' light that burned up the air betwixt Iona and all that is west of West. I was on the shore, looking at the sea. The big green waves came in like the chariots in the Holy Book. Well, it was on the black shoulder of one of them, just short of the ton o' foam that swept above it, that I saw a spar surgin' by.

'"What is that?" I said to myself. And the reason of my wondering was this: I saw that a smaller spar was swung across it. And while I was watching that thing another great billow came in with a roar, and hurled the double spar back, and not so far from me but I might have gripped it. But who would have gripped that thing if he were for seeing what I saw?

'It is Himself knows that what I say is a true thing.

'On that spar was Neil Ross, the Sin-Eater. Naked he was as the day he was born. And he was lashed, too – ay, sure, he was lashed to it by ropes round and round his legs and his waist and his left arm. It was the Cross he was on. I saw that thing with the fear upon me. Ah, poor drifting wreck that he was! *Judas on the Cross!* It was his *eric*!

'But even as I watched, shaking in my limbs, I saw that there was life in him still. The lips were moving, and his right arm was ever for swinging this way and that. 'Twas like an oar, working him off a lee shore; ay, that was what I thought.

'Then, all at once, he caught sight of me. Well he knew me, poor man, that has his share of heaven now, I am thinking!

'He waved, and called, but the hearing could not be, because of a big surge o' water that came tumbling down upon him. In the stroke of an oar he was swept close by the rocks where I was standing. In that flounderin', seethin' whirlpool I saw the white face of him for a moment, an' as he went out on the re-surge like a hauled net, I heard these words fallin' against my ears:

'"*An eirig m'anama* . . . In ransom for my soul!"

'And with that I saw the double-spar turn over and slide down the back-sweep of a drowning big wave. Ay, sure, it went out to the deep sea swift enough then. It was in the big eddy that rushes between Skerry-Mòr and Skerry-Beag. I did not see it again – no, not for the quarter of an hour, I am thinking. Then I saw just the whirling top of it rising out of the flying yeast of a great, black-blustering wave, that was rushing northward before the current that is called the Black-Eddy.

'With that you have the end of Neil Ross; ay, sure, him that was called the Sin-Eater. And that is a true thing; and may God save us the sorrow of sorrows.

'And that is all.'

THE SHINING PYRAMID

by

Arthur Machen

First published in the May and June editions
of *The Unknown World* magazine

1895

I

The Arrow-head Character

'HAUNTED, YOU SAID?'
'Yes, haunted. Don't you remember, when I saw you three years ago, you told me about your place in the west with the ancient woods hanging all about it, and the wild, domed hills, and the ragged land? It has always remained a sort of enchanted picture in my mind as I sit at my desk and hear the traffic rattling in the street in the midst of whirling London. But when did you come up?'

'The fact is, Dyson, I have only just got out of the train. I drove to the station early this morning and caught the 10.45.'

'Well, I am very glad you looked in on me. How have you been getting on since we last met? There is no Mrs Vaughan, I suppose?'

'No,' said Vaughan, 'I am still a hermit, like yourself. I have done nothing but loaf about.'

Vaughan had lit his pipe and sat in the elbow chair, fidgeting and glancing about him in a somewhat dazed and restless manner. Dyson had wheeled round his chair when his visitor entered and sat with one arm fondly reclining on the desk of his bureau, and touching the litter of manuscript.

'And you are still engaged in the old task?' said Vaughan, pointing to the pile of papers and the teeming pigeon-holes.

'Yes, the vain pursuit of literature, as idle as alchemy, and as entrancing. But you have come to town for some time I suppose; what shall we do to-night?'

'Well, I rather wanted you to try a few days with me down in the west. It would do you a lot of good. I'm sure.'

'You are very kind, Vaughan, but London in September is hard to leave. Doré could not have designed anything more wonderful and mystic than Oxford Street as I saw it the other evening; the sunset flaming, the blue haze transmuting the plain street into a road "far in the spiritual city".'

'I should like you to come down, though. You would enjoy roaming over our hills. Does this racket go on all day and night? It quite bewilders me; I wonder how you can work through it. I am sure you would revel in the great peace of my old home among the woods.'

Vaughan lit his pipe again, and looked anxiously at Dyson to see if his inducements had had any effect, but the man of letters shook his head, smiling, and vowed in his heart a firm allegiance to the streets.

'You cannot tempt me,' he said.

'Well, you may be right. Perhaps, after all, I was wrong to speak of the peace of the country. There, when a tragedy does occur, it is like a stone thrown into a pond; the circles of disturbance keep on widening, and it seems as if the water would never be still again.'

'Have you ever any tragedies where you are?'

'I can hardly say that. But I was a good deal disturbed about a month ago by something that happened; it may or may not have been a tragedy in the usual sense of the word.'

'What was the occurrence?'

'Well, the fact is a girl disappeared in a way which seems highly mysterious. Her parents, people of the name of Trevor, are well-to-do farmers, and their eldest daughter Annie was a sort of village beauty; she was really remarkably handsome. One afternoon she thought she would go and see her aunt, a widow who farms her own land, and as the two houses are only about five or six miles apart, she started off, telling her parents she would take the short cut over the hills. She never got to her aunt's, and she never was seen again. That's putting it in a few words.'

'What an extraordinary thing! I suppose there are no disused mines, are there, on the hills? I don't think you quite run to anything so formidable as a precipice?'

'No; the path the girl must have taken had no pitfalls of any description; it is just a track over wild, bare hillside, far, even, from a byroad. One may walk for miles without meeting a soul, but it is perfectly safe.'

'And what do people say about it?'

'Oh, they talk nonsense – among themselves. You have no notion as to how superstitious English cottagers are in out-of-the-way parts like mine. They are as bad as the Irish, every whit, and even more secretive.'

'But what do they say?'

'Oh, the poor girl is supposed to have "gone with the fairies", or to have been "taken by the fairies". Such stuff!' he went on, 'one would laugh if it were not for the real tragedy of the case.'

Dyson looked somewhat interested.

'Yes,' he said, '"fairies" certainly strike a little curiously on the ear in these days. But what do the police say? I presume they do not accept the fairy-tale hypothesis?'

'No; but they seem quite at fault. What I am afraid of is that

Annie Trevor must have fallen in with some scoundrels on her way. Castletown is a large seaport, you know, and some of the worst of the foreign sailors occasionally desert their ships and go on the tramp up and down the country. Not many years ago a Spanish sailor named Garcia murdered a whole family for the sake of plunder that was not worth sixpence. They are hardly human, some of these fellows, and I am dreadfully afraid the poor girl must have come to an awful end.'

'But no foreign sailor was seen by anyone about the country?'

'No; there is certainly that; and of course country people are quick to notice anyone whose appearance and dress are a little out of the common. Still it seems as if my theory were the only possible explanation.'

'There are no data to go upon,' said Dyson, thoughtfully. 'There was no question of a love affair, or anything of the kind, I suppose?'

'Oh, no, not a hint of such a thing. I am sure if Annie were alive she would have contrived to let her mother know of her safety.'

'No doubt, no doubt. Still it is barely possible that she is alive and yet unable to communicate with her friends. But all this must have disturbed you a good deal.'

'Yes, it did; I hate a mystery, and especially a mystery which is probably the veil of horror. But frankly, Dyson, I want to make a clean breast of it; I did not come here to tell you all this.'

'Of course not,' said Dyson, a little surprised at Vaughan's uneasy manner. 'You came to have a chat on more cheerful topics.'

'No, I did not. What I have been telling you about happened a month ago, but something which seems likely to affect me more personally has taken place within the last few days, and to be quite plain, I came up to town with the idea that you might be able to help me. You recollect that curious case you spoke to me about on our last meeting; something about a spectacle-maker.'

'Oh, yes, I remember that. I know I was quite proud of my acumen at the time; even to this day the police have no idea why those peculiar yellow spectacles were wanted. But, Vaughan, you really look quite put out; I hope there is nothing serious?'

'No, I think I have been exaggerating, and I want you to re-assure me. But what has happened is very odd.'

'And what has happened?'

'I am sure that you will laugh at me, but this is the story. You must know there is a path, a right of way, that goes through my land, and to be precise, close to the wall of the kitchen garden. It is not used by many people; a woodman now and again finds it useful, and five or six children who go to school in the village pass twice a day. Well, a few days ago I was taking a walk about the place before breakfast, and I happened to stop to fill my pipe just by the large doors in the garden wall. The wood, I must tell you, comes to within a few feet of the wall, and the track I spoke of runs right in the shadow of the trees. I thought the shelter from a brisk wind that was blowing rather pleasant, and I stood there smoking with my eyes on the ground. Then something caught my attention. Just under the wall, on the short grass; a number of small flints were arranged in a pattern; something like this': and Mr Vaughan caught at a pencil and piece of paper, and dotted down a few strokes.

'You see,' he went on, 'there were, I should think, twelve little stones neatly arranged in lines, and spaced at equal distances, as I have shown it on the paper. They were pointed stones, and the points were very carefully directed one way.'

'Yes,' said Dyson, without much interest, 'no doubt the children you have mentioned had been playing there on their way from school. Children, as you know, are very fond of making such devices with oyster shells or flints or flowers, or with whatever comes in their way.'

'So I thought; I just noticed these flints were arranged in a sort of pattern and then went on. But the next morning I was taking the same round, which, as a matter of fact, is habitual with me, and again I saw at the same spot a device in flints. This time it was really a curious pattern; something like the spokes of a wheel, all meeting at a common centre, and this centre formed by a device which looked like a bowl; all, you understand, done in flints.'

'You are right,' said Dyson, 'that seems odd enough. Still it is reasonable that your half-a-dozen school children are responsible for these fantasies in stone.'

'Well, I thought I would set the matter at rest. The children pass the gate every evening at half-past five, and I walked by at six, and found the device just as I had left it in the morning. The next day I was up and about at a quarter to seven, and I found the whole thing had been changed. There was a pyramid outlined in flints upon the grass. The children I saw going by an hour and a half later, and they ran past the spot without glancing to right or left. In the evening I watched them going home, and this morning when I got to the gate at six o'clock there was a thing like a half moon waiting for me.'

'So then the series runs thus: firstly ordered lines, then, the device of the spokes and the bowl, then the pyramid, and finally, this morning, the half moon. That is the order, isn't it?'

'Yes; that is right. But do you know, it has made me feel very uneasy? I suppose it seems absurd, but I can't help thinking that some kind of signalling is going on under my nose, and that sort of thing is disquieting.'

'But what have you to dread? You have no enemies?'

'No; but I have some very valuable old plate.'

'You are thinking of burglars then?' said Dyson, with an accent of considerable interest, 'but you must know your neighbours. Are there any suspicious characters about?'

'Not that I am aware of. But you remember what I told you of the sailors.'

'Can you trust your servants?'

'Oh, perfectly. The plate is preserved in a strong room; the butler, an old family servant, alone knows where the key is kept. There is nothing wrong there. Still, everybody is aware that I have a lot of old silver, and all country folks are given to gossip. In that way information may have got abroad in very undesirable quarters.'

'Yes, but I confess there seems something a little unsatisfactory in the burglar theory. Who is signalling to whom? I cannot see my way to accepting such an explanation. What put the plate into your head in connection with these flint signs, or whatever one may call them?'

'It was the figure of the Bowl,' said Vaughan. 'I happen to possess a very large and very valuable Charles II punch-bowl. The chasing is really exquisite, and the thing is worth a lot of money. The sign I described to you was exactly the same shape as my punch-bowl.'

'A queer coincidence certainly. But the other figures or devices: you have nothing shaped like a pyramid?'

'Ah, you will think that queerer. As it happens, this punch-bowl of mine, together with a set of rare old ladles, is kept in a mahogany chest of a pyramidal shape. The four sides slope upwards, the narrow towards the top.'

'I confess all this interests me a good deal,' said Dyson. 'Let us go on, then. What about the other figures; how about the Army, as we may call the first sign, and the Crescent or Half moon?'

'Ah, there is no reference that I can make out of these two. Still, you see I have some excuse for curiosity at all events. I should be very vexed to lose any of the old plate; nearly all the pieces have been in the family for generations. And I cannot get it out of my head that some scoundrels mean to rob me, and are communicating with one another every night.'

'Frankly,' said Dyson, 'I can make nothing of it; I am as much in the dark as yourself. Your theory seems certainly the only possible explanation, and yet the difficulties are immense.'

He leaned back in his chair, and the two men faced each other, frowning, and perplexed by so bizarre a problem.

'By the way,' said Dyson, after a long pause, 'what is your geological formation down there?'

Mr Vaughan looked up, a good deal surprised by the question.

'Old red sandstone and limestone, I believe,' he said. 'We are just beyond the coal measures, you know.'

'But surely there are no flints either in the sandstone or the limestone?'

'No, I never see any flints in the fields. I confess that did strike me as a little curious.'

'I should think so! It is very important. By the way, what size were the flints used in making these devices?'

'I happen to have brought one with me; I took it this morning.'

'From the Half moon?'

'Exactly. Here it is.'

He handed over a small flint, tapering to a point, and about three inches in length.

Dyson's face blazed up with excitement as he took the thing from Vaughan.

'Certainly,' he said, after a moment's pause, 'you have some curious neighbours in your country. I hardly think they can harbour any designs on your punch-bowl. Do you know this is a flint arrow-head of vast antiquity, and not only that, but an arrow-head of a unique kind? I have seen specimens from all parts of the world, but there are features about this thing that are quite peculiar.' He laid down his pipe, and took out a book from a drawer.

'We shall just have time to catch the 5.45 to Castletown,' he said.

II

The Eyes on the Wall

Mr Dyson drew in a long breath of the air of the hills and felt all the enchantment of the scene about him. It was very early morning, and he stood on the terrace in the front of the house.

Vaughan's ancestor had built on the lower slope of a great hill, in the shelter of a deep and ancient wood that gathered on three sides about the house, and on the fourth side, the south-west, the land fell gently away and sank to the valley, where a brook wound in and out in mystic esses, and the dark and gleaming alders tracked the stream's course to the eye. On the terrace in the sheltered place no wind blew, and far beyond, the trees were still. Only one sound broke in upon the silence, and Dyson heard the noise of the brook singing far below, the song of clear and shining water rippling over the stones, whispering and murmuring as it sank to dark deep pools. Across the stream, just below the house, rose a grey stone bridge, vaulted and buttressed, a fragment of the Middle Ages, and then beyond the bridge the hills rose again, vast and rounded like bastions, covered here and there with dark woods and thickets of undergrowth, but the heights were all bare of trees, showing only grey turf and patches of bracken, touched here and there with the gold of fading fronds; Dyson looked to the north and south, and still he saw the wall of the hills, and the ancient woods, and the stream drawn in and out between them; all grey and dim with morning mist beneath a grey sky in a hushed and haunted air.

Mr Vaughan's voice broke in upon the silence.

'I thought you would be too tired to be about so early,' he said. 'I see you are admiring the view. It is very pretty, isn't it, though I suppose old Meyrick Vaughan didn't think much about the scenery when he built the house. A queer, grey old place, isn't it?'

'Yes, and how it fits into the surroundings; it seems of a piece with the grey hills and the grey bridge below.'

'I am afraid I have brought you down on false pretences, Dyson,' said Vaughan, as they began to walk up and down the terrace. 'I have been to the place, and there is not a sign of anything this morning.'

'Ah, indeed. Well, suppose we go round together.'

They walked across the lawn and went by a path through the

ilex shrubbery to the back of the house. There Vaughan pointed out the track leading down to the valley and up to the heights above the wood, and presently they stood beneath the garden wall, by the door.

'Here, you see, it was,' said Vaughan, pointing to a spot on the turf. 'I was standing just where you are now that morning I first saw the flints.'

'Yes, quite so. That morning it was the Army, as I call it; then the Bowl, then the Pyramid, and, yesterday, the Half moon. What a queer old stone that is,' he went on, pointing to a block of limestone rising out of the turf just beneath the wall. 'It looks like a sort of dwarf pillar, but I suppose it is natural.'

'Oh, yes, I think so. I imagine it was brought here, though, as we stand on the red sandstone. No doubt it was used as a foundation stone for some older building.'

'Very likely.' Dyson was peering about him attentively, looking from the ground to the wall, and from the wall to the deep wood that hung almost over the garden and made the place dark even in the morning.

'Look here,' said Dyson at length, 'it is certainly a case of children this time. Look at that.' He was bending down and staring at the dull red surface of the mellowed bricks of the wall.

Vaughan came up and looked hard where Dyson's finger was pointing, and could scarcely distinguish a faint mark in deeper red.

'What is it?' he said. 'I can make nothing of it.'

'Look a little more closely. Don't you see it is an attempt to draw the human eye?'

'Ah, now I see what you mean. My sight is not very sharp. Yes, so it is, it is meant for an eye, no doubt, as you say. I thought the children learnt drawing at school.'

'Well, it is an odd eye enough. Do you notice the peculiar almond shape; almost like the eye of a Chinaman?'

Dyson looked meditatively at the work of the undeveloped artist, and scanned the wall again, going down on his knees in the minuteness of his inquisition.

'I should like very much,' he said at length, 'to know how a child in this out of the way place could have any idea of the shape of the Mongolian eye. You see the average child has a very distinct impression of the subject; he draws a circle, or something like a circle, and puts a dot in the centre. I don't think any child imagines that the eye is really made like that; it's just a convention of infantile art. But this almond-shaped thing puzzles me extremely. Perhaps it may be derived from a gilt Chinaman on a tea-canister in the grocer's shop. Still, that's hardly likely.'

'But why are you so sure it was done by a child?'

'Why! Look at the height. These old-fashioned bricks are little more than two inches thick; there are twenty courses from the ground to the sketch, if we call it so; that gives a height of three and a half feet. Now, just imagine you are going to draw something on this wall. Exactly; your pencil, if you had one, would touch the wall somewhere on the level with your eyes, that is, more than five feet from the ground. It seems, therefore, a very simple deduction to conclude that this eye on the wall was drawn by a child about ten years old.'

'Yes, I had not thought of that. Of course one of the children must have done it.'

'I suppose so; and yet as I said, there is something singularly unchildlike about those two lines, and the eyeball itself, you see, is almost an oval. To my mind, the thing has an odd, ancient air; and a touch that is not altogether pleasant. I cannot help fancying that if we could see a whole face from the same hand it would not be altogether agreeable. However, that is nonsense, after all, and we are not getting farther in our investigations. It is odd that the flint series has come to such an abrupt end.'

The two men walked away towards the house, and as they went

in at the porch there was a break in the grey sky, and a gleam of sunshine on the grey hill before them.

All the day Dyson prowled meditatively about the fields and woods surrounding the house. He was thoroughly and completely puzzled by the trivial circumstances he proposed to elucidate, and now he again took the flint arrow-head from his pocket, turning it over and examining it with deep attention. There was something about the thing that was altogether different from the specimens he had seen at the museums and private collections; the shape was of a distinct type, and around the edge there was a line of little punctured dots, apparently a suggestion of ornament. Who, thought Dyson, could possess such things in so remote a place; and who, possessing the flints, could have put them to the fantastic use of designing meaningless figures under Vaughan's garden wall? The rank absurdity of the whole affair offended him unutterably; and as one theory after another rose in his mind only to be rejected, he felt strongly tempted to take the next train back to town. He had seen the silver plate which Vaughan treasured, and had inspected the punch-bowl, the gem of the collection, with close attention; and what he saw and his interview with the butler convinced him that a plot to rob the strong box was out of the limits of inquiry. The chest in which the bowl was kept, a heavy piece of mahogany, evidently dating from the beginning of the century, was certainly strongly suggestive of a pyramid, and Dyson was at first inclined to the inept manoeuvres of the detective, but a little sober thought convinced him of the impossibility of the burglary hypothesis, and he cast wildly about for something more satisfying. He asked Vaughan if there were any gipsies in the neighbourhood, and heard that the Romany had not been seen for years. This dashed him a good deal, as he knew the gipsy habit of leaving queer hieroglyphics on the line of march, and had been much elated when the thought occurred to him. He was facing Vaughan by the old-fashioned hearth when he put the question, and leaned back in his chair in disgust at the destruction of his theory.

'It is odd,' said Vaughan, 'but the gipsies never trouble us here. Now and then the farmers find traces of fires in the wildest part of the hills, but nobody seems to know who the fire-lighters are.'

'Surely that looks like gipsies?'

'No, not in such places as those. Tinkers and gipsies and wanderers of all sorts stick to the roads and don't go very far from the farmhouses.'

'Well, I can make nothing of it. I saw the children going by this afternoon, and, as you say, they ran straight on. So we shall have no more eyes on the wall at all events.'

'No, I must waylay them one of these days and find out who is the artist.'

The next morning when Vaughan strolled in his usual course from the lawn to the back of the house he found Dyson already awaiting him by the garden door, and evidently in a state of high excitement, for he beckoned furiously with his hand, and gesticulated violently.

'What is it?' asked Vaughan. 'The flints again?'

'No; but look here, look at the wall. There; don't you see it?'

'There's another of those eyes!'

'Exactly. Drawn, you see, at a little distance from the first, almost on the same level, but slightly lower.'

'What on earth is one to make of it? It couldn't have been done by the children; it wasn't there last night, and they won't pass for another hour. What can it mean?'

'I think the very devil is at the bottom of all this,' said Dyson. 'Of course, one cannot resist the conclusion that these infernal almond eyes are to be set down to the same agency as the devices in the arrow-heads; and where that conclusion is to lead us is more than I can tell. For my part, I have to put a strong check on my imagination, or it would run wild.'

'Vaughan,' he said, as they turned away from the wall, 'has it struck you that there is one point – a very curious point – in common between the figures done in flints and the eyes drawn on the wall?'

'What is that?' asked Vaughan, on whose face there had fallen a certain shadow of indefinite dread.

'It is this. We know that the signs of the Army, the Bowl, the Pyramid, and the Half moon must have been done at night. Presumably they were meant to be seen at night. Well, precisely the same reasoning applies to those eyes on the wall.'

'I do not quite see your point.'

'Oh, surely. The nights are dark just now, and have been very cloudy, I know, since I came down. Moreover, those overhanging trees would throw that wall into deep shadow even on a clear night.'

'Well?'

'What struck me was this. What very peculiarly sharp eyesight, they, whoever "they" are, must have to be able to arrange arrow-heads in intricate order in the blackest shadow of the wood, and then draw the eyes on the wall without a trace of bungling, or a false line.'

'I have read of persons confined in dungeons for many years who have been able to see quite well in the dark,' said Vaughan.

'Yes,' said Dyson, 'there was the abbé in *Monte Cristo*. But it is a singular point.'

III

The Search for the Bowl

'Who was that old man that touched his hat to you just now?' said Dyson, as they came to the bend of the lane near the house.

'Oh, that was old Trevor. He looks very broken, poor old fellow.'

'Who is Trevor?'

'Don't you remember? I told you the story that afternoon I came to your rooms – about a girl named Annie Trevor, who disappeared in the most inexplicable manner about five weeks ago. That was her father.'

'Yes, yes, I recollect now. To tell the truth I had forgotten all about it. And nothing has been heard of the girl?'

'Nothing whatever. The police are quite at fault.'

'I am afraid I did not pay very much attention to the details you gave me. Which way did the girl go?'

'Her path would take her right across those wild hills above the house: the nearest point in the track must be about two miles from here.'

'Is it near that little hamlet I saw yesterday?'

'You mean Croesyceiliog, where the children came from? No; it goes more to the north.'

'Ah, I have never been that way.'

They went into the house, and Dyson shut himself up in his room, sunk deep in doubtful thought, but yet with the shadow of a suspicion growing within him that for a while haunted his brain, all vague and fantastic, refusing to take definite form. He was sitting by the open window and looking out on the valley and saw, as if in a picture, the intricate winding of the brook, the grey bridge, and the vast hills rising beyond; all still and without a breath of wind to stir the mystic hanging woods, and the evening sunshine glowed warm on the bracken, and down below a faint mist, pure white, began to rise from the stream. Dyson sat by the window as the day darkened and the huge bastioned hills loomed vast and vague, and the woods became dim and more shadowy: and the fancy that had seized him no longer appeared altogether impossible. He passed the rest of the evening in a reverie, hardly hearing what Vaughan said; and when he took his candle in the hall, he paused a moment before bidding his friend good-night.

'I want a good rest,' he said. 'I have got some work to do to-morrow.'

'Some writing, you mean?'

'No. I am going to look for the Bowl.'

'The Bowl! If you mean my punch-bowl, that is safe in the chest.'

'I don't mean the punch-bowl. You may take my word for it that your plate has never been threatened. No; I will not bother you with any suppositions. We shall in all probability have something much stronger than suppositions before long. Good-night, Vaughan.'

The next morning Dyson set off after breakfast. He took the path by the garden wall, and noted that there were now eight of the weird almond eyes dimly outlined on the brick.

'Six days more,' he said to himself, but as he thought over the theory he had formed, he shrank, in spite of strong conviction, from such a wildly incredible fancy. He struck up through the dense shadows of the wood, and at length came out on the bare hillside, and climbed higher and higher over the slippery turf, keeping well to the north, and following the indications given him by Vaughan. As he went on, he seemed to mount ever higher above the world of human life and customary things; to his right he looked at a fringe of orchard and saw a faint blue smoke rising like a pillar; there was the hamlet from which the children came to school, and there the only sign of life, for the woods embowered and concealed Vaughan's old grey house. As he reached what seemed the summit of the hill, he realised for the first time the desolate loneliness and strangeness of the land; there was nothing but grey sky and grey hill, a high, vast plain that seemed to stretch on for ever and ever, and a faint glimpse of a blue-peaked mountain far away and to the north. At length he came to the path, a slight track scarcely noticeable, and from its position and by what Vaughan had told him, he knew that it was the way the lost girl, Annie Trevor, must have taken. He followed the path on the bare hill-top, noticing the great limestone rocks that cropped out of the turf, grim and hideous, and of an aspect as forbidding as an idol of the South Seas; and suddenly he halted, astonished, although he had found what he searched for.

Almost without warning the ground shelved suddenly away on all sides, and Dyson looked down into a circular depression, which might well have been a Roman amphitheatre, and the ugly crags of limestone rimmed it round as if with a broken wall. Dyson walked round the hollow, and noted the position of the stones, and then turned on his way home.

'This,' he thought to himself, 'is more than curious. The Bowl is discovered, but where is the Pyramid?'

'My dear Vaughan,' he said, when he got back, 'I may tell you that I have found the Bowl, and that is all I shall tell you for the present. We have six days of absolute inaction before us; there is really nothing to be done.'

IV

The Secret of the Pyramid

'I have just been round the garden,' said Vaughan one morning. 'I have been counting those infernal eyes, and I find there are fourteen of them. For heaven's sake, Dyson, tell me what the meaning of it all is.'

'I should be very sorry to attempt to do so. I may have guessed this or that, but I always make it a principle to keep my guesses to myself. Besides, it is really not worth while anticipating events; you will remember my telling you that we had six days of inaction before us? Well, this is the sixth day, and the last of idleness. To-night, I propose we take a stroll.'

'A stroll! Is that all the action you mean to take?'

'Well, it may show you some very curious things. To be plain, I want you to start with me at nine o'clock this evening for the hills. We may have to be out all night, so you had better wrap up well, and bring some of that brandy.'

'Is it a joke?' asked Vaughan, who was bewildered with strange events and strange surmises.

'No, I don't think there is much joke in it. Unless I am much mistaken we shall find a very serious explanation of the puzzle. You will come with me, I am sure?'

'Very good. Which way do you want to go?'

'By the path you told me of; the path Annie Trevor is supposed to have taken.'

Vaughan looked white at the mention of the girl's name.

'I did not think you were on that track,' he said. 'I thought it was the affair of those devices in flint and of the eyes on the wall that you were engaged on. It's no good saying any more, but I will go with you.'

At a quarter to nine that evening the two men set out, taking the path through the wood, and up the hill-side. It was a dark and heavy night, the sky was thick with clouds, and the valley full of mist, and all the way they seemed to walk in a world of shadow and gloom, hardly speaking, and afraid to break the haunted silence. They came out at last on the steep hill-side, and instead of the oppression of the wood there was the long, dim sweep of the turf, and higher, the fantastic limestone rocks hinted horror through the darkness, and the wind sighed as it passed across the mountain to the sea, and in its passage beat chill about their hearts. They seemed to walk on and on for hours, and the dim outline of the hill still stretched before them, and the haggard rocks still loomed through the darkness, when suddenly Dyson whispered, drawing his breath quickly, and coming close to his companion:

'Here,' he said, 'we will lie down. I do not think there is any-thing yet.'

'I know the place,' said Vaughan, after a moment. 'I have often been by in the daytime. The country people are afraid to come here, I believe; it is supposed to be a fairies' castle, or something of the kind. But why on earth have we come here?'

'Speak a little lower,' said Dyson. 'It might not do us any good if we are overheard.'

'Overheard here! There is not a soul within three miles of us.'

'Possibly not; indeed, I should say certainly not. But there might be a body somewhat nearer.'

'I don't understand you in the least,' said Vaughan, whispering to humour Dyson, 'but why have we come here?'

'Well, you see this hollow before us is the Bowl. I think we had better not talk even in whispers.'

They lay full length upon the turf; the rock between their faces and the Bowl, and now and again, Dyson, slouching his dark, soft hat over his forehead, put out the glint of an eye, and in a moment drew back, not daring to take a prolonged view. Again he laid an ear to the ground and listened, and the hours went by, and the darkness seemed to blacken, and the faint sigh of the wind was the only sound.

Vaughan grew impatient with this heaviness of silence, this watching for indefinite terror; for to him there was no shape or form of apprehension, and he began to think the whole vigil a dreary farce.

'How much longer is this to last?' he whispered to Dyson, and Dyson, who had been holding his breath in the agony of attention, put his mouth to Vaughan's ear and said:

'Will you listen?' with pauses between each syllable, and in the voice with which the priest pronounces the awful words.

Vaughan caught the ground with his hands, and stretched forward, wondering what he was to hear. At first there was nothing, and then a low and gentle noise came very softly from the Bowl, a faint sound, almost indescribable, but as if one held the tongue against the roof of the mouth and expelled the breath. He listened eagerly and presently the noise grew louder, and became a strident and horrible hissing as if the pit beneath boiled with fervent heat, and Vaughan, unable to remain in suspense any longer, drew his cap half over his face in imitation of Dyson, and looked down to the hollow below.

It did, in truth, stir and seethe like an infernal caldron. The whole of the sides and bottom tossed and writhed with vague and restless forms that passed to and fro without the sound of feet, and gathered thick here and there and seemed to speak to one another in those tones of horrible sibilance, like the hissing of snakes, that he had heard. It was as if the sweet turf and the cleanly earth had suddenly become quickened with some foul writhing growth. Vaughan could not draw back his face, though he felt Dyson's finger touch him, but he peered into the quaking mass and saw faintly that there were things like faces and human limbs, and yet he felt his inmost soul chill with the sure belief that no fellow soul or human thing stirred in all that tossing and hissing host. He looked aghast, choking back sobs of horror, and at length the loathsome forms gathered thickest about some vague object in the middle of the hollow, and the hissing of their speech grew more venomous, and he saw in the uncertain light the abominable limbs, vague and yet too plainly seen, writhe and intertwine, and he thought he heard, very faint, a low human moan striking through the noise of speech that was not of man. At his heart something seemed to whisper ever 'the worm of corruption, the worm that dieth not', and grotesquely the image was pictured to his imagination of a piece of putrid offal stirring through and through with bloated and horrible creeping things. The writhing of the dusky limbs continued, they seemed clustered round the dark form in the middle of the hollow, and the sweat dripped and poured off Vaughan's forehead, and fell cold on his hand beneath his face.

Then, it seemed done in an instant, the loathsome mass melted and fell away to the sides of the Bowl, and for a moment Vaughan saw in the middle of the hollow the tossing of human arms.

But a spark gleamed beneath, a fire kindled, and as the voice of a woman cried out loud in a shrill scream of utter anguish and terror, a great pyramid of flame spired up like a bursting of a pent fountain, and threw a blaze of light upon the whole mountain. In that instant Vaughan saw the myriads beneath; the things made in the form of men but stunted like children hideously deformed, the faces with the almond eyes burning with evil and unspeakable lusts; the ghastly yellow of the mass of naked flesh and then as if by magic the place was empty, while the fire roared and crackled, and the flames shone abroad.

'You have seen the Pyramid,' said Dyson in his ear, 'the Pyramid of fire.'

V

The Little People

'Then you recognise the thing?'

'Certainly. It is a brooch that Annie Trevor used to wear on Sundays; I remember the pattern. But where did you find it? You don't mean to say that you have discovered the girl?'

'My dear Vaughan, I wonder you have not guessed where I found the brooch. You have not forgotten last night already?'

'Dyson,' said the other, speaking very seriously, 'I have been turning it over in my mind this morning while you have been out. I have thought about what I saw, or perhaps I should say about what I thought I saw, and the only conclusion I can come to is this, that the thing won't bear recollection. As men live, I have lived soberly and honestly, in the fear of God, all my days, and all I can do is believe that I suffered from some monstrous delusion, from some phantasmagoria of the bewildered senses. You know we went home together in silence, not a word passed between us as to what I fancied I saw; had we not better agree to keep silence on the subject? When I took my walk in the peaceful morning sunshine, I thought all the earth seemed full of praise, and passing by that wall I noticed there were no more signs recorded, and I blotted out those that remained. The mystery is over, and we can live quietly again. I think some poison has been working for the last few weeks; I have trod on the verge of madness, but I am sane now.'

Mr Vaughan had spoken earnestly, and bent forward in his chair and glanced at Dyson with something of entreaty.

'My dear Vaughan,' said the other, after a pause, 'what's the use of this? It is much too late to take that tone; we have gone too deep. Besides you know as well as I that there is no delusion in the case; I wish there were with all my heart. No, in justice to myself I must tell you the whole story, so far as I know it.'

'Very good,' said Vaughan with a sigh, 'if you must, you must.'

'Then,' said Dyson, 'we will begin with the end if you please. I found this brooch you have just identified in the place we have called the Bowl. There was a heap of grey ashes, as if a fire had been burning, indeed, the embers were still hot, and this brooch was lying on the ground, just outside the range of the flame. It must have dropped accidentally from the dress of the person who was wearing it. No, don't interrupt me; we can pass now to the beginning, as we have had the end. Let us go back to that day you came to see me in my rooms in London. So far as I can remember, soon after you came in you mentioned, in a somewhat casual manner, that an unfortunate and mysterious incident had occurred in your part of the country; a girl named Annie Trevor had gone to see a relative, and had disappeared. I confess freely that what you said did not greatly interest me; there are so many reasons which may make it extremely convenient for a man and more especially a woman to vanish from the circle of their relations and friends. I suppose, if we were to consult the police, one would find that in London somebody disappears mysteriously every other week, and the officers would, no doubt, shrug their shoulders, and tell you that by the law of averages it could not be otherwise. So I was very culpably careless to your story, and besides, here is another reason for my lack of interest; your tale was inexplicable. You could only suggest a blackguard sailor on the tramp, but I discarded the explanation immediately.

'For many reasons, but chiefly because the occasional criminal, the amateur in brutal crime, is always found out, especially if he selects the country as the scene of his operations. You will remember the case of that Garcia you mentioned; he strolled into a railway station the day after the murder, his trousers covered with blood, and the works of the Dutch clock, his loot, tied in a neat parcel. So rejecting this, your only suggestion, the whole tale became, as I say, inexplicable, and, *therefore*, profoundly uninteresting. Yes, therefore, it is a perfectly valid conclusion. Do you ever trouble your head about problems which you know to be insoluble? Did you ever bestow much thought on the old puzzle of Achilles and the tortoise? Of course not, because you knew it was a hopeless quest, and so when you told me the story of a country girl who had disappeared I simply placed the whole thing down in the category of the insoluble, and thought no more about the matter. I was mistaken, so it has turned out; but if you remember, you immediately passed on to an affair which interested you more intensely, because personally. I need not go over the very singular narrative of the flint signs, at first I thought it all trivial, probably some children's game, and if not that a hoax of some sort; but your showing me the arrow-head awoke my acute interest. Here, I saw, there was something widely removed from the commonplace, and matter of real curiosity; and as soon as I came here I set to work to find the solution, repeating to myself again and again the signs you had described. First came the sign we have agreed to call the Army; a number of serried lines of flints, all pointing in the same way. Then the lines, like the spokes of a wheel, all converging towards the figure of a Bowl, then the triangle or Pyramid, and last of all the Half moon. I confess that I exhausted conjecture in my efforts to unveil this mystery, and as you will understand it was a duplex or rather triplex problem. For I had not merely to ask myself: what do these figures mean? but also, who can possibly be responsible for the designing of them? And again, who can possibly possess such valuable things, and knowing their value thus throw them down by the wayside? This line of thought led me to suppose that the person or persons in question did not know the value of unique flint arrow-heads, and yet this did not lead me far, for a well-educated man might easily be ignorant on such a subject. Then came the complication of the eye on the wall, and you remember that we could not avoid the conclusion that in the two cases the same agency was at work. The peculiar position of these eyes on the wall made me inquire if there was such a thing as a dwarf anywhere in the neighbourhood, but I found that there was not, and I knew that the children who pass by every day had nothing to do with the matter. Yet I felt convinced that whoever drew the eyes must be from three and a half to four feet high, since, as I pointed out at the time, anyone who draws on a perpendicular surface chooses by instinct a spot about level with his face. Then again, there was the question of the peculiar shape of the eyes; that marked Mongolian character of which the English countryman could have no conception, and for a final cause of confusion the obvious fact that the designer or designers must be able practically to see in the dark. As you remarked, a man who has been confined for many years in an extremely dark cell or dungeon might acquire that power; but since the days of Edmond Dantès, where would such a prison be found in Europe? A sailor, who had been immured for a considerable period in some horrible Chinese *oubliette*, seemed the individual

I was in search of, and though it looked improbable, it was not absolutely impossible that a sailor or, let us say, a man employed on shipboard, should be a dwarf. But how to account for my imaginary sailor being in possession of prehistoric arrow-heads? And the possession granted, what was the meaning and object of these mysterious signs of flint, and the almond-shaped eyes? Your theory of a contemplated burglary I saw, nearly from the first, to be quite untenable, and I confess I was utterly at a loss for a working hypothesis. It was a mere accident which put me on the track; we passed poor old Trevor, and your mention of his name and of the disappearance of his daughter recalled the story which I had forgotten, or which remained unheeded. Here, then, I said to myself, is another problem, uninteresting, it is true, by itself; but what if it prove to be in relation with all these enigmas which torture me? I shut myself in my room, and endeavoured to dismiss all prejudice from my mind, and I went over everything *de novo*, assuming for theory's sake that the disappearance of Annie Trevor had some connection with the flint signs and the eyes on the wall. This assumption did not lead me very far, and I was on the point of giving the whole problem up in despair, when a possible significance of the Bowl struck me. As you know there is a "Devil's Punch-bowl" in Surrey, and I saw that the symbol might refer to some feature in the country. Putting the two extremes together, I determined to look for the Bowl near the path which the lost girl had taken, and you know how I found it. I interpreted the sign by what I knew, and read the first, the Army, thus: "there is to be a gathering or assembly at the Bowl in a fortnight (that is the Half moon) to see the Pyramid, or to build the Pyramid." The eyes, drawn one by one, day by day, evidently checked off the days, and I knew that there would be fourteen and no more. Thus far the way seemed pretty plain; I would not trouble myself to inquire as to the nature of the assembly, or as to who was to assemble in the loneliest and most dreaded place among these lonely hills. In Ireland or

China or the West of America the question would have been easily answered; a muster of the disaffected, the meeting of a secret society; vigilantes summoned to report: the thing would be simplicity itself; but in this quiet corner of England, inhabited by quiet folk, no such suppositions were possible for a moment. But I knew that I should have an opportunity of seeing and watching the assembly, and I did not care to perplex myself with hopeless research; and in place of reasoning a wild fancy entered into judgment: I remembered what people had said about Annie Trevor's disappearance, that she had been "taken by the fairies". I tell you, Vaughan, I am a sane man as you are, my brain is not, I trust, mere vacant space to let to any wild improbability, and I tried my best to thrust the fantasy away. And the hint came of the old name of fairies, "the little people", and the very probable belief that they represent a tradition of the prehistoric Turanian inhabitants of the country, who were cave dwellers: and then I realised with a shock that I was looking for a being under four feet in height, accustomed to live in darkness, possessing stone instruments, and familiar with the Mongolian cast of features! I say this, Vaughan, that I should be ashamed to hint at such visionary stuff to you, if it were not for that which you saw with your very eyes last night, and I say that I might doubt the evidence of my senses, if they were not confirmed by yours. But you and I cannot look each other in the face and pretend delusion; as you lay on the turf beside me I felt your flesh shrink and quiver, and I saw your eyes in the light of the flame. And so I tell you without any shame what was in my mind last night as we went through the wood and climbed the hill, and lay hidden beneath the rock.

'There was one thing that should have been most evident that puzzled me to the very last. I told you how I read the sign of the Pyramid; the assembly was to see a pyramid, and the true meaning of the symbol escaped me to the last moment. The old derivation from πῦρ, fire, though false, should have set me on the track, but it never occurred to me.

'I think I need say very little more. You know we were quite helpless, even if we had foreseen what was to come. Ah, the particular place where these signs were displayed? Yes, that is a curious question. But this house is, so far as I can judge, in a pretty central situation amongst the hills; and possibly, who can say yes or no, that queer, old limestone pillar by your garden wall was a place of meeting before the Celt set foot in Britain. But there is one thing I must add: I don't regret our inability to rescue the wretched girl. You saw the appearance of those things that gathered thick and writhed in the Bowl; you may be sure that what lay bound in the midst of them was no longer fit for earth.'

'So?' said Vaughan.

'So she passed in the Pyramid of Fire,' said Dyson, 'and they passed again to the underworld, to the places beneath the hills.'

THE BLACK REAPER

by

Bernard Capes

First published in the collection *At a Winter's Fire*

1899

I

NOW I AM to tell you of a thing that befell in the year 1665 of the Great Plague, when the hearts of certain amongst men, grown callous in wickedness upon that rebound from an inhuman austerity, were opened to the vision of a terror that moved and spoke not in the silent places of the fields. Forasmuch as, however, in the recovery from delirium a patient may marvel over the incredulity of neighbours who refuse to give credence to the presentments that have been *ipso facto* to him, so, the nation being sound again, and its constitution hale, I expect little but a laugh for my piety in relating of the following incident; which, nevertheless, is as essential true as that he who shall look through the knot-hole in the plank of a coffin shall acquire the evil eye.

For, indeed, in those days of a wild fear and confusion, when every condition that makes for reason was set wandering by a devious path, and all men sitting as in a theatre of death looked to see the curtain rise upon God knows what horrors, it was vouchsafed to many to witness sights and sounds beyond the compass of

Nature, and that as if the devil and his minions had profited by the anarchy to slip unobserved into the world. And I know that this is so, for all the insolence of a recovered scepticism; and, as to the unseen, we are like one that traverseth the dark with a lanthorn, himself the skipper of a little moving blot of light, but a positive mark for any secret foe without the circumference of its radiance.

Be that as it may, and whether it was our particular ill-fortune, or, as some asserted, our particular wickedness, that made of our village an inviting back-door of entrance to the Prince of Darkness, I know not; but so it is that disease and contagion are ever inclined to penetrate by way of flaws or humours where the veil of the flesh is already perforated, as a kite circleth round its quarry, looking for the weak place to strike: and, without doubt, in that land of corruption we were a very foul blot indeed.

How this came about it were idle to speculate; yet no man shall have the hardihood to affirm that it was otherwise. Nor do I seek to extenuate myself, who was in truth no better than my neighbours in most that made us a community of drunkards and forswearers both lewd and abominable. For in that village a depravity that was like madness had come to possess the heads of the people, and no man durst take his stand on honesty or even common decency, for fear he should be set upon by his comrades and drummed out of his government on a pint pot. Yet for myself I will say was one only redeeming quality, and that was the pure love I bore to my solitary orphaned child, the little Margery.

Now, our Vicar – a patient and God-fearing man, for all his predial tithes were impropriated by his lord, that was an absentee and a sheriff in London – did little to stem that current of lewdness that had set in strong with the Restoration. And this was from no lack of virtue in himself, but rather from a natural invertebracy, as one may say, and an order of mind that, yet being no order, is made the sport of any sophister with a wit for paragram. Thus it always is that mere example is of little avail without precept – of which, however, it is an important condition – and that the successful directors of men be not those who go to the van and lead, unconscious of the gibes and mockery in their rear, but such rather as drive the mob before them with a smiting hand and no infirmity of purpose. So, if a certain affection for our pastor dwelt in our hearts, no title of respect was there to leaven it and justify his high office before Him that consigned the trust; and ever deeper and deeper we sank in the slough of corruption, until was brought about this pass – that naught but some scourging despotism of the Church should acquit us of the fate of Sodom. That such, at the eleventh hour, was vouchsafed us of God's mercy, it is my purpose to show; and, doubtless, this offering of a loop-hole was to account by reason of the devil's having debarked his reserves, as it were, in our port; and so quartering upon us a soldiery that we were, at no invitation of our own, to maintain, stood us a certain extenuation.

It was late in the order of things before in our village so much as a rumour of the plague reached us. Newspapers were not in those days, and reports, being by word of mouth, travelled slowly, and were often spent bullets by the time they fell amongst us. Yet, by May, some gossip there was of the distemper having gotten a hold in certain quarters of London and increasing, and this alarmed our people, though it made no abatement of their profligacy. But presently the reports coming thicker, with confirmation of the terror and panic that was enlarging on all sides, we must take measures for our safety; though into June and July, when the pestilence was raging, none infected had come our way, and that from our remote and isolated position. Yet it needs but fear for the crown to that wickedness that is self-indulgence; and forasmuch as this fear fattens like a toadstool on the decomposition it springs from, it grew with us to the proportions that we were set to kill or destroy any that should approach us from the stricken districts.

And then suddenly there appeared in our midst *he* that was appointed to be our scourge and our cautery.

Whence he came, or how, no man of us could say. Only one day we were a community of roysterers and scoffers, impious and abominable, and the next he was amongst us smiting and thundering.

Some would have it that he was an old collegiate of our Vicar's, but at last one of those wandering Dissenters that found never as now the times opportune to their teachings – a theory to which our minister's treatment of the stranger gave colour. For from the moment of his appearance he took the reins of government, as it were, appropriating the pulpit and launching his bolts therefrom, with the full consent and encouragement of the other. There were those, again, who were resolved that his commission was from a high place, whither news of our infamy had reached, and that we had best give him a respectful hearing, lest we should run a chance of having our hearing stopped altogether. A few were convinced he was no man at all, but rather a fiend sent to thresh us with the scourge of our own contriving, that we might be tender, like steak, for the cooking; and yet other few regarded him with terror, as an actual figure or embodiment of the distemper.

But, generally, after the first surprise, the feeling of resentment at his intrusion woke and gained ground, and we were much put about that he should have thus assumed the pastorship without invitation, quartering with our Vicar; who kept himself aloof and was little seen, and seeking to drive us by terror, and amazement, and a great menace of retribution. For, in truth, this was not the method to which we were wont, and it both angered and disturbed us.

This feeling would have enlarged the sooner, perhaps, were it not for a certain restraining influence possessed of the new-comer, which neighboured him with darkness and mystery. For he was above the common tall, and ever appeared in public with a slouched hat, that concealed all the upper part of his face and showed little otherwise but the dense black beard that dropped upon his breast like a shadow.

Now with August came a fresh burst of panic, how the desolation increased and the land was overrun with swarms of infected persons seeking an asylum from the city; and our anger rose high against the stranger, who yet dwelt with us and encouraged the distemper of our minds by furious denunciations of our guilt.

Thus far, for all the corruption of our hearts, we had maintained the practice of church-going, thinking, maybe, poor fools! to hoodwink the Almighty with a show of reverence; but now, as by a common consent, we neglected the observances and loitered of a Sabbath in the fields, and thither at the last the strange man pursued us and ended the matter.

For so it fell that at the time of the harvest's ripening a goodish body of us males was gathered one Sunday for coolness about the neighbourhood of the dripping well, whose waters were a tradition, for they had long gone dry. This well was situated in a sort of cave or deep scoop at the foot of a cliff of limestone, to which the cultivated ground that led up to it fell somewhat. High above, the cliff broke away into a wide stretch of pasture land, but the face of the rock itself was all patched with bramble and little starved birch-trees clutching for foothold; and in like manner the excavation beneath was half-stifled and gloomed over with undergrowth, so that it looked a place very dismal and uninviting, save in the ardour of the dog-days.

Within, where had been the basin, was a great shattered hole going down to unknown depths; and this no man had thought to explore, for a mystery held about the spot that was doubtless the foster-child of ignorance.

But to the front of the well and of the cliff stretched a noble field of corn, and this field was of an uncommon shape, being, roughly, a vast circle and a little one joined by a neck and in suggestion not unlike an hour-glass; and into the crop thereof, which was of goodly weight and condition, were the first sickles to be put on the morrow.

Now as we stood or lay around, idly discussing of the news, and congratulating ourselves that we were featly quit of our incubus, to us along the meadow path, his shadow jumping on the corn, came the very subject of our gossip.

He strode up, looking neither to right nor left, and with the first word that fell, low and damnatory, from his lips, we knew that the moment had come when, whether for good or evil, he intended to cast us from him and acquit himself of further responsibility in our direction.

'Behold!' he cried, pausing over against us, 'I go from among ye! Behold, ye that have not obeyed nor inclined your ear, but have walked every one in the imagination of his evil heart! Saith the Lord, "I will bring evil upon them, which they shall not be able to escape; and though they shall cry unto Me, I will not hearken unto them."'

His voice rang out, and a dark silence fell among us. It was pregnant, but with little of humility. We had had enough of this interloper and his abuse. Then, like Jeremiah, he went to prophesy:

'I read ye, men of Anathoth, and the murder in your hearts. Ye that have worshipped the shameful thing and burned incense to Baal – shall I cringe that ye devise against me, or not rather pray to the Lord of Hosts, "Let me see Thy vengeance on them"? And He answereth, "I will bring evil upon the men of Anathoth, even the year of their visitation."'

Now, though I was no participator in that direful thing that followed, I stood by, nor interfered, and so must share the blame. For there were men risen all about, and their faces lowering, and it seemed that it would go hard with the stranger were he not more particular.

But he moved forward, with a stately and commanding gesture, and stood with his back to the well-scoop and threatened us and spoke.

'Lo!' he shrieked, 'your hour is upon you! Ye shall be mowed down like ripe corn, and the shadow of your name shall be swept from the earth! The glass of your iniquity is turned, and when its sand is run through, not a man of ye shall be!'

He raised his arm aloft, and in a moment he was overborne. Even then, as all say, none got sight of his face; but he fought with lowered head, and his black beard flapped like a wounded crow. But suddenly a boy-child ran forward of the bystanders, crying and screaming—

'Hurt him not! They are hurting him – oh, me! oh, me!'

And from the sweat and struggle came his voice, gasping, 'I spare the little children!'

Then only I know of the surge and the crash towards the well-mouth, of an instant cessation of motion, and immediately of men toiling hither and thither with boulders and huge blocks, which they piled over the rent, and so sealed it with a cromlech of stone.

II

That, in the heat of rage and of terror, we had gone farther than we had at first designed, our gloom and our silence on the morrow attested. True we were quit of our incubus, but on such terms as not even the severity of the times could excuse. For the man had but chastised us to our improvement; and to destroy the scourge is not to condone the offence. For myself, as I bore up the little Margery to my shoulder on my way to the reaping, I felt the burden of guilt so great as that I found myself muttering of an apology to the Lord that I durst put myself into touch with innocence. 'But the walk would fatigue her otherwise,' I murmured; and, when we were come to the field, I took and carried her into the upper or little meadow, out of reach of the scythes, and placed her to sleep amongst the corn, and so left her with a groan.

But when I was come anew to my comrades, who stood at the lower extremity of the field – and this was the bottom of the hour-glass, so to speak – I was aware of a stir amongst them, and, advancing closer, that they were all intent upon the neighbourhood of the field I had left, staring like distraught creatures, and holding well together, as if in a panic. Therefore, following the direction of their eyes, and of one that pointed with rigid finger, I turned me about, and looked whence I had come; and my heart went with a somersault, and in a moment I was all sick and dazed.

For I saw, at the upper curve of the meadow, where the well lay in gloom, that a man had sprung out of the earth, as it seemed, and was started reaping; and the face of this man was all in shadow, from which his beard ran out and down like a stream of gall.

He reaped swiftly and steadily, swinging like a pendulum; but, though the sheaves fell to him right and left, no swish of the scythe came to us, nor any sound but the beating of our own hearts.

Now, from the first moment of my looking, no doubt was in my lost soul but that this was him we had destroyed come back to verify his prophecy in ministering to the vengeance of the Lord of Hosts; and at the thought a deep groan rent my bosom, and was echoed by those about me. But scarcely was it issued when a second terror smote me as that I near reeled. Margery – my babe! put to sleep there in the path of the Black Reaper!

At that, though they called to me, I sprang forward like a madman, and running along the meadow, through the neck of the glass, reached the little thing, and stooped and snatched her into my arms. She was sound and unfrighted, as I felt with a burst of thankfulness; but, looking about me, as I turned again to fly, I had near dropped in my tracks for the sickness and horror I experienced in the nearer neighbourhood of the apparition. For, though it never raised its head, or changed the steady swing of its shoulders, I knew that it was aware of and was reaping at me. Now, I tell you, it was ten yards away, yet the point of the scythe came gliding upon me silently, like a snake, through the stalks, and at that I screamed out and ran for my life.

I escaped, sweating with terror; but when I was sped back to the men, there was all the village collected, and our Vicar to the front, praying from a throat that rattled like a dead leaf in a draught. I know not what he said, for the low cries of the women filled the air; but his face was white as a smock, and his fingers writhed in one another like a knot of worms.

'The plague is upon us!' they wailed. 'We shall be mowed down like ripe corn!'

And even as they shrieked, the Black Reaper paused, and, putting away his scythe, stooped and gathered up a sheaf in his arms and stood it on end. And, with the very act, a man – one that had been forward in yesterday's business – fell down amongst us yelling and foaming; and he rent his breast in his frenzy, revealing the purple blot thereon, and he passed blaspheming. And the reaper stooped and stooped again, and with every sheaf he gathered together one of us fell stricken and rolled in his agony, while the rest stood by palsied.

But, when at length all that was cut was accounted for, and a dozen of us were gone each to his judgment, and he had taken up his scythe to reap anew, a wild fury woke in the breasts of some of the more abandoned and reckless amongst us.

'It is not to be tolerated!' they cried. 'Let us at once fire the corn and burn this sorcerer!'

And with that, some five or six of them, emboldened by despair, ran up into the little field, and, separating, had out each his flint and fired the crop in his own place, and retreated to the narrow part for safety.

Now the reaper rested on his scythe, as if unexpectedly acquitted of a part of his labour; but the corn flamed up in these five or six directions, and was consumed in each to the compass of a single sheaf: whereat the fire died away. And with its dying the faces of those that had ventured went black as coal; and they flung up their arms, screaming, and fell prone where they stood, and were hidden from our view.

Then, indeed, despair seized upon all of us that survived, and we made no doubt but that we were to be exterminated and wiped from the earth for our sins, as were the men of Anathoth. And for an hour the Black Reaper mowed and trussed, till he had cut all from the little upper field and was approached to the neck of juncture with the lower and larger. And before us that remained, and who were drawn back amongst the trees, weeping and praying, a fifth of our comrades lay foul, and dead, and sweltering, and all blotched over with the dreadful mark of the pestilence.

Now, as I say, the reaper was nearing the neck of juncture; and so we knew that if he should once pass into the great field towards us and continue his mowing, not one of us should be left to give earnest of our repentance.

Then, as it seemed, our Vicar came to a resolution, moving forward with a face all wrapt and entranced; and he strode up the meadow path and approached the apparition, and stretched out his arms to it entreating. And we saw the other pause, awaiting him; and, as he came near, put forth his hand, and so, gently, on the good old head. But as we looked, catching at our breaths with a little pathos of hope, the priestly face was thrown back radiant, and the figure of him that would give his life for us sank amongst the yet standing corn and disappeared from our sight.

So at last we yielded ourselves fully to our despair; for if our pastor should find no mercy, what possibility of it could be for us!

It was in this moment of an uttermost grief and horror, when each stood apart from his neighbour, fearing the contamination of his presence, that there was vouchsafed to me, of God's pity, a wild and sudden inspiration. Still to my neck fastened the little Margery – not frighted, it seemed, but mazed – and other babes there were in plenty, that clung to their mothers' skirts and peeped out, wondering at the strange show.

I ran to the front and shrieked: 'The children! the children! He will not touch the little children! Bring them and set them in his path!' And so crying I sped to the neck of the meadow, and loosened the soft arms from my throat, and put the little one down within the corn.

Now at once the women saw what I would be at, and full a score of them snatched up their babes and followed me. And here we were reckless for ourselves; but we knelt the innocents in one close line across the neck of land, so that the Black Reaper should not find space between any of them to swing his scythe. And having done this, we fell back with our hearts bubbling in our breasts, and we stood panting and watched.

He had paused over that one full sheaf of his reaping; but now, with the sound of the women's running, he seized his weapon again and set to upon the narrow belt of corn that yet separated him from the children. But presently, coming out upon the tender array, his scythe stopped and trailed in his hand, and for a full minute he stood like a figure of stone. Then thrice he walked slowly backwards and forwards along the line, seeking for an interval whereby he might pass; and the children laughed at him like silver bells, showing no fear, and perchance meeting that of love in his eyes that was hidden from us.

Then of a sudden he came to before the midmost of the line, and, while we drew our breath like dying souls, stooped and snapped his blade across his knee, and, holding the two parts in his hand, turned and strode back into the shadow of the dripping well. There arrived, he paused once more, and, twisting him about, waved his hand once to us and vanished into the blackness. But there were those who affirmed that in that instant of his turning, his face was revealed, and that it was a face radiant and beautiful as an angel's.

Such is the history of the wild judgment that befell us, and by grace of the little children was foregone; and such was the stranger whose name no man ever heard tell, but whom many have since sought to identify with that spirit of the pestilence that entered into men's hearts and confounded them, so that they saw visions and were afterwards confused in their memories.

But this I may say, that when at last our courage would fetch us to that little field of death, we found it to be all blackened and blasted, so as nothing would take root there then or ever since; and it was as if, after all the golden sand of the hour-glass was run away and the lives of the most impious with it, the destroyer saw fit to stay his hand for sake of the babes that he had pronounced innocent, and for such as were spared to witness to His judgment. And this I do here, with a heart as contrite as if it were the morrow of the visitation, the which with me it ever has remained.

There will be guests at the hall.

THE ASH-TREE

by

M. R. James

First published in the collection
Ghost Stories of an Antiquary

1904

EVERYONE WHO HAS travelled over Eastern England knows the smaller country-houses with which it is studded – the rather dank little buildings, usually in the Italian style, surrounded with parks of some eighty to a hundred acres. For me they have always had a very strong attraction: with the grey paling of split oak, the noble trees, the meres with their reed-beds, and the line of distant woods. Then, I like the pillared portico – perhaps stuck on to a red-brick Queen Anne house which has been faced with stucco to bring it into line with the 'Grecian' taste of the end of the eighteenth century; the hall inside, going up to the roof, which ought always to be provided with a gallery and a small organ. I like the library, too, where you may find anything from a Psalter of the thirteenth century to a Shakespeare quarto. I like the pictures, of course; and perhaps most of all I like fancying what life in such a house was when it was first built, and in the piping times of landlords' prosperity, and not least now, when, if money is not so plentiful, taste is more varied and life quite as interesting. I wish to have one of these houses, and enough money to keep it together and entertain my friends in it modestly.

But this is a digression. I have to tell you of a curious series of events which happened in such a house as I have tried to describe. It is Castringham Hall in Suffolk. I think a good deal has been done to the building since the period of my story, but the essential features I have sketched are still there – Italian portico, square block of white house, older inside than out, park with fringe of woods, and mere. The one feature that marked out the house from a score of others is gone. As you looked at it from the park, you saw on the right a great old ash-tree growing within half a dozen yards of the wall, and almost or quite touching the building with its branches. I suppose it had stood there ever since Castringham ceased to be a fortified place, and since the moat was filled in and the Elizabethan dwelling-house built. At any rate, it had well-nigh attained its full dimensions in the year 1690.

In that year the district in which the Hall is situated was the scene of a number of witch-trials. It will be long, I think, before we arrive at a just estimate of the amount of solid reason – if there was any – which lay at the root of the universal fear of witches in old times. Whether the persons accused of this offence really did imagine that they were possessed of unusual powers of any kind; or whether they had the will at least, if not the power, of doing mischief to their neighbours; or whether all the confessions, of which there are so many, were extorted by the mere cruelty of the witchfinders – these are questions which are not, I fancy, yet solved. And the present narrative gives me pause. I cannot altogether sweep it away as mere invention. The reader must judge for himself.

Castringham contributed a victim to the *auto-da-fé*. Mrs Mothersole was her name, and she differed from the ordinary run of village witches only in being rather better off and in a more influential position. Efforts were made to save her by several reputable farmers of the parish. They did their best to testify to her character, and showed considerable anxiety as to the verdict of the jury.

But what seems to have been fatal to the woman was the evidence of the then proprietor of Castringham Hall – Sir Matthew Fell. He deposed to having watched her on three different occasions from his window, at the full of the moon, gathering sprigs 'from the ash-tree near my house'. She had climbed into the branches, clad only in her shift, and was cutting off small twigs with a peculiarly curved knife, and as she did so she seemed to be talking to herself. On each occasion Sir Matthew had done his best to capture the woman, but she had always taken alarm at some accidental noise he had made, and all he could see when he got down to the garden was a hare running across the park in the direction of the village.

On the third night he had been at the pains to follow at his best speed, and had gone straight to Mrs Mothersole's house; but he had had to wait a quarter of an hour battering at her door, and then she had come out very cross, and apparently very sleepy, as if just out of bed; and he had no good explanation to offer of his visit.

Mainly on this evidence, though there was much more of a less striking and unusual kind from other parishioners, Mrs Mothersole was found guilty and condemned to die. She was hanged a week after the trial, with five or six more unhappy creatures, at Bury St Edmunds.

Sir Matthew Fell, then Deputy-Sheriff, was present at the execution. It was a damp, drizzly March morning when the cart made its way up the rough grass hill outside Northgate, where the gallows stood. The other victims were apathetic or broken down with misery; but Mrs Mothersole was, as in life so in death, of a very different temper. Her 'poysonous Rage', as a reporter of the time puts it, 'did so work upon the Bystanders – yea, even upon the Hangman – that it was constantly affirmed of all that saw her that she presented the living Aspect of a mad Divell. Yet she offer'd no Resistance to the Officers of the Law; only she looked upon those that laid Hands upon her with so direfull and venomous an Aspect that – as one of them afterwards assured me – the meer Thought of it preyed inwardly upon his Mind for six Months after.'

However, all that she is reported to have said was the seemingly meaningless words: 'There will be guests at the Hall.' Which she repeated more than once in an undertone.

Sir Matthew Fell was not unimpressed by the bearing of the woman. He had some talk upon the matter with the Vicar of his parish; with whom he travelled home after the assize business was over. His evidence at the trial had not been very willingly given; he was not specially infected with the witch-finding mania, but he declared, then and afterwards, that he could not give any other account of the matter than that he had given, and that he could not possibly have been mistaken as to what he saw. The whole transaction had been repugnant to him, for he was a man who liked to be on pleasant terms with those about him; but he saw a duty to be done in this business, and he had done it. That seems to have been the gist of his sentiments, and the Vicar applauded it, as any reasonable man must have done.

A few weeks after, when the moon of May was at the full, Vicar and Squire met again in the park, and walked to the Hall together. Lady Fell was with her mother, who was dangerously ill, and Sir Matthew was alone at home; so the Vicar, Mr Crome, was easily persuaded to take a late supper at the Hall.

Sir Matthew was not very good company this evening. The talk ran chiefly on family and parish matters, and, as luck would have it, Sir Matthew made a memorandum in writing of certain wishes or intentions of his regarding his estates; which afterwards proved exceedingly useful.

When Mr Crome thought of starting for home, about half-past nine o'clock, Sir Matthew and he took a preliminary turn on the gravelled walk at the back of the house. The only incident that struck Mr Crome was this: they were in sight of the ash-tree which I described as growing near the windows of the building, when Sir Matthew stopped and said:

'What is that that runs up and down the stem of the ash? It is never a squirrel? They will all be in their nests by now.'

The Vicar looked and saw the moving creature, but he could make nothing of its colour in the moonlight. The sharp outline, however, seen for an instant, was imprinted on his brain, and he could have sworn, he said, though it sounded foolish, that, squirrel or not, it had more than four legs.

Still, not much was to be made of the momentary vision, and the two men parted. They may have met since then, but it was not for a score of years.

Next day Sir Matthew Fell was not downstairs at six in the morning, as was his custom, nor at seven, nor yet at eight. Hereupon the servants went and knocked at his chamber door. I need not prolong the description of their anxious listenings and renewed batterings on the panels. The door was opened at last from the outside, and they found their master dead and black. So much you have guessed. That there were any marks of violence did not at the moment appear; but the window was open.

One of the men went to fetch the parson, and then by his directions rode on to give notice to the coroner. Mr Crome himself went as quick as he might to the Hall, and was shown to the room where the dead man lay. He has left some notes among his papers which show how genuine a respect and sorrow was felt for Sir Matthew, and there is also this passage, which I transcribe for the sake of the light it throws upon the course of events, and also upon the common beliefs of the time:

'There was not any the least Trace of an Entrance having been forc'd to the Chamber: but the Casement stood open, as my poor Friend would always have it in this Season. He had his Evening Drink of small Ale in a silver vessel of about a pint measure, and to-night had not drunk it out. This Drink was examined by the Physician from Bury, a Mr Hodgkins, who could not, however, as he afterwards declar'd upon his Oath, before the Coroner's quest, discover that any matter of a venomous kind was present in it. For, as was natural, in the great Swelling and Blackness of the Corpse, there was talk made among the Neighbours of Poyson. The Body was very much Disorder'd as it laid in the Bed, being twisted after so extream a sort as gave too probable Conjecture that my worthy Friend and Patron had expir'd in great Pain and Agony. And what is as yet unexplain'd, and to myself the Argument of some Horrid and Artfull Designe in the Perpetrators of this Barbarous Murther, was this: that the Women which were entrusted with the laying-out of the Corpse and washing it, being both sad Persons and very well Respected in their Mournfull Profession, came to me in a great Pain and Distress both of Mind and Body, saying, what was indeed confirmed upon the first View, that they had no sooner touch'd the Breast of the Corpse with their naked Hands than they were sensible of a more than ordinary violent Smart and Acheing in their Palms, which, with their whole Forearms, in no long time swell'd so immoderately, the Pain still continuing, that, as afterwards proved, during many weeks they were forc'd to lay by the exercise of their Calling; and yet no mark seen on the Skin.

'Upon hearing this, I sent for the Physician, who was still in the House, and we made as carefull a Proof as we were able by the Help of a small Magnifying Lens of Crystal of the condition of the Skinn on this Part of the Body: but could not detect with the Instrument we had any Matter of Importance beyond a couple of small Punctures or Pricks, which we then concluded were the Spotts by which the Poyson might be introduced, remembering that Ring of *Pope Borgia*, with other known Specimens of the Horrid Art of the Italian Poysoners of the last age.

'So much is to be said of the Symptoms seen on the Corpse. As

to what I am to add, it is meerly my own Experiment, and to be
left to Posterity to judge whether there be anything of Value therein. There was on the Table by the Beddside a Bible of the small
size, in which my Friend – punctuall as in Matters of less Moment,
so in this more weighty one – used nightly, and upon his First
Rising, to read a sett Portion. And I taking it up – not without a
Tear duly paid to him which from the Study of this, poorer Adum-
bration was now pass'd to the contemplation of its great Originall
– it came into my Thoughts, as at such moments of Helplessness
we are prone to catch at any the least Glimmer that makes promise
of Light, to make trial of that old and by many accounted Superstitious Practice of drawing the *Sortes*: of which a Princapall Instance,
in the case of his late Sacred Majesty the Blessed Martyr King
Charles and my Lord *Falkland*, was now much talked of. I must
needs admit that by my Trial not much Assistance was afforded
me: yet, as the Cause and Origin of these Dreadful Events may
hereafter be search'd out, I set down the Results, in the case it
may be found that they pointed the true Quarter of the Mischief
to a quicker Intelligence than my own.

'I made, then, three trials, opening the Book and placing my
Finger upon certain Words: which gave in the first these words,
from Luke xiii. 7, *Cut it down*; in the second, Isaiah xiii. 20, *It shall
never be inhabited*; and upon the third Experiment, Job xxxix. 30,
Her young ones also suck up blood.'

This is all that need be quoted from Mr Crome's papers. Sir
Matthew Fell was duly coffined and laid into the earth, and his
funeral sermon, preached by Mr Crome on the following Sunday,
has been printed under the title of 'The Unsearchable Way; or,
England's Danger and the Malicious Dealings of Antichrist', it
being the Vicar's view, as well as that most commonly held in the
neighbourhood, that the Squire was the victim of a recrudescence
of the Popish Plot.

His son, Sir Matthew the second, succeeded to the title and

estates. And so ends the first act of the Castringham tragedy. It is to be mentioned, though the fact is not surprising, that the new Baronet did not occupy the room in which his father had died. Nor, indeed, was it slept in by anyone but an occasional visitor during the whole of his occupation. He died in 1735, and I do not find that anything particular marked his reign, save a curiously constant mortality among his cattle and live-stock in general, which showed a tendency to increase slightly as time went on.

Those who are interested in the details will find a statistical account in a letter to the *Gentleman's Magazine* of 1772, which draws the facts from the Baronet's own papers. He put an end to it at last by a very simple expedient, that of shutting up all his beasts in sheds at night, and keeping no sheep in his park. For he had noticed that nothing was ever attacked that spent the night indoors. After that the disorder confined itself to wild birds, and beasts of chase. But as we have no good account of the symptoms; and as all-night watching was quite unproductive of any clue, I do not dwell on what the Suffolk farmers called the 'Castringham sickness'.

The second Sir Matthew died in 1735, as I said, and was duly succeeded by his son, Sir Richard. It was in his time that the great family pew was built out on the north side of the parish church. So large were the Squire's ideas that several of the graves on that unhallowed side of the building had to be disturbed to satisfy his requirements. Among them was that of Mrs Mothersole, the position of which was accurately known, thanks to a note on a plan of the church and yard, both made by Mr Crome.

A certain amount of interest was excited in the village when it was known that the famous witch, who was still remembered by a few, was to be exhumed. And the feeling of surprise, and indeed disquiet, was very strong when it was found that, though her coffin was fairly sound and unbroken, there was no trace whatever inside it of body, bones, or dust. Indeed, it is a curious phenomenon, for at the time of her burying no such things were dreamt of as resurrection-men, and it is difficult to conceive any rational motive for stealing a body otherwise than for the uses of the dissecting-room.

The incident revived for a time all the stories of witch-trials and of the exploits of the witches, dormant for forty years, and Sir Richard's orders that the coffin should be burnt were thought by a good many to be rather foolhardy, though they were duly carried out.

Sir Richard was a pestilent innovator, it is certain. Before his time the Hall had been a fine block of the mellowest red brick; but Sir Richard had travelled in Italy and become infected with the Italian taste, and, having more money than his predecessors, he determined to leave an Italian palace where he had found an English house. So stucco and ashlar masked the brick; some indifferent Roman marbles were planted about in the entrance-hall and gardens; a reproduction of the Sibyl's temple at Tivoli was erected on the opposite bank of the mere; and Castringham took on an entirely new, and, I must say, a less engaging, aspect. But it was much admired, and served as a model to a good many of the neighbouring gentry in after-years.

One morning (it was in 1754) Sir Richard woke after a night of discomfort. It had been windy, and his chimney had smoked persistently, and yet it was so cold that he must keep up a fire. Also something had so rattled about the window that no man could get a moment's peace. Further, there was the prospect of several guests of position arriving in the course of the day, who would expect sport of some kind, and the inroads of the distemper (which continued among his game) had been lately so serious that he was afraid for his reputation as a game-preserver. But what really touched him most nearly was the other matter of his sleepless night. He could certainly not sleep in that room again.

That was the chief subject of his meditations at breakfast, and after it he began a systematic examination of the rooms to see which would suit his notions best. It was long before he found one. This had a window with an eastern aspect and that with a northern; this door the servants would be always passing, and he did not like the bedstead in that. No, he must have a room with a western look-out, so that the sun could not wake him early, and it must be out of the way of the business of the house. The housekeeper was at the end of her resources.

'Well, Sir Richard,' she said, 'you know that there is but one room like that in the house.'

'Which may that be?' said Sir Richard.

'And that is Sir Matthew's – the West Chamber.'

'Well, put me in there, for there I'll lie to-night,' said her master. 'Which way is it? Here, to be sure,' and he hurried off.

'Oh, Sir Richard, but no one has slept there these forty years. The air has hardly been changed since Sir Matthew died there.' Thus she spoke, and rustled after him.

'Come, open the door, Mrs Chiddock. I'll see the chamber, at least.'

So it was opened, and, indeed, the smell was very close and earthy. Sir Richard crossed to the window, and, impatiently, as was his wont, threw the shutters back, and flung open the casement. For this end of the house was one which the alterations had barely touched, grown up as it was with the great ash-tree, and being otherwise concealed from view.

'Air it, Mrs Chiddock, all to-day, and move my bed-furniture in in the afternoon. Put the Bishop of Kilmore in my old room.'

'Pray, Sir Richard,' said a new voice, breaking in on this speech, 'might I have the favour of a moment's interview?'

Sir Richard turned round and saw a man in black in the doorway, who bowed.

'I must ask your indulgence for this intrusion, Sir Richard. You will, perhaps, hardly remember me. My name is William Crome, and my grandfather was Vicar here in your grandfather's time.'

'Well, sir,' said Sir Richard, 'the name of Crome is always a passport to Castringham. I am glad to renew a friendship of two generations' standing. In what can I serve you? for your hour of calling – and, if I do not mistake you, your bearing – shows you to be in some haste.'

'That is no more than the truth, sir. I am riding from Norwich to Bury St Edmunds with what haste I can make, and I have called in on my way to leave with you some papers which we have but just come upon in looking over what my grandfather left at his death. It is thought you may find some matters of family interest in them.'

'You are mighty obliging, Mr Crome, and, if you will be so good as to follow me to the parlour, and drink a glass of wine, we will take a first look at these same papers together. And you, Mrs Chiddock, as I said, be about airing this chamber . . . Yes, it is here my grandfather died . . . Yes, the tree, perhaps, does make the place a little dampish . . . No; I do not wish to listen to any more. Make no difficulties, I beg. You have your orders – go. Will you follow me, sir?'

They went to the study. The packet which young Mr Crome had brought – he was then just become a Fellow of Clare Hall in Cambridge, I may say, and subsequently brought out a respectable edition of Polyænus – contained among other things the notes which the old Vicar had made upon the occasion of Sir Matthew Fell's death. And for the first time Sir Richard was confronted with the enigmatical *Sortes Biblicæ* which you have heard. They amused him a good deal.

'Well,' he said, 'my grandfather's Bible gave one prudent piece of advice – *Cut it down*. If that stands for the ash-tree, he may rest assured I shall not neglect it. Such a nest of catarrhs and agues was never seen.'

The parlour contained the family books, which, pending the arrival of a collection which Sir Richard had made in Italy, and the building of a proper room to receive them, were not many in number.

Sir Richard looked up from the paper to the bookcase.

'I wonder,' says he, 'whether the old prophet is there yet? I fancy I see him.'

Crossing the room, he took out a dumpy Bible, which, sure enough, bore on the flyleaf the inscription: 'To Matthew Fell, from his Loving Godmother, Anne Aldous, 2 September, 1659.'

'It would be no bad plan to test him again, Mr Crome. I will wager we get a couple of names in the Chronicles. H'm! what have we here? "Thou shalt seek me in the morning, and I shall not be." Well, well! Your grandfather would have made a fine omen of that, hey? No more prophets for me! They are all in a tale. And now, Mr Crome, I am infinitely obliged to you for your packet. You will, I fear, be impatient to get on. Pray allow me – another glass.'

So with offers of hospitality, which were genuinely meant (for Sir Richard thought well of the young man's address and manner), they parted.

In the afternoon came the guests – the Bishop of Kilmore, Lady Mary Hervey, Sir William Kentfield, etc. Dinner at five, wine, cards, supper, and dispersal to bed.

Next morning Sir Richard is disinclined to take his gun with the rest. He talks with the Bishop of Kilmore. This prelate, unlike a good many of the Irish Bishops of his day, had visited his see, and, indeed, resided there for some considerable time. This morning, as the two were walking along the terrace and talking over the alterations and improvements in the house, the Bishop said, pointing to the window of the West Room:

'You could never get one of my Irish flock to occupy that room, Sir Richard.'

'Why is that, my lord? It is, in fact, my own.'

'Well, our Irish peasantry will always have it that it brings the worst of luck to sleep near an ash-tree, and you have a fine growth of ash not two yards from your chamber window. Perhaps,' the Bishop went on with a smile, 'it has given you a touch of its quality already, for you do not seem, if I may say it, so much the fresher for your night's rest as your friends would like to see you.'

'That, or something else, it is true, cost me my sleep from twelve to four, my lord. But the tree is to come down to-morrow, so I shall not hear much more from it.'

'I applaud your determination. It can hardly be wholesome to have the air you breathe strained, as it were, through all that leafage.'

'Your lordship is right there, I think. But I had not my window open last night. It was rather the noise that went on – no doubt from the twigs sweeping the glass – that kept me open-eyed.'

'I think that can hardly be, Sir Richard. Here you see it from this point. None of these nearest branches even can touch your casement unless there were a gale, and there was none of that last night. They miss the panes by a foot.'

'No, sir, true. What, then, will it be, I wonder, that scratched and rustled so – ay, and covered the dust on my sill with lines and marks?'

At last they agreed that the rats must have come up through the ivy. That was the Bishop's idea, and Sir Richard jumped at it. So the day passed quietly, and night came, and the party dispersed to their rooms, and wished Sir Richard a better night.

And now we are in his bedroom, with the light out and the Squire in bed. The room is over the kitchen, and the night outside still and warm, so the window stands open.

There is very little light about the bedstead, but there is a strange movement there; it seems as if Sir Richard were moving his head rapidly to and fro with only the slightest possible sound. And now you would guess, so deceptive is the half-darkness, that he had several heads, round and brownish, which move back and forward, even as low as his chest. It is a horrible illusion. Is it nothing more? There! something drops off the bed with a soft plump, like a kitten, and is out of the window in a flash; another – four – and after that there is quiet again.

Thou shalt seek me in the morning, and I shall not be.

As with Sir Matthew, so with Sir Richard – dead and black in his bed!

A pale and silent party of guests and servants gathered under the window when the news was known. Italian poisoners, Popish emissaries, infected air – all these and more guesses were hazarded, and the Bishop of Kilmore looked at the tree, in the fork of whose lower boughs a white tom-cat was crouching, looking down the hollow which years had gnawed in the trunk. It was watching something inside the tree with great interest.

Suddenly it got up and craned over the hole. Then a bit of the edge on which it stood gave way, and it went slithering in. Everyone looked up at the noise of the fall.

It is known to most of us that a cat can cry; but few of us have heard, I hope, such a yell as came out of the trunk of the great ash. Two or three screams there were – the witnesses are not sure which – and then a slight and muffled noise of some commotion or struggling was all that came. But Lady Mary Hervey fainted outright, and the housekeeper stopped her ears and fled till she fell on the terrace.

The Bishop of Kilmore and Sir William Kentfield stayed. Yet even they were daunted, though it was only at the cry of a cat; and Sir William swallowed once or twice before he could say:

'There is something more than we know of in that tree, my lord. I am for an instant search.'

And this was agreed upon. A ladder was brought, and one of

the gardeners went up, and, looking down the hollow, could detect nothing but a few dim indications of something moving. They got a lantern, and let it down by a rope.

'We must get at the bottom of this. My life upon it, my lord, but the secret of these terrible deaths is there.'

Up went the gardener again with the lantern, and let it down the hole cautiously. They saw the yellow light upon his face as he bent over, and saw his face struck with an incredulous terror and loathing before he cried out in a dreadful voice and fell back from the ladder – where, happily, he was caught by two of the men – letting the lantern fall inside the tree.

He was in a dead faint, and it was some time before any word could be got from him.

By then they had something else to look at. The lantern must have broken at the bottom, and the light in it caught upon dry leaves and rubbish that lay there, for in a few minutes a dense smoke began to come up, and then flame; and, to be short, the tree was in a blaze.

The bystanders made a ring at some yards' distance, and Sir William and the Bishop sent men to get what weapons and tools they could; for, clearly, whatever might be using the tree as its lair would be forced out by the fire.

So it was. First, at the fork, they saw a round body covered with fire – the size of a man's head – appear very suddenly, then seem to collapse and fall back. This, five or six times; then a similar ball leapt into the air and fell on the grass, where after a moment it lay still. The Bishop went as near as he dared to it, and saw – what but the remains of an enormous spider, veinous and seared! And, as the fire burned lower down, more terrible bodies like this began to break out from the trunk, and it was seen that these were covered with greyish hair.

All that day the ash burned, and until it fell to pieces the men stood about it, and from time to time killed the brutes as they darted out. At last there was a long interval when none appeared, and they cautiously closed in and examined the roots of the tree.

'They found,' says the Bishop of Kilmore, 'below it a rounded hollow place in the earth, wherein were two or three bodies of these creatures that had plainly been smothered by the smoke; and, what is to me more curious, at the side of this den, against the wall, was crouching the anatomy or skeleton of a human being, with the skin dried upon the bones, having some remains of black hair, which was pronounced by those that examined it to be undoubtedly the body of a woman, and clearly dead for a period of fifty years.'

OUT OF THE SEA

by

A. C. Benson

First published in the collection *The Isles of Sunset*

1904

IT WAS ABOUT ten of the clock on a November morning in the little village of Blea-on-the-Sands. The hamlet was made up of some thirty houses, which clustered together on a low rising ground. The place was very poor, but some old merchant of bygone days had built in a pious mood a large church, which was now too great for the needs of the place; the nave had been unroofed in a heavy gale, and there was no money to repair it, so that it had fallen to decay, and the tower was joined to the choir by roofless walls. This was a sore trial to the old priest, Father Thomas, who had grown grey there; but he had no art in gathering money, which he asked for in a shamefaced way; and the vicarage was a poor one, hardly enough for the old man's needs. So the church lay desolate.

The village stood on what must once have been an island; the little river Reddy, which runs down to the sea, there forking into two channels on the landward side; towards the sea the ground was bare, full of sand-hills covered with a short grass. Towards the land was a small wood of gnarled trees, the boughs of which were all brushed smooth by the gales; looking landward there was the green flat, in which the river ran, rising into low hills; hardly a house was visible save one or two lonely farms; two or three church towers rose above the hills at a long distance away. Indeed Blea was much cut off from the world; there was a bridge over the stream on the west side, but over the other channel was no bridge, so that to fare eastward it was requisite to go in a boat. To seaward there were wide sands when the tide was out; when it was in, it came up nearly to the end of the village street. The people were mostly fishermen, but there were a few farmers and labourers; the boats of the fishermen lay to the east side of the village, near the river channel which gave some draught of water; and the channel was marked out by big black stakes and posts that straggled out over the sands, like awkward leaning figures, to the sea's brim.

Father Thomas lived in a small and ancient brick house near the church, with a little garden of herbs attached. He was a kindly man, much worn by age and weather, with a wise heart, and he loved the quiet life with his small flock. This morning he had come out of his house to look abroad, before he settled down to the making of his sermon. He looked out to sea, and saw with a shadow of sadness the black outline of a wreck that had come ashore a week before, and over which the white waves were now breaking. The wind blew steadily from the north-east, and had a bitter poisonous chill in it, which it doubtless drew from the fields of the upper ice. The day was dark and overhung, not with cloud, but with a kind of dreary vapour that shut out the sun. Father Thomas shuddered at the wind, and drew his patched cloak round him. As he did so, he saw three figures come up to the vicarage gate. It was not a common thing for him to have visitors in the morning, and he saw with surprise that they were old Master John Grimston, the richest man in the place, half farmer and half fisherman, a dark surly old man; his wife, Bridget, a timid and frightened woman, who found life with her harsh husband a difficult business, in spite of their wealth, which, for a place like Blea, was great; and their son Henry, a silly shambling man of forty, who was his father's butt. The three walked silently and heavily, as though they came on a sad errand.

Father Thomas went briskly down to meet them, and greeted them with his accustomed cheerfulness. 'And what may I do for you?' he said. Old Master Grimston made a sort of gesture with his head as though his wife should speak; and she said in a low and somewhat husky voice, with a rapid utterance, 'We have a matter, Father, we would ask you about – are you at leisure?' Father Thomas said, 'Ay, I am ashamed to be not more busy! Let us go within the house.' They did so; and even in the little distance to the door, the Father thought that his visitors behaved themselves very strangely. They peered round from left to right, and once or twice Master Grimston looked sharply behind them, as though they were followed. They said nothing but 'Ay' and 'No' to the Father's talk, and bore themselves like people with a sore fear on their backs. Father Thomas made up his mind that it was some question of money, for nothing else was wont to move Master Grimston's mind. So he had them into his parlour and gave them seats, and then there was a silence, while the two men continued to look furtively about them, and the goodwife sate with her eyes upon the priest's face. Father Thomas knew not what to make of this, till Master Grimston said harshly, 'Come, wife, tell the tale and make an end; we must not take up the Father's time.'

'I hardly know how to say it, Father,' said Bridget, 'but a strange and evil thing has befallen us; there is something come to our house, and we know not what it is – but it brings a fear with it.' A sudden paleness came over her face, and she stopped, and the three exchanged a glance in which terror was visibly written. Master Grimston looked over his shoulder swiftly, and made as though to speak, yet only swallowed in his throat; but Henry said suddenly, in a loud and woeful voice: 'It is an evil beast out of the sea.' And then there followed a dreadful silence, while Father Thomas felt a sudden fear leap up in his heart at the contagion of the fear that he saw written on the faces round him. But he said with all the cheerfulness he could muster, 'Come, friends, let us not begin to talk of sea-beasts; we must have the whole tale. Mistress Grimston, I must hear the story – be content – nothing can touch us here.' The three seemed to draw a faint content from his words, and Bridget began:

'It was the day of the wreck, Father. John was up betimes, before the dawn; he walked out early to the sands, and Henry with him – and they were the first to see the wreck – was not that it?' At these words the father and son seemed to exchange a very swift and secret look, and both grew pale. 'John told me there was a wreck ashore, and they went presently and roused the rest of the village; and all that day they were out, saving what could be saved. Two sailors were found, both dead and pitifully battered by the sea, and they were buried, as you know, Father, in the churchyard next day; John came back about dusk and Henry with him, and we sate down to our supper. John was telling me about the wreck, as we sate beside the fire, when Henry, who was sitting apart, rose up and cried out suddenly, "What is that?"'

She paused for a moment, and Henry, who sate with face blanched, staring at his mother, said, 'Ay, did I – it ran past me suddenly.'

'Yes, but what was it?' said Father Thomas trying to smile; 'a dog or cat, methinks.'

'It was a beast,' said Henry slowly, in a trembling voice – 'a beast about the bigness of a goat. I never saw the like – yet I did not see it clear; I but felt the air blow, and caught a whiff of it – it was salt like the sea, but with a kind of dead smell behind.'

'Was that all you saw?' said Father Thomas; 'belike you were tired and faint, and the air swam round you suddenly – I have known the like myself when weary.'

'Nay, nay,' said Henry, 'this was not like that – it was a beast, sure enough.'

'Ay, and we have seen it since,' said Bridget. 'At least I have not seen it clearly yet, but I have smelt its odour, and it turns me sick

– but John and Henry have seen it often – sometimes it lies and seems to sleep, but it watches us; and again it is merry, and will leap in a corner – and John saw it skip upon the sands near the wreck – did you not, John?'

At these words the two men again exchanged a glance, and then old Master Grimston, with a dreadful look in his face, in which great anger seemed to strive with fear, said, 'Nay, silly woman, it was not near the wreck, it was out to the east.'

'It matters little,' said Father Thomas, who saw well enough this was no light matter. 'I never heard the like of it. I will myself come down to your house with a holy book, and see if the thing will meet me. I know not what this is,' he went on, 'whether it is a vain terror that hath hold of you; but there be spirits of evil in the world, though much fettered by Christ and His Saints – we read of such in Holy Writ – and the sea, too, doubtless hath its monsters; and it may be that one hath wandered out of the waves, like a dog that hath strayed from his home. I dare not say, till I have met it face to face. But God gives no power to such things to hurt those who have a fair conscience.' And here he made a stop, and looked at the three; Bridget sate regarding him with a hope in her face; but the other two sate peering upon the ground; and the priest divined in some secret way that all was not well with them. 'But I will come at once,' he said rising, 'and I will see if I can cast out or bind the thing, whatever it be – for I am in this place as a soldier of the Lord, to fight with works of darkness.' He took a clasped book from a table, and lifted up his hat, saying, 'Let us set forth.' Then he said as they left the room, 'Hath it appeared to-day?'

'Yes, indeed,' said Henry, 'and it was ill content. It followed us as though it were angered.'

'Come,' said Father Thomas, turning upon him, 'you speak thus of a thing, as you might speak of a dog – what is it like?'

'Nay,' said Henry, 'I know not; I can never see it clearly; it is like a speck in the eye – it is never there when you look upon it – it glides away very secretly; it is most like a goat, I think. It seems to be horned, and hairy; but I have seen its eyes, and they were yellow, like a flame.'

As he said these words Master Grimston went in haste to the door, and pulled it open as though to breathe the air. The others followed him and went out; but Master Grimston drew the priest aside, and said like a man in a mortal fear, 'Look you, Father, all this is true – the thing is a devil – and why it abides with us I know not; but I cannot live so; and unless it be cast out it will slay me – but if money be of avail, I have it in abundance.'

'Nay,' said Father Thomas, 'let there be no talk of money – perchance if I can aid you, you may give of your gratitude to God.'

'Ay, ay,' said the old man hurriedly, 'that was what I meant – there is money in abundance for God, if he will but set me free.'

So they walked very sadly together through the street. There were few folk about; the men and the children were all abroad – a woman or two came to the house doors, and wondered a little to see them pass so solemnly, as though they followed a body to the grave.

Master Grimston's house was the largest in the place. It had a walled garden before it, with a strong door set in the wall. The house stood back from the road, a dark front of brick with gables; behind it the garden sloped nearly to the sands, with wooden barns and warehouses. Master Grimston unlocked the door, and then it seemed that his terrors came over him, for he would have the priest enter first. Father Thomas, with a certain apprehension of which he was ashamed, walked quickly in, and looked about him. The herbage of the garden had mostly died down in the winter, and a tangle of sodden stalks lay over the beds. A flagged path edged with box led up to the house, which seemed to stare at them out of its dark windows with a sort of steady gaze. Master Grimston fastened the door behind them, and they went all together, keeping close one to another, up to the house, the door of which opened upon a big parlour or kitchen, sparely furnished, but very clean and comfortable. Some vessels of metal glittered on a rack. There were chairs, ranged round the open fireplace. There was no sound except that the wind buffeted in the chimney. It looked a quiet and homely place, and Father Thomas grew ashamed of his fears. 'Now,' said he in his firm voice, 'though I am your guest here, I will appoint what shall be done. We will sit here together, and talk as cheerfully as we may, till we have dined. Then, if nothing appears to us,' – and he crossed himself – 'I will go round the house, into every room, and see if we can track the thing to its lair: then I will abide with you till evensong; and then I will soon return, and lie here to-night. Even if the thing be wary, and dares not to meet the power of the Church in the day-time, perhaps it will venture out at night; and I will even try a fall with it. So come, good people, and be comforted.'

So they sate together; and Father Thomas talked of many things, and told some old legends of saints; and they dined, though without much cheer; and still nothing appeared. Then, after dinner, Father Thomas would view the house. So he took his book up, and they went from room to room. On the ground floor there were several chambers not used, which they entered in turn, but saw nothing; on the upper floor was a large room where Master Grimston and his wife slept; and a further room for Henry, and a guest-chamber in which the priest was to sleep if need was; and a room where a servant-maid slept. And now the day began to darken and to turn to evening, and Father Thomas felt a shadow grow in his mind. There came into his head a verse of Scripture about a spirit which found a house 'empty, swept and garnished', and called his fellows to enter in.

At the end of the passage was a locked door; and Father Thomas said: 'This is the last room – let us enter.'

'Nay, there is no need to do that,' said Master Grimston in a kind of haste; 'it leads nowhither – it is but a room of stores.'

'It were a pity to leave it unvisited,' said the Father – and as he said the word, there came a kind of stirring from within.

'A rat, doubtless,' said the Father, striving with a sudden sense of fear; but the pale faces round him told another tale. 'Come, Master Grimston, let us be done with this,' said Father Thomas decisively; 'the hour of vespers draws nigh.'

So Master Grimston slowly drew out a key and unlocked the door, and Father Thomas marched in. It was a simple place enough. There were shelves on which various household matters lay, boxes and jars, with twine and cordage. On the ground stood chests. There were some clothes hanging on pegs, and in a corner was a heap of garments, piled up. On one of the chests stood a box of rough deal, and from the corner of it dripped water, which lay in a little pool on the floor. Master Grimston went hurriedly to the box and pushed it further to the wall. As he did so, a kind of sound came from Henry's lips. Father Thomas turned and looked at him; he stood pale and strengthless, his eyes fixed on the corner – at the same moment something dark and shapeless seemed to slip past the group, and there came to the nostrils of Father Thomas a strange sharp smell, as of the sea, only that there was a taint within it, like the smell of corruption.

They all turned and looked at Father Thomas together, as though seeking a comfort from his presence. He, hardly knowing what he did, and in the grasp of a terrible fear, fumbled with his book; and opening it, read the first words that his eye fell upon, which was the place where the Blessed Lord, beset with enemies, said that if He did but pray to His Father, He should send Him forthwith legions of angels to encompass Him. And the verse seemed to the priest so like a message sent instantly from heaven that he was not a little comforted.

But the thing, whatever the reason was, appeared to them no more at that time. Yet the thought of it lay very heavy on Father Thomas's heart. In truth he had not in the bottom of his mind believed that he would see it, but had trusted in his honest life and his sacred calling to protect him. He could hardly speak for some minutes – moreover the horror of the thing was very great – and seeing him so grave, their terrors were increased, though there was a kind of miserable joy in their minds that someone, and he a man of high repute, should suffer with them.

Then Father Thomas, after a pause – they were now in the parlour – said, speaking very slowly, that they were in a sore affliction of Satan, and that they must withstand him with a good courage – 'and look you,' he added, turning with a great sternness to the three, 'if there be any mortal sin upon your hearts, see that you confess it and be shriven speedily – for while such a thing lies upon the heart, so long hath Satan power to hurt – otherwise have no fear at all.'

Then Father Thomas slipped out to the garden, and hearing the bell pulled for vespers, he went to the church, and the three would go with him, because they would not be left alone. So they went together; by this time the street was fuller, and the servant-maid had told tales, so that there was much talk in the place about what was going forward. None spoke with them as they went, but at every corner you might see one check another in talk, and a silence fall upon a group, so that they knew that their terrors were on every tongue. There was but a handful of worshippers in the church, which was dark, save for the light on Father Thomas's book. He read the holy service swiftly and courageously, but his face was very pale and grave in the light of the candle. When the vespers were over, and he had put off his robe, he said that he would go back to his house, and gather what he needed for the night, and that they should wait for him at the churchyard gate. So he strode off to his vicarage. But as he shut to the door, he saw a dark figure come running up the garden; he waited with a fear in his mind, but in a moment he saw that it was Henry, who came up breathless, and said that he must speak with the Father alone. Father Thomas knew that somewhat dark was to be told him. So he led Henry into the parlour and seated himself, and said, 'Now, my son, speak boldly.' So there was an instant's silence, and Henry slipped on to his knees.

Then in a moment Henry with a sob began to tell his tale. He said that on the day of the wreck his father had roused him very early in the dawn, and had told him to put on his clothes and come silently, for he thought there was a wreck ashore. His father carried a spade in his hand, he knew not then why. They went down to the tide, which was moving out very fast, and left but an inch or two of water on the sands. There was but a little light, but, when they had walked a little, they saw the black hull of a ship before them, on the edge of the deeper water, the waves driving over it; and then all at once they came upon the body of a man lying on his face on the sand. There was no sign of life in him, but he clasped a bag in his hand that was heavy, and the pocket of his coat was full to bulging; and there lay, moreover, some glittering things about him that seemed to be coins. They lifted the body up, and his father stripped the coat off from the man, and then bade Henry dig a hole in the sand, which he presently did, though the sand and water oozed fast into it. Then his father, who had been stooping down, gathering somewhat up from the sand, raised the body up, and laid it in the hole, and bade Henry cover it with the sand. And so he did till it was nearly hidden. Then came a horrible thing; the sand in the hole began to move and stir, and presently a hand was put out with clutching fingers; and Henry had dropped the spade, and said, 'There is life in him,' but his father seized the spade, and shovelled the sand into the hole with a kind of silent fury, and trampled it over and smoothed it down – and then he gathered up the coat and the bag, and handed Henry the spade. By this time the town was astir, and they saw, very faintly, a man run along the shore eastward; so, making a long circuit to the west, they returned; his father had put the spade away and taken the coat upstairs; and then he went out with Henry, and told all he could find that there was a wreck ashore.

The priest heard the story with a fierce shame and anger, and turning to Henry he said, 'But why did you not resist your father, and save the poor sailor?'

'I dared not,' said Henry shuddering, 'though I would have done so if I could; but my father has a power over me, and I am used to obey him.'

Then said the priest, 'This is a dark matter. But you have told the story bravely, and now will I shrive you, my son.' So he gave him shrift. Then he said to Henry, 'And have you seen aught that would connect the beast that visits you with this thing?'

'Ay, that I have,' said Henry, 'for I watched it with my father skip and leap in the water over the place where the man lies buried.'

Then the priest said, 'Your father must tell me the tale too, and he must make submission to the law.'

'He will not,' said Henry.

'Then will I compel him,' said the priest.

'Not out of my mouth,' said Henry, 'or he will slay me too.' And then the priest said that he was in a strait place, for he could not use the words of confession of one man to convict another of his sin. So he gathered his things in haste, and walked back to the church; but Henry went another way, saying, 'I made excuse to come away, and said I went elsewhere; but I fear my father much – he sees very deep; and I would not have him suspect me of having made confession.'

Then the Father met the other two at the church gate; and they went down to the house in silence, the Father pondering heavily; and at the door Henry joined them, and it seemed to the Father that old Master Grimston regarded him not. So they entered the house in silence, and ate in silence, listening earnestly for any sound. And the Father looked oft on Master Grimston, who ate and drank and said nothing, never raising his eyes. But once the

Father saw him laugh secretly to himself, so that the blood came cold in the Father's veins, and he could hardly contain himself from accusing him. Then the Father had them to prayers, and prayed earnestly against the evil, and that they should open their hearts to God, if he would show them why this misery came upon them.

Then they went to bed; and Henry asked that he might lie in the priest's room, which he willingly granted. And so the house was dark, and they made as though they would sleep; but the Father could not sleep, and he heard Henry weeping silently to himself like a little child.

But at last the Father slept – how long he knew not – and suddenly brake out of his sleep with a horror of darkness all about him, and knew that there was some evil thing abroad. So he looked upon the room. He heard Henry mutter heavily in his sleep as though there was a dark terror upon him; and then, in the light of the dying embers, the Father saw a thing rise upon the hearth, as though it had slept there, and woke to stretch itself. And then in the half-light it seemed softly to gambol and play; but whereas when an innocent beast does this in the simple joy of its heart, and seems a fond and pretty sight, the Father thought he had never seen so ugly a sight as the beast gambolling all by itself, as if it could not contain its own dreadful joy; it looked viler and more wicked every moment; then, too, there spread in the room the sharp scent of the sea, with the foul smell underneath it, that gave the Father a deadly sickness; he tried to pray, but no words would come, and he felt indeed that the evil was too strong for him. Presently the beast desisted from its play, and looking wickedly about it, came near to the Father's bed, and seemed to put up its hairy forelegs upon it; he could see its narrow and obscene eyes, which burned with a dull yellow light, and were fixed upon him. And now the Father thought that his end was near, for he could stir neither hand nor foot, and the sweat rained down his brow; but he made a mighty effort, and in a voice which shocked himself, so dry and husky and withal of so loud and screaming a tone it was, he said three holy words. The beast gave a great quiver of rage, but it dropped down on the floor, and in a moment was gone. Then Henry woke, and raising himself on his arm, said somewhat; but there broke out in the house a great outcry and the stamping of feet, which seemed very fearful in the silence of the night. The priest leapt out of his bed all dizzy, and made a light, and ran to the door, and went out, crying whatever words came to his head. The door of Master Grimston's room was open, and a strange and strangling sound came forth; the Father made his way in, and found Master Grimston lying upon the floor, his wife bending over him; he lay still, breathing pitifully, and every now and then a shudder ran through him. In the room there seemed a strange and shadowy tumult going forward; but the Father saw that no time could be lost, and kneeling down beside Master Grimston, he prayed with all his might.

Presently Master Grimston ceased to struggle and lay still, like a man who had come out of a sore conflict. Then he opened his eyes, and the Father stopped his prayers, and looking very hard at him he said, 'My son, the time is very short – give God the glory.'

Then Master Grimston, rolling his haggard eyes upon the group, twice strove to speak and could not; but the third time the Father, bending down his head, heard him say in a thin voice, that seemed to float from a long way off, 'I slew him . . . my sin.'

Then the Father swiftly gave him shrift, and as he said the last word, Master Grimston's head fell over on the side, and the Father said, 'He is gone.' And Bridget broke out into a terrible cry, and fell upon Henry's neck, who had entered unseen.

Then the Father bade him lead her away, and put the poor body on the bed; as he did so he noticed that the face of the dead man was strangely bruised and battered, as though it had been stamped upon by the hoofs of some beast. Then Father Thomas knelt, and prayed until the light came filtering in through the shutters; and the cocks crowed in the village, and presently it was day. But that night the Father learnt strange secrets, and something of the dark purposes of God was revealed to him.

In the morning there came one to find the priest, and told him that another body had been thrown up on the shore, which was strangely smeared with sand, as though it had been rolled over and over in it; and the Father took order for its burial.

Then the priest had long talk with Bridget and Henry. He found them sitting together, and she held her son's hand and smoothed his hair, as though he had been a little child; and Henry sobbed and wept, but Bridget was very calm. 'He hath told me all,' she said, 'and we have decided that he shall do whatever you bid him; must he be given to justice?' and she looked at the priest very pitifully.

'Nay, nay,' said the priest. 'I hold not Henry to account for the death of the man; it was his father's sin, who hath made heavy atonement – the secret shall be buried in our hearts.'

Then Bridget told him how she had waked suddenly out of her sleep, and heard her husband cry out; and that then followed a dreadful kind of struggling, with the scent of the sea over all; and then he had all at once fallen to the ground and she had gone to him – and that then the priest had come.

Then Father Thomas said with tears that God had shown them deep things and visited them very strangely; and they would henceforth live humbly in His sight, showing mercy.

Then lastly he went with Henry to the storeroom; and there, in the box that had dripped with water, lay the coat of the dead man, full of money, and the bag of money too; and Henry would have cast it back into the sea, but the priest said that this might not be, but that it should be bestowed plentifully upon shipwrecked mariners unless the heirs should be found. But the ship appeared to be a foreign ship, and no search ever revealed whence the money had come, save that it seemed to have been violently come by.

Master Grimston was found to have left much wealth. But Bridget would sell the house and the land, and it mostly went to rebuild the church to God's glory. Then Bridget and Henry removed to the vicarage and served Father Thomas faithfully, and they guarded their secret. And beside the nave is a little high turret built, where burns a lamp in a lantern at the top, to give light to those at sea.

Now the beast troubled those of whom I write no more; but it is easier to raise up evil than to lay it; and there are those that say that to this day a man or a woman with an evil thought in their hearts may see on a certain evening in November, at the ebb of the tide, a goatlike thing wade in the water, snuffing at the sand, as though it sought but found not. But of this I know nothing.

GAVON'S EVE

by

E. F. Benson

First published in the 13 January edition of
The London Illustrated News

1906

IT IS ONLY the largest kind of ordnance map that records the existence of the village of Gavon, in the shire of Sutherland, and it is perhaps surprising that any map on whatever scale should mark so small and huddled a group of huts, set on a bare, bleak headland between moor and sea, and, so one would have thought, of no import at all to any who did not happen to live there. But the river Gavon, on the right bank of which stand this half-dozen of chimneyless and wind-swept habitations, is a geographical fact of far greater interest to outsiders, for the salmon there are heavy fish, the mouth of the river is clear of nets, and all the way up to Gavon Loch, some six miles inland, the coffee-coloured water lies in pool after deep pool, which verge, if the river is in order and the angler moderately sanguine, on a fishing probability amounting almost to a certainty. In any case, during the first fortnight of September last I had no blank day on those delectable waters, and up till the 15th of that month there was no day on which some one at the lodge in which I was stopping did not land a fish out of the famous Picts' pool. But after the 15th that pool was not fished again. The reason why is here set forward.

The river at this point, after some hundred yards of rapids, makes a sudden turn round a rocky angle, and plunges madly into the pool itself. Very deep water lies at the head of it, but deeper still further down on the east side, where a portion of the stream flicks back again in a swift dark backwater towards the top of the pool again. It is fishable only from the western bank, for to the east, above this backwater, a great wall of black and basaltic rock, heaved up no doubt by some fault in strata, rises sheer from the river to the height of some sixty feet. It is in fact nearly precipitous on both sides, heavily serrated at the top, and of so curious a thinness, that at about the middle of it, where a fissure breaks its topmost edge, and some twenty feet from the top, there exists a long hole, a sort of lancet window, one would say, right through the rock, so that a slit of daylight can be seen through it. Since, therefore, no one would care to cast his line standing perched on that razor-edged eminence, the pool must needs be fished from the western bank. A decent fly, however, will cover it all.

It is on the western bank that there stand the remains of that which gave its title to the pool, namely, the ruins of a Pict castle, built out of rough and scarcely hewn masonry, unmortared but on a certain large and impressive scale, and in a very well-preserved condition considering its extreme antiquity. It is circular in shape and measures some twenty yards of diameter in its internal span. A staircase of large blocks with a rise of at least a foot leads up to the main gate, and opposite this on the side towards the river is another smaller postern through which, down a rather hazard-ously steep slope, a scrambling path, where progress demands both caution and activity, conducts to the head of the pool which lies immediately beneath it. A gate-chamber still roofed over exists in the solid wall: inside there are foundation indications of three rooms, and in the centre of all a very deep hole, probably a well. Finally, just outside the postern leading to the river is a small arti-ficially levelled platform, some twenty feet across, as if made to support some super-incumbent edifice. Certain stone slabs and blocks are dispersed over it.

Brora, the post-town of Gavon, lies some six miles to the south-west, and from it a track over the moor leads to the rapids immediately above the Picts' pool, across which by somewhat extravagant striding from boulder to boulder a man can pass dry-foot when the river is low, and make his way up a steep path to the north of the basaltic rock, and so to the village. But this transit demands a steady head, and at the best is a somewhat giddy passage. Otherwise the road between it and Brora lies in a long detour higher up the moor, passing by the gates of Gavon Lodge, where I was stopping. For some vague and ill-defined reason the pool itself and the Picts' Castle had an uneasy reputation on the countryside, and several times, trudging back from a day's fishing, I have known my gillie take a longish circuit, though heavy with fish, rather than make this short cut in the dusk by the castle. On the first occasion when Sandy, a strapping yellow-bearded Viking of twenty-five, did this he gave as a reason that the ground round about the castle was 'mossy', though as a God-fearing man he must have known he lied. But on another occasion he was more frank, and said that the Picts' pool was 'no canny' after sunset. I am now inclined to agree with him, though, when he lied about it, I think it was because as a God-fearing man he feared the devil also.

It was on the evening of September 14 that I was walking back with my host, Hugh Graham, from the forest beyond the lodge. It had been a day unseasonably hot for the time of year, and the hills were blanketed with soft, furry clouds. Sandy, the gillie of whom I have spoken, was behind with the ponies, and, idly enough, I told Hugh about his strange distaste for the Picts' pool after sunset. He listened, frowning a little.

'That's curious,' he said. 'I know there is some dim local super-stition about the place, but last year certainly Sandy used to laugh at it. I remember asking him what ailed the place, and he said he thought nothing about the rubbish folk talked. But this year you say he avoids it.'

'On several occasions with me he has done so.'

Hugh smoked a while in silence, striding noiselessly over the dusky fragrant heather.

'Poor chap,' he said, 'I don't know what to do about him. He's becoming useless.'

'Drink?' I asked.

'Yes, drink in a secondary manner. But trouble led to drink, and trouble, I am afraid, is leading him to worse than drink.'

'The only thing worse than drink is the devil,' I remarked.

'Precisely. That's where he is going. He goes there often.'

'What on earth do you mean?' I asked.

'Well, it's rather curious,' said Hugh. 'You know I dabble a bit in folklore and local superstition, and I believe I am on the track of something odder than odd. Just wait a moment.'

We stood there in the gathering dusk till the ponies laboured up the hillside to us, Sandy with his six feet of lithe strength strolling easily beside them up the steep brae, as if his long day's trudging had but served to half awaken his dormant powers of limb.

'Going to see Mistress Macpherson again tonight?' asked Hugh.

'Aye, puir body,' said Sandy. 'She's auld, and she's lone.'

'Very kind of you, Sandy,' said Hugh, and we walked on.

'What then?' I asked when the ponies had fallen behind again.

'Why, superstition lingers here,' said Hugh, 'and it's supposed she's a witch. To be quite candid with you, the thing interests me a good deal. Supposing you asked me, on oath, whether I believed in witches, I should say "No". But if you asked me again, on oath, whether I suspected I believed in them, I should, I think, say "Yes". And the fifteenth of this month – to-morrow – is Gavon's Eve.'

'And what in Heaven's name is that?' I asked. 'And who is Gavon? And what's the trouble?'

'Well, Gavon is the person, I suppose, not saint, who is what we should call the eponymous hero of this district. And the trouble is Sandy's trouble. Rather a long story. But there's a long mile in front of us yet, if you care to be told.'

During that mile I heard. Sandy had been engaged a year ago to girl of Gavon who was in service at Inverness. In March last he had gone, without giving notice, to see her, and as he walked up the street in which her mistress's house stood, had met her suddenly face to face, in company with a man whose clipped speech betrayed him English, whose manner a kind of gentleman. He had a flourish of his hat for Sandy, pleasure to see him, and scarcely any need of explanation as to how he came to be walking with Catrine. It was the most natural thing possible, for a city like Inverness boasted its innocent urbanities, and a girl could stroll with a man. And for the time, since also Catrine was so frankly pleased to see him, Sandy was satisfied. But after his return to Gavon, suspicion, fungus-like, grew rank in his mind, with the result that a month ago he had, with infinite pains and blottings, written a letter to Catrine, urging her return and immediate marriage. Thereafter it was known that she had left Inverness; it was known that she had arrived by train at Brora. From Brora she had started to walk across the moor by the path leading just above the Picts' Castle, crossing the rapids to Gavon, leaving her box to be sent by the carrier. But at Gavon she had never arrived. Also it was said that, although it was hot afternoon, she wore a big cloak.

By this time we had come to the lodge, the lights of which showed dim and blurred through the thick hill-mists that had streamed sullenly down from the higher ground.

'And the rest,' said Hugh, 'which is as fantastic as this is sober fact, I will tell you later.'

Now, a fruit-bearing determination to go to bed is, to my mind, as difficult to ripen as a fruit-bearing determination to get up, and in spite of our long day, I was glad when Hugh (the rest of the men having yawned themselves out of the smoking-room) came back from the hospitable dispensing of bedroom candlesticks with a briskness that denoted that, as far as he was concerned, the distressing determination was not imminent.

'As regards Sandy,' I suggested.

'Ah, I also was thinking of that,' he said. 'Well, Catrine Gordon left Brora, and never arrived here. That is fact. Now for what remains. Have you any remembrance of a woman always alone walking about the moor by the loch? I think I once called your attention to her.'

'Yes, I remember,' I said. 'Not Catrine, surely; a very old woman, awful to look at.'

'Moustache, whiskers, and muttering to herself. Always looking at the ground, too.'

'Yes, that is she – not Catrine. Catrine! My word, a May morning! But the other – it is Mrs Macpherson, reputed witch. Well, Sandy trudges there, a mile and more away, every night to see her. You know Sandy: Adonis of the north. Now, can you account by any natural explanation for that fact? That he goes off after a long day to see an old hag in the hills?'

'It would seem unlikely,' said I.

'Unlikely! Well, yes, unlikely.'

Hugh got up from his chair and crossed the room to where a bookcase of rather fusty-looking volumes stood between windows. He took a small morocco-backed book from a top shelf.

'*Superstitions of Sutherlandshire*,' he said, as he handed it to me. 'Turn to page 128, and read.'

'September 15 appears to have been the date of what we may call this devil festival. On the night of that day the powers of darkness held pre-eminent dominion, and over-rode for any who were abroad that night and invoked their aid, the protective Providence of Almighty God.

'Witches, therefore, above all, were peculiarly potent. On this night any witch could entice to herself the heart and the love of any young man who consulted her on matters of philtre or love charm, with the result that on any night in succeeding years of the same date, he, though he was lawfully affianced and wedded, would for that night be hers. If, however, he should call on the name of God through any sudden grace of the Spirit, her charm would be of no avail. On this night, too, all witches had the power by certain dreadful incantations and indescribable profanities, to raise from the dead those who had committed suicide.'

'Top of the next page,' said Hugh. 'Leave out this next paragraph; it does not bear on this last.'

'Near a small village in this country,' I read, 'called Gavon, the moon at midnight is said to shine through a certain gap or fissure in a wall of rock close beside the river on to the ruins of a Pict castle, so that the light of its beams falls on to a large flat stone erected there near the gate, and supposed by some to be an ancient and pagan altar. At that moment, so the superstition still lingers in the countryside, the evil and malignant spirits which hold sway on Gavon's Eve are at the zenith of their powers, and those who invoke their aid at this moment and in this place, will, though with infinite peril to their immortal souls, get all that they desire of them.'

The paragraph on the subject ended here, and I shut the book.

'Well?' I asked.

'Under favourable circumstances two and two make four,' said Hugh.

'And four means—'

'This. Sandy is certainly in consultation with a woman who is supposed to be a witch, whose path no crofter will cross after nightfall. He wants to learn, at whatever cost, poor devil, what happened to Catrine. Thus I think it more than possible that to-morrow, at midnight, there will be folk by the Picts' pool. There is another curious thing. I was fishing yesterday, and just opposite the river gate of the castle, someone has set up a great flat stone, which has been dragged (for I noticed the crushed grass) from the debris at the bottom of the slope.'

'You mean that the old hag is going to try to raise the body of Catrine, if she is dead?'

'Yes, and I mean to see myself what happens. Come too.'

The next day Hugh and I fished down the river from the lodge, taking with us not Sandy, but another gillie, and ate our lunch on the slope of the Picts' Castle after landing a couple of fish there. Even as Hugh had said, a great flat slab of stone had been dragged on to the platform outside the river gate of the castle, where it rested on certain rude supports, which, now that it was in place, seemed certainly designed to receive it. It was also exactly opposite that lancet window in the basaltic rock across the pool, so that if the moon at midnight did shine through it, the light would fall on the stone. This, then, was the almost certain scene of the incantations.

Below the platform, as I have said, the ground fell rapidly away to the level of the pool, which owing to rain on the hills was running very high, and, streaked with lines of greyish bubbles, poured down in amazing and ear-filling volume. But directly underneath the steep escarpment of rock on the far side of the pool it lay foamless and black, a still backwater of great depth. Above the altar-like erection again the ground rose up seven rough-hewn steps to the gate itself, on each side of which, to the height of about four feet, ran the circular wall of the castle. Inside again were the remains of partition walls between the three chambers, and it was in the one nearest to the river gate that we determined to conceal ourselves that night. From there, should the witch and Sandy keep tryst at the altar, any sound of movement would reach us, and through the aperture of the gate itself we could see, concealed in the shadow of the wall, whatever took place at the altar or down below at the pool. The lodge, finally, was but a short ten minutes away, if one went in the direct line, so that by starting at a quarter to twelve that night, we could enter the Picts' Castle by the gate away from the river, thus not betraying our presence to those who might be waiting for the moment when the moon should shine through the lancet window in the wall of rock on to the altar in front of the river gate.

Night fell very still and windless, and when not long before midnight we let ourselves silently out of the lodge, though to the east the sky was clear, a black continent of cloud was creeping up from the west, and had now nearly reached the zenith. Out of the remote fringes of it occasional lightning winked, and the growl of very distant thunder sounded drowsily at long intervals after.

But it seemed to me as if another storm hung over our heads, ready every moment to burst, for the oppression in the air was of a far heavier quality than so distant a disturbance could have accounted for.

To the east, however, the sky was still luminously clear; the curiously hard edges of the western cloud were star-embroidered, and by the dove-coloured light in the east it was evident that the moonrise over the moor was imminent. And though I did not in my heart believe that our expedition would end in anything but yawns, I was conscious of an extreme tension and rawness of nerves, which I set down to the thunder-charged air.

For noiselessness of footstep we had both put on India-rubber-soled shoes, and all the way down to the pool we heard nothing but the distant thunder and our own padded tread. Very silently and cautiously we ascended the steps of the gate away from the river, and keeping close to the wall inside, sidled round to the river gate and peered out. For the first moment I could see nothing, so black lay the shadow of the rock-wall opposite across the pool, but by degrees I made out the lumps and line of the glimmering foam which streaked the water. High as the river was running this morning, it was infinitely more voluminous and turbulent now, and the sound of it filled and bewildered the ear with its sonorous roaring. Only under the very base of the rock opposite it ran quite black and unflecked by foam: there lay the deep still surface of the backwater. Then suddenly I saw something black move in the dimness in front of me, and against the grey foam rose up first the head, then the shoulders, and finally the whole figure of a woman coming towards us up the bank. Behind her walked another, a man, and the two came to where the altar of stone had been newly erected and stood there side by side silhouetted against the churned white of the stream. Hugh had seen too, and touched me on the arm to call my attention. So far then he was right: there was no mistaking the stalwart proportions of Sandy.

Suddenly across the gloom shot a tiny spear of light, and momentarily as we watched, it grew larger and longer, till a tall beam, as from some window cut in the rock opposite, was shed on the bank below us. It moved slowly, imperceptibly to the left till it struck full between the two black figures standing there, and shone with a curious bluish gleam on the flat stone in front of them.

Then the roar of the river was suddenly overscored by a dreadful screaming voice, the voice of a woman, and from her side her arms shot up and out as if in invocation of some power.

At first I could catch none of the words, but soon from repetition they began to convey an intelligible message to my brain, and I was listening as in paralytic horror of nightmare to a bellowing of the most hideous and un-nameable profanity. What I heard I cannot bring myself to record; suffice it to say that Satan was invoked by every adoring and reverent name, that cursing and unspeakable malediction was poured forth on Him whom we hold most holy. Then the yelling voice ceased as suddenly as it had begun, and for a moment there was silence again, but for the reverberating river.

Then once more that horror of sound was uplifted.

'So, Catrine Gordon,' it cried, 'I bid ye in the name of my master and yours to rise from where ye lie. Up with ye – up!'

Once more there was silence; then I heard Hugh at my elbow draw a quick sobbing breath, and his finger pointed unsteadily to the dead black water below the rock. And I too looked and saw.

Right under the rock there appeared a pale subaqueous light, which waved and quivered in the stream. At first it was very small and dim, but as we looked it seemed to swim upwards from remote depths and grew larger till I suppose the space of some square yard was illuminated by it.

Then the surface of the water was broken, and a head, the head of a girl, dead-white and with long, flowing hair, appeared above the stream. Her eyes were shut, the corners of her mouth drooped as in sleep, and the moving water stood in a frill round her neck. Higher and higher rose the figure out of the tide, till at last it stood, luminous in itself, so it appeared, up to the middle.

The head was bent down over the breast, and the hands clasped together. As it emerged from the water it seemed to get nearer, and was by now half-way across the pool, moving quietly and steadily against the great flood of the hurrying river.

Then I heard a man's voice crying out in a sort of strangled agony.

'Catrine!' it cried; 'Catrine! In God's name; in God's name!'

In two strides Sandy had rushed down the steep bank, and hurled himself out into that mad swirl of waters. For one moment I saw his arms flung up into the sky, the next he had altogether gone. And on the utterance of that name the unholy vision had vanished too, while simultaneously there burst in front of us a light so blinding, followed by a crack of thunder so appalling to the senses, that I know I just hid my face in my hands. At once, as if the flood-gates of the sky had been opened, the deluge was on us, not like rain, but like one sheet of solid water, so that we cowered under it. Any hope or attempt to rescue Sandy was out of the question; to dive into that whirlpool of mad water meant instant death, and even had it been possible for any swimmer to live there, in the blackness of the night there was absolutely no chance of finding him. Besides, even if it had been possible to save him, I doubt whether I was sufficiently master of my flesh and blood as to endure to plunge where that apparition had risen.

Then, as we lay there, another horror filled and possessed my mind. Somewhere close to us in the darkness was that woman whose yelling voice just now had made my blood run ice-cold, while it brought the streaming sweat to my forehead. At that moment I turned to Hugh.

'I cannot stop here,' I said. 'I must run, run right away. Where is she?'

'Did you not see?' he asked.

'No. What happened?'

'The lightning struck the stone within a few inches of where she was standing. We – we must go and look for her.'

I followed him down the slope, shaking as if I had the palsy, and groping with my hands on the ground in front of me, in deadly terror of encountering something human. The thunderclouds had in the last few minutes spread over the moon, so that no ray from the window in the rock guided our search. But up and down the bank from the stone that lay shattered there to the edge of the pool we groped and stumbled, but found nothing. At length we gave it up: it seemed morally certain that she, too, had rolled down the bank after the lightning stroke, and lay somewhere deep in the pool from which she had called the dead.

None fished the pool next day, but men with drag-nets came from Brora. Right under the rock in the backwater lay two bodies, close together, Sandy and the dead girl. Of the other they found nothing.

It would seem, then, that Catrine Gordon, in answer to Sandy's letter, left Inverness in heavy trouble. What happened afterwards can only be conjectured, but it seems likely she took the short cut to Gavon, meaning to cross the river on the boulders above the

Picts' pool. But whether she slipped accidentally in her passage, and so was drawn down by the hungry water, or whether unable to face the future, she had thrown herself into the pool, we can only guess. In any case they sleep together now in the bleak, wind-swept graveyard at Brora, in obedience to the inscrutable designs of God.

A WITCH-BURNING

by

Mrs Baillie Reynolds

First published in *The Strand Magazine*

1909

THE DUSK WAS falling upon the hard, frozen ground, covered with light, powdery snow. Gilbert Caton sat by the window of his lowly lodging, looking forth into the wide market-square of the populous New England village of Mizpah.

There before his eyes were the figures of men, warmly wrapped about from the piercing cold, busily engaged in piling faggots for the witch who was to be burned upon the morrow.

As he looked forth, the young man was raging in his heart. He could not stop this thing that was to be. Or he could stop it only as in bygone days the monk Telemachus stopped the Public Games at Rome – by being himself a martyr.

He was an Englishman, and for two years had been an exile from his country, ministering to the handful of his own faith who dwell here among the Nonconformists. He had no position, no influence. He could but sit by and see what horror men could work in the name of righteousness. He and his flock were taboo to the other inhabitants, and, though there was no open persecution now, there was a persistent hostility which gave Churchmen a poor chance in the law courts and no chance at all in the way of public posts.

And now a hideous tendency, dormant of late in the people, had awoke again in new strength. They had taken to witch-burning. Only six months before an old woman, widow of a sailor – who held the secret of a herbal preparation, brought by her husband from far countries – had been dragged to the water, flung in, and cruelly tormented before being done to death. With that the hunting instinct of the mob had been roused. Having once tasted the savage joy of pursuit, capture, and destruction, they thirsted for it again. And ere many months had passed there came tales of two witches most undoubtedly possessed of occult powers, who lived in the depths of Haranec Wood, wherein, as everybody knew, there lurked cougars, so that no woman unprotected by Satanic powers could dwell there in safety.

Day after day there sifted in tales of the skill of these women – of the marvels wrought by the mere muttering of a spell, in which the waving of hands played great and wondrous part. Two men dispatched to take the offenders came back daunted and trembling, afraid to lay a hand on either of them. And thereupon the blood lust swept raging through the town, the people turned out, and the women were hunted down with dogs and dragged to the town jail.

At first there was a division of opinion respecting their equal guilt. One of them, who was evidently the leader, had been burnt a week ago. And now news had come down that the second captive, who had been reported penitent, had been tampering with her jailers – had been bribing them to connive at her escape. So she, too, was to burn upon the morrow.

And Caton sat there, wondering what judgment God would send upon a town which, within a year, had murdered three defenceless women. He had some vague ideas floating through his head, of trying to assemble half-a-dozen men to form a rescue. But he doubted if even that were possible. And as he mused, there was sharp knocking against his door from the street without. He rose, and opened; there stood the burly form and harsh-lined face of Brading, the village constable. He held a lantern in his hand, for dusk was falling and the night would be very dark.

'His worship, in his mercy, has sent for you,' he said, in his husky tones. 'Let no man say we give not even the most degraded their fair chance. The baggage down yonder, that is to burn to-morrow, says she belongs to the English faith. So come you down and say a prayer for her, and try to turn her thoughts from Satan to the Lord, for she will not listen to the godly exhorting of Master Lupton.'

Gilbert rose and stared wide-eyed at the messenger. What? Go and speak to this poor despairing creature of the mercy of God when she was to have no mercy from man! He quailed in his heart at the task. The constable burst into a hateful, husky titter.

'He's afraid – afraid the witch'll put a spell on him,' he chuckled. 'Lord love you, man. Master Lupton, he's been in her cell nigh two hours – and that against her will – and she's not been able to hurt him, through his faith in the Lord. But you that put your trust in forms and ceremonies, ye fear, and who can wonder at it?'

A sudden impulse swept over Gilbert, calming him utterly.

Without having spoken one word, he turned to a desk which stood by his table, took his books of devotions, and stowed them in the pocket of his cassock, which, like the clergy of his day, he wore habitually. Then he took from a peg his long cloak with thick capes and his wide-brimmed hat, and intimated that he was ready to follow Brading.

It was almost night as they came out into the street and made their way – past the wide space where the pile of faggots rose a ghastly blot against the surrounding whiteness – up to the narrow throat of the street, where the houses began to cluster close, and so to the low, narrow stone archway which was the entrance to the town jail.

Brading let himself in with his own key and they stood in the small waiting-room, where two or three men were lounging by the glowing heat of a great fire. The men greeted Gilbert with half-surly respect. His powerful physique and great strength procured for him a consideration which his blameless life and sincere simplicity might not have commanded. One of them told Brading that he had been summoned to go to the house of the mayor with regard to the proceedings of to-morrow. Brading was by no means unwilling, knowing that hot supper would be forthcoming at the mayor's house; so he forthwith departed, taking his lantern with him and making a kind of apology that Gilbert must walk home in the dark.

Gilbert hardly heard. He was watching the selection of a key by a man who had risen to attend him, and who now led the way down a corkscrew stair which seemed to descend to the bowels of the earth.

The condemned cell!

All was dark and silent within. Caton took the torch from the man who held it, flashed the light round, saw an iron ring in the wall and fixed the light there.

'Knock loud when you want to come out,' said the turnkey, and retired, slamming the iron door with a bang.

Gilbert fixed his eyes upon the heap of rags huddled in a corner.

'Good evening,' he said, in his clear, high-bred voice. 'God be with you.'

There was a rustle in the straw. The heap of rags moved, turned towards him, and displayed, to his horror, the face of a young girl, hardly more than a child. She seemed all eyes – the stare of them burned his very soul. Her face was chalk-white, her streaming dark hair hung about it on either side, showing it up like a silver moon upon the dark sky. Her young, fresh mouth was piteously curved. She had that terrible dumbness of appeal which one sees in the eyes of ill-treated animals. The sight of her froze the man's blood in his veins. 'My daughter!' he said, in a voice which was almost a sob of compassion.

There came a quiver to her mouth – to her whole face. On her two hands she crawled nearer to him, a fearful questioning in her wild look. Was this really a human being speaking kind words to her? Not cursing her?

The young man threw off his cloak and hat and knelt down beside her in the straw. She laid her small hand, freezing cold, upon his outstretched palm.

'You are warm,' she said, in a murmuring voice. 'And you have brought a light! I have been in the dark – alone – so cold.'

In a transport of pity he lifted her up and drew her into his arms, holding her head in the hollow of his elbow.

'What do they mean?' he said, unsteadily. 'What do they mean by calling you a witch?'

She faintly shook her head. 'I don't – know,' she faltered, in laboured gasps. He looked about the horrible dungeon and saw on a shelf a water-pitcher and mug. In his pocket was, as it chanced, a flask of wine and some biscuit which he had taken with him to bestow upon a poor parishioner earlier in the day, and found him away. He mixed wine and water and gave her to eat and drink; in his anxiety for her bodily needs forgetting all else, as one does in such a case.

The taste of the delicate biscuit drew her to eat; the wine made the blood flow again in her veins. As she ate and drank he held her warmly wrapped in his cloak, and felt the icy rigidity of her limbs relax.

And yet – was it kindness or cruelty, he asked himself. Had it been better to leave her in her stupor of cold and hunger? Might she have cheated the flames after all? Had he not brought her back to the full sense of her misery?

'Tell me,' he said at last, as she sat silent, her head fallen sideways against his shoulder, 'what have you done? What have you said that they have condemned you for a witch?'

She sighed wearily. 'Nothing that I know of. They said Grannie was a witch; and I lived with her.'

'Was it true? Did your grandmother practise magic arts?'

'She could put them to sleep by waving her hands about. She could cure pain by stroking the place. Is that wicked?'

'Alas, I know not. Who taught her these things?'

'She learned them long ago of a nurse she had, who was a gipsy. They were very rich, my grandparents, and they had a large estate. The Indians attacked them and killed my father and mother and – and almost everybody. Only Grannie and I were left, and she was always queer after that. She would not live in the town, she was full of strange fancies. But she was good to me. We were very happy till Joseph, our servant, died.'

'How long ago was that?'

'I do not know; I forget. We buried him, and then Grannie would not stay in that house. She said she would go to my uncle, who had a fine home in England and a park with swans and a lake, and many servants. So we started off to walk to the coast, but she was old and ill. We found a little house in the wood, and rested there; and the people found us out, and they were good to us till they came hunting us. Oh!' Suddenly she sat erect, threw up her hands, and screamed. 'They will burn me! They will burn me!' she cried, madly . . . She flung her arms about his knees. 'Are you kind? Are you human?' she cried. 'Can't you save me from them? Can't you?'

The sweat stood on the young man's forehead. It had come suddenly – so suddenly. Not a moment's interval between the everyday quiet of his usual existence and this sudden plunge into a life-and-death struggle.

'Have you ever been baptised?' he asked her, hurriedly.

'Oh, yes; and confirmed, too, by a Bishop,' she said, faintly.

She was a sheep of his fold, and he must save her or die with her.

Her name, she told him, was Luna Clare. The clear shining of the moon! He thought her well named.

Rapidly his mind reviewed the position. The wild idea of passing her out in his habiliments crossed his mind. But the thing was impossible. She was much less than half his bulk. And even could he hope that, the jailers being drunk, such a plot could be carried out – once beyond the prison alone, what would become of her? She must die of exposure, be eaten by wild beasts, or re-taken.

She sat, watching with craving eyes the thoughts, the doubts, the trouble in his face. Her soft hand touched his. 'Kill me,' she breathed. 'Kill me here, with your own hand. I do not fear death – I have nothing to live for – I fear only torture – only to die shrieking with devilish men gloating on my agony. Kill me now – it is the only way.'

For a moment he thought it was. Her head fell limply against his rough cassock. He held her in his arms, his clear, grey eyes gazing out over her head, contemplating the situation.

And then, suddenly, as he reflected upon the emaciation of the slight thing he held, an idea broke upon his mind that sent the blood with a rush to his face – that made his head reel a moment, then flooded him with a calmness and strength which surprised himself.

'Luna,' he said, in a new voice, 'will you swear to do whatever I bid you?'

She moved, so that her small, white face, with its piteous, pointed chin, was upturned to his. She just breathed 'Yes,' and hung upon his words.

'Luna, you must trust me to the uttermost. In the eyes of God I am your brother – you are safe with me.'

He rose to his feet. 'Let me try how heavy you are,' he muttered; and lifted her slip of a body with an ease that astonished him.

'It can be done,' he said, through his teeth. 'God helping, it shall be done.'

From upstairs he caught a loud, vacant laugh, a snatch of drunken song. In Brading's absence the jailers were making merry.

There was a slender chance for the success of his plan. His hesitation was over; he turned upon her, short and sharp. 'I am going to put you on my back,' he said, 'and to carry you out of the prison under my cassock.' In spite of his resolution, his face flamed as he said it.

Luna looked neither afraid nor shocked. Her eye lit up. 'Oh, I will be very still,' she said, with quick breathlessness.

He was already divesting himself of his long garment, and stood before her, well-knit and sturdy, in his grey flannel shirt and knee-breeches.

'Take off your frock,' he bade her. 'We must arrange it, with a stuffing of straw, in the corner to look like you.'

She caught his idea, stripped it off her, and there she was, bare-armed and fragile, in her poor petticoat – a creature of cloud and air.

The hearts of the two young creatures throbbed with violence. They felt themselves alone against the world. Gilbert stooped and lifted the girl upon his back, so that her arms were locked about his shoulders. Her feet hung clear of the ground. With the broad sash of his cassock he bound her firmly to him to decrease the weight upon her arms. With his knife he had previously slit his cassock all up the back, from below the waist to the neckband. Now he buttoned it round them both and flung over all his big cloak, which concealed the rent behind. The weight was greater than he had anticipated, but not greater than he could bear.

All was ready. The frock, stuffed with straw, looked like a girl crouching in the corner. The imprisoned Luna hung perfectly quiet, her arms hardly perceptible under the thick cloak, whose hood concealed her head behind. He felt the warmth of her cheek against his shoulder.

Then, standing on the threshold of his venture, he spoke a brief but strenuous prayer, and heard a soft voice sigh 'Amen,' as he knocked and shouted for the turnkey to release him. The men above were so heavy with drink and the heat of their great fire that he had to knock and shout for some time before the man came.

'Can you bear it?' he asked, hastily, at the last moment. She merely answered, 'Yes.'

But the strength of ten men seemed to uphold him, as the door slowly opened.

'God be good to us! God be good to us!' he muttered, lifting his hands in horror at the failure of his mission.

'What, no success? Well, 'twasn't likely you should succeed where brother Lupton failed,' sniggered the turnkey.

'Perhaps solitude – and darkness – may prevail,' said Gilbert, harshly, taking the torch and stamping it out with his feet. 'Leave her to think over my words.'

It was more difficult than he had foreseen to ascend the narrow corkscrew stair. As he went slowly up, bumping his burden against the wall, he felt an insane desire to laugh, mingling with his fear. The sweat stood on his forehead, and his heart thumped like a machine as they emerged into the outer room, where the blaze of the fire lit up the place and threw the distorted outline of Master Caton's figure upon the wall.

The dungeon below was locked for the night – between them and their slender hope of escape stood now but one door.

Fortunately, Gilbert had a small silver coin in his pocket. At the door he bestowed it on the turnkey, whose fellow was stretched upon the bench in a drunken slumber.

'A cold night, friend,' he said. 'Here is somewhat to keep you warm.'

The turnkey muttered something inaudible. He was very tipsy indeed. He stooped to put the key in the door, and fell, a heavy mass, right across the threshold.

Gilbert turned the key at once. But he hesitated to step over the prostrate man, who was not unconscious and was struggling to arise. He knew that Luna's feet, dangling within a few inches of the ground, must brush the jailer's nether limbs, and might be perceptible, even to senses fuddled with drink. Accordingly, he held out his hand, with a friendly smile, and encouraged the man to rise, Twice in vain he essayed to gain his feet, and twice fell back, while Gilbert gasped and staggered with the strain. At the third attempt up he came, and fell upon the young man with such force as to cause him to stagger back with violence against the wall. It was quite unavoidable; he could do nothing to break the force of the impact. If the girl let forth a sound they were undone.

She remained perfectly silent, though he felt a shudder run through her limbs. He hardly knew what he said to the tipsy fool, who now, melted by the gift of the coin, flung himself upon him to embrace him.

That must be the end – discovery was now inevitable. In anguish Gilbert held up his arms – 'Man, stop, stop! My rheumatism! Have a little pity. Here, sit down on this stool – another mouthful of this will strengthen you.'

He held the glass of steaming spirits which stood on the table to the sot's lips; and in the succeeding moment had opened the door and staggered out.

Mizpah folks were early abed, and he found an empty street. He hastened along, reeling and staggering, the burden on his back seeming, like Christopher's, to grow heavier each moment. Suppose she should relax the clasp of her hands and slip to the ground? The strain must be awful. He stopped a moment to give a hoist, but the immediate slipping back which followed warned him that she was near the end of her resource. He pushed on, wild with apprehension, believing that, should he meet anyone upon the road, he must be detected. The sight of his shadow, cast by the firelight on the wall, had told him how mad a risk he ran.

His own door, with the glimmering lantern above, seemed like a ray from heaven. He lived alone, a woman coming in each day to do his 'chores', as it was called. His supper would be laid, he knew.

They must eat and then flee. What was he to do for clothes for the girl?

He almost hurled himself within, drew the great bar behind him, and, stooping under the dead weight of an apparently inert burden, found his tinder-box, made a light, and, with frantic fingers, flung away his wrappings.

The girl fell, limp and senseless, into his big chair, and lay there, in the light of his lamp, so reduced by cruelty and privation that he was inclined to think his rescue of her was too late.

The drops stood upon his forehead as he began to realise what he had done. He had broken the law, made himself responsible for a girl from nobody knew where. Flight was imperative; and how was flight possible?

His nerves were jarred with the strain of what he had undergone; but he set his teeth to the completing of his adventure, took the boiling kettle from the hot coals, made drink, and held it to her lips. By degrees she came back to consciousness. His clock told him that it was barely eight o'clock. The whole night lay before the fugitives.

When Luna was sitting up, drinking her milk and gazing timidly about, he also set to work to eat, while he tried to collect his wits and decide what he must take with him and whither shape his course. So far he had succeeded, so far they were free. But—

He started, and his face froze. There were steps and voices in the silent street without – hurried steps, coming from the direction of the prison. And as he sat, counting the hammer strokes of his heart, there was a loud and peremptory knocking upon his door.

He raised his head and looked at the fragile waif-girl who sat as if paralysed. He rose, and stood, a picture of perplexity. Then he was himself again. He crossed the room and looked at her a moment with a gaze half of command, half of appeal. She answered it as if he had spoken, rising to her feet and taking his hand. He led her across to the door of his bedroom, opened it, and said under his breath, 'In – in—'

She obeyed without words, without hesitation, and he shut and locked the door behind her, putting the key in his pocket as the knocking without was repeated, and more loudly.

He threw his cloak over his damaged cassock and went to meet Fate.

Without, in the snowy night, stood three men. They seemed to be a gentleman and his two servants. The gentleman wore a costly and much be-furred travelling suit, and his voice and courtly bow at once proclaimed him English.

'Pardon this intrusion. Do I speak to Master Gilbert Caton, the parson here?'

Gilbert admitted it.

'Dare I beg for a few minutes of your valuable time, sir? I come merely to ask a question. I am here to trace my mother and my young niece. My name is Clare – Leonard Clare, of Clare Hall, in the County of Devon. My father had a large estate west of this, which was attacked by Indians, and many of my family murdered. But I am told that my mother, with one child of my brother, escaped, and I have traced them with tolerable certainty, to this district. The town authorities, however, tell me nothing is known of them here. As they are of the Episcopal faith, I deemed that you might know something; and before leaving the place I venture to importune you.'

A sudden trembling of the limbs assailed Gilbert as he stood. With a motion to his guests to enter he turned away, and sank down into a chair, covering his face with his hands.

Then, looking up with a dawn of hope and illumination, 'Have you horses?' he eagerly demanded.

'We have horses – yes.'

'Then it will be best to fly,' said Gilbert, huskily.

Mr Clare stood, majestic and astonished, in the small room,

looking doubtfully at the young parson, whose sanity seemed questionable. 'To fly?' he echoed.

'The people of Mizpah,' said Gilbert, hoarsely, 'burnt your mother as a witch. I saw her burn, without there, in the market. They have fixed the burning of your niece for to-morrow – to-morrow. There is a holiday, that the folks may see the sight.'

Mr Clare let forth a kind of bellow. 'To burn my niece! And you urge me to fly?'

Gilbert nodded. He rose and went to his bedroom door. He threw it wide and called to the girl within. She came and stood in the doorway in her ragged petticoat – hunted, wild, shrinking, her great eyes dilated to their utmost. For one moment she stood poised there, then darted to Gilbert and clung to him with all her might.

'Don't! Don't!' she shrieked. 'Don't let them take me! Kill me – kill me yourself! Don't let me burn!'

She was so overwrought that it was long before Gilbert could make her understand that she was saved. Now that the way to act was plain to him all his energy and resource returned. He explained the situation as clearly as he could to Mr Clare.

He felt sure that it would be unwise to wait till morning and tackle the authorities. The people, baulked of their prey, would very likely break out and riot. Moreover, the inhabitants of all other villages in the district had the same blind fear and hatred of a witch, and so were potential enemies. The safest plan was to dress the girl in boy's clothes and to ride away there and then. The night lay before them clear and fine, though cold. They must travel straight through till they gained the coast, and there take ship for England. He could find something for Luna to wear, and they could lend a spare cloak.

Leonard Clare listened, with wrath in his heart, yet knowing that the advice was good. It was arranged that he should send his servants back to the inn to pay his reckoning and bring his horses and his baggage. There was a spare horse for the carriage of such things as were necessary for travel, and until they were clear of the district and could buy another horse, Luna could ride that.

There was need of urgent haste, and in the stress of the proposed flight Leonard Clare had hardly time to realise the desperate part played by the young parson.

But when Luna had been shut once more into the bedroom to wash and dress herself, the two men faced each other, and, noting the blue marks under the younger man's eyes, Clare's heart smote him for an ingrate. He spoke then in a fine, dignified way of his indebtedness. He dared not insult the young man by offer of reward, but if there were anything he could do—

Gilbert thanked him quietly. He said simply that he could not leave the girl to be murdered. He had done what he could, and God had done the rest.

He cut protestations short by sketching a map of the route he advised and giving minute directions.

In the midst of it the bedroom door softly opened, and there slipped out a slim figure in knee-breeches and shirt, with hair all gathered away under a riding-hat.

Luna's timidity was gone. Her eyes were full of a new terrible idea. Going straight up to Gilbert, she said, in her low, wondrous voice:

'And what will you do?'

He leaned across the table and looked her in the eyes.

'Stay here and do my work,' he said, quietly.

'And when they find I am gone they will seize you.'

He shrugged his shoulders. 'They may not. They may think the devil ran off with you in the night.'

'If they do *not* think so, the mob will tear you in pieces.'

'I can't help that. I have done my duty.'

The girl turned slowly from him, as if she could not tear her eyes from the dominion of his. She looked at her uncle.

'I cannot leave here unless Master Caton comes too.'

'I must humbly beg to be forgiven. I had not realised the danger that you have run by your heroic rescue of my niece,' stammered Mr Clare. 'The events of this night – I think my wits are too weak, sir. But let me repair this. Come with us tonight, and your future career shall be my care.'

Gilbert hesitated, his face aflame. Luna went close to him and took his hand. 'If he stays, I stay with him,' she said clearly.

The sound of the horses at the door was heard. Voices mingled with the tramplings. The mayor had come to express regret that Mr Clare was leaving the village with his inquiries unanswered.

They came out and spoke with him. Gilbert explained that he was going a stage with Mr Clare, who was not certain of the first ten miles before striking the main road. He mounted the spare horse, and they put the page-boy up before him.

'Mind you get back in time for the burning,' said the mayor, anxiously. 'We shall want you to say the final prayers.'

'There will be plenty of time for that,' said Gilbert, tranquilly.

THE MUSIC
ON THE HILL

by

Saki

First published in the collection
The Chronicles of Clovis

1911

SYLVIA SELTOUN ATE her breakfast in the morning-room
at Yessney with a pleasant sense of ultimate victory, such as
a fervent Ironside might have permitted himself on the morrow
of Worcester fight. She was scarcely pugnacious by temperament,
but belonged to that more successful class of fighters who are pugnacious by circumstance. Fate had willed that her life should be
occupied with a series of small struggles, usually with the odds
slightly against her, and usually she had just managed to come
through winning. And now she felt that she had brought her
hardest and certainly her most important struggle to a successful issue. To have married Mortimer Seltoun, 'Dead Mortimer'
as his more intimate enemies called him, in the teeth of the cold
hostility of his family, and in spite of his unaffected indifference
to women, was indeed an achievement that had needed some
determination and adroitness to carry through; yesterday she
had brought her victory to its concluding stage by wrenching
her husband away from Town and its group of satellite watering-
places and 'settling him down', in the vocabulary of her kind, in

this remote wood-girt manor farm which was his country house.

'You will never get Mortimer to go,' his mother had said carpingly, 'but if he once goes, he'll stay; Yessney throws almost as much a spell over him as Town does. One can understand what holds him to Town, but Yessney—' and the dowager had shrugged her shoulders.

There was a sombre, almost savage wildness about Yessney that was certainly not likely to appeal to town-bred tastes, and Sylvia, notwithstanding her name, was accustomed to nothing much more sylvan than 'leafy Kensington'. She looked on the country as something excellent and wholesome in its way, which was apt to become troublesome if you encouraged it overmuch. Distrust of town-life had been a new thing with her, born of her marriage with Mortimer, and she had watched with satisfaction the gradual fading of what she called 'the Jermyn-Street-look' in his eyes as the woods and heather of Yessney had closed in on them yesternight. Her will-power and strategy had prevailed; Mortimer would stay.

Outside the morning-room windows was a triangular slope of turf, which the indulgent might call a lawn, and beyond its low hedge of neglected fuchsia bushes a steeper slope of heather and bracken dropped down into cavernous combes overgrown with oak and yew. In its wild open savagery there seemed a stealthy linking of the joy of life with the terror of unseen things. Sylvia smiled complacently as she gazed with a School-of-Art appreciation at the landscape, and then of a sudden she almost shuddered.

'It is very wild,' she said to Mortimer, who had joined her; 'one could almost think that in such a place the worship of Pan had never quite died out.'

'The worship of Pan never has died out,' said Mortimer. 'Other newer gods have drawn aside his votaries from time to time, but he is the Nature-God to whom all must come back at last. He has been called the Father of all the Gods, but most of his children have been stillborn.'

Sylvia was religious in an honest, vaguely devotional kind of way, and did not like to hear her beliefs spoken of as mere after-growths, but it was at least something new and hopeful to hear Dead Mortimer speak with such energy and conviction on any subject.

'You don't really believe in Pan?' she asked incredulously.

'I've been a fool in most things,' said Mortimer quietly, 'but I'm not such a fool as not to believe in Pan when I'm down here. And if you're wise you won't disbelieve in him too boastfully while you're in his country.'

It was not till a week later, when Sylvia had exhausted the attractions of the woodland walks round Yessney, that she ventured on a tour of inspection of the farm buildings. A farmyard suggested in her mind a scene of cheerful bustle, with churns and flails and smiling dairymaids, and teams of horses drinking knee-deep in duck-crowded ponds. As she wandered among the gaunt grey buildings of Yessney manor farm, her first impression was one of crushing stillness and desolation, as though she had happened on some lone deserted homestead long given over to owls and cobwebs; then came a sense of furtive watchful hostility, the same shadow of unseen things that seemed to lurk in the wooded combes and coppices. From behind heavy doors and shuttered windows came the restless stamp of hoof or rasp of chain halter, and at times a muffled bellow from some stalled beast. From a distant corner a shaggy dog watched her with intent unfriendly eyes; as she drew near it slipped quietly into its kennel, and slipped out again as noiselessly when she had passed by. A few hens, questing for food under a rick, stole away under a gate at her approach. Sylvia felt that if she had come across any human beings in this wilderness of barn and byre, they would have fled wraith-like from her gaze. At last, turning a corner quickly, she came upon a living thing that did not fly from her. Astretch in a pool of mud was an enormous sow, gigantic beyond the town-woman's wildest computation of swine-flesh, and speedily alert to resent and if necessary repel the unwonted intrusion. It was Sylvia's turn to make an unobtrusive retreat. As she threaded her way past rickyards and cowsheds and long blank walls, she started suddenly at a strange sound – the echo of a boy's laughter, golden and equivocal. Jan, the only boy employed on the farm, a tow-headed, wizen-faced yokel, was visibly at work on a potato clearing half-way up the nearest hill-side, and Mortimer, when questioned, knew of no other probable or possible begetter of the hidden mockery that had ambushed Sylvia's retreat. The memory of that untraceable echo was added to her other impressions of a furtive sinister 'something' that hung around Yessney.

Of Mortimer she saw very little; farm and woods and trout-streams seemed to swallow him up from dawn till dusk. Once, following the direction she had seen him take in the morning, she came to an open space in a nut copse, further shut in by huge yew trees, in the centre of which stood a stone pedestal surmounted by a small bronze figure of a youthful Pan. It was a beautiful piece of workmanship, but her attention was chiefly held by the fact that a newly cut bunch of grapes had been placed as an offering at its feet. Grapes were none too plentiful at the manor house, and Sylvia snatched the bunch angrily from the pedestal. Contemptuous annoyance dominated her thoughts as she strolled slowly homeward, and then gave way to a sharp feeling of something that was very near fright; across a thick tangle of undergrowth a boy's face was scowling at her, brown and beautiful, with unutterably evil eyes. It was a lonely pathway, all pathways round Yessney were lonely for the matter of that, and she sped forward without waiting to give a closer scrutiny to this sudden apparition. It was not till she had reached the house that she discovered that she had dropped the bunch of grapes in her flight.

'I saw a youth in the wood today,' she told Mortimer that evening, 'brown-faced and rather handsome, but a scoundrel to look at. A gipsy lad, I suppose.'

'A reasonable theory,' said Mortimer, 'only there aren't any gipsies in these parts at present.'

'Then who was he?' asked Sylvia, and as Mortimer appeared to have no theory of his own, she passed on to recount her finding of the votive offering.

'I suppose it was your doing,' she observed; 'it's a harmless piece of lunacy, but people would think you dreadfully silly if they knew of it.'

'Did you meddle with it in any way?' asked Mortimer.

'I – I threw the grapes away. It seemed so silly,' said Sylvia, watching Mortimer's impassive face for a sign of annoyance.

'I don't think you were wise to do that,' he said reflectively. 'I've heard it said that the Wood Gods are rather horrible to those who molest them.'

'Horrible perhaps to those that believe in them, but you see I don't,' retorted Sylvia.

'All the same,' said Mortimer in his even, dispassionate tone, 'I should avoid the woods and orchards if I were you, and give a wide berth to the horned beasts on the farm.'

It was all nonsense, of course, but in that lonely wood-girt spot nonsense seemed able to rear a bastard brood of uneasiness.

'Mortimer,' said Sylvia suddenly, 'I think we will go back to Town some time soon.'

Her victory had not been so complete as she had supposed; it had carried her on to ground that she was already anxious to quit.

'I don't think you will ever go back to Town,' said Mortimer. He seemed to be paraphrasing his mother's prediction as to himself.

Sylvia noted with dissatisfaction and some self-contempt that the course of her next afternoon's ramble took her instinctively clear of the network of woods. As to the horned cattle, Mortimer's warning was scarcely needed, for she had always regarded them as of doubtful neutrality at the best: her imagination unsexed the most matronly dairy cows and turned them into bulls liable to 'see red' at any moment. The ram who fed in the narrow paddock below the orchards she had adjudged, after ample and cautious probation, to be of docile temper; today, however, she decided to leave his docility untested, for the usually tranquil beast was roaming with every sign of restlessness from corner to corner of his meadow. A low, fitful piping, as of some reedy flute, was coming from the depth of a neighbouring copse, and there seemed to be some subtle connection between the animal's restless pacing and the wild music from the wood. Sylvia turned her steps in an upward direction and climbed the heather-clad slopes that stretched in rolling shoulders high above Yessney. She had left the piping notes behind her, but across the wooded combes at her feet the wind brought her another kind of music, the straining bay of hounds in full chase. Yessney was just on the outskirts of the Devon-and-Somerset country, and the hunted deer sometimes came that way. Sylvia could presently see a dark body, breasting hill after hill, and sinking again and again out of sight as he crossed the combes, while behind him steadily swelled that relentless chorus, and she grew tense with the excited sympathy that one feels for any hunted thing in whose capture one is not directly interested. And at last he broke through the outermost line of oak scrub and fern and stood panting in the open, a fat September stag carrying a well-furnished head. His obvious course was to drop down to the brown pools of Undercombe, and thence make his way towards the red deer's favoured sanctuary, the sea. To Sylvia's surprise, however, he turned his head to the upland slope and came lumbering resolutely onward over the heather. 'It will be dreadful,' she thought, 'the hounds will pull him down under my very eyes.' But the music of the pack seemed to have died away for a moment, and in its place she heard again that wild piping, which rose now on this side, now on that, as though urging the failing stag to a final effort. Sylvia stood well aside from his path, half hidden in a thick growth of whortle bushes, and watched him swing stiffly upward, his flanks dark with sweat, the coarse hair on his neck showing light by contrast. The pipe music shrilled suddenly around her, seeming to come from the bushes at her very feet, and at the same moment the great beast slewed round and bore directly down upon her. In an instant her pity for the hunted animal was changed to wild terror at her own danger; the thick heather roots mocked her scrambling efforts at flight, and she looked frantically downward for a glimpse of oncoming hounds. The huge antler spikes were within a few yards of her, and in a flash of numbing fear she remembered Mortimer's warning, to beware of horned beasts on the farm. And then with a quick throb of joy she saw that she was not alone; a human figure stood a few paces aside, knee-deep in the whortle bushes.

'Drive it off!' she shrieked. But the figure made no answering movement.

The antlers drove straight at her breast, the acrid smell of the hunted animal was in her nostrils, but her eyes were filled with the horror of something she saw other than her oncoming death. And in her ears rang the echo of a boy's laughter, golden and equivocal.

THE TARN
OF SACRIFICE

by

Algernon Blackwood

First published in the collection *The Wolves
of God, and Other Fey Stories*

1921

J OHN HOLT, A vague excitement in him, stood at the door of
the little inn, listening to the landlord's directions as to the best
way of reaching Scarsdale. He was on a walking tour through the
Lake District, exploring the smaller dales that lie away from the
beaten track and are accessible only on foot.

The landlord, a hard-featured north countryman, half innkeeper, half sheep farmer, pointed up the valley. His deep voice had
a friendly burr in it.

'You go straight on till you reach the head,' he said, 'then take to
the fell. Follow the "sheep-trod" past the Crag. Directly you're over
the top you'll strike the road.'

'A road up there!' exclaimed his customer incredulously.

'Aye,' was the steady reply. 'The old Roman road. The same
road,' he added, 'the savages came down when they burst through
the Wall and burnt everything right up to Lancaster—'

'They were held – weren't they – at Lancaster?' asked the other,
yet not knowing quite why he asked it.

'I don't rightly know,' came the answer slowly. 'Some say they were. But the old town has been that built over since, it's hard to tell.' He paused a moment. 'At Ambleside,' he went on presently, 'you can still see the marks of the burning, and at the little fort on the way to Ravenglass.'

Holt strained his eyes into the sunlit distance, for he would soon have to walk that road and he was anxious to be off. But the landlord was communicative and interesting. 'You can't miss it,' he told him. 'It runs straight as a spear along the fell top till it meets the Wall. You must hold to it for about eight miles. Then you'll come to the Standing Stone on the left of the track—'

'The Standing Stone, yes?' broke in the other a little eagerly.

'You'll see the Stone right enough. It was where the Romans came. Then bear to the left down another "trod" that comes into the road there. They say it was the war-trail of the folk that set up the Stone.'

'And what did they use the Stone for?' Holt inquired, more as though he asked it of himself than of his companion.

The old man paused to reflect. He spoke at length.

'I mind an old fellow who seemed to know about such things called it a Sighting Stone. He reckoned the sun shone over it at dawn on the longest day right on to the little holm in Blood Tarn. He said they held sacrifices in a stone circle there.' He stopped a moment to puff at his black pipe. 'Maybe he was right. I have seen stones lying about that may well be that.'

The man was pleased and willing to talk to so good a listener. Either he had not noticed the curious gesture the other made, or he read it as a sign of eagerness to start. The sun was warm, but a sharp wind from the bare hills went between them with a sighing sound. Holt buttoned his coat about him. 'An odd name for a mountain lake – Blood Tarn,' he remarked, watching the landlord's face expectantly.

'Aye, but a good one,' was the measured reply. 'When I was a boy the old folk had a tale that the savages flung three Roman captives from that crag into the water. There's a book been written about it; they say it was a sacrifice, but most likely they were tired of dragging them along, I say. Anyway, that's what the writer said. One, I mind, now you ask me, was a priest of some heathen temple that stood near the Wall, and the other two were his daughter and her lover.' He guffawed. At least he made a strange noise in his throat. Evidently, thought Holt, he was sceptical yet superstitious. 'It's just an old tale handed down, whatever the learned folk may say,' the old man added.

'A lonely place,' began Holt, aware that a fleeting touch of awe was added suddenly to his interest.

'Aye,' said the other, 'and a bad spot too. Every year the Crag takes its toll of sheep, and sometimes a man goes over in the mist. It's right beside the track and very slippery. Ninety foot of a drop before you hit the water. Best keep round the tarn and leave the Crag alone if there's any mist about. Fishing? Yes, there's some quite fair trout in the tarn, but it's not much fished. Happen one of the shepherd lads from Tyson's farm may give it a turn with an "otter",' he went on, 'once in a while, but he won't stay for the evening. He'll clear out before sunset.'

'Ah! Superstitious, I suppose?'

'It's a gloomy, chancy spot – and with the dusk falling,' agreed the innkeeper eventually. 'None of our folk care to be caught up there with night coming on. Most handy for a shepherd, too – but Tyson can't get a man to bide there.' He paused again, then added significantly: 'Strangers don't seem to mind it, though. It's only our own folk—'

'Strangers!' repeated the other sharply, as though he had been waiting all along for this special bit of information. 'You don't mean to say there are people living up there?' A curious thrill ran over him.

'Aye,' replied the landlord, 'but they're daft folk – a man and his daughter. They come every spring. It's early in the year yet, but I mind Jim Backhouse, one of Tyson's men, talking about them last week.' He stopped to think. 'So they've come back,' he went on decidedly. 'They get milk from the farm.'

'And what on earth are they doing up there?' Holt asked.

He asked many other questions as well, but the answers were poor, the information not forthcoming. The landlord would talk for hours about the Crag, the tarn, the legends and the Romans, but concerning the two strangers he was uncommunicative. Either he knew little, or he did not want to discuss them; Holt felt it was probably the former. They were educated town-folk, he gathered with difficulty, rich apparently, and they spent their time wandering about the fell, or fishing. The man was often seen upon the Crag, his girl beside him, bare-legged, dressed as a peasant. 'Happen they come for their health, happen the father is a learned man studying the Wall' – exact information was not forthcoming.

The landlord 'minded his own business', and inhabitants were too few and far between for gossip. All Holt could extract amounted to this: the couple had been in a motor accident some years before, and as a result they came every spring to spend a month or two in absolute solitude, away from cities and the excitement of modern life. They troubled no one and no one troubled them.

'Perhaps I may see them as I go by the tarn,' remarked the walker finally, making ready to go. He gave up questioning in despair. The morning hours were passing.

'Happen you may,' was the reply, 'for your track goes past their door and leads straight down to Scarsdale. The other way over the Crag saves half a mile, but it's rough going along the scree.' He stopped dead. Then he added, in reply to Holt's good-bye: 'In my opinion it's not worth it,' yet what he meant exactly by 'it' was not quite clear.

The walker shouldered his knapsack. Instinctively he gave the little hitch to settle it on his shoulders – much as he used to give to his pack in France. The pain that shot through him as he did so was another reminder of France. The bullet he had stopped on the Somme still made its presence felt at times ... Yet he knew, as he walked off briskly, that he was one of the lucky ones. How many of his old pals would never walk again, condemned to hobble on crutches for the rest of their lives! How many, again, would never even hobble! More terrible still, he remembered, were the blind ... The dead, it seemed to him, had been more fortunate ...

He swung up the narrowing valley at a good pace and was soon climbing the fell. It proved far steeper than it had appeared from the door of the inn, and he was glad enough to reach the top and fling himself down on the coarse springy turf to admire the view below.

The spring day was delicious. It stirred his blood. The world beneath looked young and stainless. Emotion rose through him in a wave of optimistic happiness. The bare hills were half hidden by a soft blue haze that made them look bigger, vaster, less earthly than they really were. He saw silver streaks in the valleys that he knew were distant streams and lakes. Birds soared between. The dazzling air seemed painted with exhilarating light and colour. The very clouds were floating gossamer that he could touch. There were bees and dragon-flies and fluttering thistle-down. Heat vibrated. His body, his physical sensations, so-called, retired into almost nothing. He felt himself, like his surroundings, made of air and sunlight. A delicious sense of resignation poured upon him. He, too, like his surroundings, was composed of air and sunshine, of insect wings, of soft, fluttering vibrations that the gorgeous spring day produced ... It seemed that he renounced the heavy dues of bodily life, and enjoyed the delights, momentarily at any rate, of a more ethereal consciousness.

Near at hand, the hills were covered with the faded gold of last year's bracken, which ran down in a brimming flood till it was lost in the fresh green of the familiar woods below. Far in the hazy distance swam the sea of ash and hazel. The silver birch sprinkled that lower world with fairy light.

Yes, it was all natural enough. He could see the road quite clearly now, only a hundred yards away from where he lay. How straight it ran along the top of the hill! The landlord's expression recurred to him: 'Straight as a spear.' Somehow, the phrase seemed to describe exactly the Romans and all their works ... The Romans, yes, and all their works ...

He became aware of a sudden sympathy with these long-dead conquerors of the world. With them, he felt sure, there had been no useless, foolish talk. They had known no empty words, no bandying of foolish phrases. 'War to end war', and 'Regeneration of the race' – no hypocritical nonsense of that sort had troubled their minds and purposes. They had not attempted to cover up the horrible in words. With them had been no childish, vain pretence. They had gone straight to their ends.

Other thoughts, too, stole over him, as he sat gazing down upon the track of that ancient road; strange thoughts, not wholly welcome. New, yet old, emotions rose in a tide upon him. He began to wonder ... Had he, after all, become brutalised by the War? He knew quite well that the little 'Christianity' he inherited had soon fallen from him like a garment in France. In his attitude to Life and Death he had become, frankly, pagan. He now realised, abruptly, another thing as well: in reality he had never been a 'Christian' at any time. Given to him with his mother's milk, he had never accepted, felt at home with Christian dogmas. To him they had always been an alien creed. Christianity met none of his requirements ...

But what were his 'requirements'? He found it difficult to answer.

Something, at any rate, different and more primitive, he thought ...

Even up here, alone on the mountain-top, it was hard to be absolutely frank with himself. With a kind of savage, honest determination, he bent himself to the task. It became suddenly important for him. He must know exactly where he stood. It seemed he had reached a turning point in his life. The War, in the objective world, had been one such turning point; now he had reached another, in the subjective life, and it was more important than the first.

As he lay there in the pleasant sunshine, his thoughts went back to the fighting. A friend, he recalled, had divided people into those who enjoyed the War and those who didn't. He was obliged to admit that he had been one of the former – he had thoroughly enjoyed it. Brought up from a youth as an engineer, he had taken to a soldier's life as a duck takes to water. There had been plenty of misery, discomfort, wretchedness; but there had been compensations that, for him, outweighed them. The fierce excitement, the primitive, naked passions, the wild fury, the reckless indifference to pain and death, with the loss of the normal, cautious, pettifogging little daily self all these involved, had satisfied him. Even the actual killing . . .

He started. A slight shudder ran down his back as the cool wind from the open moorlands came sighing across the soft spring sunshine. Sitting up straight, he looked behind him a moment, as with an effort to turn away from something he disliked and dreaded because it was, he knew, too strong for him. But the same instant he turned round again. He faced the vile and dreadful thing in himself he had hitherto sought to deny, evade. Pretence fell away. He could not disguise from himself that he had thoroughly enjoyed the killing; or, at any rate, had not been shocked by it as by an unnatural and ghastly duty. The shooting and bombing he performed with an effort always, but the rarer moments when he had been able to use the bayonet . . . the joy of feeling the steel go home . . .

He started again, hiding his face a moment in his hands, but he did not try to evade the hideous memories that surged. At times, he knew, he had gone quite mad with the lust of slaughter; he had gone on long after he should have stopped. Once an officer had pulled him up sharply for it, but the next instant had been killed by a bullet. He thought he had gone on killing, but he did not know. It was all a red mist before his eyes and he could only remember the sticky feeling of the blood on his hands when he gripped his rifle . . .

And now, at this moment of painful honesty with himself, he realised that his creed, whatever it was, must cover all that; it must provide some sort of a philosophy for it; must neither apologise nor ignore it. The heaven that it promised must be a man's heaven. The Christian heaven made no appeal to him, he could not believe in it. The ritual must be simple and direct. He felt that in some dim way he understood why those old people had thrown their captives from the Crag. The sacrifice of an animal victim that could be eaten afterwards with due ceremonial did not shock him. Such methods seemed simple, natural, effective. Yet would it not have been better – the horrid thought rose unbidden in his inmost mind – better to have cut their throats with a flint knife . . . slowly?

Horror-stricken, he sprang to his feet. These terrible thoughts he could not recognise as his own. Had he slept a moment in the sunlight, dreaming them? Was it some hideous nightmare flash that touched him as he dozed a second? Something of fear and awe stole over him. He stared round for some minutes into the emptiness of the desolate landscape, then hurriedly ran down to the road, hoping to exorcise the strange sudden horror by vigorous movement. Yet when he reached the track he knew that he had not succeeded. The awful pictures were gone perhaps, but the mood remained. It was as though some new attitude began to take definite form and harden within him.

He walked on, trying to pretend to himself that he was some forgotten legionary marching up with his fellows to defend the Wall. Half unconsciously he fell into the steady tramping pace of his old regiment: the words of the ribald songs they had sung going to the front came pouring into his mind. Steadily and almost mechanically he swung along till he saw the Stone as a black speck on the left of the track, and the instant he saw it there rose in him the feeling that he stood upon the edge of an adventure that he feared yet longed for. He approached the great granite monolith with a curious thrill of anticipatory excitement, born he knew not whence.

But, of course, there was nothing. Common sense, still operating strongly, had warned him there would be, could be, nothing. In the waste the great Stone stood upright, solitary, forbidding, as it had stood for thousands of years. It dominated the landscape somewhat ominously. The sheep and cattle had used it as a rubbing-stone, and bits of hair and wool clung to its rough, weather-eaten edges; the feet of generations had worn a cup-shaped hollow at its base. The wind sighed round it plaintively. Its bulk glistened as it took the sun.

A short mile away the Blood Tarn was now plainly visible; he could see the little holm lying in a direct line with the Stone, while, overhanging the water as a dark shadow on one side, rose the cliff-like rock they called 'the Crag'. Of the house the landlord had mentioned, however, he could see no trace, as he relieved his shoulders of the knapsack and sat down to enjoy his lunch. The tarn, he reflected, was certainly a gloomy place; he could understand that the simple superstitious shepherds did not dare to live there, for even on this bright spring day it wore a dismal and forbidding look. With failing light, when the Crag sprawled its big lengthening shadow across the water, he could well imagine they would give it the widest possible berth. He strolled down to the shore after lunch, smoking his pipe lazily – then suddenly stood still. At the far end, hidden hitherto by a fold in the ground, he saw the little house, a faint column of blue smoke rising from the chimney, and at the same moment a woman came out of the low door and began to walk towards the tarn. She had seen him, she was moving evidently in his direction; a few minutes later she stopped and stood waiting on the path – waiting, he well knew, for him.

And his earlier mood, the mood he dreaded yet had forced himself to recognise, came back upon him with sudden redoubled power. As in some vivid dream that dominates and paralyses the will, or as in the first stages of an imposed hypnotic spell, all question, hesitation, refusal sank away. He felt a pleasurable resignation steal upon him with soft, numbing effect. Denial and criticism ceased to operate, and common sense died with them. He yielded his being automatically to the deeps of an adventure he did not understand. He began to walk towards the woman.

It was, he saw as he drew nearer, the figure of a young girl, nineteen or twenty years of age, who stood there motionless with her eyes fixed steadily on his own. She looked as wild and picturesque as the scene that framed her. Thick black hair hung loose over her back and shoulders; about her head was bound a green ribbon; her clothes consisted of a jersey and a very short skirt which showed her bare legs browned by exposure to the sun and wind. A pair of rough sandals covered her feet. Whether the face was beautiful or not he could not tell; he only knew that it attracted him immensely and with a strength of appeal that he at once felt curiously irresistible. She remained motionless against the boulder, staring fixedly at him till he was close before her. Then she spoke:

'I am glad that you have come at last,' she said in a clear, strong voice that yet was soft and even tender. 'We have been expecting you.'

'You have been expecting me!' he repeated, astonished beyond words, yet finding the language natural, right and true. A stream of sweet feeling invaded him, his heart beat faster, he felt happy and at home in some extraordinary way he could not understand yet did not question.

'Of course,' she answered, looking straight into his eyes with welcome unashamed. Her next words thrilled him to the core of his being. 'I have made the room ready for you.'

Quick upon her own, however, flashed back the landlord's words, while common sense made a last faint effort in his thought. He was the victim of some absurd mistake evidently. The lonely life, the forbidding surroundings, the associations of the desolate hills had affected her mind. He remembered the accident.

'I am afraid,' he offered, lamely enough, 'there is some mistake. I am not the friend you were expecting. I—' He stopped. A thin, slight sound as of distant laughter seemed to echo behind the unconvincing words.

'There is no mistake,' the girl answered firmly, with a quiet smile, moving a step nearer to him, so that he caught the subtle perfume of her vigorous youth. 'I saw you clearly in the Mystery Stone. I recognised you at once.'

'The Mystery Stone,' he heard himself saying, bewilderment increasing, a sense of wild happiness growing with it.

Laughing, she took his hand in hers. 'Come,' she said, drawing him along with her, 'come home with me. My father will be waiting for us; he will tell you everything, and better far than I can.'

He went with her, feeling that he was made of sunlight and that he walked on air, for at her touch his own hand responded as with a sudden fierceness of pleasure that he failed utterly to understand, yet did not question for an instant. Wildly, absurdly, madly it flashed across his mind: 'This is the woman I shall marry – *my* woman. I am her man.'

They walked in silence for a little, for no words of any sort offered themselves to his mind, nor did the girl attempt to speak. The total absence of embarrassment between them occurred to him once or twice as curious, though the very idea of embarrassment then disappeared entirely. It all seemed natural and unforced, the sudden intercourse as familiar and effortless as though they had known one another always.

'The Mystery Stone,' he heard himself saying presently, as the idea rose again to the surface of his mind. 'I should like to know more about it. Tell me, dear.'

'I bought it with the other things,' she replied softly.

'What other things?'

She turned and looked up into his face with a slight expression of surprise; their shoulders touched as they swung along; her hair blew in the wind across his coat. 'The bronze collar,' she answered in the low voice that pleased him so, 'and this ornament that I wear in my hair.'

He glanced down to examine it. Instead of a ribbon, as he had first supposed, he saw that it was a circlet of bronze, covered with a beautiful green patina and evidently very old. In front, above the forehead, was a small disk bearing an inscription he could not decipher at the moment. He bent down and kissed her hair, the girl smiling with happy contentment, but offering no sign of resistance or annoyance.

'And,' she added suddenly, 'the dagger.'

Holt started visibly. This time there was a thrill in her voice that seemed to pierce down straight into his heart. He said nothing, however. The unexpectedness of the word she used, together with the note in her voice that moved him so strangely, had a disconcerting effect that kept him silent for a time. He did not ask about the dagger. Something prevented his curiosity finding expression in speech, though the word, with the marked accent she placed upon it, had struck into him like the shock of sudden steel itself, causing him an indecipherable emotion of both joy and pain. He asked instead, presently, another question, and a very commonplace one: he asked where she and her father had lived before they came to these lonely hills. And the form of his question – his voice shook a little as he said it – was, again, an effort of his normal self to maintain its already precarious balance.

The effect of his simple query, the girl's reply above all, increased in him the mingled sensations of sweetness and menace, of joy and dread, that half alarmed, half satisfied him. For a moment she wore a puzzled expression, as though making an effort to remember.

'Down by the sea,' she answered slowly, thoughtfully, her voice very low. 'Somewhere by a big harbour with great ships coming in and out. It was there we had the break – the shock – an accident that broke us, shattering the dream we share To-day.' Her face cleared a little. 'We were in a chariot,' she went on more easily and rapidly, 'and father – my father was injured, so that I went with him to a palace beyond the Wall till he grew well.'

'You were in a chariot?' Holt repeated. 'Surely not.'

'Did I say chariot?' the girl replied. 'How foolish of me!' She shook her hair back as though the gesture helped to clear her mind and memory. 'That belongs, of course, to the other dream. No, not a chariot; it was a car. But it had wheels like a chariot – the old war-chariots. You know.'

'Disk-wheels,' thought Holt to himself. He did not ask about the palace. He asked instead where she had bought the Mystery Stone, as she called it, and the other things. Her reply bemused and enticed him farther, for he could not unravel it. His whole inner attitude was shifting with uncanny rapidity and completeness. They walked together, he now realised, with linked arms, moving slowly in step, their bodies touching. He felt the blood run hot and almost savage in his veins. He was aware how amazingly precious she was to him, how deeply, absolutely necessary to his life and happiness. Her words went past him in the mountain wind like flying birds.

'My father was fishing,' she went on, 'and I was on my way to join him, when the old woman called me into her dwelling and showed me the things. She wished to give them to me, but I refused the present and paid for them in gold. I put the fillet on my head to see if it would fit, and took the Mystery Stone in my hand. Then, as I looked deep into the stone, this present dream died all away. It faded out. I saw the older dreams again – *our* dreams.'

'The older dreams!' interrupted Holt. 'Ours!' But instead of saying the words aloud, they issued from his lips in a quiet whisper, as though control of his voice had passed a little from him. The sweetness in him became more wonderful, unmanageable; his astonishment had vanished; he walked and talked with his old familiar happy Love, the woman he had sought so long and waited for, the woman who was his mate, as he was hers, she who alone could satisfy his inmost soul.

'The old dream,' she replied, 'the very old – the oldest of all perhaps – when we committed the terrible sacrilege. I saw the High Priest lying dead – whom my father slew – and the other whom *you* destroyed. I saw you prise out the jewel from the image of the god – with your short bloody spear. I saw, too, our flight to the galley through the hot, awful night beneath the stars – and our escape . . .'

Her voice died away and she fell silent.

'Tell me more,' he whispered, drawing her closer against his side. 'What had *you* done?' His heart was racing now. Some fighting blood surged uppermost. He felt that he could kill, and the joy of violence and slaughter rose in him.

'Have you forgotten so completely?' she asked very low, as he pressed her more tightly still against his heart. And almost beneath her breath she whispered into his ear, which he bent to catch the little sound: 'I had broken my vows with you.'

'What else, my lovely one – my best beloved – what more did you see?' he whispered in return, yet wondering why the fierce pain and anger that he felt behind still lay hidden from betrayal.

'Dream after dream, and always we were punished. But the last time was the clearest, for it was here – here where we now walk together in the sunlight and the wind – it was here the savages hurled us from the rock.'

A shiver ran through him, making him tremble with an unaccountable touch of cold that communicated itself to her as well. Her arm went instantly about his shoulder, as he stooped and kissed her passionately. 'Fasten your coat about you,' she said tenderly, but with troubled breath, when he released her, 'for this wind is chill although the sun shines brightly. We were glad, you remember, when they stopped to kill us, for we were tired and our feet were cut to pieces by the long, rough journey from the Wall.' Then suddenly her voice grew louder again and the smile of happy confidence came back into her eyes. There was the deep earnestness of love in it, of love that cannot end or die. She looked up into his face. 'But soon now,' she said, 'we shall be free. For you have come, and it is nearly finished – this weary little present dream.'

'How,' he asked, 'shall we get free?' A red mist swam momentarily before his eyes.

'My father,' she replied at once, 'will tell you all. It is quite easy.'

'Your father, too, remembers?'

'The moment the collar touches him,' she said, 'he is a priest again. See! Here he comes forth already to meet us, and to bid you welcome.'

Holt looked up, startled. He had hardly noticed, so absorbed had he been in the words that half intoxicated him, the distance they had covered. The cottage was now close at hand, and a tall, powerfully built man, wearing a shepherd's rough clothing, stood a few feet in front of him. His stature, breadth of shoulder and thick black beard made up a striking figure. The dark eyes, with fire in them, gazed straight into his own, and a kindly smile played round the stern and vigorous mouth.

'Greeting, my son,' said a deep, booming voice, 'for I shall call you my son as I did of old. The bond of the spirit is stronger than that of the flesh, and with us three the tie is indeed of triple strength. You come, too, at an auspicious hour, for the omens are favourable and the time of our liberation is at hand.' He took the other's hand in a grip that might have killed an ox and yet was warm with gentle kindliness, while Holt, now caught wholly into the spirit of some deep reality he could not master yet accepted, saw that the wrist was small, the fingers shapely, the gesture itself one of dignity and refinement.

'Greeting, my father,' he replied, as naturally as though he said more modern words.

'Come in with me, I pray,' pursued the other, leading the way, 'and let me show you the poor accommodation we have provided, yet the best that we can offer.'

He stooped to pass the threshold, and as Holt stooped likewise, the girl took his hand and he knew that his bewitchment was complete. Entering the low doorway, he passed through a kitchen, where only the roughest, scantiest furniture was visible, into another room that was completely bare. A heap of dried bracken had been spread on the floor in one corner to form a bed. Beside it lay two cheap, coloured blankets. There was nothing else.

'Our place is poor,' said the man, smiling courteously, but with that dignity and air of welcome which made the hovel seem a palace. 'Yet it may serve, perhaps, for the short time that you will need it. Our little dream here is well-nigh over, now that you have come. The long weary pilgrimage at last draws to a close.' The girl had left them alone a moment, and the man stepped closer to his guest. His face grew solemn, his voice deeper and more earnest suddenly, the light in his eyes seemed actually to flame with the enthusiasm of a great belief. 'Why have you tarried thus so long, and where?' he asked in a lowered tone that vibrated in the little space. 'We have sought you with prayer and fasting, and she has spent her nights for you in tears. You lost the way, it must be. The lesser dreams entangled your feet, I see.' A touch of sadness entered the voice, the eyes held pity in them. 'It is, alas, too easy, I well know,' he murmured. 'It is too easy.'

'I lost the way,' the other replied. It seemed suddenly that his heart was filled with fire. 'But now,' he cried aloud, 'now that I have found her, I will never, never let her go again. My feet are steady and my way is sure.'

'For ever and ever, my son,' boomed the happy, yet almost solemn answer, 'she is yours. Our freedom is at hand.'

He turned and crossed the little kitchen again, making a sign that his guest should follow him. They stood together by the door, looking out across the tarn in silence. The afternoon sunshine fell in a golden blaze across the bare hills that seemed to smoke with the glory of the fiery light. But the Crag loomed dark in shadow overhead, and the little lake lay deep and black beneath it.

'Acella, Acella!' called the man, the name breaking upon his companion as with a shock of sweet delicious fire that filled his entire being, as the girl came the same instant from behind the cottage. 'The Gods call me,' said her father. 'I go now to the hill. Protect our guest and comfort him in my absence.'

Without another word, he strode away up the hillside and presently was visible standing on the summit of the Crag, his arms stretched out above his head to heaven, his great head thrown back, his bearded face turned upwards. An impressive, even a majestic figure he looked, as his bulk and stature rose in dark silhouette against the brilliant evening sky. Holt stood motionless, watching him for several minutes, his heart swelling in his breast, his pulses thumping before some great nameless pressure that rose from the depths of his being. That inner attitude which seemed a new and yet more satisfying attitude to life than he had known hitherto, had crystallised. Define it he could not, he only knew that he accepted it as natural. It satisfied him. The sight of that dignified, gaunt figure worshipping upon the hill-top enflamed him . . .

'I have brought the stone,' a voice interrupted his reflections, and turning, he saw the girl beside him. She held out for his inspection a dark square object that looked to him at first like a black stone lying against the brown skin of her hand. 'The Mystery Stone,' the girl added, as their faces bent down together to examine it. 'It is there I see the dreams I told you of.'

He took it from her and found that it was heavy, composed

apparently of something like black quartz, with a brilliant polished surface that revealed clear depths within. Once, evidently, it had been set in a stand or frame, for the marks where it had been attached still showed, and it was obviously of great age. He felt confused, the mind in him troubled yet excited as he gazed. The effect upon him was as though a wind rose suddenly and passed across his inmost subjective life, setting its entire contents in rushing motion.

'And here,' the girl said, 'is the dagger.'

He took from her the short bronze weapon, feeling at once instinctively its ragged edge, its keen point, sharp and effective still. The handle had long since rotted away, but the bronze tongue, and the holes where the rivets had been, remained, and, as he touched it, the confusion and trouble in his mind increased to a kind of turmoil, in which violence, linked to something tameless, wild and almost savage, was the dominating emotion. He turned to seize the girl and crush her to him in a passionate embrace, but she held away, throwing back her lovely head, her eyes shining, her lips parted, yet one hand stretched out to stop him.

'First look into it with me,' she said quietly. 'Let us see together.'

She sat down on the turf beside the cottage door, and Holt, obeying, took his place beside her. She remained very still for some minutes, covering the stone with both hands as though to warm it. Her lips moved. She seemed to be repeating some kind of invocation beneath her breath, though no actual words were audible. Presently her hands parted. They sat together gazing at the polished surface. They looked within.

'There comes a white mist in the heart of the stone,' the girl whispered. 'It will soon open. The pictures will then grow. Look!' she exclaimed after a brief pause, 'they are forming now.'

'I see only mist,' her companion murmured, gazing intently. 'Only mist I see.'

She took his hand and instantly the mist parted. He found

himself peering into another landscape which opened before his eyes as though it were a photograph. Hills covered with heather stretched away on every side.

'Hills, I see,' he whispered. 'The ancient hills—'

'Watch closely,' she replied, holding his hand firmly.

At first the landscape was devoid of any sign of life; then suddenly it surged and swarmed with moving figures. Torrents of men poured over the hill-crests and down their heathery sides in columns. He could see them clearly – great hairy men, clad in skins, with thick shields on their left arms or slung over their backs, and short stabbing spears in their hands. Thousands upon thousands poured over in an endless stream. In the distance he could see other columns sweeping in a turning movement. A few of the men rode rough ponies and seemed to be directing the march, and these, he knew, were the chiefs . . .

The scene grew dimmer, faded, died away completely. Another took its place:

By the faint light he knew that it was dawn. The undulating country, less hilly than before, was still wild and uncultivated. A great wall, with towers at intervals, stretched away till it was lost in shadowy distance. On the nearest of these towers he saw a sentinel clad in armour, gazing out across the rolling country. The armour gleamed faintly in the pale glimmering light, as the man suddenly snatched up a bugle and blew upon it. From a brazier burning beside him he next seized a brand and fired a great heap of brushwood. The smoke rose in a dense column into the air almost immediately, and from all directions, with incredible rapidity, figures came pouring up to man the wall. Hurriedly they strung their bows, and laid spare arrows close beside them on the coping. The light grew brighter. The whole country was alive with savages; like the waves of the sea they came rolling in enormous numbers. For several minutes the wall held. Then, in an impetuous, fearful torrent, they poured over . . .

It faded, died away, was gone again, and a moment later yet another took its place.

But this time the landscape was familiar, and he recognised the tarn. He saw the savages upon the ledge that flanked the dominating Crag; they had three captives with them. He saw two men. The other was a woman. But the woman had fallen exhausted to the ground, and a chief on a rough pony rode back to see what had delayed the march. Glancing at the captives, he made a fierce gesture with his arm towards the water far below. Instantly the woman was jerked cruelly to her feet and forced onwards till the summit of the Crag was reached. A man snatched something from her hand. A second later she was hurled over the brink.

The two men were next dragged on to the dizzy spot where she had stood. Dead with fatigue, bleeding from numerous wounds, yet at this awful moment they straightened themselves, casting contemptuous glances at the fierce savages surrounding them. They were Romans and would die like Romans. Holt saw their faces clearly for the first time.

He sprang up with a cry of anguished fury.

'The second man!' he exclaimed. 'You saw the second man!'

The girl, releasing his hand, turned her eyes slowly up to his, so that he met the flame of her ancient and undying love shining like stars upon him out of the night of time.

'Ever since that moment,' she said in a low voice that trembled, 'I have been looking, waiting for you—'

He took her in his arms and smothered her words with kisses, holding her fiercely to him as though he would never let her go. 'I, too,' he said, his whole being burning with his love, 'I have been looking, waiting for you. Now I have found you. We have found each other . . . !'

The dusk fell slowly, imperceptibly. As twilight slowly draped the gaunt hills, blotting out familiar details, so the strong dream, veil upon veil, drew closer over the soul of the wanderer, obliterating finally the last reminder of To-day. The little wind had dropped and the desolate moors lay silent, but for the hum of distant water falling to its valley bed. His life, too, and the life of the girl, he knew, were similarly falling, falling into some deep shadowed bed where rest would come at last. No details troubled him; he asked himself no questions. A profound sense of happy peace numbed every nerve and stilled his beating heart.

He felt no fear, no anxiety, no hint of alarm or uneasiness vexed his singular contentment. He realised one thing only – that the girl lay in his arms, he held her fast, her breath mingled with his own. They had found each other. What else mattered?

From time to time, as the daylight faded and the sun went down behind the moors, she spoke. She uttered words he vaguely heard, listening, though with a certain curious effort, before he closed the thing she said with kisses. Even the fierceness of his blood was gone. The world lay still, life almost ceased to flow. Lapped in the deeps of his great love, he was redeemed, perhaps, of violence and savagery . . .

'Three dark birds,' she whispered, 'pass across the sky . . . they fall beyond the ridge. The omens are favourable. A hawk now follows them, cleaving the sky with pointed wings.'

'A hawk,' he murmured. 'The badge of my old Legion.'

'My father will perform the sacrifice,' he heard again, though it seemed a long interval had passed, and the man's figure was now invisible on the Crag amid the gathering darkness. 'Already he prepares the fire. Look, the sacred island is alight. He has the black cock ready for the knife.'

Holt roused himself with difficulty, lifting his face from the garden of her hair. A faint light, he saw, gleamed fitfully on the holm within the tarn. Her father, then, had descended from the Crag, and had lit the sacrificial fire upon the stones. But what did the doings of the father matter now to him?

'The dark bird,' he repeated dully, 'the black victim the Gods of the Underworld alone accept. It is good, Acella, it is good!' He was about to sink back again, taking her against his breast as before, when she resisted and sat up suddenly.

'It is time,' she said aloud. 'The hour has come. My father climbs, and we must join him on the summit. Come!'

She took his hand and raised him to his feet, and together they began the rough ascent towards the Crag. As they passed along the shore of the Tarn of Blood, he saw the fire reflected in the ink-black waters; he made out, too, though dimly, a rough circle of big stones, with a larger flag-stone lying in the centre. Three small fires of bracken and wood, placed in a triangle with its apex towards the Standing Stone on the distant hill, burned briskly, the crackling material sending out sparks that pierced the columns of thick smoke. And in this smoke, peering, shifting, appearing and disappearing, it seemed he saw great faces moving. The flickering light and twirling smoke made clear sight difficult. His bliss, his lethargy were very deep. They left the tarn below them and hand in hand began to climb the final slope.

Whether the physical effort of climbing disturbed the deep pressure of the mood that numbed his senses, or whether the cold draught of wind they met upon the ridge restored some vital detail of To-day, Holt does not know. Something, at any rate, in him wavered suddenly, as though a centre of gravity had shifted slightly. There was a perceptible alteration in the balance of thought and feeling that had held invariable now for many hours. It seemed to him that something heavy lifted, or rather, began to lift – a weight, a shadow, something oppressive that obstructed light. A ray of light, as it were, struggled through the thick darkness that enveloped him. To him, as he paused on the ridge to recover his breath, came this vague suggestion of faint light breaking across the blackness. It was objective.

'See,' said the girl in a low voice, 'the moon is rising. It lights the sacred island. The blood-red waters turn to silver.'

He saw, indeed, that a huge three-quarter moon now drove with almost visible movement above the distant line of hills; the little tarn gleamed as with silvery armour; the glow of the sacrificial fires showed red across it. He looked down with a shudder into the sheer depth that opened at his feet, then turned to look at his companion. He started and shrank back. Her face, lit by the moon and by the fire, shone pale as death; her black hair framed it with a terrible suggestiveness; the eyes, though brilliant as ever, had a film upon them. She stood in an attitude of both ecstasy and resignation, and one outstretched arm pointed towards the summit where her father stood.

Her lips parted, a marvellous smile broke over her features, her voice was suddenly unfamiliar: 'He wears the collar,' she uttered. 'Come. Our time is here at last, and we are ready. See, he waits for us!'

There rose for the first time struggle and opposition in him; he resisted the pressure of her hand that had seized his own and drew him forcibly along. Whence came the resistance and the opposition he could not tell, but though he followed her, he was aware that the refusal in him strengthened. The weight of darkness that oppressed him shifted a little more, an inner light increased. The same moment they reached the summit and stood beside – the priest. There was a curious sound of fluttering. The figure, he saw, was naked, save for a rough blanket tied loosely about the waist.

'The hour has come at last,' cried his deep booming voice that woke echoes from the dark hills about them. 'We are alone now with our Gods.' And he broke then into a monotonous rhythmic chanting that rose and fell upon the wind, yet in a tongue that sounded strange; his erect figure swayed slightly with its cadences; his black beard swept his naked chest; and his face, turned skywards, shone in the mingled light of moon above and fire below, yet with an added light as well that burned within him rather than without. He was a weird, magnificent figure, a priest of ancient rites invoking his deathless deities upon the unchanging hills.

But upon Holt, too, as he stared in awed amazement, an inner light had broken suddenly. It came as with a dazzling blaze that at first paralysed thought and action. His mind cleared, but too abruptly for movement, either of tongue or hand, to be possible. Then, abruptly, the inner darkness rolled away completely. The light in the wild eyes of the great chanting, swaying figure, he now knew was the light of mania.

The faint fluttering sound increased, and the voice of the girl was oddly mingled with it. The priest had ceased his invocation. Holt, aware that he stood alone, saw the girl go past him carrying a big black bird that struggled with vainly beating wings.

'Behold the sacrifice,' she said, as she knelt before her father and held up the victim. 'May the Gods accept it as presently They shall accept us too!'

The great figure stooped and took the offering, and with one blow of the knife he held, its head was severed from its body. The blood spattered on the white face of the kneeling girl. Holt was aware for the first time that she, too, was now unclothed; but for a loose blanket, her white body gleamed against the dark heather in the moonlight. At the same moment she rose to her feet, stood upright, turned towards him so that he saw the dark hair streaming across her naked shoulders, and, with a face of ecstasy, yet ever that strange film upon her eyes, her voice came to him on the wind:

'Farewell, yet not farewell! We shall meet, all three, in the underworld. The Gods accept us!'

Turning her face away, she stepped towards the ominous figure behind, and bared her ivory neck and breast to the knife. The eyes of the maniac were upon her own; she was as helpless and obedient as a lamb before his spell.

Then Holt's horrible paralysis, if only just in time, was lifted.

The priest had raised his arm, the bronze knife with its ragged edge gleamed in the air, with the other hand he had already gathered up the thick dark hair, so that the neck lay bare and open to the final blow. But it was two other details, Holt thinks, that set his muscles suddenly free, enabling him to act with the swift judgment which, being wholly unexpected, disconcerted both maniac and victim and frustrated the awful culmination. The dark spots of blood upon the face he loved, and the sudden final fluttering of the dead bird's wings upon the ground – these two things, life actually touching death, released the held-back springs.

He leaped forward. He received the blow upon his left arm and hand. It was his right fist that sent the High Priest to earth with a blow that, luckily, felled him in the direction away from the dreadful brink, and it was his right arm and hand, he became aware some time afterwards only, that were chiefly of use in carrying the fainting girl and her unconscious father back to the shelter of the cottage, and to the best help and comfort he could provide . . .

It was several years afterwards, in a very different setting, that he found himself spelling out slowly to a little boy the lettering cut into a circlet of bronze the child found on his study table. To the child he told a fairy tale, then dismissed him to play with his mother in the garden. But, when alone, he rubbed away the verdigris with great care, for the circlet was thin and frail with age, as he examined again the little picture of a tripod from which smoke issued, incised neatly in the metal. Below it, almost as sharp as when the Roman craftsman cut it first, was the name Acella. He touched the letters tenderly with his left hand, from which two fingers were missing, then placed it in a drawer of his desk and turned the key.

'That curious name,' said a low voice behind his chair. His wife had come in and was looking over his shoulder. 'You love it, and I dread it.' She sat on the desk beside him, her eyes troubled. 'It was the name father used to call me in his illness.'

Her husband looked at her with passionate tenderness, but said no word.

'And this,' she went on, taking the broken hand in both her own, 'is the price you paid to me for his life. I often wonder what strange good deity brought you upon the lonely moor that night, and just in the very nick of time. You remember . . . ?'

'The deity who helps true lovers, of course,' he said with a smile, evading the question. The deeper memory, he knew, had closed absolutely in her since the moment of the attempted double crime. He kissed her, murmuring to himself as he did so, but too low for her to hear, 'Acella! *My* Acella . . . !'

HOW PAN CAME TO LITTLE INGLETON

by

Margery Lawrence

First published in the collection
Nights of the Round Table

1926

LITTLE INGLETON, DROWSY in the summer sun, lay curled like a sleepy child in the hollowed arm-curves of the mothering green hills that cradled it. Warm and white and frankly sleepy on a Sunday afternoon lay Little Ingleton, and the Reverend Thomas Minchin was cross.

In the inexplicable absence of Potts the bellringer, Mr Minchin was tolling the school-house bell for Sunday School. He tolled the bell industriously, but the wooden lych-gate gave no click to announce an entering scholar; the waiting cypresses stood tall and grim beside the old green-mossed headstones jostling each other up and down the little hill-perched graveyard, and the Reverend Thomas peered out now and again and gave the bell an extra angry tug in his annoyance – but sleep and the idleness of Midsummer Day held his parishioners, and not even Miss Rosamond Perkins, the lady teacher in the Sunday School, seemed to mean to turn up; so at last, with a primmed-up mouth and a scowl that rivalled those on the faces of the grimacing gargoyles that watched him go, the Reverend Thomas Minchin, newly installed incumbent of

Little Ingleton, clapped on his black shovel-hat and stalked forth to find his strayed flock.

The Reverend Thomas did not yet know his way about the village very well – he was aware, as he plodded up the twisting little main street looking vaguely for the turning to Miss Perkins's lodgings, that he looked an incongruous figure in his dusty black garb against the prevailing glory of blue and gold and white, and the knowledge somehow gave an added edge to his already ruffled temper.

He was a lean, stooping ascetic of a man with narrow lips and pale intolerant eyes, and his primly buttoned black clerical coat over tight black trousers and clumping square-toed boots, his flat black felt hat jammed squarely down on his head, expressed his personality as surely as any courtesan's painted smile and shadowed eyes express hers. Though, to be sure, he would have been mightily enraged at the comparison – for was he not a man of God, a celibate, a teetotaller, a non-smoker, and in a word, all the other things that a clergyman (*vide* the Press) should be?

This being so, surely he should have earned the respect and obedience of his people, so that they flocked to listen to the Word – but the remembrance of the empty school-house that afternoon brought a fresh scowl of sour anger to the face of the Reverend Thomas, and as he turned into a winding lane that seemed to resemble Miss Perkins's description of her 'road' he muttered a word that in a layman's mouth might have resembled profanity.

Had he not instituted fresh services, countless in number and strict in their ordinances? Suppressed dancing in the village hall or on the green? Closed down The George and Crown except for the sale of ginger ale and such innocuous drinks – banished from the chemist's shop *poudre de riz*, lip rouge, scents and other snares of the devil? Who but he had worked unceasingly for the regeneration of Little Ingleton – sunk as he had found it, in idle happiness, with but one or at most two services 'a Sunday, and used (low be it spoken!) to the lax ways of his predecessor, old Father Fagan, frail, gentle, kindly, who, it was whispered, at times so far forgot his duties as a clergyman as to watch and even take part in dancings and singings and junketings on the village green? Even Miss Rosamond Perkins, who wore pretty summer dresses of pink or blue and yellow patterned with gay little flowers, and had bright eyes and cherry lips – though to be sure, the Reverend Thomas had never noticed whether her lips were red or no – even Miss Perkins was reputed to have danced and laughed and played with these unregenerates before the advent of sterner ways.

Now he came to remember it, Miss Perkins had actually once or twice been guilty of murmuring on a fine Sunday in the hot classroom that it might be better to take the children out in the woods 'to play with God' – to quote her own unusual phrase – 'to play with God in His lovely world' – than drone sleepily over their Bibles; but this had greatly scandalised the new vicar, and he had spoken so severely to Miss Rosamond Perkins about it that she had wept, and looking up at his austerity with eyes like bluebells drowned in tears, subsided into silence. Subsequently, he remembered with satisfaction, she had discarded her frivolous-patterned cotton frocks, her hat with its wreath of floppy roses, and taken to brown holland and a severe straw hat with a band of ribbon only . . . This had pleased him, as showing a commendable wish to improve, but today he remembered the earlier rebellious murmur, and reviewing things grimly in his mind, decided that for some reason Miss Perkins had suddenly 'broken out' and taken her little band of scholars to the woods or fields.

He quickened his step, sending up a little cloud of light floury dust, and his lips tightened as he peered through his short-sighted eyes at the names on the gates of the cottages. 'Rose Nook' was the name of the cottage, he knew – but it was strange, it seemed much further down the lane than he had surmised from Miss Perkins's description.

'Just round the corner of Pan's Lane – you can't miss it!' Now he came to think of it, he supposed this was 'Pan's Lane'? Curious name, that – must have some connection with the old Roman times, and their crude gods; curious how traces of that sort of thing linger. The Squire had told him that King's Panton, the little town in the valley's hollow, far below high-perched Little Ingleton, was so called for its old name: 'Kynge Pan hys towne'. Strange old heathen days – how thankful one should be for modern education, and enlightenment – now where was 'Rose Nook'? It was tiring, plodding along in this heat, and the mental picture of Miss Rosamond Perkins, cool and happy in some sylvan dell, with the adoring children around her listening to some absurd fairy story – the sort of imaginative rubbish she was far too fond of telling – made his ill-temper, already sour, more acid still. He would find out from old Mrs Calder, where Miss Perkins lodged, where they had gone, and follow after them – he would come upon them suddenly in their idleness, and see them cringe in shame and confusion before his righteous wrath, hurry tearfully back to the school-house to their books and catechism! . . . And as for Miss Perkins? She must be spoken to severely – more than severely . . .

He was walking so fast in his wrathful energy that in the cloud of dust he was raising he could not see anything distinctly, and stumbling over an obstacle in his path came down full length on his respectable nose, knocking himself completely breathless.

When, winded, angry and thoroughly undignified, he sat up at last, he found the obstacle over which he had stumbled was not one, but two – the long legs of a shabby young man in travel-stained grey flannel trousers, no shoes or socks, and a torn blue shirt, who sat surveying him gravely over a half-eaten hunk of bread.

'My goodness!' said the young man, 'you did come a cropper!' He laughed and took another bite.

The Reverend Thomas was still too breathless to reply, but he blinked and stared, endeavouring to recover a touch of his lost dignity; but as he stared around him, interest in his dignity was lost in his growing astonishment. Little as he knew of Little Ingleton, he was under the impression that he certainly knew by now all the lanes that ended in field-paths or *cul-de-sacs* – but it appeared he did not, for this lane was certainly new! Somehow it seemed to have fizzled out into a mere field-path winding away over the sloping hillside. Glancing back, Mr Minchin's puzzlement increased, and he concluded that, lost in his thoughts, he must have tramped further and faster than he meant, and left the village itself far behind.

A copse of trees, through which the tiny path wound, stood at his back, and all around the stillness of a summer afternoon brooded over green hill and sleepy valley, sentinel woods and white-flecked shining sky ... Under the lee of a steep bank the strange young man sat, nodding cheerfully at him, and continued to munch his bread, throwing the crumbs to an impertinent red squirrel, that, to Mr Minchin's great amazement, sat perched and chittering at his elbow.

Transferring his attention to the young man himself, Mr Minchin frowned. He wore no hat, and his face was brown as a pinecone, his hair bleached and wiry with the sun and wind; it stood up over each eye with a comic alert whisk that gave him a curiously impertinent appearance – his face was long and thin, with a narrow chin that ran to meet a hooked nose that stood out like a wedge between two light eyes – dancing, irreverent eyes, the colour of a hawk's. The Reverend Thomas winced and looked away from those eyes, and his resentment increased. What business had this ragged vagabond to survey him with such obvious amusement! He should have lowered his own eyes in shame at his garments – they were well-cut enough, but disgracefully torn and travel-stained, and that shirt! Well, not only were the sleeves rolled up to the shoulder, but the unbuttoned front lay open almost to the waist, showing skin burnt brown as the merry face, or very nearly – thus proving indubitably that this graceless fellow was in the habit of doing without even a shirt very often! . . .

'It's so much cooler in this hot weather!' said the stranger.

He took another bite, and Mr Minchin jumped. So astonished was he that he remained sitting on the path, his hands spread each side to support him, staring at the young man who had so curiously guessed his question and answered it. Coincidence – but – odd, very! . . .

'Decent clothing is scarcely a question of convenience,' he said stiffly.

The hooked nose came down over the lean chin and the young man grinned, surveying the dusty figure before him.

'Obviously, from your point of view, or you wouldn't wear those horrible black things! Why do you?'

Mr Minchin gasped in amazement; not only at the revolutionary suggestion contained in the remark, but at the stranger's temerity in making it.

He answered severely, rising and dusting the insulted clerical garments as best he could – though he was conscious, under the scrutiny of the merry-eyed stranger, that he was not cutting his usual dignified figure.

'You do not seem aware, sir, that I am a man of God!'

The stranger twinkled again, quite unimpressed.

'I can see you are a clergyman all right – is that what you call a man of God?'

Mr Minchin was outraged.

'Sir! Are you not a Christian, that you ask me such a question?'

The stranger threw a last handful of crumbs to the waiting squirrel, and clasping his hands round his dusty knees, surveyed Mr Minchin again. Then laughed, softly, oddly.

'A Christian? I don't think I've ever been asked that before!'

'Then it's quite time you were,' said Mr Minchin virtuously.

'Time – ah, there's so much time, isn't there?' said the stranger, rather irrelevantly. 'But to continue, O Man-of-God! What brings you wandering out here this Sunday afternoon – when presumably all Men-of-God should be herding their flocks willy-nilly into church?'

The faint flavour of insolence in the stranger's tone, strangely matching his impertinent upflaming hair, stung Mr Minchin, and his response was severe.

'I agree with you. But unfortunately . . . my Sunday School class did not appear, and I came out to find them . . .'

The young man, hunching his shoulders back against the warm red earth of the bank, laughed suddenly, amusedly: a gleeful spurt of laughter like the uprush of a spring to the sunlight.

'So for once Pan won, eh? The old gods against the new – the lure of the sun and the hills and the blue, blue sky . . . ha, ha! Well, my worthy son of the Christian church, go on . . . so you came a-wandering to find your straying flock, eh?'

'Er – yes . . .' For the life of him the Reverend Thomas could not quite help an odd little feeling of trepidation under the fire of the yellow hawk's eyes that watched him, and he finished lamely, 'And I – er – wandered considerably further than I meant . . .'

'You did indeed! . . .' said the young man grimly.

There was a moment's silence while he eyed the clergyman up and down, then down came the hooked nose again in a grin, and rolling over, he stretched for a shabby knapsack reposing against a giant root.

'Down Pan's Lane – into Panton Wood – over against Pan hys towne – and all on a Midsummer Day! Oh, wonderful – amazing – my poor dear earnest-minded friend!'

He extracted a fat round bottle and tin mug from the bag as he talked – sheer nonsense to the puzzled clergyman – and uncorking the bottle with a pop that certainly sounded more than luscious and tempting to the thirsty ears of the Vicar of Ingleton, poured out a foaming crimson draught and held it out invitingly.

'Have a drink, old boy? But I'm thirsty too – so drink fair!'

Despite his iron Prohibition principles it was with quite a considerable effort that Mr Minchin waved the mug away.

'Thank you, no. I quite realise you mean it kindly – but my cloth forbids.'

'Your cloth? Good Lord!' The stranger's laugh was faintly scornful – 'I've had many a cheery drink with other fellows of your cloth, as you call it! Come, drink up!'

'I am – fortunately – not concerned with the irregularities unfortunately committed by others of my calling,' said Mr Minchin stiffly.

Unmoved, the stranger quaffed the rejected wine; over the top of the mug his piercingly bright eyes stared at the clergyman. 'Mistakes? Are you then so much better than your fellows?' He set down the mug with a flourish. 'I seem to remember – somewhere – something about a Pharisee who thanked God he was not as other men . . .'

The Reverend Thomas flushed angrily, confounded and momentarily speechless. Before he could think out a sufficiently crushing answer, the young man was off again.

'So you're the new vicar of Little Ingleton? I've heard of you! Round about King's Panton – we've been talking quite a lot about you lately . . .'

This was a sop, and though Mr Minchin was feeling a little distrustful of this remarkable young man, he smiled; cautiously, warily, but he smiled. The allusion to King's Panton relieved his mind. This was probably – now he came to think of it – one of Mr Imray's fellows from King's Panton Manor House down in the valley; the verger had told him he always had five or six studying for exams, reading for the Bar, being coached . . . doubtless this was one of his pupils. Eccentric, of course – but obviously a gentleman . . . and to a gentleman even going barefoot and wearing an open-necked shirt might be excused, though Mr Minchin secretly hoped most devoutly that the stranger would not walk down the main street of Little Ingleton thus arrayed! King's Panton – that was fifteen miles away as the crow flies – it was certainly gratifying to hear that fifteen miles away they were talking of him and of his work in cleansing, in regenerating Little Ingleton . . .

'I don't know that I should quite call it that!' said the stranger coolly.

The Reverend Thomas jumped again, and the young man laughed.

'Oh, I'm a thought reader – one of my hobbies!' His eyes danced as he watched the other's chapfallen expression. 'Great fun it is – I often guess what our fellows are thinking about, and it makes them no end annoyed. But what makes you think you have done so much for Little Ingleton?'

Mr Minchin stiffened.

'I think, if you have heard as much about me as you say, that I need hardly answer that question?'

The young man looked at him reflectively.

'That, of course, is a matter of opinion!' he commented lazily. 'You may think that driving your school-children into a stuffy room on a gorgeous day like this is doing good . . .'

Mr Minchin exploded.

'Doing good? Doesn't the Prayer Book say—'

'I know all the Prayer Book says – read it all before you were born!' said the stranger brusquely.

In his annoyance Mr Minchin failed to note this remarkable assertion from a young man at most twenty-four.

'I know God demands a certain amount of attention.' His curious, half-wistful, half-insolent gaze strayed over the brooding hills, and he paused, then went on briskly – 'but I fancy, you know, that God is a fair-minded Deity . . . and if folk come to worship Him on a Sunday morning, what harm is there if for the rest of the day they give worship to other gods – and maybe other gods than He?'

Mr Minchin gasped in horror and amazement – the poor young man was mad, surely! – Mr Imray should not have let him go out without a hat in the sun . . . As the alarming thought that he might be consorting with a raving lunatic crossed his mind, the young man jumped up, and bursting into a frank laugh, stood arms akimbo in the sun watching him. Through all the bewildered fright and anger that confused him Mr Minchin was aware of a quick stab of sheer masculine jealousy of the slim wiry frame that confronted him, muscular and lithe and brown – why, he was only just thirty-four himself, and he should be like this long-limbed, suntanned vagabond, not a lean shrivelled bone of a man buttoned into a black coat and deliberately turning away his eyes when a pretty girl glanced at him! Through the heat and confusion of his thoughts the stranger's mocking voice came to him, taunting, accusing . . .

'. . . Done for them? That's what you're trying to do – do for them! Kill joy and youth and laughter in them to implant your wizened mean little creed instead! Because of your own dour miserable narrowness, you're trying to bully them into living life your way – you, with your bigotry and prudishness that sees sin and temptation in a flower in a hat, the gay colour of a pretty gown . . .'

'Black is the Lord's colour,' croaked the Reverend Thomas, though he was growing more and more dreadfully frightened, confused, puzzled . . . why, oh why, had nice quiet Mr Imray imported this crazy young man? His inquisitor's laugh was contemptuous.

'Are you sure you know Him? He never said anything like that to me! And as far as that goes, isn't it in your dour creed that He created all things, so, what of the scarlet poppy-flower, the blue-and-purple of the hills yonder, the gold of Rosamond Perkins's hair?'

'I have never noticed the colour of Miss Perkins's hair!' said Mr Minchin stiffly – the laugh that answered him stung him like the flick of a whip.

'Poor fool! You've kept your nose so long between the leaves of your dusty Book of Duty that you almost forget you are a man at all ... almost, almost you have remade yourself into a hard religious machine grinding out texts and platitudes and conventions! And yet still because I love my people – and perhaps a little because under those black absurdities of yours I discern the germ of a real man still, one worth saving—'

'A crazy revivalist ... must be!' muttered Mr Minchin to himself, catching at the explanatory straw. Above his shrinking head the voice went on, light, laughing, yet faintly menacing in its very laughter.

'... Didn't you stop little Molly Isitt from wearing a pink sash? Tell the Squire that to start a cinema in the village meant encouraging immorality – since it would be held in the dark? Get Miss Banks's maid, Ellen, sacked because you caught her kissing a gypsy in the lane? Abolish the kindly old custom of giving bread to beggars each Friday because it encouraged pauperism? Abolish beer-drinking and the use of perfumes? Forbid dancing and singing, and refuse permission for the yearly pageant to be held in the Vicarage grounds? ...'

'All vanity – and turning their thoughts from the Lord,' snuffled the Reverend Thomas feebly, for he was very frightened – above him the voice seemed to be shaping itself into a song of triumph and of scorn together, and he was shaking, cold, despite the glowing heat ...

'From the Lord! Oh Allah! Oh Set and Horus and Osiris! Oh Kali, Shiva, and all forgotten gods!' Oh, the ringing scorn of that laughter – shrivelled tiny the wretched listener felt as the voice boomed on. 'Oh Zeus, Apollo and goat-footed Pan! In the great world is there not room – is there not room for more than one God?'

It was evening when Mr Minchin awoke, and the slanting rays of the sun were touching his bare head over the bank. Staggering to his feet, stiffly enough, for it seemed he had slept a long time, he dusted and shook himself and turned to the copse behind him. The path opened out into the end of 'Pan's Lane' up which he had trudged so wearily in the afternoon, and as the clang of the bell for Evensong rang out he hastened his steps. He had slept too long indeed – it was still a little way to the church, and he always liked to be there a good while before the service, fussing about the choirboys, heckling the patient little humpbacked organist, arranging and rearranging his books and papers. As he came down the darkening graveyard he could see the people already filing into evening service, the single bell swinging in the square tower, and he frowned.

He would have to hurry to get into his surplice and head the procession – he almost ran down the incline to the crooked little vestry-door that hid slyly behind a buttress, and rushing to the cupboard, reached for his surplice . . . and gasped! It was no longer there! Neither his own, nor the clean white surplices of the choirboys, ironed and carefully hung up every Sunday by Mrs Kitson . . . As he stared, unable to believe his eyes, the organ burst forth into full volume and he realised the dreadful truth. The service had begun without him!

Staring vaguely round the vestry, Mr Minchin pinched himself, at first doubtfully, then viciously – the shock of the pain made him realise quite definitely that he was not dreaming, and a wave of anger took possession of him. How dare they – meek little Mr Lycett, his curate, Kitson the verger, Clubb the organist, all the rest? How dared they venture to open the service without him? Was it possible that he had invited a brother priest to conduct Evensong for him, and forgotten? No – it was impossible. Frazer of King's Panton was not free, and he knew no other . . . The organ boomed and surged around him, the choirboys sang lustily and the crowding people sang too . . . Though the church was full, it seemed that a long line of dark figures, black silhouettes against the violet evening sky, still streamed towards the door, and as they came, they sang . . .

Staggering to the little window, Mr Minchin watched them come – never in all his life, certainly never since his ministry in Little Ingleton, had so great and eager a congregation besieged his church, and beneath all his bewildered anger he felt a sharp pang of compunction, of shame. Surely, surely, had he known his work as he should have known it, this throng should have trooped before to listen to his teaching? . . . Suddenly his anger left him – gave place to bewilderment and a nameless deep-seated fear – and slipping noiselessly into the dimlit church, he crouched down in a distant pew, his heart for the first time in his narrow life humbled, abashed before a thing he could not understand.

The tall windows were slips of gleaming purple where the night sky showed through, and the one rose window in the nave, of gorgeous old painted glass, shone like a glorious jewelled buckler – the high-hung gas-lamps down the centre aisle shone out, round globes of yellow, like pale marsh-flares in the velvet gloom, but it seemed either a few of these had failed or else this summer dusk was heavier than usual, for the church was dimly lit on the whole.

From his far corner Mr Minchin could see the old pulpit with its supporting stone angels shrouded in their drooping wings; a corner of the lighted choirstalls, the carved oak lectern that bore the great leather-bound Bible with its gold-tasselled marker. As he looked at this his eyes bulged and he drew an astonished breath . . . it passed in a flash, but for a moment Mr Minchin had imagined he saw an audacious red squirrel, own twin to the furry creature that had eaten crumbs so tamely from the brown hand of the strange young man, dash down the stem of the lectern and vanish beside the pulpit! It was a mere impression, of course – must be – but Mr Minchin was not quite so sure of himself as he had been a few hours ago, and the supreme assurance with which he would have said 'Imagination!' had its tail between its legs and was already sneaking ignominiously away . . . A little way beyond him stood a slim girlish figure, a child clinging to either hand: Rosamond Perkins, adorable in her pink-flowered gown, crowned with the rose-wreathed hat, her pretty mouth open as she sang, heartily, happily, her eyes fixed on the stall where sat the strange priest, grave and sedate, in the place usually sacred to the Vicar of Little Ingleton. From his position Mr Minchin could not see anything but a white-sleeve laid along the carved chair-arm, the back of a head . . . yet he had the impression that the head was young, and suddenly, completely, a miserable jealousy seized him, and he knew that he would have given anything in his lonely world to have had Rosamond Perkins look up at him like that . . . Fool that he had been – oh, fool and blind! The choir sang on; the people sang, and strange voices from every side took up the chant; voices strange and, to Mr Minchin's dazed ears, barely human at times . . . gruff and squeaky, shrill, batlike, or deep and ringing, as one, in an insane dream, might think a goat's or a ram's might be . . . Old Miss Banks stood hand in hand with pretty Ellen, her dismissed maidservant, dressed gaily as for a wedding in white muslin and ribbons, and beside Ellen stood her gypsy swain: and grim old Miss Banks's face was gay with smiles, and she wore a flower-spray pinned to her cloak! Molly Isitt's pink sash gleamed beside a pillar, and a pink frilly hat accompanied it – all the village was there, and behind them and beside them in the shadows there seemed a thousand creatures more, strange and elusive, indistinct to see, yet present, a great concourse of tossing heads and rustling hairy bodies bringing with them the scent of leaves and trampled grasses and flowers! . . . And behind these, more elusive still, others that Mr Minchin did not dare to look at; slim, elflike shadows, bright-eyed and wild, yet singing shrilly, lustily with all their hearts.

The singing stopped, and shivering, not daring to glance up, Mr Minchin knew that the Strange Preacher was in the pulpit – yet without glancing up he knew who stood there well enough – for it was the Young Man of the road, the mad student! In the lightning brilliance of those hawk's eyes that played upon him now, Mr Minchin knew the truth, and shivering, cowered in sheer terror in his shadowy corner – above him, his twin peaks of bleached shining hair like two flames under the flaring gaslight, the Preacher gave out his text . . . 'I will lift up mine eyes unto the hills!'

With all his theology-trained heart the Reverend Thomas longed to shriek 'blasphemy, blasphemy', for was it not blasphemy to have to listen, in God's Own House, to This that preached . . . why did not the outraged heavens open, the earth split and swallow up church and congregation, the very stones, consecrated by austere bishop and celibate priest, crumble upon them for this impiety? But in the hush that settled over the dusk-veiled church there seemed no note but attention, no hint of action from an outraged God . . . At last, raising his head from his hands where he had thrust his fingers into his ears, fascinated, Mr Minchin listened too, as the Preacher spoke on.

He spoke of the grave eternal hills and of their story. Of the hills in whose cradling generous arms nestle grim Druid Grove and pagan altar – fairy ring and Christian church alike. Of the rains and dews that settle in their folds and run together into streams and pools, deep lakes and mighty rivers; of the little bright unconsidered flowers that grow on the hills, and the myriad unknown creatures that live out their coloured lives of but a day, the gossamer moths and lazy painted butterflies, the grey-velvet ground spider and his black neighbour the busy ant . . . Of the forgotten forts that, built by a long-dead people, still face the sea, the green turf weaving a winding sheet over the sturdy bones of the old builders; of the cromlechs and dolmens – the strange stone rings, so old that even their purpose is forgotten now – of the battered altars to ancient creeds, so old that their very names are dead; the green groves in hidden woodland places, groves planted in honour of goddesses that rule no longer . . .

He told of trees; of the bent and crooked pine trees that face the sea-gales, the sturdy sentinels that stand guard over England and her shores; of the green willow that trails her long hair in the brooks, the sad yew with its clustering red berries; the brittle lanky elm and its twin sister the larch, slim and elegant in delicate fluttering green, like a Watteau lady, all powdered and panniered, ever whispering to her other still lovelier sister, the silver birch, superior as any Bond Street miss, and twice as fair. Of the grave oak, whose roots are planted in a Britain older even than we dream – of secret ash, and subtle thorn, that Trinity of pagan magic . . . of the little furry creatures that scamper and fight and hide beneath the great tree-boles, the quiet-eyed deer peering wary from the thickets, all the thousand-and-one shy people of the woods that live and love, happy in their untaught way . . . And then he spoke of Man and his wonder and his strength, and Woman, in her beauty – and of how Man and Woman were made for love and joy, and for the dear companioning of each other through laughing youth to hale old age. He spoke of the loveliness of love, of frank kisses betwixt honest man and maid, of the close pressure of hand in hand and heart to heart; the murmured holiness of loving speech, of marriage, and mating, and the proud bearing of sturdy children . . . and as he listened the Reverend Thomas thought of the red lips and uplifted eyes of Rosamond Perkins, and smiled and trembled, and did not turn away . . .

And above him, under the flaring gaslight, his twisting spirals of hair like pale horns, his yellow hawk's eyes roving the crowded audience, the Preacher preached on . . . and now he spoke of Others – of careless and happy things that roam the green woods in vivid lovely life, if not life as mere humans know it . . . of Those that knew and loved their Mother Earth ere ever Man had set foot upon it! Those Older Things that, retreating before Man and his noisy dusty cities, yet laugh and, shaking their wind-blown hair, withdraw deeper and deeper yet to their old fastnesses in mountain and cave and forest . . . Unbaptised, perchance – knowing no creed nor caste – merry pagan Things that own no church, yet should there not be room for all beneath the mantle of Him whose name is Love? . . . Room for even these, for elf and satyr and white-browed nymph, merry brown gnome and wandering fairy, fauns with their goat-feet, and green-eyed nixy with her dripping hair? All – the Old Ancient Things that Man denies, since dust of cities blinds his once-keen sight . . . Yet strangely, amazingly, the listener understood, and nodded happily, though his face was wet with tears, as the great Voice boomed on, that Voice that held in it the pattering of rain on summer leaves, the sweep and majesty of thunder on the cowering hills, the shrilling clearness of the stars that sing eternally in the Outer Spaces! . . . And as he listened, it seemed to the Reverend Mr Minchin that his soul shrank within him in shame at his past littleness; shrank to the smallness of a shrivelled pea, and yet swelled to a greatness and happiness utterly beyond his knowledge, a happiness too immense to even grasp as yet. Yet remembering his past harshness, his bigotry, the narrow foolish laws with which he had sought to bind and straiten the great and laughing World – his mean, harsh judgment, and lack of charity – in the shelter of the kindly pew he wept and trembled, afraid, as the Voice boomed and shouted above him, and he knew Who, for the saving of his little soul, had supplanted him to teach the people truth!

'. . . Lift up your eyes to the hills, whence cometh your help indeed! The hills whence came your fathers; the woods, the seas wherein dwell strange and lovely things undreamt of in your little lives – the aged, the eternal Mother Earth! Mother Earth from whose heart we are come, and to whose arms we return at the last. Man and Beast and stranger Folk alike! Sing praises, my people – to the dear and goodly Earth and All Those that dwell therein, each in their kind and every kind, and to all gods old and new that love the world . . . for beneath the mantle of the Great God, is there not room to shelter smaller gods? . . .'

Abruptly the wonderful voice ceased – confusedly, dazed by the tumult of emotions that possessed him, yet dimly afterwards the Reverend Thomas seemed to remember a great and wonderful acclamation in which he joined, calling feebly, his face wet with joyful tears . . . the singing of a great Magnificat in which he vaguely remembered such happy lines as he had never dreamt the dourly thunderous Psalms possessed . . .

'God is gone up with a merry sound . . . with the sound of the trumpet! . . .'

He remembered stumbling out into the churchyard, ghostly, beautiful with its black tall cypresses in the moonlight, its crowded gravestones leaning against each other in the shadows as if to listen to the happy chanting, the chorus of praise that followed him out into the open.

As if in a dream from his place on the sloping bank above the path he watched the congregation file out, two and two, like the figures in a Noah's Ark, a strung-out line of black shadows against the gorgeous sunset, rose, green and gold, singing jubilantly as they went – and smiled, without surprise, but with happy knowledge, as he saw, mingling with the village folk, Those of a different world, beast and satyr and elvish unnamed creature, all come to shout their gladness in one great festival of praise! He saw old Kitson, arm-in-arm with his wife . . . and a faun, goat-footed, leaf-crowned, pranced beside them and tweaked old Kitson's hair . . . and the old man laughed and hugged his old wife the closer! He saw sour Gertrude Pring, who ran the post-office, companioned by two merry small Things, brown-eyed and saucy, and Miss Banks, unscandalised, walk beside a sly-eyed young Bacchante, whose white breasts gleamed shamelessly beautiful in the dusk . . .

Wee Molly Isitt held a fawn in leash that trotted sedately at her side, and two slim green nixies bestrode Dame Calder's pig – sweet-breathing cows came by beside the tossing, antlered deer, the snarling village dogs, now harmless and friendly, playing between their pacing feet. Singing and waving branches of trees and garlands in the air, they wound away over the ridge that hid the village from the little church, and the sound of their singing was an echo in the listening air . . . yet Mr Minchin waited, afraid, for the Preacher had not yet come forth.

The last chanting figure vanished, silhouetted against the blazing golden sky, and from the dark church door two figures came, shadowy among the shadows of the darkened churchyard, moving each by each – and as they went they gazed into each other's faces, rapt, enthralled – and suddenly, horribly, a pang of dread caught at the Reverend Thomas's once cold heart! For it was the Preacher – the Strange Young Man, his gay hawk-eyes bent upon his companion, his arm about her waist . . . and that companion, slim and young in pink flowered gingham, swinging her rose-crowned hat by its dangling ribbons, Rosamond Perkins!

Held by a spell he could not break, the wretched listener watched them approach, whispering, murmuring to each other, with little tender foolish sounds and laughter and beneath him on the path, pause and turn, rapt in each other's eyes. He saw, sharp in the moonlight that now strove valiantly against the fading gold, the face, upraised, ecstatic, of Rosamond Perkins, her red lips pouted, her blue eyes starry with love!

He saw, bending to that kiss, the profile of the Stranger, hooked nose meeting lean chin, those dancing light eyes triumphant beneath those hornlike tufts of curling hair, his arms, now no longer surpliced, lean and muscular in the tattered shirt of the afternoon, clasped about the slender body of the girl that the miserable Thomas Minchin now realised he loved with all the yearning passion of a man at last awake to love! How it happened exactly, the clergyman never knew, but at that moment the spell seemed to snap and he stumbled wildly forward, shrieking, desperate . . . for a moment the entire universe seemed to swing round him in a whirling dance, clouds and moon and sinking sun, crowding trees and reeling churchtowers, to the tune of a wild shouting and glorious laughter . . . and shaking, dazed, Mr Minchin found himself standing on the path, a shaft of moonlight on his face, and Rosamond Perkins, quivering, smiling in his arms, her lips upturned to his! Dimly through a haze of rioting emotions he heard her voice – loving, eager, human.

'Yes, yes! I love you – I've loved you all along! Darling – I felt you loved me – and after your sermon tonight I knew, I knew! . . .'

'My sermon?' The Reverend gentleman was still dazed, but she patted his cheek with her hand and laughed triumphantly.

'Your sermon – your wonderful sermon! If you could have heard yourself – the glorious theme – the fire and eloquence! . . . If I had not loved you from the beginning, I should have loved you after tonight! You seemed all of a sudden to have dropped all your funny little stilted ways, your stiffness – the grim hardness and intolerance, that – (forgive me!) – seems to have so long enclosed your great and generous heart like the hard shell of a nut that is all sweet and wholesome and tender within . . . but tonight all this fell away, and you spoke like one who, long-prisoned in a dark tower, looks out into the open and sees the wide and lovely sky . . .'

Still dazed, but with his hand fast-locked in hers, Mr Minchin turned towards the listening hills, the dark woods that seemed to watch him, the dusk-filled valley from which he still vaguely thought came an echo of joyous singing . . . They had gone again back to Their secret places, these dear strange People who had turned aside to teach him wisdom, and his heart swelled within him in love and sorrow that he could not thank Them, bless Them, tell Them his humility, his deep-hearted gratitude!

Mystified, the girl watched him, as, moving away a step, on an irresistible impulse he flung out both arms to the deep and smiling sky, and his voice, limpid, tremulous, rose to a joyful note that was almost a song.

'Oh great god Pan, I know Thee! – I thank Thee – I bless

Thee ... Thee and all Thy People great and small – for indeed, indeed beneath the mantle of the God whose name is Love, is there not room for all in His world to shelter?'

So Pan and his merry crew came to Little Ingleton, and so departed – and so the Reverend Thomas Minchin learnt humility. But deeply as he is now loved and revered by his flock – and indeed you would not know him for the same man – it is generally admitted that he has never again attained to quite the pitch of eloquence of that memorable Midsummer Day.

Through cautious questioning of his betrothed, the young clergyman established, much to his own private relief, that not one of the congregation that night, not even Miss Perkins at the moment when Pan, playing his last elvish trick, literally thrust them into each other's arms, had the remotest idea that any but their own accustomed priest had led the service ... the truth lay hid in Mr Minchin's breast, and there it was buried, gratefully and thankfully. Not one had dreamt of the Things of so strange life and shape and form that had elbowed them during that amazing Evensong – and in his undreamt-of happiness with his pretty wife the Reverend Thomas looks back upon that enchanted Midsummer Night with a deep and humble thankfulness ... For since that marvellous hour of sight – when for a little while the veil before his eyes was torn away and he saw horned beast of the field, wilful elf and goblin, faun and nymph, mingling with village maid and man, jostle together singing prayer and praise in the Church of Christ, he has walked humbly, tremblingly before men, and in his gentleness and understanding, his loving-kindness and readiness to forgive sin, his old cruel bigotry is long forgotten.

Only on one day in the year does he mystify the village a little, and that is on Midsummer Day – now a great holiday in Little Ingleton, when parson and flock betake themselves to the fields and woods, dancing and singing and feasting as in the old days, for joy of the dear green world, the warm sun and the merry pagan winds of heaven . . . And there is no stinting of the feast these days – good ale and foaming golden beer shoulder prim lemonade and gingerpop, and there is no lack of junket, and syllabub, of Granny Calder's recipe, to eat with the cakes and pies, the plum-starred buns . . . and the village foots it to the tune of ragged Peter's fiddle and old Dad Verity's drum till the moon rises glimmering over the tree-tops, and busy little Mrs Minchin begins to gather up the food for distribution on the morrow to her beloved poor. But then her husband comes, and despite her eager puzzled questions, so frequent at first (though now she laughs and shrugs and lets it go, since he merely smiles and shakes his head!), silently, reverently the Reverend Thomas chooses a portion of cake, of fruit and wine, the best that remains, and disappears silently into the wood with his offering. There on a log or clear space of mossy turf, he lays his tribute, and after standing a moment with bowed head, goes softly away through the green shadows back to his flock, leaving behind him his yearly offering, libation to the old God who taught him wisdom, the God who was old when Christ was a stammering babe . . . the Great God Pan, who, in a whimsy moment, came and played parson to save a parson's soul.

ALL HALLOWS

by

Walter de la Mare

First published in the collection
The Connoisseur, and Other Stories

1926

And because time in itselfe . . . can receive no alteration, the hal-
lowing . . . must consist in the shape or countenance which we
put upon the affaires that are incident in these days.

RICHARD HOOKER

IT WAS ABOUT half-past three on an August afternoon when I
found myself for the first time looking down upon All Hallows.
And at glimpse of it, fatigue and vexation passed away. I stood 'at
gaze', as the old phrase goes – like the two children of Israel sent in
to spy out the Promised Land. How often the imagined transcends
the real. Not so All Hallows. Having at last reached the end of my
journey – flies, dust, heat, wind – having at last come limping out
upon the green sea-bluff beneath which lay its walls – I confess the
actuality excelled my feeble dreams of it.

What most astonished me, perhaps, was the sense not so much
of its age, its austerity, or even its solitude, but its air of abandonment. It lay couched there as if in hiding in its narrow sea-bay.
Not a sound was in the air; not a jackdaw clapped its wings among
its turrets. No other roof, not even a chimney, was in sight; only

the dark-blue arch of the sky; the narrow snowline of the ebbing tide; and that gaunt coast fading away into the haze of a west over which were already gathering the veils of sunset.

We had met, then, at an appropriate hour and season. And yet – I wonder. For it was certainly not the 'beauty' of All Hallows, lulled as if into a dream in this serenity of air and heavens, which was to leave the sharpest impression upon me. And what kind of first showing would it have made, I speculated, if an autumnal gale had been shrilling and trumpeting across its narrow bay – clots of wind-borne spume floating among its dusky pinnacles – and the roar of the sea echoing against its walls! Imagine it frozen stark in winter, icy hoar-frost edging its every boss, moulding, finial, crocket, cusp!

Indeed, are there not works of man, legacies of a half-forgotten past, scattered across this human world of ours from China to Peru, which seem to daunt the imagination with their incomprehensibility? Incomprehensible, I mean, in the sense that the passion that inspired and conceived them is incomprehensible. Viewed in the light of the passing day, they might be the monuments of a race of demi-gods. And yet, if we could but free ourselves from our timidities, and follies, we might realise that even we ourselves have an obligation to leave behind us similar memorials – testaments to the creative and faithful genius not so much of the individual as of Humanity itself.

However that may be, it was my own personal fortune to see All Hallows for the first time in the heat of the Dog Days, after a journey which could hardly be justified except by its end. At this moment of the afternoon the great church almost cheated one into the belief that it was possessed of a life of its own. It lay, as I say, couched in its natural hollow, basking under the dark dome of the heavens like some half-fossilised monster that might at any moment stir and awaken out of the swoon to which the wand of the enchanter had committed it. And with every inch of the sun's descending journey it changed its appearance.

That is the charm of such things. Man himself, says the philosopher, is the sport of change. His life and the life around him are but the flotsam of a perpetual flux. Yet, haunted by ideals, egged on by impossibilities, he builds his vision of the changeless; and time diversifies it with its colours and its 'effects' at leisure. It was drawing near to harvest now; the summer was nearly over; the corn would soon be in stook; the season of silence had come, not even the robins had yet begun to practise their autumnal lament. I should have come earlier.

The distance was of little account. But nine flinty hills in seven miles is certainly hard commons. To plod (the occupant of a cloud of dust) up one steep incline and so see another; to plod up that and so see a third; to surmount that and, half-choked, half-roasted, to see (as if in unbelievable mirage) a fourth – and always stone walls, discoloured grass, no flower but ragged ragwort, whited fleabane, moody nettle, and the exquisite stubborn bindweed with its almond-burdened censers, and always the glitter and dazzle of the sun – well, the experience grows irksome. And then that endless flint erection with which some jealous Lord of the Manor had barricaded his verdurous estate! A fly-infested mile of the company of that wall was tantamount to making one's way into the infernal regions – with Tantalus for fellow-pilgrim. And when a solitary and empty dung-cart had lumbered by, lifting the dumb dust out of the road in swirling clouds into the heat-quivering air, I had all but wept aloud.

No, I shall not easily forget that walk – or the conclusion of it – when footsore, all but dead beat – dust all over me, cheeks, lips, eyelids, in my hair, dust in drifts even between my naked body and my clothes – I stretched my aching limbs on the turf under the straggle of trees which crowned the bluff of that last hill still blessedly green and verdant, and feasted my eyes on the cathedral beneath me. How odd Memory is – in her sorting arrangements. How perverse her pigeon-holes.

It had reminded me of a drizzling evening many years ago. I had stayed a moment to listen to an old Salvation Army officer preaching at a street corner. The sopped and squalid houses echoed with his harangue. His penitents' drum resembled the block of an executioner. His goatish beard wagged at every word he uttered. 'My brothers and sisters,' he was saying, 'the very instant our fleshly bodies are born they begin to perish; the moment the Lord has put them together, time begins to take them to pieces again. *Now* at this very instant if you listen close, you can hear the nibblings and frettings of the moth and rust within – the worm that never dies. It's the same with human causes and creeds and institutions – just the same. O, then, for that Strand of Beauty where all that is mortal shall be shed away and we shall appear in the likeness and verisimilitude of what in sober and awful truth we are!'

The light striking out of an oil-and-colourman's shop at the street corner lay across his cheek and beard and glassed his eye. The soaked circle of humanity in which he was gesticulating stood staring and motionless – the lassies, the probationers, the melancholy idlers. I had had enough. I went away. But it is odd that so utterly inappropriate a recollection should have edged back into my mind at this moment. There was, as I have said, not a living soul in sight. Only a few seabirds – oyster-catchers maybe – were jangling on the distant beach.

It was now a quarter to four by my watch, and the usual pensive 'lin-lan-lone' from the belfry beneath me would soon no doubt be ringing to evensong. But if at that moment a triple bob-major had suddenly clanged its alarm over sea and shore I couldn't have stirred a finger's breadth. Scanty though the shade afforded by the wind-shorn tuft of trees under which I lay might be – I was ineffably at peace.

No bell, as a matter of fact, loosed its tongue that stagnant half-hour. Unless then the walls beneath me already concealed a few such chance visitors as myself, All Hallows would be empty.

A cathedral not only without a close but without a congregation – yet another romantic charm. The Deanery and the residences of its clergy, my old guide-book had long since informed me, were a full mile or more away. I determined in due time, first to make sure of an entry, and then having quenched my thirst, to bathe.

How inhuman any extremity – hunger, fatigue, pain, desire – makes us poor humans. Thirst and drought so haunted my mind that again and again as I glanced towards it I supped up in one long draught that complete blue sea. But meanwhile, too, my eyes had been steadily exploring and searching out this monument of the bygone centuries beneath me.

The headland faced approximately due west. The windows of the Lady Chapel therefore lay immediately beneath me, their fourteenth-century glass showing flatly dark amid their traceries. Above it, the shallow V-shaped, leaden ribbed roof of the chancel converged towards the unfinished tower, then broke away at right angles – for the cathedral was cruciform. Walls so ancient and so sparsely adorned and decorated could not but be inhospitable in effect. Their stone was of a bleached bone-grey; a grey that none the less seemed to be as immaterial as flame – or incandescent ash. They were substantial enough, however, to cast a marvellously lucent shadow, of a blue no less vivid but paler than that of the sea, on the shelving sward beneath them. And that shadow was steadily shifting as I watched. But even if the complete edifice had vanished into the void, the scene would still have been of an incredible loveliness. The colours in air and sky on this dangerous coast seemed to shed a peculiar unreality even on the rocks of its own outworks.

So, from my vantage place on the hill that dominates it, I continued for a while to watch All Hallows; to spy upon it; and no less intently than a sentry who, not quite trusting his own eyes, has seen a dubious shape approaching him in the dusk. It may sound absurd, but I felt that at any moment I too might surprise

All Hallows in the act of revealing what in very truth it looked like – and *was*, when no human witness was there to share its solitude.

Those gigantic statues, for example, which flanked the base of the unfinished tower – an intense bluish-white in the sunlight and a bluish-purple in shadow – images of angels and of saints, as I had learned of old from my guide-book. Only six of them at most could be visible, of course, from where I sat. And yet I found myself counting them again and yet again, as if doubting my own arithmetic. For my first impression had been that seven were in view – though the figure furthest from me at the western angle showed little more than a jutting fragment of stone which might perhaps be only part and parcel of the fabric itself.

But then the lights even of day may be deceitful, and fantasy plays strange tricks with one's eyes. With exercise, none the less, the mind is enabled to detect minute details which the unaided eye is incapable of particularising. Given the imagination, man himself indeed may some day be able to distinguish what shapes are walking during our own terrestrial midnight amid the black shadows of the craters in the noonday of the moon. At any rate, I could trace at last frets of carving, minute weather marks, crookednesses, incrustations, repairings, that had before passed unnoticed. These walls, indeed, like human faces, were maps and charts of their own long past.

In the midst of this prolonged scrutiny, the hypnotic air, the heat, must suddenly have overcome me. I fell asleep up there in my grove's scanty shade; and remained asleep, too, long enough (as time is measured by the clocks of sleep) to dream an immense panoramic dream. On waking, I could recall only the faintest vestiges of it, and found that the hand of my watch had crept on but a few minutes in the interval. It was eight minutes past four.

I scrambled up – numbed and inert – with that peculiar sense of panic which sometimes follows an uneasy sleep. What folly to have been frittering time away within sight of my goal at an hour when no doubt the cathedral would soon be closed to visitors, and abandoned for the night to its own secret ruminations. I hastened down the steep rounded incline of the hill, and having skirted under the sunlit expanse of the walls, came presently to the south door, only to discover that my forebodings had been justified, and that it was already barred and bolted. The discovery seemed to increase my fatigue fourfold. How foolish it is to obey mere caprices. What a straw is a man!

I glanced up into the beautiful shell of masonry above my head. Shapes and figures in stone it showed in plenty – symbols of an imagination that had flamed and faded, leaving this signature for sole witness – but not a living bird or butterfly. There was but one faint chance left of making an entry. Hunted now, rather than the hunter, I hastened out again into the full blazing flood of sunshine – and once more came within sight of the sea; a sea so near at last that I could hear its enormous sallies and murmurings. Indeed I had not realised until that moment how closely the great western doors of the cathedral abutted on the beach.

It was as if its hospitality had been deliberately designed, not for a people to whom the faith of which it was the shrine had become a weariness and a commonplace, but for the solace of pilgrims from over the ocean. I could see them tumbling into their cockleboats out of their great hollow ships – sails idle, anchors down; see them leaping ashore and straggling up across the sands to these all-welcoming portals – 'Parthians and Medes and Elamites; dwellers in Mesopotamia and in the parts of Egypt about Cyrene; strangers of Rome, Jews and Proselytes – we do hear them speak in our own tongue the wonderful works of God.'

And so at last I found my way into All Hallows – entering by a rounded dwarfish side-door with zigzag mouldings. There hung for corbel to its dripstone a curious leering face, with its forked tongue out, to give me welcome. And an appropriate one, too, for the figure I made!

But once beneath that prodigious roof-tree, I forgot myself and everything that was mine. The hush, the coolness, the unfathomable twilight drifted in on my small human consciousness. Not even the ocean itself is able so completely to receive one into its solacing bosom. Except for the windows over my head, filtering with their stained glass the last western radiance of the sun, there was but little visible colour in those great spaces, and a severe economy of decoration. The stone piers carried their round arches with an almost intimidating impassivity.

By deliberate design, too, or by some illusion of perspective, the whole floor of the building appeared steadily to ascend towards the east, where a dark wooden multitudinously figured rood-screen shut off the choir and the high altar from the nave. I seemed to have exchanged one universal actuality for another: the burning world of nature, for this oasis of quiet. Here, the wings of the imagination need never rest in their flight out of the wilderness into the unknown.

Thus resting, I must again have fallen asleep. And so swiftly can even the merest freshet of sleep affect the mind, that when my eyes opened, I was completely at a loss.

Where was I? What demon of what romantic chasm had swept my poor drowsy body into this immense haunt? The din and clamour of an horrific dream whose fainting rumour was still in my ear became suddenly stilled. Then at one and the same moment, a sense of utter dismay at earthly surroundings no longer serene and peaceful, but grim and forbidding, flooded my mind, and I became aware that I was no longer alone. Twenty or thirty paces away, and a little this side of the rood-screen, an old man was standing.

To judge from the black and purple velvet and tassel-tagged gown he wore, he was a verger. He had not yet realised, it seemed, that a visitor shared his solitude. And yet he was listening. His head was craned forward and leaned sideways on his rusty shoulders.

As I steadily watched him, he raised his eyes, and with a peculiar stealthy deliberation scanned the complete upper regions of the northern transept. Not the faintest rumour of any sound that may have attracted his attention reached me where I sat. Perhaps a wild bird had made its entry through a broken pane of glass and with its cry had at the same moment awakened me and caught his attention. Or maybe the old man was waiting for some fellow-occupant to join him from above.

I continued to watch him. Even at this distance, the silvery twilight cast by the clerestory windows was sufficient to show me, though vaguely, his face: the high sloping nose, the lean cheekbones and protruding chin. He continued so long in the same position that I at last determined to break in on his reverie.

At sound of my footsteps his head sunk cautiously back upon his shoulders; and he turned; and then motionlessly surveyed me as I drew near. He resembled one of those old men whom Rembrandt delighted in drawing: the knotted hands, the black drooping eyebrows, the wide thin-lipped ecclesiastical mouth, the intent cavernous dark eyes beneath the heavy folds of their lids. White as a miller with dust, hot and draggled, I was hardly the kind of visitor that any self-respecting custodian would warmly welcome, but he greeted me none the less with every mark of courtesy.

I apologised for the lateness of my arrival, and explained it as best I could. 'Until I caught sight of you,' I concluded lamely, 'I hadn't ventured very far in: otherwise I might have found myself a prisoner for the night. It must be dark in here when there is no moon.'

The old man smiled – but wryly. 'As a matter of fact, sir,' he replied, 'the cathedral is closed to visitors at four – at such times, that is, when there is no afternoon service. Services are not as frequent as they were. But visitors are rare too. In winter, in particular, you notice the gloom – as you say, sir. Not that I ever spend the night here: though I am usually last to leave. There's the risk of fire to be thought of and ... I think I should have detected your presence here, sir. One becomes accustomed after many years.'

There was the usual trace of official pedantry in his voice, but it was more pleasing than otherwise. Nor did he show any wish to be rid of me. He continued his survey, although his eye was a little absent and his attention seemed to be divided.

'I thought perhaps I might be able to find a room for the night and really explore the cathedral to-morrow morning. It has been a tiring journey; I come from B——'

'Ah, from B——; it *is* a fatiguing journey, sir, taken on foot. I used to walk in there to see a sick daughter of mine. Carriage parties occasionally make their way here, but not so much as once. We are too far out of the hurly-burly to be much intruded on. Not that them who come to make their worship here are intruders. Far from it. But most that come are mere sightseers. And the fewer of them, I say, in the circumstances, the better.'

Something in what I had said or in my appearance seemed to have reassured him. 'Well, I cannot claim to be a regular church-goer,' I said. 'I am myself a mere sightseer. And yet – even to sit here for a few minutes is to be reconciled.'

'Ah, reconciled, sir,' the old man repeated, turning away. 'I can well imagine it after that journey on such a day as this. But to live here is another matter.'

'I was thinking of that,' I replied in a foolish attempt to retrieve the position. 'It must, as you say, be desolate enough in the winter – for two-thirds of the year, indeed.'

'We have our storms, sir – the bad with the good,' he agreed, 'and our position is specially prolific of what they call sea-fog. It comes driving in from the sea for days and nights together – gale and mist, so that you can scarcely see your open hand in front of your eyes even in broad daylight. And the noise of it, sir, sweeping across overhead in that wooliness of mist, if you take me, is most peculiar. It's shocking to a stranger. No, sir, we are left pretty much to ourselves when the fine-weather birds are flown ... You'd be astonished at the power of the winds here. There was a mason – a local man too – not above two or three years ago was blown clean off the roof from under the tower – tossed up in the air like an empty sack. But,' – and the old man at last allowed his eyes to stray upwards to the roof again – 'but there's not much doing now.' He seemed to be pondering. 'Nothing open.'

'I mustn't detain you,' I said, 'but you were saying that services are infrequent now. Why is that? When one thinks of—' But tact restrained me.

'Pray don't think of keeping me, sir. It's a part of my duties. But from a remark you let fall I was supposing you may have seen something that appeared, I understand, not many months ago in the newspapers. We lost our dean – Dean Pomfrey – last November. To all intents and purposes, I mean; and his office has not yet been filled. Between you and me, sir, there's a hitch – though I should wish it to go no further. They are greedy monsters – those newspapers: no respect, no discretion, no decency, in my view. And they copy each other like cats in a chorus.

'We have never wanted to be a notoriety here, sir, and not of late of all times. We must face our own troubles. You'd be astonished how callous the mere sightseer can be. And not only them from over the water whom our particular troubles cannot concern – but far worse – parties as English as you or me. They ask you questions you wouldn't believe possible in a civilised country. Not that they care what becomes of us – not one iota, sir. We talk of them masked-up Inquisitors in olden times, but there's many a human being in our own would enjoy seeing a fellow-creature on the rack if he could get the opportunity. It's a heartless age, sir.'

This was queerish talk in the circumstances: and after all I myself was of the glorious company of the sightseers. I held my peace. And the old man, as if to make amends, asked me if I would care to see any particular part of the building. 'The light is smalling,'

323

he explained, 'but still if we keep to the ground level there'll be a few minutes to spare; and we shall not be interrupted if we go quietly on our way.'

For the moment the reference eluded me: I could only thank him for the suggestion and once more beg him not to put himself to any inconvenience. I explained, too, that though I had no personal acquaintance with Dr Pomfrey, I had read of his illness in the newspapers. 'Isn't he,' I added a little dubiously, 'the author of *The Church and the Folk*? If so, he must be an exceedingly learned and delightful man.'

'Ay, sir.' The old verger put up a hand towards me. 'You may well say it: a saint if ever there was one. But it's worse than "illness", sir – it's oblivion. And, thank God, the newspapers didn't get hold of more than a bare outline.'

He dropped his voice. 'This way, if you please'; and he led me off gently down the aisle, once more coming to a standstill beneath the roof of the tower. 'What I mean, sir, is that there's very few left in this world who have any place in their minds for a sacred confidence – no reverence, sir. They would as lief All Hallows and all it stands for were swept away to-morrow, demolished to the dust. And that gives me the greatest caution with whom I speak. But sharing one's troubles is sometimes a relief. If it weren't so, why do those Catholics have their wooden boxes all built for the purpose? What else, I ask you, is the meaning of their fasts and penances?

'You see, sir, I am myself, and have been for upwards of twelve years now, the dean's verger. In the sight of no respecter of persons – of offices and dignities, that is, I take it – I might claim to be even an elder brother. And our dean, sir, was a man who was all things to all men. No pride of place, no vauntingness, none of your apron-and-gaiter high-and-mightiness whatsoever, sir. And then that! And to come on us without warning; or at least without warning as could be taken as *such*.' I followed his eyes into the darkening stony spaces above us; a light like tarnished silver lay over the soundless vaultings. But so, of course, dusk, either of evening or daybreak, would affect the ancient stones. Nothing moved there.

'You must understand, sir,' the old man was continuing, 'the procession for divine service proceeds from the vestry over yonder out through those wrought-iron gates and so under the rood-screen and into the chancel there. Visitors are admitted on showing a card or a word to the verger in charge; but not otherwise. If you stand a pace or two to the right, you will catch a glimpse of the altar-screen – fourteenth-century work, Bishop Robert de Beaufort – and a unique example of the age. But what I was saying is that when we proceed for the services *out* of here *into* there, it has always been our custom to keep pretty close together; more seemly and decent, sir, than straggling in like so many sheep.

'Besides, sir, aren't we at such times in the manner of an *array*, "marching as to war", if you take me: it's a lesson in objects. The third verger leading: then the choristers, boys and men, though sadly depleted; then the minor canons; then any other dignitaries who may happen to be present, with the canon in residence; then myself, sir, followed by the dean.

'There hadn't been much amiss up to then, and on that afternoon, I can vouch – and I've repeated it *ad naushum* – there was not a single stranger out in this beyond here, sir – nave or transepts. Not within view, that is: one can't be expected to see through four feet of Norman stone. Well, sir, we had gone on our way, and I had actually turned about as usual to bow Dr Pomfrey into his stall, when I found to my consternation, to my consternation, I say, he wasn't there! It alarmed me, sir, and as you might well believe if you knew the full circumstances.

'Not that I lost my presence of mind. My first duty was to see all things to be in order and nothing unseemly to occur. My feelings were another matter. The old gentleman had left the vestry with us: that I knew: I had myself robed 'im as usual, and he in his own manner, smiling with his "Well, Jones, another day gone; another day gone." He was always an anxious gentleman for *time*, sir. How we spend it and all.

'As I say, then, he was behind me when we swepp out of the gates. I saw him coming on out of the tail of my eye – we grow accustomed to it, to see with the whole of the eye, I mean. And then – not a vestige; and me – well, sir, nonplussed, as you may imagine. I gave a look and sign at Canon Ockham, and the service proceeded as usual, while I hurried back to the vestry thinking the poor gentleman must have been taken suddenly ill. And yet, sir, I was not surprised to find the vestry vacant, and him not there. I had been expecting matters to come to what you might call a head.

'As best I could I held my tongue, and a fortunate thing it was that Canon Ockham was then in residence and not Canon Leigh Shougar, though perhaps I am not the one to say it. No, sir, our beloved dean – as pious and unworldly a gentleman as ever graced the Church – was gone for ever. He was not to appear in our midst again. He had been' – and the old man with elevated eyebrows and long lean mouth nearly whispered the words into my ear – 'he had been absconded – abducted, sir.'

'Abducted!' I murmured.

The old man closed his eyes, and with trembling lids added, 'He was found, sir, late that night up there in what they call the Trophy Room – sitting in a corner there, weeping. A child. Not a word of what had persuaded him to go or misled him there, not a word of sorrow or sadness, thank God. He didn't know us, sir – didn't know *me*. Just simple; harmless; memory all gone. Simple, sir.'

It was foolish to be whispering together like this beneath these enormous spaces with not so much as a clothes-moth for sign of life within view. But I even lowered my voice still farther: 'Were there no premonitory symptoms? Had he been failing for long?'

The spectacle of grief in any human face is afflicting, but in a face as aged and resigned as this old man's – I turned away in remorse the moment the question was out of my lips; emotion is a human solvent and a sort of friendliness had sprung up between us.

'If you will just follow me,' he whispered, 'there's a little place where I make my ablutions that might be of service, sir. We would converse there in better comfort. I am sometimes reminded of those words in Ecclesiastes: "And a bird of the air shall tell of the matter." There is not much in our poor human affairs, sir, that was not known to the writer of that book.'

He turned and led the way with surprising celerity, gliding along in his thin-soled, square-toed, clerical spring-side boots; and came to a pause outside a nail-studded door. He opened it with a huge key, and admitted me into a recess under the central tower. We mounted a spiral stone staircase and passed along a corridor hardly more than two feet wide and so dark that now and again I thrust out my finger-tips in search of his black velveted gown to make sure of my guide.

This corridor at length conducted us into a little room whose only illumination I gathered was that of the ebbing dusk from within the cathedral. The old man with trembling rheumatic fingers lit a candle, and thrusting its stick into the middle of an old oak table, pushed open yet another thick oaken door. 'You will find a basin and a towel in there, sir, if you will be so kind.'

I entered. A print of the Crucifixion was tin-tacked to the panelled wall, and beneath it stood a tin basin and jug on a stand. Never was water sweeter. I laved my face and hands and drank deep; my throat like a parched river-course after a drought. What appeared to be a tarnished censer lay in one corner of the room; a pair of seven-branched candlesticks shared a recess with a mouse-trap and a book. My eyes passed wearily yet gratefully from one to another of these mute discarded objects while I stood drying my hands.

When I returned, the old man was standing motionless before the spike-barred grill of the window, peering out and down.

'You asked me, sir,' he said, turning his lank waxen face into the feeble rays of the candle, 'you asked me, sir, a question which, if I understood you aright, was this: Was there anything that had occurred *previous* that would explain what I have been telling you? Well, sir, it's a long story, and one best restricted to them perhaps that have the goodwill of things at heart. All Hallows, I might say, sir, is my second home. I have been here, boy and man, for close on fifty-five years – have seen four bishops pass away and have served under no less than five several deans, Dr Pomfrey, poor gentleman, being the last of the five.

'If such a word could be excused, sir, it's no exaggeration to say that Canon Leigh Shougar is a greenhorn by comparison; which may in part be why he has never quite hit it off, as they say, with Canon Ockham. Or even with Archdeacon Trafford, though he's another kind of gentleman altogether. And *he* is at present abroad. He had what they call a breakdown in health, sir.

'Now in my humble opinion, what was required was not only wisdom and knowledge but simple common sense. In the circumstances I am about to mention, it serves no purpose for any of us to be talking too much; to be for ever sitting at a table with shut doors and finger on lip, and discussing what to most intents and purposes would hardly be called evidence at all, sir. What is the use of argufying, splitting hairs, objurgating about trifles, when matters are sweeping rapidly on from bad to worse. I say it with all due respect and not, I hope, thrusting myself into what doesn't concern me: Dr Pomfrey might be with us now in his own self and reason if only common caution had been observed.

'But now that the poor gentleman is gone beyond all that, there is no hope of action or agreement left, none whatsoever. They meet and they meet, and they have now one expert now another down from London, and even from the continent. And I don't say they are not knowledgeable gentlemen either, nor a pride to their profession. But why not tell *all*? Why keep back the very secret of what we know? That's what I am asking. And, what's the answer? Why simply that what they don't want to believe, what runs counter to their hopes and wishes and credibilities – and comfort – in this world, that's what they keep out of sight as long as decency permits.

'Canon Leigh Shougar *knows*, sir, what *I* know. And how, I ask, is he going to get to grips with it at this late day if he refuses to acknowledge that such things are what every fragment of evidence goes to prove that they are. It's *we*, sir, and not the rest of the heedless world outside, who in the long and the short of it are responsible. And what I say is: no power or principality here or hereunder can take possession of a place while those inside have faith enough to keep them out. But once let that falter – the seas are in. And when I say no power, sir, I mean – with all deference – even Satan himself.' The lean lank face had set at the word like a wax mask. The black eyes beneath the heavy lids were fixed on mine with an acute intensity and – though more inscrutable things haunted them – with an unfaltering courage. So dense a hush hung about us that the very stones of the walls seemed to be of silence solidified. It is curious what a refreshment of spirit a mere tin basinful of water may be. I stood leaning against the edge of the table so that the candlelight still rested on my companion.

'What is *wrong* here?' I asked him baldly.

He seemed not to have expected so direct an inquiry. 'Wrong, sir? Why, if I might make so bold,' he replied with a wan, far-away smile and gently drawing his hand down one of the velvet lapels of his gown, 'if I might make so bold, sir, I take it that you have come as a direct answer to prayer.'

His voice faltered. 'I am an old man now, and nearly at the end of my tether. You must realise, if you please, that I can't get any help that I can understand. I am not doubting that the gentlemen I have mentioned have only the salvation of the cathedral at heart – the cause, sir; and a graver responsibility yet. But they refuse to see how close to the edge of things we are: and how we are drifting.

'Take mere situation. So far as my knowledge tells me, there is no sacred edifice in the whole kingdom – of a piece, that is, with All Hallows not only in mere size and age but in what I might call sanctity and tradition – that is so open – open, I mean, sir, to attack of this peculiar and terrifying nature.'

'Terrifying?'

'*Terrifying*, sir; though I hold fast to what wits my Maker has bestowed on me. Where else, may I ask, would you expect the powers of darkness to congregate in open besiegement than in this narrow valley? First, the sea out there. Are you aware, sir, that ever since living remembrance flood-tide has been gnawing and mumbling its way into this bay to the extent of three or four feet *per annum*? Forty inches, and forty inches, and forty inches corroding on and on: Watch it, sir, man and boy as I have these sixty years past and then make a century of it. Not to mention positive leaps and bounds.

'And now, think a moment of the floods and gales that fall upon us autumn and winter through and even in spring, when this valley is liker paradise to young eyes than any place on earth. They make the roads from the nearest towns well-nigh impassable; which means that for some months of the year we are to all intents and purposes clean cut off from the rest of the world – as the Schindels out there are from the mainland. Are you aware, sir, I continue, that as we stand now we are above a mile from traces of the nearest human habitation, and them merely the relics of a burnt-out old farmstead? I warrant that if (and which God forbid) you had been shut up here during the coming night, and it was a near thing but what you weren't – I warrant you might have shouted yourself dumb out of the nearest window if window you could reach – and not a human soul to heed or help you.'

I shifted my hands on the table. It was tedious to be asking questions that received only such vague and evasive replies: and it is always a little disconcerting in the presence of a stranger to be spoken to so close, and with such positiveness.

'Well,' I smiled, 'I hope I should not have disgraced my nerves to such an extreme as that. As a small boy, one of my particular fancies was to spend a night in a pulpit. There's a cushion, you know!'

The old man's solemn glance never swerved from my eyes. 'But I take it, sir,' he said, 'if you had ventured to give out a text up there in the dark hours, your jocular young mind would not have been prepared for any kind of a congregation?'

'You mean,' I said a little sharply, 'that the place is haunted?' The absurd notion flitted across my mind of some wandering tribe of gipsies chancing on a refuge so ample and isolated as this, and taking up its quarters in its secret parts. The old church must be honeycombed with corridors and passages and chambers pretty much like the one in which we were now concealed: and what does 'cartholic' imply but an infinite hospitality within prescribed limits? But the old man had taken me at my word.

'I mean, sir,' he said firmly, shutting his eyes, 'that there are devilish agencies at work here.' He raised his hand. 'Don't, I entreat you, dismiss what I am saying as the wanderings of a foolish old man.' He drew a little nearer. 'I have heard them with these ears; I have seen them with these eyes; though whether they have any positive substance, sir, is beyond my small knowledge to declare. But what indeed might we expect their substance to *be*? First: "I take it," says the Book, "to be such as no man can by learning define, nor by wisdom search out." Is that so? Then I go by the Book. And next: what does the same Word or very near it (I speak of the Apocrypha) say of their *purpose*? It says – and correct me if I go astray – "Devils are creatures made by God, and *that for vengeance*."

'So far, so good, sir. We stop when we can go no further. Vengeance. But of their power, of what they can *do*, I can give you definite evidences. It would be a byword if once the rumour was spread abroad. And if it is *not* so, why, I ask, does every expert that comes here leave us in haste and in dismay? They go off with their tails between their legs. They see, they grope in, but they don't believe. They *invent* reasons. And they *hasten* to leave us!' His face shook with the emphasis he laid upon the word. 'Why? Why, because the experience is beyond their knowledge, sir.' He drew back breathless and, as I could see, profoundly moved.

'But surely,' I said, 'every old building is bound in time to show symptoms of decay. Half the cathedrals in England, half its churches, even, of any age, have been "restored" – and in many cases with ghastly results. This new grouting and so on. Why, only the other day . . . All I mean is, why should you suppose mere wear and tear should be caused by any other agency than—'

The old man turned away. 'I must apologise,' he interrupted me with his inimitable admixture of modesty and dignity. 'I am a poor mouth at explanations, sir. Decay – stress – strain – settling – dissolution: I have heard those words bandied from lip to lip like a game at cup and ball. They fill me with nausea. Why, I am speaking not of dissolution, sir, but of *repairs*, *restorations*. Not decay, *strengthening*. Not a corroding loss, an awful *progress*. I could show you places – and chiefly obscured from direct view and difficult of a close examination, sir, where stones lately as rotten as pumice and as fretted as a sponge have been replaced by others fresh-quarried – and nothing of their kind within twenty miles.

'There are spots where massive blocks a yard or more square have been *pushed* into place by sheer force. All Hallows is safer at this moment than it has been for three hundred years. They meant well – them who came to see, full of talk and fine language, and went dumb away. I grant you they meant well. I allow that. They hummed and they hawed. They smirked this and they shrugged that. But at heart, sir, they were cowed – horrified: all at a loss. Their very faces showed it. But if you ask me for what purpose such doings are afoot – I have no answer; none.

'But now, supposing you yourself, sir, were one of them, with *your* repute at stake, and you were called in to look at a house which the owners of it and them who had it in trust were disturbed by its being re-edificated and restored by some agency unknown to them. Supposing that! *Why*,' and he rapped with his knuckles on the table, 'being human *and not one of us* mightn't you be going away too with mouth shut, because you didn't want to get talked about to your disadvantage? And wouldn't you at last dismiss the whole thing as a foolish delusion, in the belief that living in out-of-the-way parts like these cuts a man off from the world, breeds maggots in the mind?

'I assure you, sir, they don't – not even Canon Ockham himself to the full – they don't believe even me. And yet, when they have their meetings of the Chapter they talk and wrangle round and round about nothing else. I can bear the other without a murmur. What God sends, I say, we humans deserve. We have laid ourselves open to it. But when you buttress up blindness and wickedness with downright folly, why then, sir, I sometimes fear for my own reason.'

He set his shoulders as square as his aged frame would permit, and with fingers clutching the lapels beneath his chin, he stood gazing out into the darkness through that narrow inward window.

'Ah, sir,' he began again, 'I have not spent sixty years in this solitary place without paying heed to my own small wandering thoughts and instincts. Look at your newspapers, sir. What they call the Great War is over – and he'd be a brave man who would take an oath before heaven that *that* was only of human designing – and yet what do we see around us? Nothing but strife and juggleries and hatred and contempt and discord wherever you look. I am no scholar, sir, but so far as my knowledge and experience carry me, we human beings are living to-day merely from hand to mouth. We learn to-day what ought to have been done yesterday, and yet are at a loss to know what's to be done to-morrow.

'And the Church, sir. God forbid I should push my way into what does not concern me; and if you had told me half an hour gone by that you were a regular churchman, I shouldn't be pouring out all this to you now. It wouldn't be seemly. But being not so gives me confidence. By merely listening you can help me, sir; though you can't help *us*. Centuries ago – and in my humble judgement, rightly – we broke away from the parent stem and rooted ourselves in our own soil. But, right or wrong, doesn't that of itself, I ask you, make us all the more open to attack from him who never wearies in going to and fro in the world seeking whom he may devour?

'I am not wishing you to take sides. But a gentleman doesn't scoff; you don't find him jeering at what he doesn't rightly understand. He keeps his own counsel, sir. And that's where, as I say, Canon Leigh Shougar sets me doubting. He refuses to make allowances; though up there in London things may look different. He gets his company there; and then for him the whole kallyidoscope changes, if you take me.'

The old man scanned me an instant as if inquiring within himself whether, after all, I too might not be one of the outcasts. 'You see, sir,' he went on dejectedly, 'I can bear what may be to come. I can, if need be, live on through what few years may yet remain to me and keep going, as they say. But only if I can be assured that my own inmost senses are not cheating and misleading me. Tell me the worst, and you will have done an old man a service he can never repay. Tell me, on the other hand, that I am merely groping along in a network of devilish *delusion*, sir – well, in that case I hope to be with my master, with Dr Pomfrey, as soon as possible. We were all children once; and now there's nothing worse in this world for him to come into, in a manner of speaking.

'Oh, sir, I sometimes wonder if what we call childhood and growing up isn't a copy of the fate of our ancient forefathers. In the beginning of time there were Fallen Angels, we are told; but even if it weren't there in Holy Writ, we might have learnt it of our own fears and misgivings. I sometimes find myself looking at a young child with little short of awe, sir, knowing that within its mind is a scene of peace and paradise of which we older folk have no notion, and which will fade away out of it, as life wears on, like the mere tabernacling of a dream.'

There was no trace of unction in his speech, though the phraseology might suggest it, and he smiled at me as if in reassurance. 'You see, sir – if I have any true notion of the matter – then I say, heaven is dealing very gently with Dr Pomfrey. He has gone back, and, I take it, his soul is elsewhere and at rest.'

He had come a pace or two nearer, and the candlelight now cast grotesque shadows in the hollows of his brows and cheekbones, silvering his long scanty hair. The eyes, dimming with age, were fixed on mine as if in incommunicable entreaty. I was at a loss to answer him.

He dropped his hands to his sides. 'The fact is,' he looked cautiously about him, 'what I am now being so bold as to suggest, though it's a familiar enough experience to me, may put you in actual physical danger. But then, duty's duty, and a deed of kindness from stranger to stranger quite another matter. You seem to have come, if I may say so, in the nick of time; that was all. On the other hand, we can leave the building at once if you are so minded. In any case we must be gone well before dark sets in; even mere human beings are best not disturbed at any night-work they may be after. The dark brings recklessness: conscience cannot see as clear in the dark. Besides, I once delayed too long myself. There is not much of day left even now, though I see by the almanac there should be a slip of moon to-night – unless the sky is overclouded. All that I'm meaning is that our all-in-all, so to speak, is the calm untrammelled evidence of the outer senses, sir. And there comes a time when – well, when one hesitates to trust one's own.'

I have read somewhere that it is only its setting – the shape, the line, the fold, the angle of the lid and so on – that gives its finer shades of meaning and significance to the human eye. Looking into his, even in that narrow and melancholy illumination, was like pondering over a grey, salt, desolate pool – such as sometimes neighbours the sea on a flat and dangerous coast.

Perhaps if I had been a little less credulous, or less exhausted, I should by now have begun to doubt this old creature's sanity. And yet, surely, at even the faintest contact with the insane, a sentinel in the mind sends up flares and warnings; the very landscape changes; there is a sense of insecurity. If, too, the characters inscribed by age and experience on a man's face can be evidence of goodness and simplicity, then my companion was safe enough. To trust in his sagacity was another matter.

But then, there was All Hallows itself to take into account. That first glimpse from my green headland of its louring yet lovely walls had been strangely moving. There are buildings (almost as though they were once copies of originals now half-forgotten in the human mind) that have a singular influence on the imagination. Even now in this remote candle-lit room, immured between its massive stones, the vast edifice seemed to be gently and furtively fretting its impression on my mind.

I glanced again at the old man: he had turned aside as if to leave me, unbiased, to my own decision. How would a lifetime spent between these sombre walls have affected *me*, I wondered? Surely it would be an act of mere decency to indulge their worn-out hermit! He had appealed to me. If I were ten times more reluctant to follow him, I could hardly refuse. Not at any rate without risking a retreat as humiliating as that of the architectural experts he had referred to – with my tail between my legs.

'I only wish I could hope to be of any real help.'

He turned about; his expression changed, as if at the coming of a light. 'Why, then, sir, let us be gone at once. You are with me, sir: that was all I hoped and asked. And now there's no time to waste.'

336

He tilted his head to listen a moment – with that large, flat, shell-like ear of his which age alone seems to produce. 'Matches and candle, sir,' he had lowered his voice to a whisper, 'but – though we mustn't lose each other; you and me, I mean – *not*, I think, a naked light. What I would suggest, if you have no objection, is your kindly grasping my gown. There is a kind of streamer here, you see – as if made for the purpose. There will be a good deal of up-and-downing, but I know the building blindfold and, as you might say, inch by inch. And now that the bell-ringers have given up ringing it is more in my charge than ever.'

He stood back and looked at me with folded hands, a whimsical childlike smile on his aged face. 'I sometimes think to myself I'm like the sentry, sir, in that play by William Shakespeare. I saw it, sir, years ago, on my only visit to London – when I was a boy. If ever there were a villain for all his fine talk and all, commend me to that ghost. I see him yet.'

Whisper though it was, a sort of chirrup had come into his voice, like that of a cricket in a baker's shop. I took tight hold of the velveted tag of his gown. He opened the door, pressed the box of safety matches into my hand, himself grasped the candlestick and then blew out the light. We were instantly marooned in an impenetrable darkness. 'Now, sir, if you would kindly remove your walking shoes,' he muttered close in my ear, 'we should proceed with less noise. I shan't hurry you. And please to tug at the streamer if you need attention. In a few minutes the blackness will be less intense.'

As I stooped down to loose my shoe-laces I heard my heart thumping merrily away. It had been listening to our conversation apparently! I slung my shoes round my neck – as I had often done as a boy when going paddling – and we set out on our expedition.

I have endured too often the nightmare of being lost and abandoned in the stony bowels of some strange and prodigious building to take such an adventure lightly. I clung, I confess, desperately tight to my lifeline and we groped steadily onward – my guide ever and again turning back to mutter warning or encouragement in my ear.

Now I found myself steadily ascending; and then in a while, feeling my way down flights of hollowly worn stone steps, and anon brushing along a gallery or corkscrewing up a newel staircase so narrow that my shoulders all but touched the walls on either side. In spite of the sepulchral chill in these bowels of the cathedral, I was soon suffocatingly hot, and the effort to see became intolerably fatiguing. Once, to recover our breath we paused opposite a slit in the thickness of the masonry, at which to breathe the tepid sweetness of the outer air. It was faint with the scent of wild flowers and cool of the sea. And presently after, at a barred window, high overhead, I caught a glimpse of the night's first stars.

We then turned inward once more, ascending yet another spiral staircase. And now the intense darkness had thinned a little, the groined roof above us becoming faintly discernible. A fresher air softly fanned my cheek; and then trembling fingers groped over my breast, and, cold and bony, clutched my own.

'Dead still here, sir, if you please.' So close sounded the whispered syllables the voice might have been a messenger's within my own consciousness. 'Dead still, here. There's a drop of some sixty or seventy feet a few paces on.'

I peered out across the abyss, conscious, as it seemed, of the huge superincumbent weight of the noble fretted roof only a small space now immediately above our heads. As we approached the edge of this stony precipice, the gloom paled a little, and I guessed that we must be standing in some coign of the southern transept, for what light the evening skies now afforded was clearer towards the right. On the other hand, it seemed the northern windows opposite us were most of them boarded up, or obscured in some fashion. Gazing out, I could detect scaffolding poles – like knitting needles – thrust out from the walls and a balloon-like spread of canvas above them. For the moment my ear was haunted by what appeared to be the droning of an immense insect. But this presently ceased. I fancy it was internal only.

'You will understand, sir,' breathed the old man close beside me – and we still stood, grotesquely enough, hand in hand – 'the scaffolding over there has been in position a good many months now. It was put up when the last gentleman came down from London to inspect the fabric. And there it's been left ever since. Now, sir! – though I implore you to be cautious.'

I hardly needed the warning. With one hand clutching my box of matches, the fingers of the other interlaced with my companion's, I strained every sense. And yet I could detect not the faintest stir or murmur under that wide-spreading roof. Only a hush as profound as that which must reign in the Royal Chamber of the pyramid of Cheops faintly swirled in the labyrinths of my ear.

How long we stayed in this position I cannot say; but minutes sometimes seem like hours. And then, without the slightest warning, I became aware of a peculiar and incessant vibration. It is impossible to give a name to it. It suggested the remote whirring of an enormous mill-stone, or that – though without definite pulsation – of revolving wings, or even the spinning of an immense top.

In spite of his age, my companion apparently had ears as acute as mine. He had clutched me tighter a full ten seconds before I myself became aware of this disturbance of the air. He pressed closer. 'Do you see that, sir?'

I gazed and gazed, and saw nothing. Indeed even in what I had seemed to *hear* I might have been deceived. Nothing is more treacherous in certain circumstances – except possibly the eye – than the ear. It magnifies, distorts, and may even invent. As instantaneously as I had become aware of it, the murmur had ceased. And then – though I cannot be certain – it seemed the dingy and voluminous spread of canvas over there had perceptibly trembled, as if a huge cautious hand had been thrust out to draw it aside. No time was given me to make sure. The old man had hastily withdrawn me into the opening of the wall through which we had issued; and we made no pause in our retreat until we had come again to the narrow slit of window which I have spoken of and could refresh ourselves with a less stagnant air. We stood here resting awhile.

'Well, sir?' he inquired at last, in the same flat muffled tones.

'Do you ever pass along here alone?' I whispered.

'Oh, yes, sir. I make it a habit to be the last to leave – and often the first to come; but I am usually gone by this hour.'

I looked close at the dim face in profile against that narrow oblong of night. 'It is so difficult to be sure of oneself,' I said. 'Have you ever actually *encountered* anything – near at hand, I mean?'

'I keep a sharp look-out, sir. Maybe they don't think me of enough importance to molest – the last rat, as they say.'

'But *have* you?' – I might myself have been communicating with the phantasmal *genius loci* of All Hallows – our muffled voices; this intense caution and secret listening; the slight breathlessness, as if at any instant one's heart were ready for flight: 'But *have* you?'

'Well yes, sir,' he said. 'And in this very gallery. They nearly had me, sir. But by good fortune there's a recess a little further on – stored up with some old fragments of carving, from the original building, sixth-century, so it's said: stone-capitals, heads and hands, and such like. I had had my warning, and managed to leap in there and conceal myself. But only just in time. Indeed, sir, I confess I was in such a condition of terror and horror I turned my back.'

'You mean you heard, but didn't look? And – something came?'

'Yes, sir, I seemed to be reduced to no bigger than a child, huddled up there in that corner. There was a sound like clanging metal – but I don't think it was metal. It drew near at a furious speed, then passed me, making a filthy gust of wind. For some instants I couldn't breathe; the air was gone.'

'And no other sound?'

'No other, sir, except out of the distance a noise like the sounding of a stupendous kind of gibberish. A calling; or so it seemed – no human sound. The air shook with it. You see, sir, I myself wasn't of any consequence, I take it – unless a mere obstruction in the way. But – I have heard it said somewhere that the rarity of these happenings is only because it's a pain and torment and not any sort of pleasure for such beings, such apparitions, sir, good or bad, to visit our outward world. That's what I have heard said; though I can go no further.

'The time I'm telling you of was in the early winter – November. There was a dense sea-fog over the valley, I remember. It eddied through that opening there into the candlelight like flowing milk. I never light up now: and, if I may be forgiven the boast, sir, I seem to have almost forgotten how to be afraid. After all, in any walk of life a man can only do his best, and if there weren't such opposition and hindrances in high places I should have nothing to complain of. What is anybody's life, sir (come past the gaiety of youth), but marking time . . . Did you hear anything *then*, sir?'

His gentle monotonous mumbling ceased and we listened together. But every ancient edifice has voices and soundings of its own: there was nothing audible that I could put a name to, only what seemed to be a faint perpetual stir or whirr of grinding such as (to one's over-stimulated senses) the stablest stones set one on top of the other with an ever slightly varying weight and stress might be likely to make perceptible in a world of matter. A world which, after all, they say, is itself in unimaginably rapid rotation, and under the tyranny of time.

'No, I hear nothing,' I answered, 'but please don't think I am doubting what you say. Far from it. You must remember I am a stranger, and that therefore the influence of the place cannot but be less apparent to me. And you have no help in this now?'

'No, sir. Not now. But even at the best of times we had small company hereabouts, and no money. Not for any substantial outlay,

I mean. And not even the boldest suggests making what's called a public appeal. It's a strange thing to me, sir, but whenever the newspapers get hold of anything, they turn it into a byword and a sham. Yet how can they help themselves? – with no beliefs to guide them and nothing to stay their mouths except about what for sheer human decency's sake they daren't talk about. But then, who am I to complain? And now, sir,' he continued with a sigh of utter weariness, 'if you are sufficiently rested, would you perhaps follow me on to the roof? It is the last visit I make – though by rights perhaps I should take in what there is of the tower. But I'm too old now for that – clambering and climbing over naked beams; and the ladders are not so safe as they were.'

We had not far to go. The old man drew open a squat, heavily ironed door at the head of a flight of wooden steps. It was latched but not bolted, and admitted us at once to the leaden roof of the building and to the immense amphitheatre of evening. The last faint hues of sunset were fading in the west; and silver-bright Spica shared with the tilted crescent of the moon the serene lagoon-like expanse of sky above the sea. Even at this height, the air was audibly stirred with the low lullaby of the tide.

The staircase by which we had come out was surmounted by a flat penthouse roof about seven feet high. We edged softly along, then paused once more; to find ourselves now all but *tête-à-tête* with the gigantic figures that stood sentinel at the base of the buttresses to the unfinished tower.

The tower was so far unfinished, indeed, as to wear the appearance of the ruinous; besides which, what appeared to be scars and stains as if of fire were detectable on some of its stones, reminding me of the legend which years before I had chanced upon, that this stretch of coast had more than once been visited centuries ago by pillaging Norsemen.

The night was unfathomably clear and still. On our left rose the conical bluff of the headland crowned with the solitary grove of trees beneath which I had taken refuge from the blinding sunshine that very afternoon. Its grasses were now hoary with faintest moonlight. Far to the right stretched the flat cold plain of the Atlantic – that enormous darkened looking-glass of space; only a distant lightship ever and again stealthily signalling to us with a lean phosphoric finger from its outermost reaches.

The mere sense of that abysm of space – its waste powdered with the stars of the Milky Way; the mere presence of the stony leviathan on whose back we two humans now stood, dwarfed into insignificance beside these gesturing images of stone, were enough of themselves to excite the imagination. And – whether matter-of-fact or pure delusion – this old verger's insinuations that the cathedral was now menaced by some inconceivable danger and assault had set my nerves on edge. My feet were numb as the lead they stood upon; while the tips of my fingers tingled as if a powerful electric discharge were coursing through my body.

We moved gently on – the spare shape of the old man a few steps ahead, peering cautiously to right and left of him as we advanced. Once, with a hasty gesture, he drew me back and fixed his eyes for a full minute on a figure – at two removes – which was silhouetted at that moment against the starry emptiness: a forbidding thing enough, viewed in this vague luminosity, which seemed in spite of the unmoving stare that I fixed on it to be perceptibly stirring on its windworn pedestal.

But no; 'All's well!' the old man had mutely signalled to me, and we pushed on. Slowly and cautiously; indeed I had time to notice in passing that this particular figure held stretched in its right hand a bent bow, and was crowned with a high weather-worn stone coronet. One and all were frigid company. At last we completed our circuit of the tower, had come back to the place we had set out from, and stood eyeing one another like two conspirators in the clear dusk. Maybe there was a tinge of incredulity on my face.

'No, sir,' murmured the old man, 'I expected no other. The night is uncommonly quiet. I've noticed that before. They seem to leave us at peace on nights of quiet. We must turn in again and be getting home.'

Until that moment I had thought no more of where I was to sleep or to get food, nor had even realised how famished with hunger I was. Nevertheless, the notion of fumbling down again out of the open air into the narrow inward blackness of the walls from which we had just issued was singularly uninviting. Across these wide flat stretches of roof there was at least space for flight, and there were recesses for concealment. To gain a moment's respite, I inquired if I should have much difficulty in getting a bed in the village. And as I had hoped, the old man himself offered me hospitality.

I thanked him; but still hesitated to follow, for at that moment I was trying to discover what peculiar effect of dusk and darkness a moment before had deceived me into the belief that some small animal – a dog, a spaniel I should have guessed – had suddenly and surreptitiously taken cover behind the stone buttress nearby. But that apparently had been a mere illusion. The creature, whatever it might be, was no barker at any rate. Nothing stirred now; and my companion seemed to have noticed nothing amiss.

'You were saying,' I pressed him, 'that when repairs – restorations – of the building were in contemplation, even the experts were perplexed by what they discovered? What did they actually say?'

'Say, sir!' Our voices sounded as small and meaningless up here as those of grasshoppers in a noonday meadow. 'Examine that balustrade which you are leaning against at this minute. Look at that gnawing and fretting – that furrowing above the lead. All that is honest wear and tear – constant weathering of the mere elements, sir – rain and wind and snow and frost. That's honest *nature*-work, sir. But now compare it, if you please, with this St Mark here; and remember, sir, these images were intended to be part and parcel of the fabric as you might say, sentries on a castle – symbols, you understand.'

I stooped close under the huge grey creature of stone until my eyes were scarcely more than six inches from its pedestal. And, unless the moon deceived me, I confess I could find not the slightest trace of fret or friction. Far from it. The stone had been grotesquely decorated in low relief with a gaping crocodile – a two-headed crocodile; and the angles, knubs and undulations of the creature were cut as sharp as with a knife in cheese. I drew back.

'Now cast your glance upwards, sir. Is that what you would call a saintly shape and gesture?'

What appeared to represent an eagle was perched on the image's lifted wrist – an eagle resembling a vulture. The head beneath it was poised at an angle of defiance – its ears abnormally erected on the skull; the lean right forearm extended with point-ing forefinger as if in derision. Its stony gaze was fixed upon the stars; its whole aspect was hostile, sinister and intimidating. I drew aside. The faintest puff of milk-warm air from over the sea stirred on my cheek.

'Ay, sir, and so with one or two of the rest of them,' the old man commented, as he watched me, 'there are other wills than the Almighty's.'

At this, the pent-up excitement within me broke bounds. This nebulous insinuatory talk! – I all but lost my temper. 'I can't, for the life of me, understand what you are saying,' I exclaimed in a voice that astonished me with its shrill volume of sound in that intense lofty quiet. 'One doesn't *repair* in order to destroy.'

The old man met me without flinching. 'No, sir? Say you so? And why not? Are there not two kinds of change in this world? – a building-up and a breaking-down? To give strength and endur-ance for evil or misguided purposes, would that be power wasted, if such was your aim? Why, sir, isn't that true even of the human mind and heart? We here are on the outskirts, I grant, but where would you expect the enemy to show himself unless in the outer defences? An institution may be beyond saving, sir: it may be being restored for a worse destruction. And a hundred trumpeting voices would make no difference when the faith and life within is tottering to its fall.'

Somehow, this muddle of metaphors reassured me. Obviously the old man's wits had worn a little thin: he was the victim of an intelligible but monstrous hallucination.

'And yet you are taking it for granted,' I expostulated, 'that, if what you say is true, a stranger could be of the slightest help. A visitor – mind you – who hasn't been inside the doors of a church, except in search of what is old and obsolete, for years.'

The old man laid a trembling hand upon my sleeve. The folly of it – with my shoes hanging like ludicrous millstones round my neck!

'If you please, sir,' he pleaded, 'have a little patience with me. I'm preaching at nobody. I'm not even hinting that them outside the fold circumstantially speaking aren't of the flock. All in good time, sir; the Almighty's time. Maybe – with all due respect – it's from them within we have most to fear. And indeed, sir, believe an old man: I could never express the gratitude I feel. You have given me the occasion to unbosom myself, to make a clean breast, as they say. All Hallows is my earthly home, and – well, there, let us say no more. You couldn't *help me* – except only by your presence here. God alone knows who can!'

At that instant, a dull enormous rumble reverberated from within the building – as if a huge boulder or block of stone had been shifted or dislodged in the fabric; a peculiar grinding nerve-wracking sound. And for the fraction of a second the flags on which we stood seemed to tremble beneath our feet.

The fingers tightened on my arm. 'Come, sir; keep close; we must be gone at once,' the quavering old voice whispered; 'we have stayed too long.'

But we emerged into the night at last without mishap. The little western door, above which the grinning head had welcomed me on my arrival, admitted us to *terra firma* again, and we made our way up a deep sandy track, bordered by clumps of hemp agrimony and fennel and hemlock, with viper's bugloss and sea-poppy blooming in the gentle dusk of night at our feet. We turned when we reached the summit of this sandy incline and looked back. All Hallows, vague and enormous, lay beneath us in its hollow, resembling some natural prehistoric outcrop of that sea-worn rock-bound coast; but strangely human and saturnine.

The air was mild as milk – a pool of faintest sweetnesses – gorse, bracken, heather; and not a rumour disturbed its calm, except only the furtive and stertorous sighings of the tide. But far out to sea and beneath the horizon summer lightnings were now in idle play – flickering into the sky like the unfolding of a signal, planet to planet – then gone. That alone, and perhaps too this feeble moonlight glinting on the ancient glass, may have accounted for the faint vitreous glare that seemed ever and again to glitter across the windows of the northern transept far beneath us. And yet how easily deceived is the imagination. This old man's talk still echoing in my ear, I could have vowed this was no reflection but the glow of some light shining fitfully from within outwards.

We paused together beside a flowering bush of fuchsia at the wicket-gate leading into his small square of country garden. 'You'll forgive me, sir, for mentioning it; but I make it a rule as far as possible to leave all my troubles and misgivings outside when I come home. My daughter is a widow, and not long in that sad condition, so I keep as happy a face as I can on things. And yet: well, sir, I wonder at times if – if a personal sacrifice isn't incumbent on them that have their object most at heart. I'd go out myself very willingly, sir, I can assure you, if there was any certainty in my mind that it would serve the cause. It would be little to me if—' He made no attempt to complete the sentence.

On my way to bed, that night, the old man led me in on tiptoe to show me his grandson. His daughter watched me intently as I stooped over the child's cot – with that bird-like solicitude which all mothers show in the presence of a stranger.

Her small son was of that fairness which almost suggests the unreal. He had flung back his bedclothes – as if innocence in this world needed no covering or defence – and lay at ease, the dews of sleep on lip, cheek, and forehead. He was breathing so quietly that not the least movement of shoulder or narrow breast was perceptible.

'The lovely thing!' I muttered, staring at him. 'Where is he now, I wonder?' His mother lifted her face and smiled at me with a drowsy ecstatic happiness, then sighed.

And from out of the distance, there came the first prolonged whisper of a wind from over the sea. It was eleven by my watch, the storm after the long heat of the day seemed to be drifting inland; but All Hallows, apparently, had forgotten to wind its clock.

RANDALLS ROUND

by

Eleanor Scott

First published in the collection *Randalls Round*

1929

'OF COURSE, I don't pretend to be aesthetic and all that,' said Heyling in that voice of half contemptuous indifference that often marks the rivalry between Science and Art, 'but I must say that this folk-song and dance business strikes me as pretty complete rot. I dare say there may be some arguments in favour of it for exercise and that, but I'm dashed if I can see why a chap need leap about in fancy braces because he wants to train down his fat.'

He lit a cigarette disdainfully.

'All revivals are a bit artificial, I expect,' said Mortlake in his quiet, pleasant voice, 'but it's not a question of exercise only in this case, you know. People who know say that it's the remains of a religious cult – sacrificial rites and that. There certainly are some very odd things done in out-of-the-way places.'

'How d'you mean?' asked Heyling, unconvinced. 'You can't really think that there's any kind of heathen cult still practised in this country?'

'Well,' said Mortlake, 'there's not much left now. More in Wales, I believe, and France, than here. But I believe that if we could find a place where people had never lost the cult, we might run into some queer things. There are a few places like that,' he went on, 'places where they're said to perform their own rite occasionally. I mean to look it up some time. By the way,' he added, suddenly sitting upright, 'didn't you say you were going to a village called Randalls for the weekend?'

'Yes – little place in the Cotswolds somewhere. Boney gave me an address.'

'Going to work, or for an easy?'

'Not to work. Boney's afraid of my precious health. He thinks I'm overworking my delicate constitution.'

'Well, if you've the chance, I wish you'd take a look at the records in the old Guildhall there and see if you can find any references to folk customs. Randalls is believed to be one of the places where there is a genuine survival. They have a game I think, or a dance, called Randalls Round. I'd very much like to know if there are any written records – anything definite. Not if you're bored you know, or don't want to. Just if you're at a loose end.'

'Right, I will,' said Heyling; and there the talk ended.

It is unusual for Oxford undergraduates to take a long week-end off in the Michaelmas term with the permission of the college authorities; but Heyling, from whom his tutor expected great things, had certainly been reading too hard. The weather that autumn was unusually close and clammy, even for Oxford; and Heyling was getting into such a state of nerves that he was delighted to take the chance of getting away from Oxford for the weekend.

The weather, as he cycled out along the Woodstock Road, was moist and warm; but as the miles slipped by and the ground rose, he became aware of the softness of the air, the pleasant lines of the bare, sloping fields, the quiet of the low, rolling clouds. Already he felt calmer, more at ease.

The lift of the ground became more definite, and the character of the country changed. It became more open, bleaker; it had something of the quality of moorland, and the little scattered stone houses had that air of being one with the earth that is the right of moorland houses.

Randalls was, as Heyling's tutor had told him, quite a small place, though it had once boasted a market. Round a little square space, grass-grown now, where once droves of patient cattle and flocks of shaggy Cotswold sheep had stood to be sold, were grouped houses, mostly of the seventeenth or early eighteenth century, made of the beautiful mellow stone of the Cotswolds; and Heyling noticed among these one building of exceptional beauty, earlier in date than the others, long and low, with a deep square porch and mullioned windows.

'That's the Guildhall Mortlake spoke of I expect,' he said to himself as he made his way to the Flaming Hand Inn, where his quarters were booked. 'Quite a good place to look up town records. Queer how that sort of vague rot gets hold of quite sensible men.'

Heyling received a hearty welcome at the inn. Visitors were not very frequent at that time of year, for Randalls is rather far from the good hunting country. Even a chance weekender was something of an event. Heyling was given a quite exceptionally nice room (or rather, a pair of rooms – for two communicated with one another) on the ground floor. The front one, looking out on to the old square, was furnished as a sitting-room; the other gave on to the inn yard, a pleasant cobbled place surrounded by a moss-grown wall and barns with beautiful lichened roofs. Heyling began to feel quite cheerful and vigorous as he lit his pipe and prepared to spend a lazy evening.

As he was settling down in his chair with one of the inn's scanty supply of very dull novels, he was mildly surprised to hear children's voices chanting outside. He reflected that Guy Fawkes' Day was not due yet, and that in any case the tune they sang was not the formless huddle usually produced on that august occasion. This was a real melody – rather an odd, plaintive air, ending with an abrupt drop that pleased his ear. Little as he knew folklore, and much as he despised it, Heyling could not but recognise that this was a genuine folk air, and a very attractive one.

The children did not appear to be begging; their song finished, they simply went away; but Heyling was surprised when some minutes later he heard the same air played again, this time on a flute or flageolet. There came also the sound of many feet in the market square. It was evident that the whole population had turned out to see some sight. Mildly interested, Heyling rose and lounged across to the bay window of his room.

The tiny square was thronged with villagers, all gazing at an empty space left in the centre. At one end of this space stood a man playing on a long and curiously sweet pipe: he played the same haunting plaintive melody again and again. In the very centre stood a pole, as a maypole stands in some villages; but instead of garlands and ribbons, this pole had flung over it the shaggy hide of some creature like an ox. Heyling could just see the blunt heavy head with its short thick horns. Then, without a word or a signal, men came out from among the watchers and began a curious dance.

Heyling had seen folk-dancing done in Oxford, and he recognised some of the features of the dance; but it struck him as being a graver, more barbaric affair than the performances he had seen before. It was almost solemn.

As he watched, the dancers began a figure that he recognised. They took hands in a ring, facing outwards; then, with their hands lifted, they began to move slowly round, counter-clockwise. Memory stirred faintly, and two things came drifting into Heyling's mind: one, the sound of Mortlake's voice as the two men had stood watching a performance of the Headington Mummers – 'That's the Back Ring. It's supposed to be symbolic of death – a survival of a time when a dead victim lay in the middle and the dancers turned away from him.' The other memory was dimmer, for he could not remember who had told him that to move in a circle counter-clockwise was unlucky. It must have been a Scot, though, for he remembered the word 'widdershins'.

These faint stirrings of memory were snapped off by a sudden movement in the dance going on outside. Two new figures advanced – one a man, whose head was covered by a mask made in the rough likeness of a bull; the other shrouded from head to foot in a white sheet, so that even the sex was indistinguishable. Without a sound these two came into the space left in the centre of the dance. The bull-headed man placed the second figure with its back to the pole where hung the hide. The dancers moved more and more slowly. Evidently some crisis of the dance was coming.

Suddenly the bull-headed man jerked the pole so that the shaggy hide fell outspread on the shrouded figure standing before it.

It gave a horrid impression – as if the creature hanging limp on the pole had suddenly come to life, and with one swift, terrible movement had engulfed and devoured the helpless victim standing passively before it. Heyling felt quite shocked – startled, as if he ought to do something. He even threw the window open, as though he meant to spring out and stop the horrid rite. Then he drew back, laughing a little at his own folly. The dance had come to an end: the bull-headed man had lifted the hide from the shrouded figure and thrown it carelessly over his shoulder. The flute-player had stopped his melody, and the crowd was melting away.

'What a queer performance!' said Heyling to himself. 'I see now what old Mortlake means. It does look like a survival of some sort. Where's that book of his?'

He rummaged in his rucksack and produced a book that Mortlake had lent him – one volume of a very famous book on folklore. There were many accounts of village games and 'feasts', all traced in a sober and scholarly fashion to some barbaric, primitive rite. He was interested to see how often mention was made of animal masks, or of the hides or tails of animals being worn by performers in these odd revels. There was nothing fantastic or strained in these accounts – nothing of the romantic type that Heyling scornfully dubbed 'aesthetic'. They were as careful and well authenticated as the facts in a scientific treatise. Randalls was mentioned, and the dance described – rather scantily, Heyling thought, until, reading on, he found that the author acknowledged that he had not himself seen it, but was indebted to a friend for the account of it. But Heyling found something that interested him.

'The origin of this dance,' he read, 'is almost certainly sacrificial. Near Randalls is one of those "banks" or mounds, surrounded by a thicket, which the villagers refuse to approach. These mounds are not uncommon in the Cotswolds, though few seem to be regarded with quite as much awe as Randalls Bank, which the country people avoid scrupulously. The bank is oval in shape, and is almost certainly formed by a long barrow of the Palæolithic age. This theory is borne out by the fact that at one time the curious Randalls Round was danced about the mound, the "victim" being led into the fringe of the thicket that surrounds it.' (A footnote added, 'Whether this is still the case I cannot be certain.') 'Permission to open the tumulus has always been most firmly refused.'

'That's amusing,' thought Heyling, as he laid down the book and felt for a match. 'Jove, what a lark it would be to get into that barrow!' he went on, drawing at his pipe. 'Wonder if I could get leave? The villagers seem to have changed their ways a bit – they do their show in the village now. They mayn't be so set on their blessed mound as they used to be. Where exactly is the place?'

He drew out an ordnance map, and soon found it – a field about a mile and a half north-west of the village, with the word 'Tumulus' in Gothic characters.

'I'll have a look at that tomorrow,' Heyling told himself, folding up the map. 'I must find out who owns the field, and get leave to investigate a bit. The landlord would know who the owner is, I expect.'

Unfortunately for Heyling's plans, the next day dawned wet,

although occasional gleams gave hope that the weather would clear later. His interest had not faded during the night, and he determined that as soon as the weather was a little better he would cycle out to Randalls Bank and have a look at it. Meanwhile, it might not be a bad plan to see whether the Guildhall held any records that might throw a light on his search as Mortlake had suggested. He accordingly hunted out a worthy who was, among many other offices, Town Clerk, and was led by him to the fifteenth-century building he had noticed on his way to the Flaming Hand.

It was very cool and dark inside the old Guildhall. The atmosphere of the place pleased Heyling; he liked the simple groining of the roof and the worn stone stair that led up to the Record Room. This was a low, pleasant place, with deep windows and a singularly beautiful ceiling; Heyling noticed that it also served the purpose of a small reference library.

While the Town Clerk pottered with keys in the locks of chests and presses, Heyling idly examined the titles of the books ranged decorously on the shelves about the room. His eye was caught by the title, *Prehistoric Remains in the Cotswolds*. He took the volume down. There was an opening chapter dealing with prehistoric remains in general, and, glancing through it, he saw mentions of long and round barrows. He kept the book in his hand for closer inspection. He really knew precious little about barrows, and it would be just as well to find out a little before beginning his exploration. In fact, when the Town Clerk left him alone in the Record Room, that book was the first thing he studied.

It was a mere text-book, after all, but to Heyling's ignorance it revealed a few facts of interest. Long barrows, he gathered, were older than round, and more uncommon, and were often objects of superstitious awe among the country folk of the district, who generally opposed any effort to explore them; but the whole chapter was very brief and skimpy, and Heyling had soon exhausted its interest.

The town records, however, were more amusing, for he very soon found references to his particular field. There was a lawsuit in the early seventeenth century which concerned it, and the interest to Heyling was redoubled by the vagueness of certain evidence. A certain Beale brought charges of witchcraft against 'diuers Persouns of ys Towne'. He had reason for alarm, for apparently his son, 'a yong and comely Lad of 20ann.', had completely disappeared: 'wherefore ye sd. Jno. Beale didd openlie declare and state yt ye sd. Son Frauncis hadd been led away by Warlockes in ye Daunce (for yt his Ringe, ye wh. he hadd long worne, was found in ye Fielde wh. ye wot of) and hadd by ym beene done to Deathe in yr Abhominable Practicinges.' The case seemed to have been hushed up, although several people cited by 'ye sd. Jno. Beale' admitted having been in the company of the missing youth on the night of his disappearance – which, Heyling was interested to notice, was that very day, 31st October.

Another document, of a later date, recorded the attempted sale of the 'field wh. ye wot of' – (no name was ever given to the place) – and the refusal of the purchaser to fulfil his contract owing to 'ye ill repute of the place, the wh. was unknowen to Himm when he didd entre into his Bargayn'.

The only other documents of interest to Heyling were some of the seventeenth century, wherein the authorities of the Commonwealth inveighed against 'ye Lewd Games and Dauncyng, ye wh. are Seruice to Sathanas and a moste strong Abhominatioun to ye Lorde'. These spoke openly of devil worship and 'loathlie Ceremonie at ye Banke in ye Fielde'. It seemed that more than one person had stood trial for conducting these ceremonies, and against one case (dated 7th November, 1659) was written, '*Conuicti et combusti.*'

'Good Lord – burnt!' exclaimed Heyling aloud. 'What an appalling business! I suppose the poor beggars were only doing much the same thing as those chaps I saw yesterday.'

He sat lost in thought for some time. He thought how that odd tune and dance had gone on in this remote village for centuries; had there been more to it once, he wondered? Did that queer business with the hide mean – well, some real devilry? Pictures floated into his mind – odd, squat little men, broad of shoulder and long of arm, naked and hairy, dancing in solemn, ghastly worship, dim ages ago ... This business was getting a stronger hold of him than he would have thought possible.

'Strikes me that if there is anything of the old devilry left, it'll be in that field,' he concluded at last. 'The dance they do now is all open and above board; but if they still avoid the field, as that book of Mortlake's seems to think, that might be a clue. I'll find out.'

He rose and went down to inform the Town Clerk that his researches were over, and then went back to the inn in a comfortable frame of mind. Certainly his weekend was bringing him distraction from his work: no thought of it had entered his head since he first heard the children singing outside the inn.

The landlord of the Flaming Hand was a solid man who gave the impression of honesty and sense. Heyling felt that he could depend upon him for a reasonable account of 'the fielde which ye wot of'. He accordingly tackled him after lunch, and was at once amused, surprised and annoyed to find that the man hedged as soon as he was questioned on the subject. He quite definitely opposed any idea of exploration.

'I'm not like some on 'em, sir,' he said. 'I wouldn't go for to say that it'd do any 'arm for you to take a turn in the field while it was light, like. But it ain't 'ealthy after dark, sir, that field aren't. Nor it ain't no sense to go a-diggin' and a-delvin' in that there bank. I've lived in this 'ere place a matter of forty year, man and boy, and I know what I'm a-sayin' of.'

'But why isn't it healthy? Is it marshy?'

'No, sir, it ain't not to say marshy.'

'Don't the farmers ever cultivate it?'

'Well, sir, all I can say is I been in this place forty year, man and boy, and it ain't never been dug nor ploughed nor sown nor reaped in my mem'ry. Nor yet in my father's, nor in my grandfather's. Crops wouldn' do, sir, not in that field.'

'Well, I want to go and examine the mound. Who's the owner? – I ought to get his leave, I suppose.'

'You won't do that, sir.'

'Why not?'

''Cause I'm the owner, sir, and I won't 'ave anyone, not the King 'isself nor yet the King's son, a-diggin' in that bank. Not for a wagon-load of gold, I won't.'

Heyling saw it was useless.

'Oh, all right! If you feel like that about it!' he said carelessly.

The stubborn, half-frightened look left the host's eyes. 'Thank you, sir,' he said, quite gratefully.

But he had not really gained the victory. Heyling was as obstinate as he, and he had determined that before he left Randalls he would have investigated that barrow. If he could not get permission, he would go without. He decided that as soon as darkness fell he would go out on the quiet and explore in earnest. He would borrow a spade from the open cart-shed of the inn – a spade and a pick, if he could find one. He began to feel some of the enthusiasm of the explorer.

He decided that he would spend part of the afternoon in examining the outside of the mound. It was not more than a ten minutes' ride to the field, which lay on the road. It was, as the landlord had said, uncultivated. Almost in the middle of it rose a mass of stunted trees and bushes – a thick mass of intertwining boughs that would certainly take some strength to penetrate. Was it really a tomb, Heyling wondered? And he thought with some awe of the strange prehistoric being who might lie there, his rude jewels and arms about him.

He returned to the inn, his interest keener than ever. He would most certainly get into that barrow as soon as it was dark enough to try. He felt restless now, as one always does when one is looking forward with some excitement to an event a few hours distant. He fidgeted about the room, one eye constantly on his watch.

He wanted to get to the field as soon as possible after dark, for his casual inspection of the afternoon had shown him that the task of pushing through the bushes, tangled and interwoven as they were, would be no light one; and then there was the opening of the tumulus to be done – that soil, untouched by spade or plough for centuries, to be broken by the pick until an entrance was forced into the chamber within. He ought to be off as soon as he could safely secure the tools he wanted to borrow.

But Fate was against him. There seemed to be a constant flow of visitors to the Flaming Hand that evening – not ordinary labourers dropping in for a drink, but private visitors to the landlord, who went through to his parlour behind the bar and left by the yard at the side of the inn. It really did seem like some silly mystery story, thought Heyling impatiently; the affair in the marketplace, the landlord's odd manner over the question of the field, and now this hushed coming and going from the landlord's room!

He went to his bedroom window and looked out into the yard. He wanted to make quite sure that the pick and spade were still in the open cart-shed. To his relief they were; but as he looked he got yet another shock. A man slipped out from the door of the inn kitchen and slipped across the yard into the lane that lay behind the inn. Another followed him, and a little later another; and all three had black faces. Their hands showed light, and their necks; but their faces were covered with soot, so that the features were quite indistinguishable.

'This is too mad!' exclaimed Heyling half aloud. 'Jove, I didn't expect to run into this sort of farce when I came here. Wonder if *all* old Cross's mysterious visitors have had black faces? Anyway,

I wish they'd buck up and clear out. I may not have another chance to go to that mound if I don't get off soon.'

The queer happenings at the inn now appeared to him solely as obstacles to his own movements. If their import came into his mind at all, it was to make him wonder whether there were any play like a mummers' show which the village kept up; or games, perhaps, like those played in Scotland at Hallowe'en ... By Jove! That probably was the explanation. It *was* All Hallows' Eve! Why couldn't they buck up and get on with it, anyhow?

His patience was not to be tried much longer. Soon after nine the noises ceased; but to make doubly sure, Heyling did not leave his room till ten had struck from Randalls church.

He got cautiously out of his bedroom window and landed softly on the cobbles of the yard. The tools still leaned against the wall of the open shed – trusting man, Mr Cross, of the Flaming Hand! The shed where his cycle stood was locked, though, and he swore softly at the loss of time this would mean in getting to the field. It would take him twenty-five minutes to walk.

As a matter of fact, it did not take him quite so long, for impatience gave him speed. The country looked very beautiful under the slow-rising hunter's moon. The long bare lines of the fields swept up to the ridges, black against the dark serene blue of the night sky. The air was cool and clean, with the smell of frost in it. Heyling, hurrying along the rough white road, was dimly conscious of the purity and peace of the night.

At last the field came in sight, empty and still in the cold moonlight. Only the mound, black as a tomb, broke the flood of light. The gate was wide open, and even in his haste this struck Heyling as odd.

'I could have sworn I shut that gate,' he said to himself. 'I remember thinking I must, in case anyone spotted I'd been in. It just shows that people don't avoid the place as much as old Cross would like me to believe.'

He decided to attack the barrow on the side away from the road, lest any belated labourer should pass by. He walked round the mound, looking for a thin spot in its defence of thorn and hazel bushes; but there was none. The scrub formed a thick belt all round the barrow, and was so high that he could not see the top of the mound at all. The confounded stuff might grow half-way up the tumulus for all he could see.

He abandoned any idea of finding an easy spot to begin operations. It was obviously just a question of breaking through. Then, just as he was about to take this heroic course, he stopped short, listening. It sounded to him as if some creature were moving within the bushes – something heavy and bulky, breaking the smaller branches of the undergrowth.

'Must be a fox, I suppose,' he thought, 'but he must be a monster. It sounds more like a cow, though of course it can't be. Well, here goes.'

He turned his back to the belt of thick undergrowth, ducked his head forward, and was just about to force his backwards way through the bushes when again he stopped to listen. This time it was a very different sound that arrested him – it was the distant playing of a pipe. He recognised it – the plaintive melody of Randalls Round.

He paused, listening. Yes – feet were coming up the road – many feet, pattering unevenly. There *was* some village game afoot, then!

The words of Mortlake's book came back to his mind. The author had said that at one time the barrow was the centre of the dance. Was it possible that it was so still – that there was a second form, less decorous perhaps, which took place at night?

Anyhow, he mustn't be seen, that was certain. Lucky the mound was between him and the road. He stole cautiously towards the hedge on the far side of the field. Thank goodness it was a hedge and not one of those low stone walls that surround most fields in the Cotswolds.

As he took cautious cover he couldn't help feeling a very complete fool. Was it really necessary to take this precaution? And then he remembered the look of stubborn determination on the landlord's face. Yes, if he were to investigate the barrow he must keep dark. Besides, there might be something to see in this business – something to delight old Mortlake's heart.

The tune came nearer, and the sound of footsteps was muffled. They were in the grassy field, then. Heyling cautiously raised his head from the ditch where he lay; but the mound blocked his view as yet. What luck that he'd happened to go to Randalls just at that time – Hallowe'en! He remembered the documents in the Guildhall, and Jno. Beale's indictment of the men who, he averred, had made away with his son at Hallowe'en. Heyling's blood tingled with excitement.

The playing came closer, and now Heyling could see the figures of men moving into the circle they formed for Randalls Round. Again he was struck by the queer barbaric look of the thing and by the gravity of their movements; and then his heart gave a sudden heavy thump. The dancers had all the blackened mask-like faces of the men he had seen leaving the inn. How odd! thought Heyling. They perform quite openly in the village square, and then steal away at night, disguising their faces . . .

The dance was extraordinarily impressive, seen in that empty field under the quiet moon. There was no sound but the whispering of their feet on the long dry grass and the melancholy music of the pipe. Then, quite suddenly, Heyling heard again the cracking, rustling sound from the dense bushes about the mound. It was exactly like the stirring of some big clumsy animal. The dancers heard it too; there came a sort of shuddering gasp; Heyling saw one man glance at his neighbour, and his eyes shone light and terrified in his blackened face.

The melody came slower, and with a kind of horror Heyling knew that the crisis of the dance was near. Slowly the dancers formed the ring, their faces turned away from the mound; then from outside the circle came a shrouded figure led by a man wearing a mask like a bull's head. The veiled form was led into the ring. The pipe mourned on.

Again, shattering the quiet, came a snapping, crashing noise from the inmost recesses of the bushes about the barrow. There *was* some big animal in there, crashing his way out . . .

Then he saw it, bulky and black in the pure white light – some horrible primitive creature, with heavy lowered head. The dancers circled slowly; the air of the flute grew faint.

Heyling felt cold and sick. This was loathsome, devilish . . . He buried his head in his arms and tried to drown the sound of that mourning melody.

Sounds came through the muffling hands over his ears – a crunching, tearing sound, and then a horrible noise like an animal lapping. Sweat broke out on Heyling's back. It sounded like bones . . . He could not think, or move, or pray . . . The haunting music still crooned on . . .

The crashing, snapping noise again as the branches broke. *It*, whatever it was, was going back into its lair. The tune grew fainter and fainter. Steps sounded again on the road – slow steps, with no life in them. The horrible rite was over.

Very cautiously Heyling got to his feet. His knees trembled, and his breath came short and rough. He felt sick with horror and with personal fear as he skirted the mound. His fascinated eyes saw the break in the hazels and thorns; then they fell upon a dark mark on the ground – dark and wet, soaking into the dry grass. A white rag, dappled with dark stains, lay near . . .

Heyling could bear no more. He gave a strangled cry as he rushed, blindly stumbling, falling sometimes, out of the field and down the road.

THE FIRST SHEAF

by

H. R. Wakefield

First published in the collection
The Clock Strikes Twelve

1940

'IF ONLY THEY realised what they were doing!' laughed old
Porteous, leaning over the side of the car. 'They' were a clut-
ter of rustics, cuddling vegetable marrows, cauliflowers, apples,
and other stuffs, passing into a village church some miles south of
Birmingham. 'Humanity has been doing that, performing that rite,
since thousands of years before the first syllable of recorded time,
I suppose; though not always in quite such a refined manner. And
then there are maypoles, of all indecorous symbols, and beating the
bounds, a particularly interesting survival with, originally, a dual
function; first they beat the bounds to scare the devils out, and then
they beat the small boys that their tears might propitiate the Rain
Goddess. Such propitiation having been found to be superfluous in
this climate, they have ceased to beat the urchins; a great pity, but
an admirable example of myth-adaptation. Great Britain swarms
with such survivals, some as innocuous and bland as this harvest
festival, others far more formidable and guarded secrets; at least
that was so when I was a boy. Did I ever tell you how I lost my arm?'

'No,' I replied, yawning. 'Go ahead. But I hope the tale has
entertainment value, for I am feeling deliciously sleepy.'

Old Porteous leaned back and lit a cigar. He had started his career with fifty pounds, and turned this into seven figures by sheer speculative genius; he seemed to touch nothing which did not appreciate. He is fat, shrewd, cynical, and very charitable in an individual, far-sighted way. A copious but discriminating eater and drinker, to all appearances just a superb epitome of a type. But he has a less mundane side which is highly developed, being a devoted amateur of music with a trained and individual taste. And he owns the finest collection of keyboard instruments in Europe, the only one of his many possessions I very greatly envy him. Music, indeed, was the cause of our being together that Sunday morning in August, for I make my living out of attempting to criticise it, and we were driving to Manchester for a Harty Sibelius concert.

When I was a boy of thirteen [he began] my father accepted the living of Reedley End in Essex. There was little competition for the *curé* as the place had a notable reputation for toughness in the diocese, and the stipend was two hundred and fifty pounds a year and a house which, in size and amenities, somewhat resembled a contemporary poor-house. However, the prospect appealed to my dear old dad's zeal, for he was an Evangelist by label and temperament. Reedley End was in one of those remote corners of the country which are 'backwaterish' to this day; and was then almost as cut off from the world as a village in Tibet. It sprawled along the lower slopes of a short, narrow valley, was fifteen miles from a railway station, and its only avenue to anywhere was a glorified cart-track. It was peopled by a strange tribe, aloof, dour, bitter, and revealing copious signs of intensive interbreeding. They greeted my father's arrival with contemptuous nonchalance, spurned his ministrations, and soon enough broke his spirit.

'I can do nothing with them!' he groaned, half to himself and half to me. 'They seem to worship other gods than mine!'

There was a very real justification for their bitterness. Reedley

End was, perhaps, the most arid spot in Britain; drought, save in very good years, was endemic in that part of Essex, and I believe a bad spring and dry summer still causes great inconvenience and some hardship to this day. There had been three successive drought years before our arrival, with crop failures, heavy mortality amongst the beasts, and actual thirst the result. The distress was great and growing, and a mood of venomous despair had come with it. There was no one to help them – the day of Governmental paternalism had not yet dawned, and my father's predecessor's prayers for rain had been a singularly ineffectual substitute. They were off the map and left to stew in their own juice – or rather perish from the lack of it. Men in such a pass, if they cannot look forward for succour, many times look back.

In February they went forth to sow again, and my father told me they seemed to him in a sinister and enigmatic mood. (I may say my mother had died five years before, I was an only child, and through being my father's confidant, was old and 'wise' for my age.) Their habitual aloofness had become impenetrable, and all – even the children – seemed imbued with some communal purpose, sharers of some communal secret.

One morning my father went to visit an ancient, bedridden crone who snubbed him with less consistent ruthlessness than the rest of his fearsome flock. To his astonishment he found the village entirely deserted. When he entered the ancient's cottage she abruptly told him to be gone.

'It is no day for you to be abroad, parson,' she said peremptorily. 'Go home and stay indoors!'

In his bewilderment my father attempted to solve the humiliating mystery, and decided to visit one of the three small farmers who strove desperately to scrape a living for themselves and their hinds from the parched acres; and who had treated him with rough courtesy. His farmhouse was some two miles away and my father set out to walk there. But, on reaching the outskirts of the village, he found his way barred by three men placed like sentries across the track. They waved him back without a word, and when he made some show of passing them, grew so threatening and their gestures so unmistakable, that my father cut short his protests and came miserably home again.

That night I couldn't sleep; my father's disturbed mood had communicated itself to me. Some time in the course of it I went to my window and leaned out. A bitter northerly wind was blowing, and suddenly down it came a horrid, thin cry of agony that seemed to have been carried from afar. It came once again, diminished and cut short. I crept shivering and badly scared back to bed.

If my father had heard it he made no reference to it next morning, when the village seemed itself again. And though the children were brooding and subdued, their elders were almost in good spirits, ruthlessly jocund, like homing lynchers. (I made that comparison, of course, long afterwards, but I know it to be psychologically true.)

My father had made valiant and pathetic attempts to get hold of the village youth and managed to coax together a meagre attendance at a Sunday school. On the next Sunday one of the dozen was missing. This was a girl of about my own age, the only child of a farm-labourer and his wife. He was a 'foreigner', a native of Sussex, and a sparklingly handsome fellow of the pure Saxon type. His wife had some claims to be a beauty, too, and was much fairer than the average of those parts. The result was an oddly lovely child, as fair and rosy as her father. She shone out in the village like a Golden Oriole in a crew of crows. She aroused my keenest curiosity, the bud of love, I suppose; and I spent much of my time spying on her from a shy distance. When she failed to turn up that Sunday, my father went round to her parents' cottage. They were both at home. The man was pacing up and down the kitchen, his face revealing fury and grief. The mother was sitting in front of the fire, wearing an expression my father found it hard to analyse. It reminded him of the appearance often shown by religious maniacs in their less boisterous moments; ecstatic, exalted, yet essentially unbalanced. When he asked after the little girl, the father clenched his fists and swore fiercely; the woman, without turning her head, muttered, 'She'll be coming to school no more.' This ultimatum was naturally not good enough for my father, who was disagreeably affected by the scene. He asked where she was. She'd been sent away. 'Where to?' he asked. But at this she became a raging virago and ordered my father to go and mind his own business. He turned to the man, who seemed on the verge of an outburst, but she muttered something my father couldn't catch and he ran from the room.

Late that night my dad heard a tap on his study window. It was the father.

'Sir,' he said, 'I'm away. They're devils here!'

'Your little girl?' asked my father, horrified.

'They've taken her,' he replied hoarsely. 'I don't know why, and I don't know where she's gone. But I know I shan't see her no more. As for my wife, I hate her for what she's done. She says they'll kill me if I try to find her. They'd kill me if they knew I was here!'

My father implored him to tell him more; promised him sanctuary and protection, but all he said was, 'Avenge her, sir!' and vanished into the night.

Naturally my father was at a loss what to do. He even enlisted my more than willing aid. But all I succeeded in doing was verifying the agonising fact that my darling had gone, and taking a terrific beating from persons unknown one night when I was snooping near the cottage.

In the end my father wrote a confidential letter to the Colchester police outlining the circumstances. But I suppose his tale was so vague and discreet that, though some enquiries were made by a thick-skulled, pot-bellied constable, nothing whatsoever came of them. But my father was a marked man from the moment of this peeler's appearance, and audible and impertinent interruptions punctuated his services.

Realising he was beaten, he made up his mind, with many tears and self-reproaches, to resign at the end of the year.

The week after the little girl's disappearance there was a lovely two days' rain, and the spring and summer were a farmer's Elysian dream. My father, with pathetic optimism, hoped this copious, if belated, answer to his prayers would improve his status with his iron-fleeced flock. Instead he experienced a unanimous and shattering ostracism. In despair he wrote to his bishop, but the episcopal counsel was couched in too general and booming terms to be efficacious in converting the denizens of Reedley End.

And one day it was August, the fields shone with a mighty harvest, and it was time to bring it home.

The valley divided the corn-lands of Reedley into two areas tilled against the slight slopes. Those facing north were noticeably less productive than those on the south and do not concern us. Those southern fields were open and treeless, with one exception, a comparatively small circular field in the very middle of the tilled expanse. This was completely hemmed in by evergreens, yews, and holm-oaks; not a single deciduous tree interrupted the dark barrier. In the centre of this field was a stone pillar about eight feet high. I was forced to be by myself for many hours a day; and I spent many of them roaming the countryside and peopling it with the folk of my fancy. The local youth regarded me without enthusiasm, but young blood is thicker than old and they did not keep me in rigid 'Coventry', though they were very guarded in their replies to my questions.

This circular field stirred an intense curiosity within me, and all my wanderings on the southern slopes seemed to bring me, sooner or later, to its boundaries. Eventually I summoned up courage to ask a lad who had shown traces of cordiality if the field had a name – for some reason I was sure it had. He looked at me oddly – nervously and angrily – and replied, 'It's the Good Field; and nought to do with you!' After the little girl's disappearance I was convinced, vaguely but certainly, that this field was concerned with it; intuition I suppose.

'Now that,' I interrupted, 'is a word that baffles me; and the dictionary seems to know no more than I do.'

'In a way I agree,' laughed old Porteous. 'I could answer you negatively and quite accurately by saying that it is a mode of apprehension unknown to women. But I believe an intuitive judgment to be a syllogism of which the premises are in the Unconscious, the conclusion in the Conscious, though retrospective meditation can sometimes resolve it into a normal thought process. I have often done so in the case of big deals. It is the speed of the intuitive process which is so valuable. And now I hope you are a wiser man!'

Anyway, I conceived a fascinated horror of the field, a shivering curiosity concerning it I longed to satisfy.

One evening, early in March, I determined to do what I had never dared before, walk out into the field and examine the stone pillar. It was almost dusk and not a soul in sight. When I'd surmounted a small but deep ditch, broken through between two yews, and stood out in that strange place under a hurrying, unstable sky, I felt a sense of extreme isolation; not, I think, the isolation of being alone in a deserted place, but such as one would experience if alone and horribly conspicuous amongst a hostile crowd. However, I fought down my fears and strode forward. When I reached the pillar I found it was square and surrounded by a small, cleared expanse of neatly tiled stone. This stone was thickly stained with what appeared to be red rust. The pillar itself was heavily pitted and indented about a third from its top, with such regularity as suggested an almost obliterated inscription of some kind. I clasped the pillar with my arms, tucked my legs round it, and heaved myself up till I could touch its top. This I found to be hollowed out into a cup. I stretched up farther and pushed my fingers down. The next moment I was lying on my back and wringing my fingers; for if I had dipped my hand into molten lead I couldn't have known a sharper scald. This emptied my little bag of courage and, with 'zero at the bone', I got up and ran for it. As I stumbled forward I took one look over my shoulder, and it seemed to me there was a dark figure standing by the pillar and reaching high above its top; and all the time I gasped homewards I felt I had a follower, and the pursuit was not called off till I flung myself through the rectory door.

'What's the matter?' asked my father. 'You shouldn't run like that. And you've cut your hand. Go and bathe it.'

They started to reap in the second week of August and I found the process of great interest, for it was the first harvest I had seen. I hovered about the outskirts of the activity, fearing my reception if I ventured nearer. I found they were working in towards the Round Field from all points of the compass; and, young and inexperienced as I was, it seemed to me the people were in a strange mood, or rather mood-cycle, for at times there would be outbursts of wild singing, with horse-play and gesticulation, and at others they would be even more morose and silent than had been their sombre wont. And day after day they drew nearer the Round Field.

They reached it from all sides almost simultaneously by about noon on a superbly fine day. And then to my astonishment, they all stopped work and went home. That was on a Tuesday, and they did nothing the next day in the fields, though they were anything but idle. There was incessant activity in the village of a sort which perplexed my father greatly. It struck him that something of great importance was being prepared. The hive was seething. Needless to say, no knowledge of it was vouchsafed to him. He discovered by humiliating experience that a meeting of the older men was held in what was known as 'Odiues Field', for the sentries posted round all the approaches to it brusquely and menacingly refused him entrance.

Now whether it was our old friend, Intuition, or not, I was convinced these plans and consultations concerned the Round Field, and that something was due to be done there on the morrow.

So I crept out of the house an hour before dawn, leaving a note on the hall-table telling my father not to worry. I took with me three slices of bread-and-butter and a bottle of water. I made my way to the Round Field by a devious route so as to avoid passing through the village, creeping along the hedgerows and keeping a sharp look-out with eye and ear. I have said that a ditch encircled the field, and in it I crouched down between two yews, well away from the gates. By creeping into the space where their branches touched, I believed I could spy out undetected.

Dawn broke fine, but very heavy and close, and there were red strata of clouds to the east as the sun climbed through them.

To my surprise no one appeared at six, their usual hour for starting work, nor at seven, eight, or nine, when I ate half my bread-and-butter and sipped the bottle. By ten o'clock I had made up my mind that nothing would happen and I'd better go home, when I heard voices in the field behind me and knew it was too late to retreat if I'd wanted to. I could see nothing ahead of me save the high, white wheat, but presently I heard more voices and two men with sickles came cutting their way past me, and soon I could see an arc of a ring of them slashing towards the centre. When they had advanced some fifty yards I had a better view to right and left, and a very strange sight I beheld. The villagers, mostly old people and children, were streaming through the gates. All were clad in black with wreaths of corn around their necks. They formed in line behind the reapers and moved slowly forward. They made no sound – I heard not a single child's cry – but stared in a rapt way straight before them. Slowly and steadily the reapers cut their way forward. By this time the sun had disappeared and a dense cloud-bank was spreading from the east. By four o'clock the reapers had met in the centre round the last small patch of wheat by the stone pillar. And there they stopped, laid down their sickles, and took their stand in front of the people. For, perhaps, five minutes they all stayed motionless with bowed heads. And then they lifted their faces to the sky and began to chant. And a very odd song they sang, one which made me shiver beneath the yew branches. It was mainly in the minor mode, but at perfectly regular intervals it transposed into the major in a tremendous, but perfectly controlled, cry of exaltation and ecstasy. I have heard nothing like it since, though a 'Spiritual', sung by four thousand god-drunk worshippers in Georgia, faintly reminded me of it. But this was something far more formidable, far more primitive; in fact it seemed like the old-est song ever sung. The last, fierce, sustained shout of triumph made me tremble with some unnameable emotion, and I longed to be out there shouting with them. When it ended they all knelt down save one old, white-bearded man with a wreath of corn around his brow who, taking some of the corn in his right hand, raised it above his head and stared into the sky. At once four men came forward and, with what seemed like large trowels, began digging with them. The people then rose to their feet, somewhat obstructing my view. But soon the four men had finished their work and stood upright. Then the old man stepped out again and I could see he was holding what appeared to be a short iron bar. With this he pounded the earth for some moments. Then, picking up something, it looked as if he dropped it into a vessel, a dark, metal pot, I fancied, and paced to the stone pillar, raised his right arm, and poured the contents into the cup at the pillar's top. At that moment a terrific flash of light-ning cut down from the clouds and enveloped the pillar in mauve and devilish flame; and there came such a piercing blast of thunder that I fell backwards into the ditch. When I'd struggled back, the rain was hurling itself down in such fury that it was bouncing high off the lanes of stiff soil. Dimly through it I could see that all the folk had prostrated themselves once more. But in two minutes the thunder-cloud had run with the squall and the sun was blazing from a clear sky. The four men then bound up the corn in that last patch and placed the sheaf in front of the pillar. After which the old man, leading the people, paced the length of the field, scattering something from the vessel in the manner of one sowing. And he led them out of the gate and that was the last I saw of them.

Now somehow I felt that if they knew I'd been watching them, it would have gone hard with me. So I determined to wait for dusk. I was stiff, cold, and hungry, but I stuck it till the sun went flaming down and the loveliest after-glow I ever remember had faded. While I waited there a resolve had been forming in my mind. I had the most intense desire to know what the old man had dropped in the hollow on the pillar, and curiosity is in all animals the strongest foe of fear. Every moment that emotion grew more compelling, and when at last it was just not dark it became over-mastering. I stumbled across as fast as I could to the pillar, looking neither to right nor left, clambered up, and thrust down my hand. I could feel small pieces of what might have been wood, and then it was as if my forefinger was caught and gripped. The most agonising pain shot up my arm and through my body. I fell to the ground and shook my hand wildly to free my finger from that which held it. In the end it clattered down beside me and splintered on the stone. And then the blood streamed from my finger, which had been punctured to the bone. Somehow I struggled home, leaving a trail of blood behind me.

The next day my arm was swollen up like a black bladder; the morning after it was amputated at the shoulder. The surgeon who operated on me came up to my father in the hospital and held something out to him. 'I found this embedded in your son's finger,' he said.

'What is it?' asked my father.

'A child's tooth,' he replied. 'I suppose he's been fighting someone, someone with a very dirty mouth!'

'And that's why,' said old Porteous, 'though I have none of my own, I have ever since shown the greatest respect to the gods of others.'

CWM GARON

by

L. T. C. Rolt

First published in the collection *Sleep No More*

1948

A FTER A LONG winter spent in the fog and grime of London, this Welsh Borderland was balm to the eye. Spring had only just touched the soot-blackened trees in the squares with the lightest film of green, but here she had already run riot, dressing the whole countryside in fresh splendour. So thought John Carfax as the labouring branch-line train bore him slowly over the last stage of his long journey to Wales. The map lay disregarded on his knees as he watched the moving panorama of hills stippled with April cloud shadows, of neat farms buried in the white mist of fruit orchards, and of rich meadows dotted with sheep or the red cattle of Herefordshire. He was in that mood of exhilaration and heightened perception which only a well-earned and long-awaited holiday in new surroundings can awaken, and he sniffed delightedly at the limpid air, crystalline as spring water yet somehow filled with unidentifiable sweetness, which blew in through the open window. He was alone in the compartment now, but it had evidently been market day in the town where he had left the London express, for the little train standing at the bay platform had been filled with country folk. Black-gaitered farmers and their plump, basket-laden wives, all had gone, but still he seemed to smell sheep-dip and carbolic, to hear the lilt of their Border speech, and to see the lithe Welsh sheep-dog which had sat between his master's legs, regarding him with wall-eyed suspicion.

The rhythm of wheels over rail joints slowed, and Carfax could tell from the labouring exhaust beats of the engine that they were climbing steeply. A chasm-like cutting hewn through the old red sandstone cut off the view and plunged the compartment into sudden twilight. As suddenly, the train emerged and, with a hollow reverberation, crossed a swift mountain torrent, before swinging round a curve so sharp that the wheel flanges grunted and squealed in protest. As it did so, the carriage window framed a picture which made Carfax start and catch his breath in wonder, so startling was it in its wild grandeur after looking so long on the smooth fields and hills of England. A towering mountain wall had suddenly arisen to enclose the whole western horizon, and to dominate and dwarf the familiar landscape of the foreground. Seen thus against the westering light of late afternoon, the shadowed face of this great massif presented so marked a contrast to the sunlit levels below as to seem unreal and as menacing as a thunder-cloud. So impenetrable was the shadow on the mountain that its contours were invisible, and the long, level line of the ridge, sharply etched across the sky's brightness, appeared to mark the lip of a precipice the height of which seemed monstrously magnified.

Reluctantly, John Carfax turned his attention from the window to the map. Then, as he felt the brakes applied, he got up and lifted his rucksack down from the luggage rack. This must be Pont Newydd; he would have to step out if he was to cross the mountain and reach the inn at Llangaron Abbey by nightfall. A good map-reader, he had no doubt of his ability to find his way through strange country by daylight, but to be overtaken by darkness on an open mountain was a very different matter. He welcomed the prospect of the long, hard walk after the inactivity of the train journey, and set off at a smart pace up the narrow road from the station. Behind him, he heard the train pant heavily out of earshot. It seemed to symbolise the last link between him and the civilisation he had so lately left, and as he turned to glance at the thin plume of steam fast vanishing into the distance, he felt something of the sensation a voyager feels when, landed on some remote, far distant island, he sees the ship that has brought him fade over the horizon. He experienced momentarily a strange feeling of loneliness, realising that the train was an intruder from that world of elaborate artifice by means of which man had shut himself away from the eternal world of earth and sky as though fearful of their elemental mystery. It had ruffled a still pool of silence, but now the last ripples died away into stillness, until there remained no sounds but his own footfall, a distant rumour of birdsong and the sibilant voice of the little brook which ran beside the road.

He had been walking for the best part of an hour before he came in sight of the first of the landmarks he had previously noted on his map, a grey, ruined tower set upon a conical mound and surrounded by a ditch. He conjectured correctly that it was one of the border keeps erected by the Norman Lords Marcher in their efforts to subdue the Silurians of the mountains. Here, turning off the metalled road into a rutted, high-banked lane, he set his face towards the mountain wall which had hitherto marched on his left hand. Pressing on, he passed by two small white-washed farms where sheep-dogs ran out to bark and sniff at his heels, but though the lane climbed continuously, the skyline of the ridge seemed to retreat elusively before him. At length, however, he emerged on to a level plateau, treeless except for a few stunted thorn bushes, and patterned by crumbling, dry stone walls which had proved powerless to resist the downward march of the bracken. Here he came within the mountain's shadow, so that his eyes could, for the first time, penetrate its darkness to discern the steep diagonal path which scaled the ridge. Following its upward course he could see, too, the shallow notch cut in the skyline of the ridge which marked the pass, if 'pass' it could be called, for his map told him that the path climbed almost to the 2,000 feet contour. The premature dusk of the shadow spurred him on, and he had soon passed through a rickety gate on to the open mountain and was tackling the steep ascent. Pausing on the break-neck path to regain his breath, he turned and saw that already the plateau, which had seemed so high and windswept, now looked insignificant, merging imperceptibly into a vast chequer-work of field and copse whose folds this height had now smoothed out. He plodded on, and had nearly reached the summit before he stopped and turned again to find that the familiar landscape had shrunk to a remote perspective, while the evening sunlight on the farther fields looked pallid and unreal, as though seen through a veil. Glancing about him, he saw the reason. A white wall of cloud was rolling along the ridge out of the north-west, and in the next instant the scene below was lost in swirling mist. No rain fell, but his rough tweed jacket was soon pearled with beads of moisture, while a chill wind blew about him.

The sudden coming of the mist brought with it a feeling of utter isolation, intensifying the loneliness he had felt when he left the station. It seemed to mark a further stage in some inexorable progress designed deliberately to cut him off from the familiar world of his fellow-men. Sole occupant of a minute island of mountain turf, heather and whinberry, that familiar world already seemed incredibly remote. Fortunately for him, the path was clearly defined, so that he was able to press on without pause or doubt. And as he did so, some curious trick of the silver light threw his shadow upon the white curtain before him so that it seemed that a figure, monstrous, yet tenuous as the mist itself, was leading him onward towards the summit of the pass. Watching it, he thought he could understand the stories he had heard of the creatures which were believed to haunt the mountain mists, and he felt he knew the terror that might come with this loneliness as terror comes with darkness

382

to the child. His heart seemed to beat in his ears like a muffled drum, for the stillness was intense, even his footfall was muffled now by the resilient turf of the path. When, faint and far off, his ear caught the cry of a curlew, the sound brought no comforting sense of companionship, but by its plaintive wildness, seemed only to accentuate the silence and the loneliness. Suddenly, the path swung right-handed, levelled out, and he found himself passing through a narrow defile which he knew must mark the spine of the ridge. Immediately beyond the pass, the track skirted a mawne pit, a hole from which peats had once been dug, but which had now become a quagmire ringed by livid green moss and tufted cotton-grass. A luckless mountain pony had evidently floundered into it at some time and, unable to extricate itself, had perished miserably. Now that ravens, crows and mountain foxes had done their work, all that remained was a skeleton of whitened bones wrapped in the hide as in a winding-sheet. Carfax paused for a moment at this desolate sight, and as he did so the curlew cried again, nearer at hand this time, and the mist seemed to eddy more densely about him. He shivered involuntarily and went on, happy to find that the path was now leading him downwards as steeply as it had climbed. As he stumbled along, his feet pressing uncomfortably into the toes of his shoes, he noticed that the mist was now thinning, and that its whiteness was becoming suffused with golden light, although the invisible depths into which he was descending still seemed dark. Not only was he walking out of the mists, but the cloud itself appeared to be lifting, sweeping up the steep flank of the mountain like steam out of a cauldron until, with breathtaking and dramatic suddenness, the veil which had imprisoned and blinded him lifted like a curtain to reveal the whole wild prospect clearly before him. 'You'll find the valley enchanting' – he suddenly recalled the words of the friend who had first suggested his holiday, not in their original sense as a conventional overstatement, but with a new, and strangely literal significance.

He stood in the last stormy light of a sun that was just about to set behind the rim of yet another mountain ridge which marched parallel with that upon which he stood, and which appeared to be of equal, if not greater height. It could not be much more than a mile by crow-flight, he judged, from ridge to ridge, yet between them yawned Cwm Garon, a stupendous furrow which, in the course of unnumbered centuries, the Afon Garon had carved into the heart of the mountains. Already this valley was wrapped in the blue shades of a premature twilight, yet Carfax could sense rather than see the intense green of the meadows along the floor of the Cwm. Here and there, lights gleamed from farmhouse windows. Faintly there rose into the thin mountain air the resinous incense of pine-wood smoke, and the murmur of the swiftly flowing river. At one point the valley widened into a natural amphitheatre, in the centre of which stood the grey shape of a building larger than a mountain farm. This Carfax took to be his destination, the ruined Abbey of Llangaron and its adjoining inn. After the cloud-blinded solitude of the mountain-top, the sight of his goal raised his spirits to high good humour, and he strode on down the steep path at a great pace, his mind occupied with the prospect of a blazing fire, a well-earned dinner and a foaming tankard.

Great anticipations are often the prelude to disillusionment, but in this instance John Carfax was not disappointed. The dinner was excellent, and he gave a sigh of contentment as he stirred his coffee and extended his slippered feet towards the friendly flame of the log fire. Its warmth was welcome, for the spring nights were chilly in this valley which the sun so soon forsook. In the opposite chimney-corner, likewise toasting his toes, sat his only fellow-guest at the inn. He was busily writing in what appeared to Carfax to be a large journal or diary which he balanced on his knee, and the tireless scratching of his pen mingled with the comfortable crackling of the fire, and the occasional faint bubbling sound which Carfax's pipe made when he drew deeply. In London, he thought, it is never truly quiet, but here one becomes conscious of the slightest sound. He had exchanged generalities with his companion during their meal when they had sat together, but the latter had not been very forthcoming. He was much older than Carfax; in middle age he had obviously been a man of great strength, tall and broad in proportion. Now the wide shoulders stooped, and a suit of rough, grey tweed hung loosely about his gaunt frame. Yet it was obvious that he was still very active, nor had his presence lost its power of command. A fine head of white hair and a short, pointed beard meticulously trimmed made a fitting frame for the massive brow and the distinguished features. The most remarkable thing about these features, Carfax thought, were the eyes, bright blue eyes which had no need of glasses and whose keenness quite belied his age. When he had spoken he had regarded his fellow-guest with a penetrating, unblinking gaze that was almost hypnotic in its intensity and which, in a lesser man, would have seemed mere ill-mannered arrogance. Carfax found it disconcerting, for it gave him the impression that a keen intelligence, possessing a store of secret knowledge, was coolly taking the measure of his own mind while it remained itself inscrutable, permitting him no such liberty. He recalled with a slight feeling of resentment that whereas he had straightway introduced himself, the other had not responded similarly.

He yawned and must have dozed, for he suddenly became conscious that the fire had burned lower, and that the bole of his pipe was cold. He hoped that he had not snored, and glanced apprehensively at his companion. If he had, it would seem that his bad manners had passed unnoticed, for the other's head was still bent over his book and his pen travelled imperturbably on. He glanced at his watch. The hour was not late, but the long journey, the keen air and the warmth of the fire had told upon him, and his eyelids were heavy with sleep. He rose to go to bed, but before doing so, some chance impulse made him walk to the window, part the curtains and look out.

The night was clear, and a bright moon, near the full, rode above a wrack of clouds which was drifting like smoke from lip to lip of the defile. Yet despite the swiftly moving clouds overhead an absolute stillness held the valley, for the trees stood motionless. Only the unseen river, rushing over its rocky bed, sounded incessantly. The window looked directly up the roofless nave of the Abbey, and the great columns threw upon the moonlit grass, shadows so dense that the eye could scarcely distinguish image from substance. Beyond, above the site of the high altar, the great east window, devoid of tracery, framed the dark brooding shape of the mountain which Carfax had crossed that evening. The scene was so extravagant in its chiaroscuro, so humiliating in its grandeur, that he could not restrain a muttered exclamation—

'Oh who will tell me where
He found thee at that dead and silent hour?
What hallowed solitary ground did bear
So rare a flower
Within whose sacred leaves did lie
The fullness of the Deity?'

It was appropriate that these lines of the Silurist should have sprung to his mind, for it was not surprising, he reflected, that this country should have been the inspiration of Vaughan and Traherne. Here, truly, heaven seemed nearer earth . . .

'And hell, too, maybe.'

Carfax started, not only because the voice sounded close at his elbow, but because he was not aware that he had spoken his thoughts aloud. He realised that his taciturn companion had moved silently from his chair and was gazing out into the night with those strange, unblinking eyes of his.

'Yes,' he went on in a soft, ruminative tone, as though he were speaking more to himself than to Carfax, 'it is certainly very beautiful, so beautiful that it distils some influence – call it magic if you like – which turns men's minds from material to spiritual things.

Unless I am much mistaken, it set you thinking of the Dominicans who built their great church in this solitude, and of the Silurists, Traherne and Vaughan.'

Carfax turned back into the room, letting the curtain fall across the window. The uncanny accuracy with which the other had read his thoughts disturbed him.

His expression must have revealed this disquiet, for the other chuckled. 'I must really apologise,' he went on, 'if I startled you. I can assure you I am not really such an accomplished thought-reader. Let me explain: I have visited this valley on numerous occasions spread over a period of years, and I know that on first acquaintance it always casts this same spell over visitors who, like yourself, are gifted with imagination. All I have done was to observe in you the familiar symptoms.'

Carfax was somewhat mollified, though he still felt slightly irritated by the other's self-assurance, and by the way in which he talked of what had been to him a profound spiritual experience as though it were a cold in the head. Nevertheless, his companion's words had roused his curiosity.

'What exactly do you mean by saying "on first acquaintance"?' he asked. 'Are you suggesting that my present impression of Cwm Garon is likely to change? And what did you mean by your odd remark about hell?'

'Taking the first question first,' replied the other, 'if I have judged you correctly, then I think your impressions will change, but I don't propose to bias your mind by suggesting how that change may come, or what form it will take. Explore the valley for yourself tomorrow and then, if you should feel so disposed, I should be most interested to hear your views. As to your second question,' he went on, 'I regret the remark, and do not know what prompted me to make it. I would prefer not to explain myself further for the moment, except to suggest that a belief in heaven implies a corresponding belief in hell.'

Despite renewed questioning, the older man refused to commit himself further, and it was a puzzled and thoughtful Carfax who eventually bid his fellow-guest good-night, lit his candle, and made his way up the narrow, stone newel stair to his bed in the tower room.

He slept soundly, rose early and breakfasted alone. He was about to set out on his tour of exploration, in fact he was standing in the hall of the inn packing sandwiches into his haversack, when he noticed the visitors' book and remembered that he had not yet signed it. As he turned the pages to remedy this omission, he discovered the identity of his fellow-guest, for in the last occupied space was written 'Charles Elphinstone, Oxford', in a fluent, scholarly hand. The name seemed familiar, but for the life of him he could not place it.

By the time he had reached the valley floor the previous night, darkness had prevented him from forming an adequate picture of his new surroundings, and now the weather conditions could scarcely have been less favourable. The portents of a stormy sunset and an ominously clear night had been fulfilled. The mountain walls upon either hand were hidden by a moving wrack of clouds whose tattered fringe had descended almost to the upper limit of the cultivated fields. A fine but deceptively penetrating rain was falling, and although occasional strong gusts of wind came eddying off the mountains, now from this direction, now from that, the air was humid and stifling. The swollen Garon and the innumerable small torrents cascading down the steep slopes filled the valley with the sound of falling water. Nevertheless, knowing how swiftly the mountain climate could change, Carfax was not unduly downcast and, buttoning up the collar of his mackintosh, he set off resolutely up the valley. The lane was narrow and high banked, and was never far away from the line of alder and hazel which overhung the shallow gorge through which the river flowed. He noticed that the small fields, both pasture and arable, looked clean and well tended, their hedges neatly laid and trimmed, but he saw no one at work in them. The small farms seemed equally deserted, and had he not scented wood-smoke as he passed them he would have thought that they were empty. No doubt the weather accounted for this suspension of activity. It struck him as ironical that the only fellow-mortal he encountered in the morning's solitude he passed by unawares. Only a chance glance over his shoulder had revealed the figure of a man sheltering beneath a tree which he had lately passed. The man stood so still, and the old brown overcoat, together with the sack which he had thrown over head and shoulders against the wet, blended so exactly with the colour of the tree bole at his back, that Carfax stopped for a moment to confirm his first glance. The man ignored his scrutiny, but when, at the bend of the road, he looked back again, he was no longer to be seen.

He had been walking for the best part of an hour when he saw on the left of the road what he took to be the ruins of a church. The valley was narrower here, and its walls more precipitous, for the clouds revealed glimpses of naked crags and desolate screes of shattered boulders. As though these features had not already made the site of the church sombre enough, a dense belt of pine-trees had been planted beside it. This must be Capel Cwm Garon, he reflected, recalling his study of the map during breakfast. He thought he had never seen so gloomy a place; it would seem dark even in sunlight, and, as the ruined church appeared to be of no architectural merit, he walked on. He conjectured that he must be nearing the head of the valley, for the lane grew rougher and commenced to climb steeply until he presently gained the open mountain. The rain had stopped, the sky looked brighter ahead, while the clouds showed signs of lifting. The rain, the lowering clouds and the oppressive humid warmth of the valley had between them damped his spirits, but now he stepped out cheerfully, a cooler and drier wind in his face which made him feel as one who passes into fresh night air out of some overheated room.

By the time he had reached the head of the pass and could look down on the great landscape of hill and vale spread out beneath him, there was blue sky overhead, and a moving pattern of sunlight and shadow was dappling the slopes of the mountains. Carfax felt very well content as he sat with his back against a sheltering boulder and munched his sandwiches. Not far away a little group of mountain ponies were grazing, while high overhead a buzzard soared on moth-like wings. A shepherd was gathering his sheep off the north face of the mountain; Carfax could see his tiny foreshortened figure on the plateau far below, and his shrill whistle as he worked his dogs was borne up to him on the wind. These things brought a sense of life and companionship, dispelling the feeling of loneliness that had been growing upon him since he left the train on the previous day. He took out his map and checked his position. He had reached the central massif of the range. From it, the long ridges stretched southward like the fingers of an outspread hand. Between them, and to the west, lay two valleys, the Llan Fawr and the Llan Fechan, running parallel with Cwm Garon. As the weather seemed to have set fair, and there was plenty of time, he decided he would walk back down the Llan Fawr valley, cross the intervening ridge at a point well below Llangaron, and so return to the inn from the opposite direction.

He found that the valley of Llan Fawr was physically very similar to that of Cwm Garon. If anything, it was even narrower, while the mountain walls were equally high. Yet somehow the atmosphere of the place seemed quite different; 'more friendly' was the description which at once occurred to him. Obviously the improvement in the weather must be responsible, he decided; this mountain country was strangely temperamental. Owing to the more restricted area of cultivated land, the small farms were spaced farther apart than those in Cwm Garon, yet there seemed to be no lack of life and activity. A hedger at work beside the lane, and a swarthy individual leading a pair of jennets with pack-saddles, bid him a lilting good day as he passed. In one farmyard three small children paused from play to stare round-eyed as he went by, while in a nearby field, sown with oats, a farmer was working a two-horse roll. Finally, just before he turned off the road to climb back over the ridge, he met a woman driving three cows to the evening milking.

When he had finished the climb and begun the steep descent, the sun was still lighting the fields on the farther side of Cwm Garon, but he noticed that they looked just as deserted as they had done that morning. There still seemed to be neither sight nor sound of any activity. Silence seemed to well up from the valley like water from a spring, in fact the distant murmur of the Garon seemed to symbolise and accentuate it. He began to recall all the small workaday noises which he had heard but not remarked in Llan Fawr, and the lower he descended, the louder his footfalls seemed to sound. Despite the sunlight and the clear air he found the feeling of loneliness and of strange oppression inexplicably returning. There was a sense of menacing constriction about the towering walls which hemmed in this valley and cut him off from the outer world, and yet, after his experience in Llan Fawr, he knew that it could not merely be a case of claustrophobia.

He had not gone far along the road back to Llangaron when he came in sight of a small public-house, and decided that a glass of beer would help him over the last lap of the way. Probably, too, he would find company there which would dispel this curious illusion that the valley was deserted.

The dim, low-ceilinged room – there was no bar – was snug and spotless. The stone-flagged floor looked newly scrubbed, and the dark polished surfaces of table, settle and high-backed Welsh dresser caught the light of the cheerful fire which burned in the hob grate. But the room was empty and silent save for the small settling sounds of the fire and the measured ticking of the grandfather clock. Carfax coughed and scuffed his feet on the flags.

A latch clicked in the back of the house, and as the unseen door opened, he heard a deep rumble of male voices. A woman appeared, and when she had fetched his drink he made some trivial pleasantry, but she seemed either shy or taciturn, for she answered in monosyllables, and after standing awkwardly for a moment, retired again to what he imagined to be the kitchen. The indistinguishable murmur of male talk went on. Carfax took a deep and gratifying draught, and then stooped to knock out his pipe in the ash-tray. As he did so, he realised that the dottle already in the tray was warm, and that the cigarette stub beside it was still smouldering. Looking round the room curiously, he then saw that a man's cap lay in the chimney-corner of the settle, and that two knarled hazel sticks were propped against the wall near the door. At any other time and place, Carfax would not have observed such trivialities, and even if he had he would have attached no importance to them. But now they bred in him a disquieting suspicion which refused to be dispelled. It was that his approach had been discreetly observed by the late occupants of the room, and that for reasons best known to themselves they had retreated to the kitchen. The uncomfortable feeling of unwelcome intrusion which this suspicion prompted scarcely encouraged him to linger. The room seemed to have grown suddenly hostile, so much so that he did not even pause to refill his pipe, but drained his glass and set out once more upon his way.

The sunlight had now crept away from the fields, so that although the higher slopes of the eastern ridge were still suffused with golden light, the shadows in the valley were already thickening into twilight. His experience at the inn had exerted a curious influence over his mind, he discovered, for although the farms he passed seemed as still and deserted as those he had seen that morning, they no longer gave him the impression of being uninhabited. On the contrary, he imagined that every window concealed a watcher, that every house was the centre of some intense and secret life which, at his approach, was instantly suspended. The farther he went the more certain did he become that his every movement was the subject of furtive scrutiny, yet it was a certainty which his reason was powerless either to confirm or to disprove. Time and again he would stop and look back quickly, hoping to surprise the swaying of a curtain, the movement of a door, or to see in the shadows of tree or hedge some tangible shape. He looked in vain. Yet the feeling and the fear continued to grow upon him despite his senses' negative evidence. It was no longer confined to the houses he passed and to the people who might or might not lurk within them; it was a fear distilled by the valley itself. The brooding mountains, the still pines, even the heavy, windless air itself seemed to have suspended some secret activity to join in this silent and malign watch. As he walked resolutely on, fear stalked at his elbow, and he felt as if he was the focal point of some great burning-glass of hostile forces. Just as the first lightning flash and thunder-clap puts a welcome end to the breath-bating suspense that precedes the storm, Carfax found himself wishing that something, however fearful, might happen. But no material event took place, and he reached the inn at Llangaron in good time for dinner. In the cheerful light of the dining-room he felt inclined to dismiss the matter as so much hallucination, but he could not deny that, as his fellow-guest had prophesied, his first impression of the valley had undergone radical revision.

'Well,' queried Elphinstone as they drew their chairs to the fire after dinner, 'what's the verdict now?'

Carfax hesitated. Considered in retrospect, his fears seemed so intangible and groundless that he felt foolish and doubted his ability to express them in so many words. With the other's encouragement, however, he presently gave as detailed and faithful an account of his day as he was able. During his narration Elphinstone nodded occasionally, but seemed to evince no surprise. When Carfax had finished speaking he remained silent for a few moments, pulling at a thin, black cheroot.

'Interesting,' he said at length. 'Very interesting, but not, I can assure you, a unique experience by any means. For years, I might safely say for centuries, strangers have been made aware, by some such means as you describe, that they were not welcome in this valley.'

'But it's not just the people,' put in Carfax. 'It's as though the valley . . .'

'I know, I know,' the older man cut him short. 'It's not as simple as that, is it? "An angel satyr walks these hills",' he quoted; 'know who wrote that? Why, Kilvert. "Angel satyr" – a curious association of opposites – what do you suppose induced a mild little Victorian curate to use such a term?'

'I think I can understand now,' Carfax admitted. 'And yet,' he went on, 'I refuse to believe that this sense of evil is a natural emanation of the place itself. As a Christian, I hold that both good and evil are human concepts, and that they do not exist in nature.'

'Well put,' said the other, 'and probably true, but if, as a Christian, you believe that there are spiritual as well as material powers, then don't you think it possible that man might abuse and pervert the former no less than the latter?'

Carfax nodded. 'Yes,' he agreed, thoughtfully, 'I suppose such a thing is possible.'

'I am sure of it,' Elphinstone went on, 'and what's more I consider that this valley can prove my contention.'

'Go on,' prompted Carfax.

'I believe,' the other continued, 'that some evil force dominates Cwm Garon. I think it is a natural force which man, in some remote time, released and harnessed to secret and perverted ends. For centuries this dark power has been, as it were, dammed up in this valley until it has soaked into the very stones of the place. That is why a more superficial mind than yours might imagine that it is a natural phenomenon. Outside interference has an effect upon it like that of a stone flung into a still pool. That's why Cwm

Garon and its people have always implacably resisted intrusion.'
He paused.

'But is that really so?' queried Carfax. 'What evidence have you?'

'Apart from many similar experiences to your own,' the older man replied, 'there is ample historical evidence. Take this Abbey, for instance.' He made a sweeping gesture. 'It did not survive until the Dissolution. What happened? The community dwindled. Its numbers could not be maintained. Finally, a new Abbey of Llangaron was built in the safe, flat lands beside the Wye, and the old was abandoned. It has been said that it was too solitary, too open to attack by wolves or raiding hillmen. Do you find that explanation convincing? Do you think that a Church which deliberately sought the solitudes, and which established flourishing communities at such places as Valle Crucis or Strata Florida, would be defeated merely by the loneliness of Cwm Garon? No, I suggest that they went because they feared something more potent but less tangible than wolves or robbers.

'You say you saw the ruined church at Capel Cwm Garon; do you know the history of that? It was built by a nineteenth-century religious sect headed by a man who called himself Brother Jeremy. What happened? History repeated itself; the community dwindled; misfortune followed misfortune. The eventual result you have seen for yourself. It's not only the efforts of the Church that have failed,' he went on. 'On the slope of the mountain just behind here you'll find the ruins of a house. There's not much to see, but it is all that's left of the place that Alaric Stephenson the artist tried to build for himself. I say "tried" because it was never finished. He apparently had some grandiose notion that he was going to make a sort of miniature paradise for himself here, but he soon found he was mistaken. Everything went wrong. No local contractors would work for him. What was done during the day was undone at night. Even the trees he tried to plant were uprooted. I could quote several other examples of the same kind of thing, but the repetition would be boring.'

'But do these . . . these forces manifest themselves in any way?' questioned Carfax.

'That depends,' was the answer. 'Unless you deliberately seek them or try to interfere with them, I should say no; you might stay here a month without experiencing any more than the sense of hostility and surveillance which you felt today!'

Elphinstone rose to his feet and lit the candle on the side-table.

'What is this extraordinary influence, and how exactly does it affect the people who live in Cwm Garon?' Carfax persisted.

The other was standing in the doorway about to bid him good-night. His keen eyes glittered in the flickering candle flame as he smiled and shook his head.

'I cannot answer that question,' he replied. 'At least, not yet. I think I have a shrewd idea, but one day – soon perhaps – I hope to know.'

The conversation had filled Carfax's head with disturbing specu-lations, and despite his long day in the mountain air it was some time before he lost consciousness. Even so, it must have been a light doze instead of his usual sound sleep, for he presently awoke and, glancing at the luminous dial of his wrist-watch, saw that it was nearly midnight. He became aware of stealthy movement in the room overhead at the top of the tower, movement betrayed by sounds so slight that he could never have detected them but for the profound stillness. Then he heard the pad of stealthy feet descend-ing the stone stairs. A thin pencil of light flickered momentarily beneath his door and was gone. Carfax climbed softly out of the bed and crossed to the open window. He was in time to see a tall, slightly stooping figure, which he recognised unmistakably as that of Charles Elphinstone, cross the grass below and disappear beyond the ruined wall of the cloister garth. As he watched, he suddenly recalled the association of the name which had eluded him all day – Professor Charles Elphinstone, probably the greatest authority on folklore and magic since Frazer. 'One day – soon perhaps – I hope to know.' He seemed to hear an echo of his last words. Though Carfax was by no means of a timid disposition, he felt a reluctant, even envious feeling of admiration for the intrepid old man. Admittedly, on the face of it, a midnight stroll in this quiet Welsh valley seemed to call for no particular display of courage. The night was clear and brightly moonlit, the scene the same as before, the same black shadows of the nave arches on the dew-laden grass, the same black grandeur of mountains framed in the gaping east window, the same stillness. Yet this time, Carfax had no thought of Vaughan or Traherne, for he knew the fear that lurked in this silence. Were those lights, moving and dancing along the slopes of the mountains, or was it merely a trick of moonlight shining upon stone? Somewhere near at hand an owl hooted mournfully, and there came into his mind a line from the thirteenth chapter of Isaiah: 'Owls shall dwell there, and satyrs shall dance there.' He shivered, and returned to the welcome warmth of the bed.

The Professor did not appear at breakfast. Doubtless he was making up for lost sleep, thought Carfax, but the reflection could not dispel a vague sense of uneasiness which refused to be quieted. He deliberately loitered in the dining-room, hoping Elphinstone would come. When, at half-past ten, his place was still empty, Carfax determined to settle his fears. He climbed the tower stairs to the Professor's room. A can stood outside his door. It was full, and the water was quite cold. He knocked softly, then more loudly. There was no response. Turning the handle very gently, he opened the door a few inches and looked in. The room was empty.

Some instinct prompted Carfax to set out on his search in the same direction as he had taken the previous day, towards the ruined church of Capel Cwm Garon. He was still trying to reassure himself that his fears were groundless. Though Elphinstone had not, it appeared, warned the inn of any intended absence, he might well have decided to stay out on such a fine morning, while even involuntary absence might be caused by no worse mishap than a sprained ankle. Yet the feeling of foreboding would not be appeased. He realised that the date was May the first, that last night, in fact, had been 'Eve of May' of ancient celebration, and somehow this knowledge by no means allayed his concern. Meanwhile, his senses observed the same atmosphere of hostility and watchfulness, but now, preoccupied with fresh fears, he no longer turned to peer at vacant windows or into the shadows beneath the trees, knowing that to do so would be fruitless. So he strode on until he came in sight of the crags of Black Daren, which towered above the ruined church. As his eyes roamed over the precipice, he thought he detected a movement among the boulders of the screes below. He fumbled for his binoculars, and focused them hurriedly. Two men appeared to be bending over something which lay behind a rock invisible to him. 'No doubt a sheep has fallen from the crags,' whispered reason, but dread lent wings to his feet.

Professor Charles Elphinstone had obviously slipped and fallen from a great height in attempting to scale the crags, and his body lay against the rock in that attitude of macabre abandonment which betokens shattered bones. His hat had fallen off, and the luxuriant white hair was matted with congealed blood. Carfax, who was familiar with death in many forms, was not dismayed by these gruesome commonplaces of violent dissolution. What drained the blood from his face and impelled him quickly to replace the sack which covered the body, was the expression on the face. He would not have believed that the features he had lately seen so calm and self-confident could have been moulded by terror to such hideous contortion. It may be thought that Carfax would have no desire ever to revisit the valley; he would certainly have subscribed to this view himself when he left Llangaron on the day following the tragic accident. Everything about Cwm Garon had become repulsive to him and, as many others, it seemed, had done before him, he retired defeated. Never did the mundane environment of the outside world seem so friendly and welcoming. When the train pulled in to the little station at Pont Newydd he could scarcely resist the impulse to run up to the footplate and shake the driver by the hand. Yet – and to those who have never visited Cwm Garon this will seem the most improbable part of this strange story – as the weeks went by after his return to London, fear turned to curiosity, and repulsion to an attraction which he found increasingly difficult to resist. It was almost as though some powerful influence was luring him back.

Be that as it may, Carfax did return to the valley, and a sultry night on the eve of August the first found him once again walking up the lane toward Capel Cwm Garon. The heat in the valley that day had been stifling. Everything had felt hot to the touch, and the outlines of the mountain ridges shimmered in a haze which mingled with the acrid smoke of a heather fire. Never had the atmosphere seemed so surcharged with still suspense. Even the interminable voice of the Garon had been muted by weeks of drought. Only occasionally, far away over the mountains toward Radnor, faint thunder growled and muttered. At evening a grey veil of cloud had spread slowly across the sky so that the night fell black and starless. Yet the heat was still insufferable and there was no breath of wind. Everything, from towering mountain to individual leaf or grass blade, seemed poised in tense expectancy as though awaiting some tremendous event.

I will not attempt to analyse Carfax's state of mind as he strode on through the dark of the high-banked lane. Though still beyond the reach of his five senses, his reason no longer questioned the reality of a malign, unsleeping watch. Yet still, 'For lust of knowing what should not be known', he held on purposefully. Somewhere above the invisible crags of the Black Daren a heather fire was still burning, a livid wheal of flickering flame twisting snake-like across the face of the mountain. But Carfax also saw other lights in the darkness, moving points of light which no comfortable theory could explain. They appeared to move swiftly along and down the mountain walls, converging, it would seem, upon the church at Capel Cwm Garon. There must, he thought, be another fire just beyond the church, for the ruined walls were visible against its dull red glare. As he approached more closely, however, he saw, with a new fear stirring in his heart, that he was mistaken, and that the light was actually coming from within the church itself.

While fascination fought with terror within him, he drew nearer, leaving the lane for the short turf of the field where his footfalls made no sound, until he reached a position from which he could see into the roofless nave. In the centre of the church stood a brazier which glowed redly and sent up swirling clouds of smoke whose pungent aromatic odour drifted across to where Carfax stood. Around and about the brazier moved a considerable company of men and women. They were naked, and as they moved, their bodies seemed to capture and reflect the ruddy glare of the fire as though they were lacquered. When he glimpsed them momentarily in the firelight, Carfax thought that the faces of a few of the taller ones seemed vaguely familiar, but the majority of the company appeared to be very short in stature, so short, in fact, that at the first instant of vision he thought they must be children. Their bodies, however, belied this impression, as did their faces, for their countenances were such that Carfax was grateful for the smoke which prevented him from seeing them clearly. Sometimes the company moved in slow and stately dance, sometimes the pace quickened to a frenzy accompanied by gesture and posture indescribably obscene. Naked feet moved silently and there was no sound of music, yet always they seemed obedient to the measure of some inaudible rhythm. Now and again the smoke whirled aside to reveal, in the shadows beyond the brazier, a horned figure seated upon some kind of throne. Carfax marked this inhuman shape with a renewed access of fear until he realised that it was a man clothed in skins and wearing a horned head-dress. He knew then that he was beholding the celebration of rites unbelievably ancient, and temporarily his interest overcame his revulsion and his fear. But only momentarily, for it dawned upon him that this spectacle, for all its diabolic depravity, was human, and that it inspired a purely physical emotion, whereas the malignant power which brooded over the valley itself was something more or less than human. These forms which writhed in the firelight might conjure or appease that power, but they were not the power itself; their monstrous celebration had not abated the tense expectancy of the stillness. The valley still awaited some greater event.

Suddenly, a blinding flash of lightning, followed immediately by a crash of thunder, tore through the veil of darkness and silence. Reverberating like great drums, the mountains took up the roar of sound and flung it from wall to wall, echoing and re-echoing down Cwm Garon. The figures round the fire had ceased their dance and flung themselves prostrate on the ground. The fire itself burnt low. The thunder died away with a sound like the closing of some vast door, and with its passing there seized Carfax a terror of the soul so abject that it was as though the valley yawned like the mouth of hell. For there fell about him a silence that was like the soundless desolation of outer space, and a sightless darkness blacker than any midnight. Though his eyes were blinded and his ears heard no sound, he knew that there stalked through the valley something intangible, unearthly, monstrous and very terrible. Though no leaf moved, something stirred in his hair. It seemed to pass as a storm cloud passes, sweeping down Cwm Garon, and with that passage the spell which had bound senses and held limbs from motion lifted. Carfax screamed, and, slipping and stumbling, he ran towards the crags of Black Daren. At the sound of his voice, two squat figures left the circle round the fire. Their pale forms glimmered in the darkness as they followed lithely after, moving in swift silence over the screes.

THE SUMMER PEOPLE

by

Shirley Jackson

First published in the September
edition of *Charm* magazine

1950

THE ALLISONS' COUNTRY cottage, seven miles from the near-est town, was set prettily on a hill; from three sides it looked down on soft trees and grass that seldom, even at midsummer, lay still and dry. On the fourth side was the lake, which touched against the wooden pier the Allisons had to keep repairing, and which looked equally well from the Allisons' front porch, their side porch or any spot on the wooden staircase leading from the porch down to the water. Although the Allisons loved their summer cottage, looked forward to arriving in the early summer and hated to leave in the fall, they had not troubled themselves to put in any improve-ments, regarding the cottage itself and the lake as improvement enough for the life left to them. The cottage had no heat, no run-ning water except the precarious supply from the backyard pump, and no electricity. For seventeen summers, Janet Allison had cooked on a kerosene stove, heating all their water; Robert Allison had brought buckets full of water daily from the pump and read his paper by kerosene light in the evenings; and they had both, sanitary city people, become stolid and matter-of-fact about their back-house. In the first two years they had gone through all the standard vaudeville and magazine jokes about backhouses and by now, when they no longer had frequent guests to impress, they had subsided to a comfortable security which made the backhouse, as well as the pump and the kerosene, an indefinable asset to their summer life.

In themselves, the Allisons were ordinary people. Mrs Allison was fifty-eight years old and Mr Allison sixty; they had seen their children outgrow the summer cottage and go on to families of their own and seashore resorts; their friends were either dead or settled in comfortable year-round houses, their nieces and nephews vague. In the winter they told one another they could stand their New York apartment while waiting for the summer; in the summer they told one another that the winter was well worth while, waiting to get to the country.

Since they were old enough not to be ashamed of regular habits, the Allisons invariably left their summer cottage the Tuesday after Labor Day, and were as invariably sorry when the months of September and early October turned out to be pleasant and almost insufferably barren in the city; each year they recognised that there was nothing to bring them back to New York, but it was not until this year that they overcame their traditional inertia enough to decide to stay in the cottage after Labor Day.

'There isn't really anything to take us back to the city,' Mrs Allison told her husband seriously, as though it were a new idea, and he told her, as though neither of them had ever considered it, 'We might as well enjoy the country as long as possible.'

Consequently, with much pleasure and a slight feeling of adventure, Mrs Allison went into their village the day after Labor Day and told those natives with whom she had dealings, with a pretty air of breaking away from tradition, that she and her husband had decided to stay at least a month longer at their cottage.

'It isn't as though we had anything to take us back to the city,' she said to Mr Babcock, her grocer. 'We might as well enjoy the country while we can.'

'Nobody ever stayed at the lake past Labor Day before,' Mr Babcock said. He was putting Mrs Allison's groceries into a large cardboard carton, and he stopped for a minute to look reflectively into a bag of cookies. 'Nobody,' he added.

'But the city!' Mrs Allison always spoke of the city to Mr Babcock as though it were Mr Babcock's dream to go there. 'It's so hot – you've really no idea. We're always sorry when we leave.'

'Hate to leave,' Mr Babcock said. One of the most irritating native tricks Mrs Allison had noticed was that of taking a trivial statement and rephrasing it downward into an even more trite statement. 'I'd hate to leave myself,' Mr Babcock said, after deliberation, and both he and Mrs Allison smiled. 'But I never heard of anyone ever staying out at the lake after Labor Day before.'

'Well, we're going to give it a try,' Mrs Allison said, and Mr Babcock replied gravely, 'Never know till you try.'

Physically, Mrs Allison decided, as she always did when leaving the grocery after one of her inconclusive conversations with Mr Babcock, physically, Mr Babcock could model for a statue of Daniel Webster, but mentally . . . it was horrible to think into what old New England Yankee stock had degenerated. She said as much to Mr Allison when she got into the car, and he said, 'It's generations of inbreeding. That and the bad land.'

Since this was their big trip into town, which they made only once every two weeks to buy things they could not have delivered, they spent all day at it, stopping to have a sandwich in the newspaper and soda shop, and leaving packages heaped in the back of the car. Although Mrs Allison was able to order groceries delivered regularly, she was never able to form any accurate idea of Mr Babcock's current stock by telephone, and her lists of odds and ends that might be procured was always supplemented, almost beyond their need, by the new and fresh local vegetables Mr Babcock was selling temporarily, or the packaged candy which had just come in. This trip Mrs Allison was tempted, too, by the set of glass baking dishes that had found themselves completely by chance in the hardware and clothing and general store, and which had seemingly been waiting there for no one but Mrs Allison, since the country people, with their instinctive distrust of anything that did not look as permanent as trees and rocks and sky, had only recently begun to experiment in aluminum baking dishes instead of ironware, and had, apparently within the memory of local inhabitants, discarded stoneware in favor of iron.

Mrs Allison had the glass baking dishes carefully wrapped, to endure the uncomfortable ride home over the rocky road that led up to the Allisons' cottage, and while Mr Charley Walpole, who, with his younger brother Albert, ran the hardware-clothing-general store (the store itself was called Johnson's because it stood on the site of the old Johnson cabin, burned fifty years before Charley Walpole was born), laboriously unfolded newspapers to wrap around the dishes, Mrs Allison said, informally, 'Course, I *could* have waited and gotten those dishes in New York, but we're not going back so soon this year.'

'Heard you was staying on,' Mr Charley Walpole said. His old fingers fumbled maddeningly with the thin sheets of newspaper, carefully trying to isolate only one sheet at a time, and he did not look up at Mrs Allison as he went on, 'Don't know about staying on up there to the lake. Not after Labor Day.'

'Well, you know,' Mrs Allison said, quite as though he deserved an explanation, 'it just seemed to us that we've been hurrying back to New York every year, and there just wasn't any need for it. You know what the city's like in the fall.' And she smiled confidingly up at Mr Charley Walpole.

Rhythmically he wound string around the package. He's giving me a piece long enough to save, Mrs Allison thought, and she looked away quickly to avoid giving any sign of impatience. 'I feel sort of like we belong here, more,' she said. 'Staying on after everyone else has left.' To prove this, she smiled brightly across the store at a woman with a familiar face, who might have been the woman who sold berries to the Allisons one year, or the woman who occasionally helped in the grocery and was probably Mr Babcock's aunt.

'Well,' Mr Charley Walpole said. He shoved the package a little across the counter, to show that it was finished and that for a sale well made, a package well wrapped, he was willing to accept pay. 'Well,' he said again. 'Never been summer people before, at the lake after Labor Day.'

Mrs Allison gave him a five-dollar bill, and he made change methodically, giving great weight even to the pennies. 'Never after Labor Day,' he said, and nodded at Mrs Allison, and went soberly along the store to deal with two women who were looking at cotton house dresses.

As Mrs Allison passed on her way out she heard one of the women say acutely, 'Why is one of them dresses one dollar and thirty-nine cents and this one here is only ninety-eight?'

'They're great people,' Mrs Allison told her husband as they went together down the sidewalk after meeting at the door of the hardware store. 'They're so solid, and so reasonable, and so *honest*.'

'Makes you feel good, knowing there are still towns like this,' Mr Allison said.

'You know, in New York,' Mrs Allison said, 'I might have paid a few cents less for these dishes, but there wouldn't have been anything sort of personal in the transaction.'

'Staying on to the lake?' Mrs Martin, in the newspaper and sandwich shop, asked the Allisons. 'Heard you was staying on.'

'Thought we'd take advantage of the lovely weather this year,' Mr Allison said.

Mrs Martin was a comparative newcomer to the town; she had married into the newspaper and sandwich shop from a neighbouring farm, and had stayed on after her husband's death. She served bottled soft drinks, and fried egg and onion sandwiches on thick bread, which she made on her own stove at the back of the store.

Occasionally when Mrs Martin served a sandwich it would carry with it the rich fragrance of the stew or the pork chops cooking alongside for Mrs Martin's dinner.

'I don't guess anyone's ever stayed out there so long before,' Mrs Martin said. 'Not after Labor Day, anyway.'

'I guess Labor Day is when they usually leave,' Mr Hall, the Allisons' nearest neighbour, told them later, in front of Mr Babcock's store, where the Allisons were getting into their car to go home. 'Surprised you're staying on.'

'It seemed a shame to go so soon,' Mrs Allison said. Mr Hall lived three miles away; he supplied the Allisons with butter and eggs, and occasionally, from the top of their hill, the Allisons could see the lights in his house in the early evening before the Halls went to bed.

'They usually leave Labor Day,' Mr Hall said.

The ride home was long and rough; it was beginning to get dark, and Mr Allison had to drive very carefully over the dirt road by the lake. Mrs Allison lay back against the seat, pleasantly relaxed after a day of what seemed whirlwind shopping compared with their day-to-day existence; the new glass baking dishes lurked agreeably in her mind, and the half-bushel of red eating apples, and the package of coloured thumbtacks with which she was going to put up new shelf edging in the kitchen. 'Good to get home,' she said softly as they came in sight of their cottage, silhouetted above them against the sky.

'Glad we decided to stay on,' Mr Allison agreed.

Mrs Allison spent the next morning lovingly washing her baking dishes, although in his innocence Charley Walpole had neglected to notice the chip in the edge of one; she decided, wastefully, to use some of the red eating apples in a pie for dinner, and, while the pie was in the oven and Mr Allison was down getting the mail, she sat out on the little lawn the Allisons had made at the top of the hill, and watched the changing lights on the lake, alternating grey and blue as clouds moved quickly across the sun.

Mr Allison came back a little out of sorts; it always irritated him to walk the mile to the mailbox on the state road and come back with nothing, even though he assumed that the walk was good for his health. This morning there was nothing but a circular from a New York department store, and their New York paper, which arrived erratically by mail from one to four days later than it should, so that some days the Allisons might have three papers and frequently none. Mrs Allison, although she shared with her husband the annoyance of not having mail when they so anticipated it, pored affectionately over the department store circular, and made a mental note to drop in at the store when she finally went back to New York, and check on the sale of wool blankets; it was hard to find good ones in pretty colours nowadays. She debated saving the circular to remind herself, but after thinking about getting up and getting into the cottage to put it away safely somewhere, she dropped it into the grass beside her chair and lay back, her eyes half closed.

'Looks like we might have some rain,' Mr Allison said, squinting at the sky.

'Good for the crops,' Mrs Allison said laconically, and they both laughed.

The kerosene man came the next morning while Mr Allison was down getting the mail; they were getting low on kerosene and Mrs Allison greeted the man warmly; he sold kerosene and ice, and, during the summer, hauled garbage away for the summer people. A garbage man was only necessary for improvident city folk; country people had no garbage.

'I'm glad to see you,' Mrs Allison told him. 'We were getting pretty low.'

The kerosene man, whose name Mrs Allison had never learned, used a hose attachment to fill the twenty-gallon tank which supplied light and heat and cooking facilities for the Allisons; but today, instead of swinging down from his truck and unhooking the hose from where it coiled affectionately around the cab of the truck, the man stared uncomfortably at Mrs Allison, his truck motor still going.

'Thought you folks'd be leaving,' he said.

'We're staying on another month,' Mrs Allison said brightly. 'The weather was so nice, and it seemed like—'

'That's what they told me,' the man said. 'Can't give you no oil, though.'

'What do you mean?' Mrs Allison raised her eyebrows. 'We're just going to keep on with our regular—'

'After Labor Day,' the man said. 'I don't get so much oil myself after Labor Day.'

Mrs Allison reminded herself, as she had frequently to do when in disagreement with her neighbors, that city manners were no good with country people; you could not expect to overrule a country employee as you could a city worker, and Mrs Allison smiled engagingly as she said, 'But can't you get extra oil, at least while we stay?'

'You see,' the man said. He tapped his finger exasperatingly against the car wheel as he spoke. 'You see,' he said slowly, 'I order this oil. I order it down from maybe fifty, fifty-five miles away. I order back in June, how much I'll need for the summer. Then I order again . . . oh, about November. Round about now it's starting to get pretty short.' As though the subject were closed, he stopped tapping his finger and tightened his hands on the wheel in preparation for departure.

'But can't you give us *some*?' Mrs Allison said. 'Isn't there anyone else?'

'Don't know as you could get oil anywheres else right now,' the man said consideringly. 'I can't give you none.' Before Mrs Allison could speak, the truck began to move; then it stopped for a minute and he looked at her through the back window of the cab. 'Ice?' he called. 'I could let you have some ice.'

Mrs Allison shook her head; they were not terribly low on ice, and she was angry. She ran a few steps to catch up with the truck, calling, 'Will you try to get us some? Next week?'

'Don't see's I can,' the man said. 'After Labor Day, it's harder.' The truck drove away, and Mrs Allison, only comforted by the thought that she could probably get kerosene from Mr Babcock, or, at worst, the Halls, watched it go with anger. 'Next summer,' she told herself. 'Just let *him* try coming around next summer!'

There was no mail again, only the paper, which seemed to be coming doggedly on time, and Mr Allison was openly cross when he returned. When Mrs Allison told him about the kerosene man he was not particularly impressed.

'Probably keeping it all for a high price during the winter,' he commented. 'What's happened to Anne and Jerry, do you think?'

Anne and Jerry were their son and daughter, both married, one living in Chicago, one in the Far West; their dutiful weekly letters were late; so late, in fact, that Mr Allison's annoyance at the lack of mail was able to settle on a legitimate grievance. 'Ought to realise how we wait for their letters,' he said. 'Thoughtless, selfish children. Ought to know better.'

'Well, dear,' Mrs Allison said placatingly. Anger at Anne and Jerry would not relieve her emotions toward the kerosene man. After a few minutes she said, 'Wishing won't bring the mail, dear. I'm going to go call Mr Babcock and tell him to send up some kerosene with my order.'

'At least a postcard,' Mr Allison said as she left.

As with most of the cottage's inconveniences, the Allisons no longer noticed the phone particularly, but yielded to its eccentricities without conscious complaint. It was a wall phone, of a type still seen in only few communities; in order to get the operator,

Mrs Allison had first to turn the sidecrank and ring once. Usually it took two or three tries to force the operator to answer, and Mrs Allison, making any kind of telephone call, approached the phone with resignation and a sort of desperate patience. She had to crank the phone three times this morning before the operator answered, and then it was still longer before Mr Babcock picked up the receiver at his phone in the corner of the grocery behind the meat table. He said 'Store?' with the rising inflection that seemed to indicate suspicion of anyone who tried to communicate with him by means of this unreliable instrument.

'This is Mrs Allison, Mr Babcock. I thought I'd give you my order a day early because I wanted to be sure and get some—'

'What say, Mrs Allison?'

Mrs Allison raised her voice a little; she saw Mr Allison, out on the lawn, turn in his chair and regard her sympathetically. 'I said, Mr Babcock, I thought I'd call in my order early so you could send me—'

'Mrs Allison?' Mr Babcock said. 'You'll come and pick it up?'

'Pick it up?' In her surprise Mrs Allison let her voice drop back to its normal tone and Mr Babcock said loudly, 'What's that, Mrs Allison?'

'I thought I'd have you send it out as usual,' Mrs Allison said.

'Well, Mrs Allison,' Mr Babcock said, and there was a pause while Mrs Allison waited, staring past the phone over her husband's head out into the sky. 'Mrs Allison,' Mr Babcock went on finally, 'I'll tell you, my boy's been working for me went back to school yesterday and now I got no one to deliver. I only got a boy delivering summers, you see.'

'I thought you *always* delivered,' Mrs Allison said.

'Not after Labor Day, Mrs Allison,' Mr Babcock said firmly. 'You never been here after Labor Day before, so's you wouldn't know, of course.'

'Well,' Mrs Allison said helplessly. Far inside her mind she was saying, over and over, can't use city manners on country folk, no use getting mad.

'Are you *sure?*' she asked finally. 'Couldn't you just send out an order today, Mr Babcock?'

'Matter of fact,' Mr Babcock said, 'I guess I couldn't, Mrs Allison. It wouldn't hardly pay, delivering, with no one else out at the lake.'

'What about Mr Hall?' Mrs Allison asked suddenly, 'the people who live about three miles away from us out here? Mr Hall could bring it out when he comes.'

'Hall?' Mr Babcock said. 'John Hall? They've gone to visit her folks upstate, Mrs Allison.'

'But they bring all our butter and eggs,' Mrs Allison said, appalled.

'Left yesterday,' Mr Babcock said. 'Probably didn't think you folks would stay on up there.'

'But I told Mr Hall . . .' Mrs Allison started to say, and then stopped. 'I'll send Mr Allison in after some groceries tomorrow,' she said.

'You got all you need till then,' Mr Babcock said, satisfied; it was not a question, but a confirmation.

After she hung up, Mrs Allison went slowly out to sit again in her chair next to her husband. 'He won't deliver,' she said. 'You'll have to go in tomorrow. We've got just enough kerosene to last till you get back.'

'He should have told us sooner,' Mr Allison said.

It was not possible to remain troubled long in the face of the day; the country had never seemed more inviting, and the lake moved quietly below them, among the trees, with the almost incredible softness of a summer picture. Mrs Allison sighed deeply, in the pleasure of possessing for themselves that sight of the lake, with the distant green hills beyond, the gentleness of the small wind through the trees.

✦ ✦ ✦

The weather continued fair; the next morning Mr Allison, duly armed with a list of groceries, with 'kerosene' in large letters at the top, went down the path to the garage, and Mrs Allison began another pie in her new baking dishes. She had mixed the crust and was starting to pare the apples when Mr Allison came rapidly up the path and flung open the screen door into the kitchen.

'Damn car won't start,' he announced, with the end-of-the-tether voice of a man who depends on a car as he depends on his right arm.

'What's wrong with it?' Mrs Allison demanded, stopping with the paring knife in one hand and an apple in the other. 'It was all right on Tuesday.'

'Well,' Mr Allison said between his teeth, 'it's not all right on Friday.'

'Can you fix it?' Mrs Allison asked.

'No,' Mr Allison said, 'I cannot. Got to call someone, I guess.'

'Who?' Mrs Allison asked.

'Man runs the filling station, I guess.' Mr Allison moved purposefully toward the phone. 'He fixed it last summer one time.'

A little apprehensive, Mrs Allison went on paring apples absentmindedly, while she listened to Mr Allison with the phone, ringing, waiting, finally giving the number to the operator, then waiting again and giving the number again, giving the number a third time, and then slamming down the receiver.

'No one there,' he announced as he came into the kitchen.

'He's probably gone out for a minute,' Mrs Allison said nervously; she was not quite sure what made her so nervous, unless it was the probability of her husband's losing his temper completely. 'He's there alone, I imagine, so if he goes out there's no one to answer the phone.'

'That must be it,' Mr Allison said with heavy irony. He slumped into one of the kitchen chairs and watched Mrs Allison paring apples. After a minute, Mrs Allison said soothingly, 'Why don't you go down and get the mail and then call him again?'

Mr Allison debated and then said, 'Guess I might as well.' He rose heavily and when he got to the kitchen door he turned and said, 'But if there's no mail—' and leaving an awful silence behind him, he went off down the path.

Mrs Allison hurried with her pie. Twice she went to the window to glance at the sky to see if there were clouds coming up. The room seemed unexpectedly dark, and she herself felt in the state of tension that preceded a thunderstorm, but both times when she looked the sky was clear and serene, smiling indifferently down on the Allisons' summer cottage as well as on the rest of the world. When Mrs Allison, her pie ready for the oven, went a third time to look outside, she saw her husband coming up the path; he seemed more cheerful, and when he saw her, he waved eagerly and held a letter in the air.

'From Jerry,' he called as soon as he was close enough for her to hear him, 'at last – a letter!' Mrs Allison noticed with concern that he was no longer able to get up the gentle slope of the path without breathing heavily; but then he was in the doorway, holding out the letter. 'I saved it till I got here,' he said.

Mrs Allison looked with an eagerness that surprised her on the familiar handwriting of her son; she could not imagine why the letter excited her so, except that it was the first they had received in so long; it would be a pleasant, dutiful letter, full of the doings of Alice and the children, reporting progress with his job, commenting on the recent weather in Chicago, closing with love from all; both Mr and Mrs Allison could, if they wished, recite a pattern letter from either of their children.

Mr Allison slit the letter open with great deliberation, and then he spread it out on the kitchen table and they leaned down and read it together.

'*Dear Mother and Dad,*' it began, in Jerry's familiar, rather child-ish, handwriting, '*Am glad this goes to the lake as usual, we always thought you came back too soon and ought to stay up there as long as you could. Alice says that now that you're not as young as you used to be and have no demands on your time, fewer friends, etc., in the city, you ought to get what fun you can while you can. Since you two are both happy up there, it's a good idea for you to stay.*'

Uneasily Mrs Allison glanced sideways at her husband; he was reading intently, and she reached out and picked up the empty envelope, not knowing exactly what she wanted from it. It was addressed quite as usual, in Jerry's handwriting, and was post-marked 'Chicago'. Of course it's postmarked Chicago, she thought quickly, why would they want to postmark it anywhere else? When she looked back down at the letter, her husband had turned the page, and she read on with him: '—*and of course if they get measles, etc., now, they will be better off later. Alice is well, of course; me too. Been playing a lot of bridge lately with some people you don't know, named Carruthers. Nice young couple, about our age. Well, will close now as I guess it bores you to hear about things so far away. Tell Dad old Dickson, in our Chicago office, died. He used to ask about Dad a lot. Have a good time up at the lake, and don't bother about hurrying back. Love from all of us, Jerry.*'

'Funny,' Mr Allison commented.

'It doesn't sound like Jerry,' Mrs Allison said in a small voice. 'He never wrote anything like . . .' She stopped.

'Like what?' Mr Allison demanded. 'Never wrote anything like what?' Mrs Allison turned the letter over, frowning. It was impos-sible to find any sentence, any word, even, that did not sound like Jerry's regular letters. Perhaps it was only that the letter was so late, or the unusual number of dirty fingerprints on the envelope.

'I don't *know*,' she said impatiently.

'Going to try that phone call again,' Mr Allison said. Mrs Alli-son read the letter twice more, trying to find a phrase that sounded wrong. Then Mr Allison came back and said, very quietly, 'Phone's dead.'

'What?' Mrs Allison said, dropping the letter.

'Phone's dead,' Mr Allison said.

The rest of the day went quickly; after a lunch of crackers and milk, the Allisons went to sit outside on the lawn, but their afternoon was cut short by the gradually increasing storm clouds that came up over the lake to the cottage, so that it was as dark as evening by four o'clock. The storm delayed, however, as though in loving anticipation of the moment it would break over the summer cottage, and there was an occasional flash of lightning, but no rain. In the evening Mr and Mrs Allison, sitting close together inside their cottage, turned on the battery radio they had brought with them from New York. There were no lamps lighted in the cottage, and the only light came from the lightning outside and the small square glow from the dial of the radio.

The slight framework of the cottage was not strong enough to withstand the city noises, the music and the voices, from the radio, and the Allisons could hear them far off echoing across the lake, the saxophones in the New York dance band wailing over the water, the flat voice of the girl vocalist going inexorably out into the clean country air. Even the announcer, speaking glowingly of the virtues of razor blades, was no more than an inhuman voice sounding out from the Allisons' cottage and echoing back, as though the lake and the hills and the trees were returning it unwanted.

During one pause between commercials, Mrs Allison turned and smiled weakly at her husband. 'I wonder if we're supposed to . . . *do* anything,' she said.

'No,' Mr Allison said consideringly. 'I don't think so. Just wait.'

Mrs Allison caught her breath quickly, and Mr Allison said, under the trivial melody of the dance band beginning again, 'The car had been tampered with, you know. Even I could see that.'

Mrs Allison hesitated a minute and then said very softly, 'I suppose the phone wires were cut.'

'I imagine so,' Mr Allison said.

After a while, the dance music stopped and they listened attentively to a news broadcast, the announcer's rich voice telling them breathlessly of a marriage in Hollywood, the latest baseball scores, the estimated rise in food prices during the coming week. He spoke to them, in the summer cottage, quite as though they still deserved to hear news of a world that no longer reached them except through the fallible batteries on the radio, which were already beginning to fade, almost as though they still belonged, however tenuously, to the rest of the world.

Mrs Allison glanced out the window at the smooth surface of the lake, the black masses of the trees, and the waiting storm, and said conversationally, 'I feel better about that letter of Jerry's.'

'I knew when I saw the light down at the Hall place last night,' Mr Allison said.

The wind, coming up suddenly over the lake, swept around the summer cottage and slapped hard at the windows. Mr and Mrs Allison involuntarily moved closer together, and with the first sudden crash of thunder, Mr Allison reached out and took his wife's hand. And then, while the lightning flashed outside, and the radio faded and sputtered, the two old people huddled together in their summer cottage and waited.

THE LADY
ON THE GREY

by

John Collier

First published in the 16 June edition of
The New Yorker magazine

1951

Ringwood was the last of an Anglo-Irish family which had played the devil in County Clare for a matter of three centuries. At last all their big houses were sold up, or burned down by the long-suffering Irish, and of all their thousands of acres not a single foot remained. Ringwood, however, had a few hundred a year of his own, and if the family estates had vanished, he at least inherited a family instinct which prompted him to regard all Ireland as his domain and to rejoice in its abundance of horses, foxes, salmon, game, and girls.

In pursuit of these delights, Ringwood ranged and roved from Donegal to Wexford through all the seasons of the year. There were not many hunts he had not led at some time or other on a borrowed mount, nor many bridges he had not leaned over through half a May morning, nor many inn parlours where he had not snored away a wet winter afternoon in front of the fire.

He had an intimate by the name of Bates, who was another of the same breed and the same kidney. Bates was equally long and lean, and equally hard-up, and he had the same wind-flushed bony face, the same shabby arrogance, and the same seignorial approach to the little girls in the cottages and cowsheds.

Neither of these blades ever wrote a letter, but each generally knew where the other was to be found. The ticket collector, respectfully blind as he snipped Ringwood's third-class ticket in a first-class compartment, would mention that Mr Bates had travelled that way only last Tuesday, stopping off at Killorglin for a week or two after the snipe. The chambermaid, coy in the clammy bedroom of a fishing inn, would find time to tell Bates that Ringwood had gone on up to Lough Corrib for a go at the pike. Policemen, priests, bagmen, gamekeepers, even the tinkers on the roads, would pass on this verbal *pateran*. Then, if it seemed his friend was on to a good thing, the other would pack up his battered kitbag, put rods and guns into their cases, and drift off to join in the sport.

So it happened that one winter afternoon, when Ringwood was strolling back from a singularly blank day on the bog of Ballyneary, he was hailed by a one-eyed horse dealer of his acquaintance, who came trotting by in a gig, as people still do in Ireland. This worthy told our friend that he had just come down from Galway, where he had seen Mr Bates, who was on his way to a village called Knockderry, and who had told him very particularly to mention it to Mr Ringwood if he came across him.

Ringwood turned this message over in his mind, and noted that it was a very particular one, and that no mention was made as to whether it was fishing or shooting his friend was engaged in, or whether he had met with some Croesus who had a string of hunters that he was prepared to lend. 'He certainly would have put a name to it if it was anything of that sort! I'll bet my life it's a pair of sisters he's got on the track of. It must be!'

At this thought, he grinned from the tip of his long nose like a fox, and he lost no time in packing his bag and setting off for this place Knockderry, which he had never visited before in all his roving up and down the country in pursuit of fur, feather, and girls.

He found it was a long way off the beaten track, and a very quiet place when he got to it. There were the usual low, bleak hills all around, and a river running along the valley, and the usual ruined tower up on a slight rise, girdled with a straggly wood and approached by the remains of an avenue.

The village itself was like many another: a few groups of shabby cottages, a decaying mill, half-a-dozen beer shops, and one inn at which a gentleman, hardened to rural cookery, might conceivably put up.

Ringwood's hired car deposited him there, and he strode in and found the landlady in the kitchen, and asked for his friend Mr Bates.

'Why, sure, your honour,' said the landlady, 'the gentleman's staying here. At least, he is, so to speak, and then, now, he isn't.'

'How's that?' said Ringwood.

'His bag's here,' said the landlady, 'and his things are here, and my grandest room taken up with them (though I've another every bit as good), and himself staying in the house best part of a week. But the day before yesterday he went out for a bit of a constitutional, and – would you believe it, sir? – we've seen neither hide nor hair of him since.'

'He'll be back,' said Ringwood. 'Show me a room, and I'll stay here and wait for him.'

Accordingly, he settled in, and waited all the evening, but Bates failed to appear. However, that sort of thing bothers no one in Ireland, and Ringwood's only impatience was in connection with the pair of sisters, whose acquaintance he was extremely anxious to make.

During the next day or two he employed his time in strolling up and down all the lanes and bypaths in the neighbourhood, in the hope of discovering these beauties, or else some other. He was not particular as to which it should be, but on the whole he would have preferred a cottage girl, because he had no wish to waste time on elaborate approaches.

It was on the second afternoon, just as the early dusk was falling, he was about a mile outside the village and he met a straggle of muddy cows coming along the road, and a girl driving them. Our friend took a look at this girl, and stopped dead in his tracks, grinning more like a fox than ever.

This girl was still a child in her teens, and her bare legs were spattered with mud and scratched by brambles, but she was so pretty that the seignorial blood of all the Ringwoods boiled in the veins of their last descendant, and he felt an overmastering desire for a cup of milk. He therefore waited a minute or two, and then followed leisurely along the lane, meaning to turn in as soon as he saw the byre, and beg the favour of this innocent refreshment, and perhaps a little conversation into the bargain.

They say, though, that blessings never come singly, any more than misfortunes. As Ringwood followed his charmer, swearing to himself that there couldn't be such another in the whole county, he heard the fall of a horse's hoofs, and looked up, and there, approaching him at a walking pace, was a grey horse, which must have turned in from some bypath or other, because there certainly had been no horse in sight a moment before.

A grey horse is no great matter, especially when one is so urgently in need of a cup of milk, but this grey horse differed from all others of its species and colour in two respects. First, it was no sort of a horse at all, neither hack nor hunter, and it picked up its feet in a queer way, and yet it had an arch to its neck and a small head and a wide nostril that were not entirely without distinction. And, second – and this distracted Ringwood from all curiosity as to breed and bloodline – this grey horse carried on its back a girl who was obviously and certainly the most beautiful girl he had ever seen in his life.

Ringwood looked at her, and as she came slowly through the dusk she raised her eyes and looked at Ringwood. He at once forgot the little girl with the cows. In fact, he forgot everything else in the world.

The horse came nearer, and still the girl looked, and Ringwood looked, and it was not a mere exchange of glances, it was wooing and a marriage, all complete and perfect in a mingling of the eyes.

Next moment, the horse had carried her past him, and, quickening its pace a little, it left him standing on the road. He could hardly run after it, or shout; in any case, he was too overcome to do anything but stand and stare.

He watched the horse and rider go on through the wintry twilight, and he saw her turn in at a broken gateway just a little way along the road. Just as she passed through, she turned her head and whistled, and Ringwood noticed that her dog had stopped by him, and was sniffing about his legs. For a moment he thought it was a smallish wolfhound, but then he saw it was just a tall, lean, hairy lurcher. He watched it run limping after her, with its tail down, and it struck him that the poor creature had had an appalling thrashing not so long ago; he had noticed the marks where the hair was thin on its ribs.

However, he had little thought to spare for the dog. As soon as he got over his first excitement, he moved on in the direction of the gateway. The girl was already out of sight when he got there, but he recognised the neglected avenue which led up to the battered tower on the shoulder of the hill.

Ringwood thought that was enough for the day, so he made his way back to the inn. Bates was still absent, but that was just as well. Ringwood wanted the evening to himself in order to work out a plan of campaign.

'That horse never cost two ten-pound notes of anybody's money,' said he to himself. 'So, she's not so rich. So much the better! Besides, she wasn't dressed up much; I don't know what she had on – a sort of cloak or something. Nothing out of Bond Street, anyway. And lives in that old tower! I should have thought it was all tumbled down. Still, I suppose there's a room or two left at the bottom. Poverty Hall! One of the old school, blue blood and no money, pining away in this Godforsaken hole, miles away from everybody. Probably she doesn't see a man from one year's end to another. No wonder she gave me a look. God! If I was sure she was there by herself, I wouldn't need much of an introduction. Still, there might be a father or a brother or somebody. Never mind, I'll manage it.'

When the landlady brought in the lamp: 'Tell me,' said he. 'Who's the young lady who rides the cobby-looking, old-fashioned-looking grey?'

'A young lady, sir?' said the landlady doubtfully. 'On a grey?'

'Yes,' said he. 'She passed me on the lane up there. She turned in on the old avenue, going up to the tower.'

'Oh, Mary bless and keep you!' said the good woman. 'That's the beautiful Murrough lady you must have seen.'

'Murrough?' said he. 'Is that the name? Well! Well! Well! That's a fine old name in the West here.'

'It is so, indeed,' said the landlady. 'For they were kings and queens in Connaught before the Saxon came. And herself, sir, has the face of a queen, they tell me.'

'They're right,' said Ringwood. 'Perhaps you'll bring me in the whiskey and water, Mrs Doyle, and I shall be comfortable.'

He had an impulse to ask if the beautiful Miss Murrough had anything in the shape of a father or a brother at the tower, but his principle was, 'Least said, soonest mended,' especially in little affairs of this sort. So he sat by the fire, recapturing and savouring the look the girl had given him, and he decided he needed only the barest excuse to present himself at the tower.

Ringwood had never any shortage of excuses, so the next after-noon he spruced himself up and set out in the direction of the old avenue. He turned in at the gate, and went along under the forlorn and dripping trees, which were so ivied and overgrown that the darkness was already thickening under them. He looked ahead for a sight of the tower, but the avenue took a turn at the end, and it was still hidden among the clustering trees.

Just as he got to the end, he saw someone standing there, and he looked again, and it was the girl herself, standing as if she was waiting for him.

'Good afternoon, Miss Murrough,' said he, as soon as he got into earshot. 'Hope I'm not intruding. The fact is, I think I had the pleasure of meeting a relation of yours, down in Cork, only last month . . .' By this time he had got close enough to see the look in her eyes again, and all this nonsense died away in his mouth, for this was something beyond any nonsense of that sort.

'I thought you would come,' said she.

'My God!' said he. 'I had to. Tell me – are you all by yourself here?'

'All by myself,' said she, and she put out her hand as if to lead him along with her.

Ringwood, blessing his lucky stars, was about to take it, when her lean dog bounded between them and nearly knocked him over.

'Down!' cried she, lifting her hand. 'Get back!' The dog cowered and whimpered, and slunk behind her, creeping almost on its belly. 'He's not a dog to be trusted,' she said.

'He's all right,' said Ringwood. 'He looks a knowing old fellow. I like a lurcher. Clever dogs. What? Are you trying to talk to me, old boy?'

Ringwood always paid a compliment to a lady's dog, and in fact the creature really was whining and whimpering in the most extraordinary fashion.

'Be quiet!' said the girl, raising her hand again, and the dog was silent.

'A cur,' said she to Ringwood. 'Did you come here to sing the praises of a half-bred cur?' With that, she gave him her eyes again, and he forgot the wretched dog, and she gave him her hand, and this time he took it and they walked toward the tower.

Ringwood was in seventh heaven. 'What luck!' thought he. 'I might at this moment be fondling that little farm wench in some damp and smelly cowshed. And ten to one she'd be snivelling and crying and running home to tell her mammy. This is something different.'

At that moment, the girl pushed open a heavy door, and, bidding the dog lie down, she led our friend through a wide, bare, stone-flagged hall and into a small vaulted room which certainly had no resemblance to a cowshed except perhaps it smelt a little damp and mouldy, as these old stone places so often do. All the same, there were logs burning on the open hearth, and a broad, low couch before the fireplace. For the rest, the room was furnished with the greatest simplicity, and very much in the antique style. 'A touch of the Kathleen ni Houlihan,' thought Ringwood. 'Well, well! Sitting in the Celtic twilight, dreaming of love. She certainly doesn't make much bones about it.'

The girl sat down on the couch and motioned him down beside her. Neither of them said anything; there was no sound but the wind outside, and the dog scratching and whimpering timidly at the door of the chamber.

At last, the girl spoke. 'You are of the Saxon,' said she gravely.

'Don't hold it against me,' said Ringwood. 'My people came here in 1656. Of course, that's yesterday to the Gaelic League, but still I think we can say we have a stake in the country.'

'Yes, through its heart,' said she.

'Is it politics we're going to talk?' said he, putting an Irish turn to his tongue. 'You and I, sitting here in the firelight?'

'It's love you'd rather be talking of,' said she with a smile. 'But you're the man to make a blunder and a mockery of the poor girls of Eire.'

'You misjudge me entirely,' said Ringwood. 'I'm the man to live alone and sorrowful, waiting for the one love, though it seemed something beyond hoping for.'

'Yes,' said she. 'But yesterday you were looking at one of the Connell girls as she drove her kine along the lane.'

'Looking at her? I'll go so far as to say I did,' said he. 'But when I saw you I forgot her entirely.'

'That was my wish,' said she, giving him both her hands. 'Will you stay with me here?'

'Ah, that I will!' cried he in rapture.

'Always?' said she.

'Always,' cried Ringwood. 'Always and for ever!' For he felt it better to be guilty of a slight exaggeration than to be lacking in courtesy to a lady. But as he spoke she fixed her eyes on him, looking so much as if she believed him that he positively believed himself.

'Ah,' he cried. 'You bewitch me!' And he took her in his arms.

He pressed his lips to hers, and at once he was over the brink. Usually he prided himself on being a pretty cool hand, but this was an intoxication too strong for him; his mind seemed to dissolve in sweetness and fire, and at last the fire was gone, and his senses went with it. As they failed, he heard her saying, 'For ever! For ever!' and then everything was gone and he fell asleep.

He must have slept some time. It seemed he was awakened by the heavy opening and closing of a door. For a moment, he was all confused and hardly knew where he was.

The room was now quite dark, and the fire had sunk to a dim glow. He blinked, and shook his ears, trying to shake some sense into his head. Suddenly he heard Bates talking to him, muttering as if he, too, was half asleep, or half drunk more likely. 'You *would* come here,' said Bates. 'I tried hard enough to stop you.'

'Hullo!' said Ringwood, thinking he must have dozed off by the fire in the inn parlour. 'Bates? God, I must have slept heavy! I feel queer. Damn it – so it was all a dream! Strike a light, old boy. It must be late. I'll yell for supper.'

'Don't, for heaven's sake,' said Bates, in his altered voice. 'Don't yell. She'll thrash us if you do.'

'What's that?' said Ringwood. 'Thrash us? What the hell are you talking about?'

At that moment a log rolled on the hearth, and a little flame flickered up, and he saw his long and hairy forelegs, and he knew.

BIND YOUR HAIR

by

Robert Aickman

First published in the collection *Dark Entries*

1964

N O O N E S E E M E D able to fathom Clarinda Hartley. She had
a small but fastidious flat near Church Street, Kensington;
and a responsible job in a large non-committal commercial organ-
isation. No one who knew her now had ever known her in any
other residence or any other job. She entertained a little, never
more nor less over the years; went out not infrequently with men;
and for her holidays simply disappeared, returning with brief references to foreign parts. No one seemed to know her really well; and
in the course of time there came to be wide differences of opinion
about her age, and recurrent speculation about her emotional life.
The latter topic was not made less urgent by a certain distinction in
her appearance, and also in her manner. She was very tall (a great
handicap, of course, in the opinion of many) and well-shaped; she
had very fair, very fine, very abundant hair, to which plainly she
gave much attention; her face had interesting planes (for those
who could appreciate them), but also soft curves, which went with
her hair. She had a memorable voice: high-pitched, but gentle. She
was in fact, thirty-two. Everyone was greatly surprised when she
announced her engagement to Dudley Carstairs.

Or rather it was Carstairs who announced it. He could not keep it to himself as long as there was anyone within earshot who was ignorant of it; and well might he be elated, because his capture followed a campaign of several years' continuance, and supported by few sweeping advantages. He worked in the same office as Clarinda, and in a not unsatisfactory position for his thirty years; and was in every way a thoroughly presentable person: but even in the office there were a number of others like him, and it would have seemed possible that Clarinda could have further extended her range of choice by going outside.

The weekend after the engagement Dudley arranged for her to spend with him and his parents in Northamptonshire. Mr Carstairs, Senior, had held an important position on the administrative side of the Northampton boot and shoe industry; and when he retired upon a fair pension, had settled in a small but comfortable house in one of the remote parts of a county where the remote parts are surprisingly many and extensive. Mr Carstairs had been a pioneer in this particular, because others similarly placed had tended upon retirement to emigrate to the Sussex Coast or the New Forest; but his initiative, as often happens in such cases, had been imitated, until the little village in which he had settled was now largely populated by retired industrial executives and portions of their families.

Clarinda would have been grateful for more time in which to adjust herself to Dudley in the capacity of accepted lover; but Dudley somehow did not seem to see himself in that capacity, and to be reluctant in any way to defer Clarinda's full involvement with her new family position. Clarinda having said yes to what was believed to be the major question, smiled slightly and said yes to the minor.

Mr Carstairs, Senior, met them at Roade station.

'Hullo, Dad.' The two men gazed at one another's shoes, not wanting to embrace and hesitating to shake hands. Mr Carstairs was smiling, benignly expectant. Plainly he was one who considered that life had treated him well. Almost, one believed, he was ready to accept his son's choice of a bride as, for him, joy's crown of joy.

'Dad. This is Clarinda.'

'I *say*, my boy . . .'

Outside the station was a grey Standard, in which Mr Carstairs drove them many miles to the west. Already the sun was sinking. Soon after they arrived they had settled down, with Mrs Carstairs and Dudley's sister Elizabeth, to crumpets in the long winter dusk. Elizabeth had a secretarial position in Leamington, and bicycled there and back every day. All of them were charmed with Clarinda. She exceeded their highest, and perhaps not very confident, hopes.

Clarinda responded to their happy approval of her, and smiled at Dudley's extreme pleasure at being home. An iced cake had been baked for her specially, and she wondered whether these particular gilt-edged cups were in daily use. They neither asked her questions, nor talked mainly about themselves: they all made a warm-hearted, not unskilful effort to make her feel completely one with them from the outset. She and Elizabeth discovered a common interest in the theatre (shared only in a lesser degree by Dudley).

'But Leamington's so stuffy that no one's ever made a theatre pay there.'

'Not since the war,' said Mr Carstairs in affectionate qualification.

'Not since the *first* war,' said Elizabeth.

'Is Leamington the nearest town?' asked Clarinda.

'It's the nearest as the crow flies, or as Elizabeth cycles,' said Dudley, 'but it's not the quickest when you're coming from London. Narrow lanes all the way.'

'Fortunately we've got our own friends by now in the village,' said Mrs Carstairs. 'I've asked some of them in for drinks, so that you can meet them at once.'

And indeed almost immediately the bell rang, and the first of the visitors was upon them. Mr Carstairs went round the room putting on lights and drawing the curtains. Every now and then he gave some jocular direction to Dudley, who was complementarily engaged. A domestic servant of some kind, referred to by Mrs Carstairs as 'Our local woman', had removed the remains of tea; and by the time Elizabeth had borne in a tray of drinks, three more visitors had added themselves to the first two.

'Can I help?' Clarinda had said.

'No,' the Carstairs family had replied. 'Certainly not. Not *yet*.'

Altogether there were eleven visitors, only two of whom were under forty. All eleven of them Clarinda liked very much less than she liked the Carstairs family. Then just as several of them were showing signs of departure, a twelfth arrived; who made a considerable change. A woman of medium height and in early middle age, she had a lined and sallow face, but an alert expression and large deeply set black eyes. She had untidy, shoulder-length, black hair which tended to separate itself into distinct compact strands. Her only make-up appeared to be an exceptionally vivid lipstick, abundantly applied to her large square mouth. She entered in a luxuriant fur coat, but at once cast it off, so that it lay on the floor, and appeared in a black corduroy skirt and a black silk blouse, cut low, and with long tight sleeves. On her feet were heel-less golden slippers.

'I've been so *busy*.' She seized both of Mrs Carstairs's hands. Her voice was very deep and melodious, but marred by a certain hoarseness, or uncertainty of timbre. 'Where is she?'

Mrs Carstairs was smiling amiably as ever; but all conversation in the room had stopped.

'Do go on talking.' The newcomer addressed the party at random. She had now observed Clarinda. 'Introduce me,' she said to Mrs Carstairs, as if her hostess were being a little slow with her duties. 'Or am I too late?' Her sudden quick smile was possibly artificial but certainly bewitching. For a second, various men in the room missed the thread of their resumed conversations.

'Of course you're not too late,' said Mrs Carstairs. Then she made the introduction. 'Clarinda Hartley. Mrs Pagani.'

'Nothing whatever to do with the restaurant,' said Mrs Pagani.

'How do you do?' said Clarinda.

Mrs Pagani had a firm and even but somewhat bony hand-shake. She was wearing several large rings, with heavy stones in them, and round her neck a big fat locket on a thick golden chain.

By now Mrs Carstairs had brought Mrs Pagani a drink. 'Here's to the future,' said Mrs Pagani, looking into Clarinda's eyes, and as soon as Mrs Carstairs had turned away, drained the glass.

'Thank you,' said Clarinda.

'Do sit down,' said Mrs Pagani, as if the house were hers.

'Thank you,' said Clarinda, falling in with the illusion.

Mrs Pagani stretched out an arm (Clarinda noticed that her arms, in their tight black sleeves, were uncommonly long) and pulled up a chair, upon which she sat. Clarinda noticed also that when she was seated, her hips too looked bony and obtrusive. Altogether Mrs Pagani gave an impression of unusual physical power, only partly concealed by her conventional clothes. It was as if suddenly she might arise and tear down the house.

'You cannot imagine,' said Mrs Pagani, 'how much it means to me to have someone new in the village, especially someone more or less my own age. Or perhaps you can?'

'But I'm not going to *live* here,' said Clarinda, clutching hold of the main point.

'Well, of course not. But there'll be frequent weekends. What-ever else may be said for or against Dudley, he's devoted to his home.'

Clarinda nodded thoughtfully. She was aware that every-one's eyes were upon them, and realised that Mrs Pagani had so far acknowledged the presence of none of the other guests, well though she must presumably know them.

'Who would want to know any of these people?' enquired Mrs Pagani in a husky, telepathic, undertone.

One trouble was that Clarinda rather agreed with her.

'Why do *you* live here?'

'I can't live in towns. And in the country people are the same wherever you go. Most people, I mean. You don't live in the country for the local society.'

Clarinda failed to ask why you did live in the country.

Elizabeth came up with more drinks.

'Hullo, Elizabeth,' said Mrs Pagani.

For some reason Elizabeth went very red.

'Hullo, Mrs Pagani.' She left two drinks with them, and hurried away on her errand of hospitality. Mrs Pagani's eyes followed her for a few seconds. Then she turned back to Clarinda, and said: 'We two will be seeing a lot of one another.'

Again Clarinda could only nod.

'I needn't tell you that you're not what I expected. Do you know where I live?'

Clarinda, still silent, shook her head.

'Have you been round the village yet?'

'No.'

'Not seen the church?'

'It was getting dark when I arrived.'

'I live in the churchyard.' Mrs Pagani suddenly shouted with laughter. 'It always surprises people.' She placed her long bony left hand on Clarinda's knee. 'There used to be a chapel in the church-yard, with a room over it. This is a thinly populated district, and they brought the corpses from the farmhouses and cottages, often a long slow journey, and left the coffin in the chapel waiting for the funeral the next day. And the mourners passed the night upstairs, watching and, of course, drinking. When all this became unne-cessary, the chapel fell into ruin. The Parish Council was glad to sell it to me. The vicar's a hundred and one anyway. I restored it and I live in it. The ground had to be specially deconsecrated for me.' Mrs Pagani removed her hand and picked up her glass. 'Come and see me.' For the second time she toasted Clarinda. 'I call it the Charnel House. Not quite correct, of course: a charnel house is where the dead lie *after* the funeral. But I thought the name rather suited me.' Suddenly her attention was distracted. Without moving her eyes, she inclined her head slightly sideways. 'Just look at Mr Appleby. Used to be Managing Director of an important company. Appleby's Arterial Bootlaces.'

Clarinda could not see that Mr Appleby, with whom she had been talking before Mrs Pagani's arrival, was doing anything much out of the ordinary. He seemed simply to be telling stories to two or three other guests, who admittedly seemed less interested than he was. But Clarinda was unaccustomed to making twelve or fifteen intimate acquaintances for life en bloc; and all coming within the, at best, uncertain category of friends' friends.

Again Mrs Pagani had drained her glass. 'I must be going. I only looked in for a minute. I have a lot to do tonight.' She rose and held out her hand. 'Tomorrow then?'

'Thank you very much, but I'm not quite sure. I expect Mr and Mrs Carstairs have some plans for me.'

Mrs Pagani looked her in the eyes, then nodded. 'Yes. You mustn't quarrel with them. That's very important. Well: come if you can.'

'Thank you, I'd like to.'

Mrs Pagani was resuming her expensive sable coat, and saying good-bye to Mrs Carstairs.

'You've nothing to worry about,' Clarinda heard her say, 'Dudley's chosen well.'

'Darling.' It was Dudley standing behind Clarinda's chair. He kissed the top of her head. 'Don't mind her. She's far round the bend, of course, but good-hearted at bottom. Anyway she's the only one of her kind in the village. Pots of money too.'

'What makes you think that, Dudley?' asked the marzipan voice of Mr Appleby. Conversation about Mrs Pagani was now general.

'Couldn't behave as she does if she hadn't, Mr Appleby,' replied Dudley.

That seemed to be the consensus of opinion.

When everyone had gone, they listened to the radio. Then they had supper, and Clarinda was permitted, after strenuous application, to participate in the washing up. As they retired in a warm mist of gently affectionate demonstrativeness, the thought crossed Clarinda's mind that she might like to sleep with Dudley. It was still not an urgent wish, only a thought; but in Dudley there was no evidence that it was even a thought. For him the fateful outer wall of the fortress had been successfully battered down after a long siege; the course of time would bring the later degrees of capitulation.

The next morning Clarinda had to admit to herself that she was very depressed. As she lay in bed watching wisps of late autumn fog drift and swirl past her window, she felt that inside the house was a warm and cosy emptiness in which she was about to be lost. She saw herself, her real self, for ever suspended in blackness, howling in the lonely dark, miserable and unheard; while her other, outer self went smiling through an endless purposeless routine of love for and compliance with a family and a community of friends which, however excellent, were exceedingly unlike her, in some way that she did not fully understand. Elizabeth might bill and coo about the theatre, but it could hardly be said that any one of them had a sense of drama. They lived in the depths of the country, but had no idea of the wilderness. They were constantly together, but knew one another too well to be able to converse. Individuality had been eroded from all of them by the tides of common sentiment. Love me, said Dudley in effect, his eyes softly glowing; love mine. His London personality seemed merely a bait with which to entice her into the capacious family lobster pot. Mrs Pagani was certainly different from the rest of them; but Clarinda was far from sure that Mrs Pagani was her idea of an ally.

Then she got up, turned on the big electric heater, and felt that her thoughts had been the morbid product of lying too long abed. Moreover, the flying swathes of fog were most beautiful. She stood in her nightdress by the window looking at them; with the heater behind her sending ripples of warmth up her back. It was an old sash window with the original well-proportioned glazing bars. The new white paint covered numerous under-currents in the surface of earlier coats. Clarinda liked such details in the house; always kept neat and spruce, like an old dandy whom people still cared about.

But from breakfast onwards her spirits once more began to sink. One trouble was that the Carstairs family, in fact, had no plans for her whatever, and nor had Dudley individually. There was a half-hearted suggestion of church, which no one seemed wishful to keep alive; and after that a sequence of minor interruptions and involved jobs which Clarinda felt could be much better organised, but which everyone else seemed quietly to enjoy as they were. The whole family, Dudley included, seemed to like even the most point-less chores simply because they were being undertaken collectively. The four of them did all they could to give Clarinda a place in the various undertakings; and Clarinda hated the perverse barrier which seemed more and more to isolate her from their kindness. But when by the middle of the afternoon (Sunday luncheon was a substantial reaping of the morning's seedtime) no one had even suggested a walk, she did something precipitate. Without speaking to Dudley, who was helping his father in the garden, she went up to her bedroom, changed into a pair of trousers and a sweater, donned her mackintosh, wrote on the inside of a cigarette box 'Gone for a walk. Back soon', and quietly left the house.

The swathes of fog were still sweeping before the wind, but, though damp, it was not a cold wind nor unfriendly. Immediately she was away from the house, Clarinda felt alive again. After walking a few hundred yards rather furtively, she ascended a roadside bank from which the grass had recently been sickled, and looked about her. She was looking for the church; and when, through a break in the mist, she saw the battlemented top of the yellow stone tower, with a jutting gargoyle at each corner, she knew which way she would go. She turned her back on the church, and walked away from the few cottages which made up the village. Mrs Pagani had possibly served a purpose as serio-comic relief the previous evening, but Clarinda had no wish to enlarge the acquaintance-ship.

The patches of cloud and fog drifted and lifted, making constant changes of scene. There was no hope of sunshine, but the mist was uncharged with smoke, and served to melt the sharp air of winter and to enclose Clarinda with an advancing tent of invisibility. Other than Clarinda's light quick step on the granite chips of the old-fashioned narrow road, the only sound was the dripping of water from the trees, the hedges, the occasional gates. At the tip of every leaf was a fat pearl about to drop and vanish. Clarinda realised that her hair was becoming damp. She bundled it on to the top of her head, soaking her hands in the process; then drew a long black scarf from her mackintosh pocket, and twisted it into a tight turban. The road seemed to be lined with dripping trees, which appeared dimly one at a time, grew into a fullness of detail which had seemed impossible a minute before, and then dissolved away, even from the backward glance; but the air also was itself heavy with soft wetness. Soft and wet, but good on the face . . . 'Let there be wet', quoted Clarinda to herself in her clear gentle voice. 'Oh let there be wet.'

She had seen no one in the village, and if there were animals in the fields, the mist cut off sight and hearing of them. Clarinda was aware that she might have some difficult personal problems almost immediately ahead of her; but she thought nothing of them as the renewal of contact with the country, the adventurous loneliness of her walk, suffused her with their first freshness. Out of the mist advanced a small square notice-board lopsided on top of a sloping wooden pole: 'No Rite of Way,' read Clarinda. 'Persons Proceed Beyond This Point By Favour Only.'

It was perhaps an unusual announcement, and not made more convincing by the misspelling, and by the crudeness of the erection; but Clarinda had heard of landowners who close gates on one day each year in order to prevent the establishment of an easement, and there seemed to be no change whatever in the nature or surface of the road, at least in the short distance ahead which was visible. Clarinda continued her walk.

No one, however, is entirely unaffected, either towards carefulness, or towards challenge, by passing such a notice; and in due course Clarinda realised that she was walking more slowly. Then she perceived that the road itself had for some time been rising slightly but continuously. It also seemed narrower, and the hedges higher. Clarinda stopped and looked at her watch. Despite the muffling mist, she could hear its ticking with extreme clarity, so silent were the hidden pastures around her. It had been something before three o'clock when she had crept out of the house; it was now something after half past. She had possibly another hour of daylight. If she went on for a quarter of that hour, there would be as much time in which to return as she had taken upon the outward journey, and the way back was along a known road, and one which inclined downhill. Moreover, there had not been a single crossroads or doubtful turning. And in any case Clarinda liked walking in the dark. Certainly neither her mind nor her stomach was inclined to a cosy crumpet tea with the Carstairs family, or to a further session bound, like Catherine upon her wheel, to the mark of interrogation which Dudley remained for her. Again, therefore, she continued her walk.

443

The gradient increased, but the trees came more quickly, imperceptibly losing, tree by tree, the moment of clear detail which had previously characterised each of them. The road had begun to wind steeply upwards through a wood. Now the hedges, lately so high, had ceased, but the road, although the antique metalling seemed more and more lost in the damp loamy soil, remained distinct. Intermittently, the going had become a little muddy, but the softness underfoot made a change from the angular granite. The trees had now become dim and uniform shapes which passed so quickly and monotonously that sometimes they seemed almost to move, as in a very early cinematograph.

Then, unmistakably, something else was moving. From among the tall thin trees, and out of the veiling mist, came a small animal. It crossed the track ten or twelve feet in front of Clarinda, and disappeared again almost at once. It neither walked nor ran, but slowly ambled. It was not quite silent, but the atmosphere made the sound of its passage seem insufficient; it whispered and sighed its way through the undergrowth. Clarinda could not think what animal it was. Probably a dog which the mist had misshaped. She checked for a moment, then went on.

Swiftly and momentarily the mist cleared a larger area around her, as she had seen it do several times before. She could see many trees, and could now perceive also that they were beeches. Dotted about the bare earth which surrounds beech trees even in a thick wood, were many more of the animals. They were pigs.

Each of the pigs seemed very intent about its business, softly snuffling after unknown sweets in the naked soil. None grunted or squeaked; but the dead, brown-paper leaves rustled slightly as the herd rooted. The pigs were on both sides of the track, and again Clarinda hesitated briefly before advancing through the midst of them.

At first they took no notice of her, perhaps, she thought, unafraid of man because little knowing him; and the tent of mist, temporarily a marquee, advanced with her on to the wooded heights ahead. Then, most unexpectedly, there came from the obscurity thirty yards away on Clarinda's right a shattering animal shriek; short but so loud and high as to pain the ear. All the pigs looked up, stood motionless for a second, then massed together in the direction the sound had come from, some of them crossing the track behind and ahead of her for the purpose. Again they stood, an indistinct agglomeration on the edge of the mist; then suddenly swept back the way they had come. The whole herd, packed tightly together, charged across the track and disappeared into the mist on the left. The pigs had passed no more than five or six feet in front of Clarinda; who was able to observe that in the very middle of the throng was a creature much larger than the rest, a bristling, long-snouted boar, with large curving bluish-white tusks. He it was, she suspected, that had cried from the enveloping mist. She had never before seen such a creature, and was slightly alarmed.

The scampering flight of the pigs could be heard for a few seconds after the fog had surrounded them. Then the wood was silent again. It was as if the pigs had been the last creatures left alive in it. The fog had now closed up again, scudding across the track on a wind which seemed colder and stronger than it had been in the village at the beginning of Clarinda's walk. But the track was now rising steeply, and the extra exertion kept her warm. The long drawn-out winter dusk must have begun, because not until she was right upon them did Clarinda notice two figures on the path.

They were children. They did not seem to be either ascending or descending, but to be quietly waiting by the side of the track for someone to pass. They were identically dressed in one-piece waterproof garments, like small trim diving suits, bright blue in colour, and provided with hoods. One child had its hood over its head, but the other was bareheaded and displayed a curly mass of silky flaxen hair, much the colour of Clarinda's own in childhood. The bareheaded child had blue eyes very widely spaced, and a pale skin. The face of the other child was shadowed by its hood, and from Clarinda's altitude amounted to little more than a long red mouth. Both children, Clarinda noticed, had long red mouths. She was unable to determine their sex.

'Excuse me,' said the bareheaded child, very politely. Clarinda decided it was a girl. The girl spoke well.

Clarinda stopped.

The little girl smiled charmingly. 'Have you seen the pigs?' She spoke as if the pigs were a matter of common interest to them, and automatically identifiable; as if a straggler from a hunt had asked, Had she seen the hounds?

'Yes,' said Clarinda. 'Are they your pigs?'

'How long ago?' asked the child, with a child's disregard of side issues.

'About five minutes ago.' Clarinda looked at her watch. Quarter to four. Time to go back. 'As a matter of fact, I'm afraid I frightened them.'

'Silly old pigs,' said the child, fortunately taking Clarinda's side. 'Which way did they go? *This* way? Or *that* way?' She indicated up the hill or down. Clarinda thought that she was about eight.

'That way, I'm afraid,' said Clarinda pointing vaguely into the mist. 'I hope they'll not get lost in the fog.'

'There's always a fog,' said the child.

Clarinda let that one go.

'What happens if I get to the top?' she asked.

The hooded child, who had said nothing, suddenly made an odd movement. It raised one foot and stamped on the ground. It was as if its whole small body were swept by a spasm. The movement reminded Clarinda of an animal which had been startled, and pawed the earth: a large animal, moreover. In the child seemed to be a disproportionate strength. Clarinda was really frightened by it.

'There's a lovely view some days,' said the bareheaded child helpfully.

'Not much good this evening.'

The child shook its head, smiling politely. The hooded child snatched at the bareheaded child's sleeve and pulled it sharply.

'There's a maze.' The bareheaded child was showing off slightly but meaning to help also.

'What kind of maze? With hedges? I don't believe it.' To Clarinda a maze meant Hampton Court.

'An ordinary maze. You have to look for it though.'

'How far away?'

'Quite near.'

'Where do I look?' Clearly the child was speaking the truth, and Clarinda was interested.

'In among the bushes. There's a little path.'

Clarinda noticed that the second child had cocked up its head and was looking at her. It seemed to have sharp, sallow features, and big eyes. In its hood it was not unlike a falcon.

'Shall I get lost in the maze?'

The bareheaded child appeared unable to understand this question and looked at Clarinda disappointedly.

'Well, that's up to me,' said Clarinda coming to the rescue.

The child nodded. She had still not understood. 'Thank you for telling us about the pigs.'

'Thank you for telling me about the maze.'

The little girl smiled her pretty smile. Really I never saw such a beautiful child, thought Clarinda. The children departed quickly down the hill. In a moment they had vanished.

Clarinda again looked at her watch. Three-fifty. She decided that she would give fifteen minutes to looking for the child's maze, and that even then she would be back soon after five.

Before long she reached a gate. It was at the edge of the wood and the end of the track. Outside the wood was short, downlike grass, mossy with moisture. Clarinda's feet sank into it, as into very soft rubber. There were frequent, irregularly placed clumps of thorny scrub, and no sign of even the sketchiest path. The wind was still growing chillier, and the mist was darkening all the time. Clarinda had not gone fifty yards from the gate when she decided to return. The question of whether or not it would be worth looking for the maze did not arise. On top of the hill it would be easy to lose oneself without entering a maze.

In the dim light she perceived that a man was leaning against the gate and facing her. He had red curly hair which had receded slightly at the sides, and a prominent nose. He wore pale-hued riding breeches and dark boots. Across his shoulders was a fur cape, which Clarinda vaguely connected with the idea of aviation. As Clarinda approached, he neither spoke nor moved. She saw that in his right hand he held a long thick shepherd's crook. It was black, and reached from the ground to his shoulder.

Clarinda put her hand on the wooden drawbar of the gate. She assumed that this action would make the man move. But he continued leaning on the gate and regarding her. If she opened the gate, he would fall.

'I want to go through.' It was not an occasion for undue politeness.

Without change of expression, the man swiftly placed his left hand on the other end of the drawbar. Clarinda pushed at it, but it would not give. Not given to panic, Clarinda momentarily considered the situation, and began to climb the gate.

'*Hullo*,' said a voice behind her. 'Rufo! What do you suppose you're doing?' Unmistakably it was the voice of Mrs Pagani.

Clarinda stepped down. Mrs Pagani was also wearing high boots, and her head was enveloped like Clarinda's in a dark scarf; but, strangely, she was wearing the capacious and opulent fur coat in which Clarinda had first seen her. The top of her boots were hidden beneath it.

'Rufo!' Mrs Pagani spoke to the man by the gate as if she were calling off a foolish and over-demonstrative dog. The man said something in a strange language. It was so unlike any language Clarinda had heard that at first she thought he had a defect in his speech.

Mrs Pagani, however, replied to him in what was presumably the same tongue. In her mouth it sounded less unfamiliar because she lacked his oddly throaty delivery. Clarinda wondered whether this might be Romany.

The man was remonstrating against Mrs Pagani's reproof. Her reply was curious: she was fluently pantomimic, and Clarinda could not but gather that Rufo was being told that she, Clarinda, was to be admitted where others were to be denied. The man scowled, and leered, then shuffled off. Although young and apparently strong, he stumbled in his gait and leaned on his crook. There was now very little light, but after he had gone a few paces, he appeared to draw his fur cape high over the back of his head.

'What can you think of Rufo?'

Clarinda often found Mrs Pagani's remarks difficult to answer.

'Will you forgive him? And me?'

'There's nothing to forgive. I didn't know he couldn't speak English.'

'How could you?' Clarinda got the impression that the tone of this was not apologetic, but amicably ironical. Not for the first time she thought that Mrs Pagani implied some understanding between them which did not exist.

'And *will* you come back?'

It was ridiculous. But Mrs Pagani had saved her from a menacing situation, and she had to say something.

'When should I come back?'

'Tonight.' The intonation made it plain that no other time could be in question.

'Here?'

449

Mrs Pagani said nothing, but dropped her head to one side and smiled.

It was almost impossible after that to seek a reason.

Moreover, Mrs Pagani left no time.

'You've bound your hair very well.'

Clarinda had been noticing how carefully Mrs Pagani's own thick locks had been turbanned.

'It was getting wet.'

Mrs Pagani nodded and smiled. She was looking Clarinda over. *'Au revoir.'*

Clarinda had not expected that either.

'Good-bye. Thank you for rescuing me.'

'My dear, we wouldn't lose *you*.' Mrs Pagani strode off. The plural was a new mystery, for Clarinda felt that it could not refer to Rufo.

Although by now it was night, Clarinda leaped and ran down the dark track. At one time she thought she heard the pigs softly rooting in the invisible undergrowth. But she did not stop to listen, and duly reached the house only a few minutes after five.

Dudley seemed to take her escapade for granted (although she provided no details). Clarinda wondered whether this suggested that already he was growing accustomed to her, or whether it was evidence that he would be a good and unexacting husband, prepared to allow her due liberty and no questions asked. She certainly valued his success in persuading his family to adopt the same attitude.

'Out at night in winter,' said Mrs Carstairs, 'when you don't have to be!' And upon her gentle mark of exclamation, the matter dropped and tea began. Clarinda wondered whether their surprising equanimity was a product of Dudley's leadership in a full discussion during her absence. She liked Dudley for not fussing, whatever his reasons.

Elizabeth had got out a quantity of clothes and ranged them

round the room for inspection and comparison by Clarinda. This was a lengthy undertaking. In the end there was a knock at the door.

'Liz.' It was Dudley's voice outside.

'One moment.' Elizabeth drew on a sweater. 'Now.'

Dudley entered. 'I've been sent up to fetch you both downstairs.' He smiled fraternally.

'We're ready,' said Elizabeth, looking at Clarinda as woman to woman.

On the dark landing outside, Dudley held Clarinda back for a moment and embraced her. 'Go on, Liz, you fool.' Elizabeth went on. 'You understand?' said Dudley to Clarinda. 'At least I hope you do. I've been trying to keep out of sight as far as possible so that you can get to know the family. That walk of yours. I've been wondering.'

Clarinda squeezed his hand.

'It's all right? And you do like them?'

'Of course it's all right. And I like them very much.'

Every Sunday evening, Clarinda understood, Mr Carstairs read aloud from about half past six until they had supper at eight. Tonight the start had been delayed by her walk and by the discussion in Elizabeth's bedroom; but still there was time for four chapters of *Persuasion*. Mr Carstairs read well, Clarinda thought; and the book was new to her.

Dudley, who could be convincing in such matters, had somehow contrived to arrange that both of them could arrive late at the office the next day: otherwise they would have had to return to London that same night. Soon after supper Elizabeth had disappeared upstairs, saying she had some letters to write, and that she probably would not be coming down again. She bade Clarinda good-night, and kissed her affectionately on the cheekbone. About half an hour later, Mr and Mrs Carstairs also withdrew. Dudley went to assist his father with stoking up the boiler for the night.

The clock struck half past nine. Otherwise the house was very quiet. Clarinda supposed that she and Dudley were being purposefully left to themselves.

'I wish *we* could live in the country,' said Dudley when he reappeared.

'I expect we could.'

'Not the real country. Not unless I get another job.'

'Where does the real country begin?'

'About Berkhamstead. Or perhaps Tring. Nowadays, that is.'

'The country stretches in this direction only.' Clarinda smiled at him.

'For me it does, darling.' She had not yet got into the habit of his calling her 'darling'. 'I *belong* around here.'

'But surely until recently you lived in a town? Northampton is a town isn't it?' She really wasn't quite sure.

'Yes, but I was always out and about.'

Clarinda had observed that every normal English male believes that he wants to live in the country, and said no more.

Dudley talked for some time about the advantages of the arrangement. Then he stopped, and Clarinda perceived that he was waiting for her assent. There was a slight pause.

'Dudley,' said Clarinda. 'How well do your father and mother know Mrs Pagani?'

'Not very well,' said Dudley, faintly disappointed. 'What you would call a bare acquaintanceship. Why?'

'They asked her to the party.'

'Actually, they didn't. She heard about it and just came. Not the first time she's done it, either. But you can't put on side in a small village, and she's not a bad old bird really.'

'How do you know?'

'I don't,' said Dudley, grinning at her earnestness. 'So what?'

'What does she do with herself? Live on, I mean?'

'I don't know what she lives on, darling. Little children, I expect, like Red Riding Hood's grandmother. You know she occupies an old ruin in the churchyard?'

'So she told me. I should like to go and see it.'

'What, *now*?'

'Will you come with me?'

'It's a bit late for calls in the country.'

'I'm not suggesting a call. I just want to have a look round.'

'She might think that a trifle nosey, mightn't she?'

Clarinda nodded. 'Of course, you know Mrs Pagani better than I do.' She suddenly remembered a nocturnal stroll in Marseilles with a fellow tourist, who had proved unexpectedly delightful.

'Tell you what I'll do,' said Dudley, 'I'll whistle you round before we push off to Roade tomorrow.'

'We mustn't miss the train.'

'Never missed a train in my life.'

Clarinda's second night was worse than her first, because now she couldn't sleep at all. Dudley had considered that they should go their separate ways soon after eleven, in order, as he said, not to disturb Mr and Mrs Carstairs; and when the church clock, brooding over Mrs Pagani's romantic residence, struck one, Clarinda was still tense and tumultuous in the prickly dark. Without switching on the light, she got out of bed and crossed to the window. She hoped that the sudden chill would numb her writhing nerves. When, an hour and a half before, she had drawn back the curtains, and opened the window at top and bottom, she had noticed that the mist seemed at last to have vanished, although it was so black that it was hard to be sure. Now the moon was rising, low and enormous, as if at the horizon the bottom edge of it dragged against the earth, and Clarinda saw that indeed all was clear, the starry sky, and the mist withdrawn to the distant shadowy hills. In the foreground there was nothing to be seen but the silent fields and naked trees.

Swiftly a bat loomed against the night and flew smack against the outer sash. Another two feet higher or two feet lower and he would have been in. Clarinda softly shivered for a moment, then watched the bat skid into invisibility. The silver-gilt autumn night was somehow warmer and more welcoming than Clarinda's unadventurous bed; fellow-bed, twin-bed to a thousand others in a thousand well-ordered houses. The grave self-sufficiency of the night was seeping into Clarinda's bloodstream, renewing her audacity, inflaming her curiosity; and its moonlit beauty agitating her heart. By the light of the big moon she began to dress.

When, upon her return from the woods, she had taken off her walking shoes, she had thought them very wet; but now they seemed dried, as if by the moon's rays. She opened the door of her room. Again a bat struck the window at the end of the passage outside. There was no other sound but that of disturbed breathing; which, however, seemed all around her. The other occupants of the house slept, but, as it appeared, uneasily. She descended the stairs and creaked into her mackintosh before trying the door. She expected difficulty here, but it opened at a touch. Doubtless it would be side to lock one's doors in a village.

The moon shone on the gate and on the lane beyond; but the long path from the front door was in darkness. With the moon so low, the house cast a disproportionate shadow. As Clarinda walked down the narrow strip of paving, a hare scuttered across her feet. She could feel his warmth on her ankles as he nearly tripped her. The gate had a patent catch which had caused her trouble before, and she had to stand for half a minute fumbling.

As she walked along the road, passed the 'By Favour Only' notice, and began to ascend into the wood, she never doubted that at the top of the hill would be some remarkable warrant for her efforts; and she was resolved to find out what it was. Now the regular roadside trees were as clear-cut and trim as a guard of honour, and the owls seemed to be passing a message ahead of her into the thickets. Once or twice, when entering a straighter part of the road, she thought she saw a shambling figure rounding the distant corner ahead, but she decided that it was probably only a shadow. The bats were everywhere, hurtling in and out of the dark patches, and fluting their strange cries, which Clarinda was always so glad that she was among those who are privileged to hear. There were even some surviving or revitalised moths; and a steadily rising perfume of moisture and decay.

The gate at the hilltop was shut. But as soon as Clarinda drew near, she saw the little blue girl standing by it.

'Hullo.'

'Hullo,' said Clarinda.

'You're rather late.'

'I'm very sorry. I didn't know.'

'It's important to be punctual.' The child spoke in a tone of earnest helpfulness.

'I'll try to remember,' said Clarinda humbly.

The child had opened the gate and was leaning back against the end of it, her chin stuck in her neck and her feet in the ground, holding it for Clarinda.

Clarinda passed through. The moon was now higher, and the soft grass glistened and gleamed. Even in the almost bright light there was no sign of a continuing path.

'I shall get my feet wet.'

'Yes, you will. You should wear boots.' Clarinda observed the legs of the child's blue garment were stuck into close-fitting black wellingtons. Also its hood was now over its head.

There was no sign of the other child.

The little girl had carefully shut the gate. She stood looking ruefully at Clarinda's feet. Then, apparently deciding there was nothing to be done about them, she said very politely, 'Shall I show you where you change?'

'Can I change my shoes?' asked Clarinda, humouring her.

'No, I don't think you can change your shoes,' said the child very seriously. 'Only everything else.'

'I don't want to change anything else.'

The child regarded her, all at sea. Then, perhaps considering that she must have misunderstood, said, 'It's over there. Follow me. And do take care of your feet.'

It certainly was very wet, but the grass proved to be tussocky, and Clarinda did her best to keep dry by striding from tussock to tussock in the moonlight.

'Rufo's in there already,' said the child conversationally. 'You see you're the last.'

'I've said I'm sorry.'

'It doesn't matter.' This was uttered with that special magnanimity only found in the very young.

The little girl waded on, and Clarinda struggled after her. There was no sign of anyone else: indeed the place looked a hilltop of the dead. The lumpy saturated grass and the rank and stunted vegetation compared most unfavourably with the handsome trees behind.

There was one place where the briars and ragged bushes were particularly dense and abundant, constituting a small prickly copse. Round the outskirts of this copse, the child led the way until Clarinda saw that embedded in its perimeter was a rickety shed. Possibly constructed for some agricultural purpose but long abandoned by its maker, it drooped and sagged into the ground. From it came a penetrating and repugnant odour, like all the bad smells of nature and the stockyard merged together.

'That's it,' said the little girl pointing. They were still some yards off, but the feral odour from the shed was already making Clarinda feel sick.

'I don't think I want to go in there.'

'But you *must*. Rufo's in there. All the others changed long ago.'

Apart from other considerations, the shed seemed too small to house many; and Clarinda could now see that the approach to it was thick with mud, which added its smell to the rest. She was sure that the floor of the shed was muddy almost to the knees.

The child's face was puckered with puzzlement.

'I'm sorry,' said Clarinda, 'but you know I don't want to change at all.'

Clearly she was behaving in quite the wrong way. But the child took a grip on the situation and said, 'Wait here. I'll go and ask.'

'All right,' said Clarinda. 'But I'll wait over there, if you don't mind.' The child seemed not to notice the awful smell, but Clarinda was not going to be the first to mention it.

'*There*,' said the child, pointing to an exact spot. Clarinda took up her stance upon it. 'Mind you don't move.'

'Not if you hurry.' The smell was still very detectable.

'Quite still,' insisted the child.

'Quite still,' said Clarinda.

Swiftly the child ran three times round Clarinda in a large circle. The light was so clear that Clarinda could see the drops of water flying up from her feet.

'*Hurry*,' urged Clarinda; and, the third circle complete, the child darted away round the edge of the copse in the direction from which they had come.

Left alone in the still moonlight, Clarinda wondered whether this were not her great chance to return home to safety and certainty. Then she saw a figure emerging from the dilapidated hut.

The figure walked upright, but otherwise appeared to be a large furry animal, such as a bear or ape. From its distinctive staggering uncertainty of gait, Clarinda would have recognised Rufo, even without the statements of the little girl. Moreover, he was still leaning upon his long crook, which stuck in the mud and had to be dragged out at every step. He too was going back round the edge of the copse, the same way as the child. Although he showed no sign of intending to molest Clarinda, she found him a horrifying sight, and decided upon retreat. Then she became really frightened; because she found she could not move.

The hairy slouching figure drew slowly nearer, and with him came an intensification of the dreadful smell, sweet and putrid and commingled. The animal skin was thick and wrinkled about his neck and almost covered his face, but Clarinda saw his huge nose and expressionless eyes. Then he was past, and the child had re-appeared.

'I ran all the way.' Indeed it seemed as if she had been gone only an instant. 'You're not to bother about changing because it's too late anyway.' Clearly she was repeating words spoken by an adult. 'You're to come at once, although of course you'll have to be hidden. But it's all right,' she added reassuringly. 'There've been people before who've had to be hidden.' She spoke as if the period covered by her words were at least a generation. 'But you'd better be quick.'

Clarinda found that she could move once more. Rufo, moreover, had disappeared from sight.

'Where do I hide?'

'I'll show you. I've often done it.' Again she was showing off slightly. 'Bind your hair.'

'What?'

'Bind your hair. Do be quick.' The little girl was peremptory but not unsympathetic. She was like a mother addressing an unusually slow child she was none the less rather fond of. 'Haven't you got that thing you had before?'

'It was raining then.' But Clarinda in fact had replaced the black scarf in her mackintosh pocket after drying it before the Carstairs' kitchen fire. Now, without knowing why, she drew it out.

'Go on.' Clarinda's sluggishness was making the child frantic.

But Clarinda refused to be rattled. With careful grace she went through the moonlit ritual of twisting the scarf round her head and enveloping her abundant soft hair.

The child led her back halfway round the copse to where there was a tiny path between the bushes. This path also was exceedingly muddy; ploughed up, as Clarinda could plainly see, by innumerable hoofmarks.

'I'd better go first,' said the little girl; adding with her customary good manners, 'I'm afraid it's rather spiky.'

It was indeed. The little girl, being little, appeared to advance unscathed; but Clarinda, being tall, found that her clothes were torn to pieces, and her face and hands lacerated. The radiance of the moon had sufficed outside, but in here failed to give warning of the thick tangled briars and rank whipcord suckers. Everywhere was a vapour of ancient cobwebs, clinging and greasy, amid which strange night insects flapped and flopped.

'We're nearly there,' said the little girl. 'You'd better be rather quiet.'

It was impossible to be quiet, and Clarinda was almost in tears with the discomfort.

'*Quieter*,' said the little girl; and Clarinda did not dare to answer back.

The slender muddy trail, matted with half-unearthed roots, wriggled on for another minute or two; and then the little girl whispered, 'Under here.'

She was making a gap in the foliage of a tall round bush. Clarinda pushed in. 'Ssh,' said the little girl.

Inside it was like a small native hut. The foliage hung all round, but there was room to stand up and dry ground beneath the feet.

'Stand on this,' whispered the little girl, pointing to a round, sawn section of tree, about two feet high and four in diameter. 'I call it my fairy dinner table.'

'What about you?'

'I'm all right, thank you. I'm always here.'

Clarinda climbed on to the section of tree, and made a cautious aperture in the boscage before her.

The sight beyond was one which she would not easily forget.

Clearly, to begin with, this was the maze, although Clarinda had never seen or heard of such a maze before. It filled a clearing in the copse about twenty or thirty yards wide and consisted in a labyrinth of little ridges, all about nine inches high. The general pattern of the labyrinth was circular, with involved inner convolutions everywhere, and at some points flourishes curving beyond the main outer boundary, as if they had once erupted like boils or volcanic blow-holes. In the valleys between the ridges, grass grew, but the ridges themselves were trodden bare. At the centre of the maze was a hewn block of stone, which put Clarinda in mind of the Stone of Scone.

Little of this, however, had much immediate significance for Clarinda; because all over the maze, under the moon, writhed and slithered and sprawled the smooth white bodies of men and women. There were scores of them; all apparently well-shaped and comely; all (perhaps for that reason) weirdly impersonal; all recumbent and reptilian, as in a picture Clarinda remembered having seen; all completely and impossibly silent beneath the silent night. Clarinda saw that all round the maze were heaps of furry skins. She then noticed that the heads of all of the women were bound in black fillets.

At the points where the coils of the maze surged out beyond the main perimeter were other, different figures. Still wrapped in furs, which distorted and made horrible the outlines of their bodies, they clung together as if locked in death. Down to the maze the ground fell away a few feet from Clarinda's hiding place. Immediately below her was one of these groups, silent as all the rest. By one of the shapeless figures she noticed a long thick staff. Then the figure soundlessly shifted, and the white moonlight fell upon the face of the equally shapeless figure in its arms. The eyes were blank and staring, the nostrils stretched like a running deer, and the red lips not so much parted as drawn back to the gums: but Clarinda recognised the face of Mrs Pagani.

Suddenly there was a rustling in the hiding-place. Though soft, it was the first sound of any kind since Clarinda had looked out on the maze.

'Go away, you silly little boy,' muttered the little girl.

Clarinda looked over her shoulder.

Inside the bower, the moonlight, filtered through the veil of foliage, was dim and deceitful; but she could see the big eyes and bird-of-prey mien of the other child. He was still wearing his bright blue hooded garment; but now the idea occurred to Clarinda that he might not be a child at all, but a well-proportioned dwarf. She looked at the black ground before stepping down from the tree trunk; and instantly he leapt at her. She felt a sharp, indefinite pain in her ankle and saw one of the creature's hands yellow and claw-like where a moonbeam through the hole above fell on the pale wood of the cut tree. Then in the murk the little girl did something which Clarinda could not see at all, and the hand jerked into passivity. The little girl was crying.

Clarinda touched her torn ankle, and stretched her hand into the beam of light. There was duly a mess of blood.

The little girl clutched at Clarinda's wrist. 'Don't let them see,' she whispered beseechingly through her tears. 'Oh please don't let them see.' Then she added with passionate fury, 'He always spoils *everything*. I hate him. I hate him. I hate him.'

Clarinda's ankle hurt badly, and there was palpable danger of blood poisoning, but otherwise the injury was not severe.

'Shall I be all right if I go?'

'Yes. But I think you'd better run.'

'That may not be so easy.'

The little girl seemed desolated with grief.

'Never mind,' said Clarinda. 'And thank you.'

The little girl stopped sobbing for a moment. 'You *will* come back?'

'I don't think so,' said Clarinda.

The sobbing recommenced. It was very quiet and despairing.

'Well,' said Clarinda, 'I'll see.'

'Punctually? That makes all the difference, you know.'

'Of course,' said Clarinda.

The child smiled at her in the faint moonlight. She was being brave. She was remembering her manners.

'Shall I come with you?'

'No need,' said Clarinda rather hastily.

'I mean to the end of the little path.'

'Still no need,' said Clarinda. 'Thank you again though. Good-bye.'

'Good-bye,' said the little girl. 'Don't forget. Punctual.'

Clarinda crept along the involved muddy path: then she sped across the soft wet sward, which she spotted with her blood; through the gate where she had seen Rufo, and down the hill where she had seen the pigs; past the ill-spelled notice; and home. As she fumbled with the patent catch, the church clock which kept ward over Mrs Pagani's abode struck three. The mist was rising again everywhere; but, in what remained of the moonlight, Clarinda, before entering the house, unwound the black scarf from her head and shook her soft abundant locks.

The question of Mrs Pagani's unusual dwelling-place arose, of course, the next morning, as they hurriedly ate the generously over-large breakfast which Mrs Carstairs, convinced that London meant starvation, pressed upon them.

'Please not,' said Clarinda, her mouth full of golden syrup. She was wearing ankle socks to conceal her careful bandage. 'I just don't want to go.'

The family looked at her; but only Dudley spoke. 'Whatever you wish, darling.'

There was a pause; after which Mr Carstairs remarked that he supposed the good lady would still be in bed anyway.

But here, most unusually, Mr Carstairs was wrong. As Dudley and Clarinda drove away, they saw the back of Mrs Pagani walking towards the church and not a couple of hundred yards from their own gate. She wore high, stout boots, caked with country mud, and an enveloping fur coat against the sharpness of the morning. Her step was springy, and her thick black hair flew in the wind like a dusky gonfalon.

As they overtook her, Dudley slowed. 'Good morning,' he shouted. 'Back to the grindstone.'

Mrs Pagani smiled affectionately.

'Don't be late,' she cried, and kissed her hand to them.

ACKNOWLEDGEMENTS

I'D LIKE TO thank everyone who pledged their support and helped bring this spooky anthology to life, including those who helped to spread the word through social media and elsewhere. At Unbound, special thanks to John Mitchinson, who first approached me out of the blue with the suggestion of perhaps collaborating on a book project. Thanks to Benjamin Myers for his wonderful foreword. I'm a particular fan of his brutal 2014 novel, *Beastings*, and was thrilled he agreed to take part. Thank you to Martha Sprackland, Mark Ecob and the rest of the team at Unbound for shepherding the project through its editorial and design stages. Thank you to Johnny Mains for his sage editorial words of wisdom, and to Anne Billson, Andrew Male, Edward Parnell and Stephen Volk for their fantastic suggestions of additional tales to include. Thanks to Mom, Dad, Michael and Max for the continued support, and helping to keep me sane during what became something of a mammoth lockdown lino-cutting project. Finally, thanks to the Old Gods for guiding my lino-cutting hand (probably) . . .

✦ ✦ ✦

'Bind Your Hair' taken from *Dark Entries*. Copyright the Estate of Robert Aickman and reproduced by permission of Faber & Faber Ltd.

ACKNOWLEDGEMENTS

'All Hallows' by Walter de la Mare is reproduced by kind permission of the Literary Trustees of Walter de la Mare and the Society of Authors as their representative.

'The Lady on the Grey' by John Collier © 1951 by John Collier. Reprinted by permission of Harold Matson – Ben Camardi, Inc.

'The Summer People' from *Dark Tales* by Shirley Jackson © Laurence Jackson Hyman, J. S. Holly, Sarah Hyman DeWitt and Barry Hyman, 2016. Published by Penguin Classics and reproduced here by permission of Penguin Books Limited.

'How Pan Came to Little Ingleton' by Margery Lawrence first appeared in *Nights of the Round Table* (Hutchinson, 1926) and is reproduced here by kind permission of David Higham Associates Ltd.

'Cwm Garon' by L. T. C. Rolt is reproduced here by kind permission of the L. T. C. Rolt estate.

'Randalls Round' by Eleanor Scott first appeared in *Randalls Round*, 1929, and is reproduced here by kind permission of the Leys family.

SUPPORTERS

Unbound is the world's first crowdfunding publisher, established in 2011.

We believe that wonderful things can happen when you clear a path for people who share a passion. That's why we've built a platform that brings together readers and authors to crowdfund books they believe in – and give fresh ideas that don't fit the traditional mould the chance they deserve.

This book is in your hands because readers made it possible. Everyone who pledged their support is listed below. Join them by visiting unbound.com and supporting a book today.

Joe Abel
Marty Abercrombie
Geoff Adams
Molly Adams
Racheal Adams
Tracey Adams-Moody
Jo Adlam
ADW Decorators
 (Lancaster)
Daniel Agnew
Gordon Aitken
James Aitken

James Akers
Chris Aldis
David Aldridge
Ashley Allen
Steve Allen
Joe Allocco
Tom Allport
Jon Alsbury
Richard Angliss
Sara Appleton
Peter Appleyard
Kerry Apps

Sandra Armor
Gareth Armstrong
Nick Arthurs
Lauren Ashley
Madeleine Ashton
Rebecca Aston
Lucy, Tom &
 Robin Atherton
Nathan Atherton
Tom Atkinson
Barrie Auty and
 Mark Miller

James Aylett
Dai Baddley
Martin Bain
Duncan Baines
Josh Baker
Luke Baker
Mark Baker
Peter Bakewell
Florence Ballard
Simon Ballard
Jason Ballinger
Patricia Balster
Lori Baluta
Bannerless Games
John Bannister
Dr Matt Barber
Jon Barbour
George Barker
Bridie Barrett
Dom Barringer
Simon Barton
Jacob Bartynski
Anderson Bass
Morten Basse
Matthew Batten
Ross Battersby
Stephen Bauer
Rebecca Baumann
Luke Bauserman
Melissa Bavington
Adam Baylis-West
Emma Bayliss
Vikki Bayman
Suzanna Beaupré
Carol Beck
Sam Begley
Richard Bell
Jo Bellamy
Beth Bennett
Giles Bennett

Richard Bennett
Julian Benton
Rachel Berardinelli
Adam Bertolett
Lucy Beth
Clare Bewick
Patrick Binks
Matthew Binswanger
Wiebke Bird
Eloise Birnam-Wood
Steve Birt
Christian Bishop
John Bishop
Chris Bissette
Gustav Black
Graham Blenkin
Amy Blessington
Harry E. Blevins, Jr.
Joe Blitgen
Anniken Blomberg
Jeffrey Blomquist
Adam Blumenau
Graham Blunt
Rob Bodger
Alex Bollard
Brad Bone
Justin Booher
Jacqueline Boston
John Bowditch
Matt Bowskill
Brandon Boyer
Ian Boyle
Jo Boyles
Becca Bradford
Dominic Bradley
Elizabeth Bradley
Steve Bradley
Catharine Braithwaite
Philip Brennan
Orla Breslin

Joseph Brett
Polly Brewster
Marc Bright
Scott Broadfoot
River Broadley-Hale
Helen Brocklebank
Mark Bromley
Jen Brook
Henry Brookfield
Andrew Brooks
Antony Brown
Karen Brown
Sarah Brown
Tim Bryars
A BS
Alistair Buchan
Charlotte Buchet
Laura Buckley
Clark Buckner
Elaine Buckton
Emma Bull
Anwen Bullen
Steve Bulman
Rachel Burch
Neil Burgess
Stephen Burnette
John Burnham
Claire Burton
Samantha Buswell
Andrew Butler
Matthew Butler-Hart
Matteo Alfredo Buttu
Adam Byfield
Jonathan Bygraves
Jake Byrne
John Byrne
Hanna Cadell
Stacey Cahan
Colin Cairnes
Jamie Cairney

Sophie Calalesina
Ian Calcutt
James Caldwell
Dan Callahan
Christopher Calvert
James Cameron
Joseph Camilleri
Ben Campbell
Dominic Campbell
Jonny Campbell
Kristine Campbell
Matthew Campbell
Michael Campbell
Alexis Candelaria
Ian Capes
Jonathan Capp-Isaksen
Paul Capps
Brittany Cardwell
Victoria Cargill-James
DC Carlile
Claira Carnell
Geraldine Carr
Jonathan Carr
Thomas Carr
Johnny Carrington
Calin Carter
Carter
Scan Casserly
Cerise Cauthron
Inge Cederberg
Michael Cerliano
Justin Cetinich
Jon Chadwick
Richard Chalk
Rob Challis
Barbara Chamberlin
Zoe Chan
Adam Chard
David Chaudoir
Paul Childs

Daniel Chisham
Ryan Chittenden
Oliver Chmell
Mae Cichella Parcher
William Cini
John Clark
Kerri Clark
Paul Clark
Stuart Clark
Brandon Clauser
Philip Clements
Tom Clements
Wendy Clements
Troy Cleven
Michael Clifton
Garrett Coakley
James Coccaro
Genevieve Cogman
Gary Colbert-Owen
GMark Cole
Joe Coleman
Sarah J. Coleman
Sean Coleman
Garry Colfer
Ruth Collard-Stayte
Gina R. Collia
Deborah Collington
Katherine Collins
Mike Collins
Mark Collyer
Paul Colnaghi
Montse Cols
Jo Conlon
Patrick Connelly
Tom Connelly
Maria Connor
Jane Conway
Ethan Cook
John Peyton Cooke
Charlotte Coombs

Sarah Coomer
Fiona Cooper
Nigel Cooper
Rachael Cooper
Brett Copeland
Alex Corbin
Kate Cornish
Andrew Correia
Jack Cottam
Aaron Cotton
Alex Cotton
Kaitlyn Cottrell
Nicky Coulbeck
Ben Coulson-Gilmer
Paul Coward
Sophie Cowles
Laura-beth Cowley
Geoff Cox
Natasha Cox
Simon Cox
Dan Coxon
Wayne Crampton
Sal Creber
Alice Crick
Philip Crinnan
Meghan Crockett
Brenda Croskery
Alasdair Cross
Marshall Crow
Steven Croxford
Ian Cruickshank
Kate Cryer
CrystalLake-
   Managment
Kristofer
   Cullum-Fernandez
Helen Culyer
Peter Cumiskey
Morvern Cunningham
Alexandru Curea

Heather Curtis
Joel Curtis
Samantha Curtis
Paul Cutting
Hannah Dalgleish
Maya Dancey
Angharad Dando
Gill Dare
John Darrington
Laura Darrington
Nirvana Davidson
Stuart Davidson
Jo Davies
Alice Davis
Charlie Davis
Laura Davis
Simon Davis
Edward Daw
Suzanne Dawson
Marcel de Jong
Tom de Ville
Celia Deakin
Clare Dean
Jon Dear
Leah Delaney
Clement Deneux
Alex Dennis
Andrew Denny
Lara Derham
Bobby Derie
Emma Dermott
John DiCarlo
Ava Dickerson
Daniel DiTommaso
Chad Diver
Simon Dixey
Cara Dixon
Richard Dixon
Richard Dobell
Fabian Dodt

Mariusz Doering
Stephen Dolamore
Steven Dole
Barry Donnelly
Linda Doughty
John Douglas-Field
Dave Dow
James Downs
Liz Drabble
Keith Draper
Mike Drew
Etienne du Celliée
    Muller
Stephane Dube
Shana DuBois
Stanisław
    Dunin-Wilczyński
Jory Dunworth-Warby
Mitch Durette
Jennifer Durkan
Alice Durose
Jo Dyrlaga
Drew Dyson
Yvette Earl
Echo Echo
Giles Edwards
Zoe Edwards
Joshua Elcombe
Adrian Elder
Caitlin Elliman
Gary Ellis
Marie Ellis
Kane Elwell
Dónal Emerson
Emma @RedImpala
Vicent Escorihuela
Robert Espy
Andrew Evans
David Evans
Sally Evans

Scott Fairgrieve
Steven Falconer
Sorcha Fane
    Henderson
Nick Farrer
John Paul Feehily
Jacqueline Feeney
Teri Feeney
Steve Fenton
Tim Ferro
Stace Fiendish
Hannah Filipski
Emma
    Finlayson-Palmer
Robby Finley
Heiko Fischer
Catherine Fisher
Colin Fisher
Karl Fitzgerald
Lindsey Fitzharris
Steve Fleming
Ben Fleming-Yates
Fabrizio Foni
Stuart Forbes
Matthew Ford
Stuart Forsyth
Oliver Fosdike
Holly Foskett
Paul Foster
Mike Fowler
Adrian Francis
Jodie Francis
Lisa Frankis
Con Franklin
Kyla Fraser
Karen Frazer
Rob French
Clayton Freund
Jo Friend
Ed G

Hannah Gabriel
Kerry Gaffney
Patrick Gaffney
Stephanie Gallon
Majda Gama
Mark Gamble
Karsten Gandor
Neil Gardner
Elizabeth Garner
Graham Garner
Neil Gateley
Deborah Gatty
Richard Geddes
Chris Gibbons
Clara Gibbons
Marina Gibbons
Jennifer Gibson
Kim Giddings
Tim Gilbert
Wendy Gilbert
Tommy Gillard
Anna Gillespie
Craig Gillespie
Carya Gish
David Gleave
Rob Glover
Catherine Gogerty
Kathryn Golden
Caroline Goldsmith
Thomas Goldsworthy
Ricardo Gomez
Jeremy Gonzales
Gustavo Gonzalez
Jess Goodwin
Nathaniel Goss
Jenny Graham-Jones
Maxine Grant
Stephen Graves
Kenneth Gray
Mark Gray

Al Green
Bob Green
Dan Green
Harry Green
Henry Green
Justine Green
Marc Green
Stephen Green
Helen Greenwood
Amy Griffiths
•Barry• Griffiths
Lisa Grimm
Rebecca Groves
Mark Guerin
Katie Gunn
Leyla Gurr
Nicholas Habib
Thora Skye Hadfield
Simon Hagberg
Gary Haigh
Emma Hall
Haley Hall
Neil Hall
Liam Hallett
Chris Halliday
Niklas Hallin
Sara Halpin
Samu Hämäläinen
Sam Hamer
Daniel Hamilton
Robert G Hamilton
Stuart Hamilton
Stephen Hampshire
Russell Handelman
Holly Hang
Jeremy Hanks
Sophie Hanlon
Ewan Hannay
Robert Hanss
Max Harding

Caroline Hargreaves
James Harkness
Graham Harley
Karla Harlow
Katie Harper
Becca Harper-Day
Peter Harries
Jay Harris
Jim Harris
Libby Harris
Sagan Harris
Kate Harrison
Matt Harrison
Johnny Hartin
Max Hartshorn
Laurence R. Harvey
Phil Harvey 'The Hairy
    Horror'!
Krispijn Hasebos
Jo Haseltine
Lucy Haskell
Simon Haslam
Hastie
Jonathan Hatfull
Glen Hattersley
Katherine Hawes
Oliver Hayes
Sam Healy
Peter Hearn
Andrew Hearse
James Hedges
Cuyler Hedlund
Jo Heeley
Tyler Heil
Mary Heinz
Hannah Hellevnag
Spencer Hemming
Lynne Henderson
Sandra Henriques
Stuart Herkes

Conor Herlihy
Eric Hernandez
Alex Heron
Benedict Heywood
Jason Hicks
Max Higgins
Richard Higson
Ian Hill
Kayley Hill
Sarah Hill
Aaron Hillier
Matt Hinds
Richard Hing
Kody Hinkel
Jacky Ho
James Hoare
Amy Hoddinott
Sigrun Hodne
Maxime Hoek
Gareth Hogan
Michael Holiday
Daniel Holland
Wayne Hollis
Ray Holman
Steve Holness
Vee Holt
Christian Holte
Matt Hooper
Matthew Hooper
Matthew Hopkins
Katy Horan
Eileen A Horansky
John Hornor Jacobs
Remy Hoskings
T Houghton
Antony Howard
Jonathan L. Howard
Joanne Howe
Bob Howell
Becca Hoy

Lachezar Hubanov
Mark Huckerby
Scott Huggett
Philip Huggins
Billy Hughes
Jeff Hughes
Jennifer Hughes
Hoyt Hughie
Klive Humberstone
Jon Humphreys
Trent Humphreys
Sarah Hunt
Ian F Hunter
Rowan Hunter
Jessica Hurtgen
Lee Hutchinson
Sally-Anne Huxtable
Ross Hyman
Elanor Ibbotson-Butt
Catherine Illingworth
Kaye Inglis
Ted Irvine
Brent Isaacs
Suzanne Isaacs
Giles Ivey
Daniel Jackson
Judith Jackson
Peter Jackson
Riley Jackson
Catherine Jacob
Marilie Jacob
Andrew James
Tobias James
Michael Janes
Sally Japp
Sarah Jarvis
Jay
Anders Jeffrey
Laura Jellicoe
Paul Jenner

Douglas Jensen
Evan Jensen
Martin Jensen
Peter Jervis
Andri Johannsson
Derek John
Tristan John
Charlotte Johnson
Elizabeth Johnson
Derek Johnston
Graeme Johnston
Arwel Jones
Chris Jones
David Heulun Jones
Dickie Jones
Jolene Jones
Laura Jones
Nate Jones
Phillip M Jones
Sally Jones
Anna Jordan
Mary Jordan-Smith
Jack Joslin
Bernd Kalker
Chris Kalley
Jane Karg
Oliver Kassman
Jessica Kaufmann
Helen Keenlyside
Dawn Kelly
Eugene Kelly
Jonathan Kelly
Robert Kelly
Helen Kemp
Hilary Kemp
Zoey Kennedy
Daryl Kent
Debbie, Graeme,
  Rigby, Charlie &
  Dudley Kerr

Laura Ketcham
Jennifer Kettell
Dan Kieran
Robert Killheffer
Tom Killingbeck
Rebecca King
E Kinsey
Ivan Kirby
Nicola Kirby
Al Kitching
Candis Klaila
Katie Knight
Marco Kohlschmidt
Phil Konecky
Rachel Koning
R.S. Konjek
Susanna Krawczyk
Karin L. Kross
Farran Kruse
Fabrice Kutting
Mit Lahiri
Alastair Laing
Evelyn Laing
Paige Lamb
Ian Land
Suzie Landgrebe
Francine Lane
Autumn Lanman
Nick Lansbury
Ben Larson
Alisha Latham
Brian Lavelle
Eoin Lawlor
Bethany Lawrence
Eric Lawrence
Robert Laws
Alison Layland
Catherine Layne
Ben Lazenby
Kim Le Patourel

Robert Martin Lea
Enda Leaney
Claire Louise Lee
Stephen Lee
Carolyn Leedy
Emilia Leese
Rob Leinheiser
Jason LeMaitre
Milada Leonova
Johan Leuris
Véronique Levrier
Sam Lewin –
    MadeofRats
Antony Lias
Katie Liddane
Ben Lieberman
Jonathan Light
Emily Limb
Chris Lincé
Beth Lincoln
Clare Lindley
Roy Lines
Ian Lipthorpe
Nathan Llewellyn
Gareth Lloyd
Keith Lloyd
Ryan Lloyd
JacqueLyn Lobelle
Beatrice Rose
    Locock-Jones
Camille Lofters
Andrew Lohrum
Gareth Lonnen
Gary Lord
Åmid Lorestani
Cat Lovejoy
Ross Lovelock
Jennifer Lovely
Catriona M. Low
Iain Lowson

Gem Luca
Will Ludwigsen
Jari Luiten
Paul Luke
Adam Lungberg
Tim Lutton
Marty Lyons
Vincent Lyte
Rainy M.
Hamish Mabon-Ross
Sean MacDhai
Thom Mackey
Adrian Mackinder
Des MacLeod
Joshua Peter
    MacLeod
Theresa Macourek
Gareth Madeley
Ashley Madigan
Edward Madson
Jay Mahone
Phil Mahoney
Sam Mahony
Jamie Makin
Allison Malenfant
Grey Malkin
Tony Malone
Scott Malthouse
Simon Manby
Gerrit Manger
Kenneth Mann
Richard Hunty
    Mansfield
Adam Marshall
Danny Marshall
Jade Marshall
Beverley Martin
Hannah Martin
Rafael Martín
Ashley Martinez

Matthew Martyniuk
Liam Marx
Callum Mason
Lu Mason
Adam Mastrud
Alejandro Mathe
David Matkins
Karen May
MB
Molly McCarthy
Adrian McConnell
James McConnell
Megan McCormick
Ian McDonald
Helen McElwee
Daniel McGachey
Sean McGeady
John A C McGowan
Lucy McGranaghan
David McGroarty
David McGuigan
Maura McHugh
Shane McHugh
John McKenzie
Patrick McKitrick
Max McLaughlan
Patrick McLaughlin
Brian Mcleish
Becky Mcleod
Ryan McMahon
Steven McNally
Thomas McNamara
Scott McNee
Joel Meador
Santiago Medín
Tommy Medley
Melissa
Rob Melocha
Taous Merakchi
Jason R. Merrill

Bryan Merto
Kristina Meschi
Dave Miatt
Matthew Michael
Patch Middleton
Alex Miell
Sarah Miles
Edward Millar
Dustin Miller
Kayleigh Miller
Peter Miller
Silas & Emily Miller
Geoff Millington
Kat Milne
Neill Milton
Hannah Miodrag
Daniel Mitchell
Neil Mitchell
Celandine Mitchell
   Cotts
John Mitchinson
Casey Mix
Magnus Mjørud
James Moakes
Deborah Moffat
Carl Mole
Jonathan Molyneux
Nadia Lee
   Monaghan
Hazel Monforton
Alan Montgomery
Ross Montgomery
Paul Moody
Jac Ifan Moore
Julian Moore
Nathan Moore
Vesta Moore
Elizabeth Morant
Nathaniel Mordain
Lou Morgan

Nathan Morgan
Hugh Morgan-Platt
Morganlefey
Rowena Morley
Beth Morris
Andrew Morton
Chloe Morton
Caroline Mosley
Bernard Moxham
Joerg Mueller-Kindt
Patrick Mulcahy
Laura Mulkeen
Linda Muller
Tom Mulligan
Gareth Mulvenna
Will Munday
Frieda Munro
Patrick Murdough
Euan Murray
James Murray
Mark Mzyk
Annie Nagem
Luke Nagle
Emmett Nahil
Fergal Nally
Stu Nathan
Alistair Nattrass
Carlo Navato
Adrian Neesam
David Neesam
Andrew Nelson
Leocie Nelson
Mark Nelson
Bri Neumann
John New
Laura Newberry
Paddy Newman
James Newman-Shah
Chris Newsom
Andy Nichol

Amy Nicholls
Babs Nienhuis
Marie-Jose Nieuwkoop
Michael Nimmo
Mark Nixon
Miriam Nolting
Sally Noonan
Jo Norcup
Johnnemann
  Nordhagen
Badger North
Adam Northall
Lesley Northfield
Caleb Nyberg
Rosencranz O'Dowd
Penn O'Gara
Ruth O'Leary
Mark O'Neill
Karen O'Sullivan
Angie Oakwood
Rick Oates
Elvia Olive
James Oliver
William Onions
Mark Osborne
Tom Osborne
Kiyomi Oswald
Christopher A. Otto
Kyle Overholt
Simon Page
Kate Paice
Kayla Painter
Sally Painter
Michael Paley
Emily Pallett
Henrik Palm
Edwin Palmer
Sarah Palmer
Judith Panetta
Jacky Pankhurst

David Parker
Eleanor Parker
Sam Parker
Edward Parnell
George Parr
Katy Parrett
Callum Paterson
Scott Patient
James Patmore
Trish Paton
Linkat Paul
Carol Paxton
Selene Paxton-Brooks
Hywel Payne
John Payne
Sam Payne
Jordan Peach
Gordon Peake
Michelle Pearce
Oliver Pearcey
Jared Pease
Garrett Pedigo
Jayme Pendergraft
Vanda Penny-Roberts
Sheena E. Perez
Maria Perez Cuervo
Fernando
  Pérez-García
Simon Perry
Ms Frances Perty
Amy Peters
Dale Peters
Dan Peters
Bethanie Petitpas
Sindre Pettersen
Patrick Petterson
Debbie Phillips
Sophie Phillips-Jones
Sarah Pickles
Karen F. Pierce

Phil Pinel
Jane Pink
Kristin Plant
Clare Plater
Victoria Pohlen
Lizbeth
  Poirier-Morissette
Matthew Poke
Justin Pollard
Jenni Pope
Valentin Potey
Holly Potier
Mandy Powell
Nick Powell
Sian Powell
Richard Prangle
Charles Prepolec
Alison Price
Abby Prince
Mat Pringle
Ben Prior
Adam Pritchett
Julian Prokaza
Joel Proudfoot
Scott Pryde
Gaynor Pugh
Kieron Purcell
Jordan Putinski
Stephen Queralt
Joe Quinn
Christian Radl
Ciarán Raftery
Kaitlyn Rak
Laurence Ranger
Monica Ras
Janet Rawlings
Stephen Rawlinson
Becca Read
Nicolas Rebholz
El Redman

Kris Rees
Stevie Reeve
John A. Reimers
Bärbel Reinecke
Tamsin Reinsch
Bill Rennie
Claire Reynolds
Julian Reynolds
Chris Rhodes
Electra Rhodes
Nick Riddle
Ben Ridgeon
Leslie Rieth
Anna Rixson
Jacqueline Roach
Ian Roberts
Imogen Robertson
Jenna Robertson
Maxime Robinet
Andrew Robinson
Jenn Rodriguez
Elina Rodriguez
  Millan
Ben Rogers
Chris Rogers
Constanza
  Rojas-Molina
Eilish Rolfe
Delmotte Romain
Alan Roos
Rebecca Rose
Tom Rose-Jones
Jesse Ross
Grace Rosser
Benjamin Rostance
Janice Rostance
Steven Rostance
Andres Rothschild
Anna Route
Mark Routledge

Stephen Routledge
Nick Rowe
Paul Rowe
George Royer
Jim Rudge
Rachel Ruetz
Melissa Rung-Blue
Sean J Ruppert
Ally Russell
Joseph Russell
Dana Russomano
Jackie Ruth
Michael Rutherford
Eoin Ryan
Beverley &
  Chris Rye
Andreas Ryttersgaard
  Alving
Josh Saco
Brian Safdie
Katie Sajnog
Chris Salt
Zannah Salter
Hernan Sanchez
Charles Sanders
Matt Sanders
Helen Sanders-Smith
Alexander Sanderson
Gustavo Sandoval
  Vega
Beverly Sanford
Alexandra Sansome
Lyni Sargent
Thelonia Saunders
Kat Savage
Nathan Savant
Sophie Sawicka-Sykes
Melle Schakel
Rinus Scheldeman
Christopher Schelling

Jordan Schmid
Tjark Schöneck
Martin Schoonmaker
Janis Schorsch
Philip Schrimpf
Julian Schröger
Janette Schubert
Johanna Schuepbach
Daniel Schuhmann
William P. Schumacher
Cavan Scott
Christine M. Scott
Gemma Scott
Jack Scott-Keyser
Jo Seaman
Christine Seigneur
Neil Sellers
Chris Senior
Marcello Seri
Belynda J. Shadoan
Grace Shalloo
Nichola Shanks
Joseph Shape
Graeme Shaw
Simon Shaw
Steve J Shaw
Meghan Shearer
Reece Shearsmith
Richard Sheehan
John Sheeran
Adnan Sheikh
Hilary Shenton
Joanne Sheppard
Jessie Sheridan
Yemin Shi
Lewis Short
Jim Shorter
Stephen Shovlin
Edward Shull
Jared Shurin

Silhouby
Damian Silverton
Christian Simcock
Yuna Simeon
Peter Simmons
Alan Sims
Helena Sinclair
Brad Singer
Holly Sismore
Rebecca Sivieri
Joe Skade
@skionar
John David Slavney
Ross Sleight
Eli John Smith
Kelly Smith
Michael Smith
Peter Smith
Simon Smith
Glyn Smyth
Michael Soares
Graeme Soeder
Neil Solan
John Sommerville
Kevin Sommerville
Richard Soundy
Rebecca Southwell
Chris Spalton
spectralisle.co.uk
Connor Spilsbury
Miranda Spraggs
Kelda Sproston
Teresa Squires
Kathleen Clara Molitor
  St. John
Ruth Stanley
Jenny Staples
Charlotte Stark
Brian Stauffer
Clare Stebbings

Toby Steedman
Martin Steel
Laura Steele
Sean Steele
Amanda Stefaniuk
Jonathan Stephen
Chris Stephens
Alex Stevens
Julie Stevens
Linda Stevens
Penny Stevens
Alistair Stevenson
Lorraine Stevenson
Thomas Stevenson
Gordon Stewart
Sam Stewart
Nick Stockdale
Andrew Stone
Corinne Stone
Nathan Stone
Beth Storey
Pamela Strachman
Caroline Strack
Brice Stratford
Samantha Streeter
Nicolo Strella
Kaitlin Stringer
Andrew Stuart
Tobias Sturt
Thomas Styring
Jean-Baptiste Suara
Ander Suarez
Gary Sullivan
Kirstie Summers
Glen Supple
Matt Swanson
Trever Swearingen
Curtis Swenson
Nick Swift
Kirsty Syder

Amélie Taddei
Tracey Taggart
Peter Tags &
  Kim Jarvis
Rosie Talbot
John Tarrow
Claire Taylor
John Taylor
Josie Taylor
Louise Taylor
Martha Taylor
Margaret Tedford
Edward Thomas
Lydia Thomas
Martyn Thomas
Brian Thompson
Carrie Thompson
Helen Thompson
Jason Thompson
Katie Thompson
Michael John
  Thompson
Nicholas Thompson
Shannon Thomson
Nick Thorpe
James Thresher
Ellee Thunfeldt
Helen Tiley
Ksenia Timchik
Joanna Tindall
Keith Tomlinson
Sophie Tomlinson
Damia Torhagen
Laura Touhey
Peter Townend
Carolyn Townsend
Lyndsay Townsend
Rebecca Traquair
Lucy Traves
Bry Tribuna

Jacqui Trowsdale
Menno Simon
  Troyer
Mark Truesdale
Jason Tsimplakos
Noel Tuazon
Callum Tucker
Emma Tucker
Alexander Turner
Daniel S Turner
Jonathan Turner
Rob Turpin
Laura Twist
Emma Tyers
Laura-Faye Underhill
Dan Usztan
Oscar-Torjus Utaaker
A. Valliard
Davy Van Obbergen
Mark Van Pee
Tommaso Vannocci
Simon Vargheese
Elizabeth Vegvary
Mark Vent
Elizabeth Verbraak
Désirée Verkaar
Neil Vidler
Shelly Vingis
Alice Violett
Stephanie Volk
James Voller
Leslie Wainger
Richard Wainman
Martyn Waites
Dominic Wakeford
Imogen Walker
Julie Walker
Matthew Walker
Tony Walker

Jeff Wall
Caitlin Wallace
Anthony Waller
Jonathan Walmsley
Brendan Walsh
Damian Walter
Meg Walters
Ashley Walton
Jeffery Wang
Adam Ward
Lee Ward
Paul Wardell
Erik Warfield
David Warley
Stephanie Wasek
Alice Watson
Ben J. Watson
Derek Watson
Molly Watson
Connor Webb
Matthew Webb
Martin Webber
Nathan Weber
Ange Weeks
Joe Weinmunson
Scott Crawford
  Weller
Michael Wells
Shelley Wells
Alexandra Welsby
Jordan Welsh
Devon Brooks West
Ian Wheeler
Luke Whiston
Andrew White
James White
Diana White Smith
Alan Whitehill
Scott Whitehouse

Cassie Whittell
Roger Whittington
James Wilde
Paul Wilde
Andrew Wileman
John Wilkinson
Joy Wilkinson
Emma Williams
Jordan Williams
Neil Williams
Izzy Williamson
Neil Williamson
Thom Willis
Derek Wilson
Fiona Wilson
Johanna Wilson
Lawrence Wilson
Marcus Wilson
Robbie Wilson
Rachel Winner
Stephen Wise
Pamela Wishbow
Sophie Witcombe
Barry Wolf
George Woo
Alisdair Wood
Eilidh Wood
Lucy Wood
Matthew Wood
Mike Wood
Peter Wood
Josh Woodfin
Paul Woodgate
John Woodruff
Janina Woods
Zoe Woods
Angie Wright
Richard Wright
Louise Wykes

Akhlys Wynn
Andrew Yates
Ian Yates
Georgia Young
Katie Young

Zane Zarakovska
Zachary Zelazny
Pete Ziegel
Violet Venables
Ziminski

Grace Zimmerman
Gavin Zollo
Sophie Zurybida